A LAST SHRED

Here, in the sunlight, [...] her cheek, her neck, [...] her breasts and waist and hips, until he moved his lips away from hers, and gazed down at her, as she lay half on his lap, half upon the grass.

"I really think it's time, my love," Julian said, "to end this troublesome matter of your maidenhood. So, if you agree, and you're sure no one's coming. . . ." Slowly the Viscount pulled the top of her gown down and admired what he uncovered.

"We can't . . . out here!" Eliza whispered frantically, pulling up her dress.

He grinned like a boy. "Then . . . where?" he asked.

"My house is nearby," she said. "Will you come home with me . . . ?"

EDITH LAYTON, one of the most widely read and acclaimed Regency writers, is winner of the 1984 Reviewers Choice Award and the Romantic Times Award for Best New Regency Author, the 1985 Reviewers Choice Award for Best Regency Novel (*Lord of Dishonor*), and the 1986 Reviewers Choice Award for Best Regency. Her first Super Regency, *Love in Disguise*, won her the 1987 Romantic Times Award for Best Regency Author, the 1987 Romantic Writers Association Golden Leaf Award for Best Historical Novel, and the 1987 Reviewers Choice Special Achievement Award for Best Hero.

SURRENDER TO LOVE

by
Edith Layton

A SIGNET BOOK

NEW AMERICAN LIBRARY

PUBLISHER'S NOTE

This book is a work of fiction. Names, characters, places, and incidents either are the product of the author's imagination or are used fictiously, and any resemblance to actual persons, living or dead, events, or locales is entirely coincidental.

NAL BOOKS ARE AVAILABLE AT QUANTITY DISCOUNTS
WHEN USED TO PROMOTE PRODUCTS OR SERVICES.
FOR INFORMATION PLEASE WRITE TO PREMIUM MARKETING DIVISION,
NEW AMERICAN LIBRARY, 1633 BROADWAY,
NEW YORK, NEW YORK 10019.

SIGNET TRADEMARK REG. U.S. PAT. OFF. AND FOREIGN COUNTRIES
REGISTERED TRADEMARK—MARCA REGISTRADA
HECHO EN DRESDEN, TN, U.S.A.

SIGNET, SIGNET CLASSIC, MENTOR, ONYX, PLUME, MERIDIAN and NAL BOOKS are published by NAL PENGUIN INC., 1633 Broadway, New York, New York 10019

First Printing, March, 1989

1 2 3 4 5 6 7 8 9

PRINTED IN THE UNITED STATES OF AMERICA

. . . I obtained from these books a notion of an English coachman, as an idealized being, a combination of Phoebus Apollo, a Roman Charioteer, and the Prince Regent . . .

—Alice Morse Earle,
Stage Coach and Tavern Days, 1900

Love conquers all things;
let us too surrender to Love.

—Virgil, *Georgics I*

1

THE SUN RODE the sky at its highest point so that nothing beneath it cast a shadow, and generous shade became a memory. The gentleman driving the light carriage down the long palm avenue had only the brim of his hat to shelter him from the heat and stunning brightness of noon, but it was enough, he had been cold for so long. In fact, after he'd surrendered his team and coach to a servant, and escaped the blaze of noon, he felt the relative coolness in his house most keenly as he paced through its long corridors.

It was not so much cool as it was less hot within the elegant white house. The high ceilings staved off the sun, the white walls blunted its glare, and the tiled veranda the gentleman strode to was filled with ferns that ate up the blinding light. But here he could see outdoors as though he were still there, and so here he settled to read the mail that he'd brought with him from the harbor. He took off his hat before he settled in his favorite chair, and for a moment it was as though he'd carried a bit of the blazing afternoon in with him, the way a man might shed water from his clothing after coming in from a rainstorm. For his hair was gilt on gold and it shone brilliantly even in the filtered light of the fern-filled room. But it was light without heat and the illusion was gone when he shuddered from the slight change in temperature as he sorted through the letters. He was done with the heat the moment he'd stepped out of it, but it would take more than slight physical discomfort to distract him now, for the ship had been late, and so the mail was overdue.

There was little to divert his attention even if he were

less anxious to read his post. It was quiet in the spare and spacious parlor. Or at least as quiet as the tropics ever got, for it only grew comparatively hushed at this precise moment at the height of noon. The palms outside the open windows had ceased to clash their swordlike fronds as the breeze from the constant trade winds faltered, the raucous birds and insects paused for breath, and even the little yellow birds high on the walls only fluffed their feathers after they'd dashed to the sides of their ornate cages in startled reaction to the sudden entrance of the gentleman. He heard none of it, neither the subtle sounds nor the absence of them. He was engrossed in his letters.

He read for a long while; there were a great many letters, in several languages, from several lands, to be got through. But one letter was read first, put down and then read again, and then perused again at the last. He'd smiled when he'd first seen it, but then frowned, and he'd worn a distracted air ever since he'd first read the first paragraph of it.

After a while the gentleman rose and put the letter aside and stared out into the afternoon as the sky began to darken, for the midday rains were gathering. They'd be brief and torrential and it would be cool only just as they fell, for so soon as the clouds rolled away until the next day's rains, the heat would rise up from the earth to touch the heat that would pour down from the sky again. That was part of the lure of this place, he thought, the eternal predictability of it. And that was part of the fault with it too, of course.

He only remained inactive for a brief time. It was not in his style to linger when action was needful. He turned then, even as a little breeze sprang up, and tugged a bell pull to summon a servant to him. When the footman appeared, he gave one soft command, and then he went to the pagoda-shaped cage that hung near to the window. The little yellow bird within flew up to the roof of it in alarm, for though it thrived and sang, it never had made peace with humankind.

When the little girl appeared in the doorway, her solemn face lit with gentle joy and she said with pleasure, "You're home!"

"Not yet," he answered, smiling, though his answer made her frown in incomprehension.

She looked to the bird cage in his hands in confusion as he opened the door to it and held it high, near to the open window.

"It's time for them to go home," he explained as the bird paused and stilled and looked out at an unbarred day for the first time in months, and appeared to be unwilling to believe what it saw. But then it clearly recognized the shape of freedom, and gathered itself and launched up and out and soared away into the trees at the edge of the long lawns that surrounded the house.

"Won't he be hungry? Where will he sleep? What will he do?" the child asked fearfully.

"He'll remember everything," he answered as he went to the next cage and brought it to the window, "and eat the fruits he did before he knew us, and sleep in his favorite trees, and play with all his old friends," he said gravely, pausing with his hand on the cage door, watching the sober little face until he saw she understood and accepted that, as she accepted all that he told and gave her.

And then he smiled.

"They're going home again," he explained, "just as I am. As we are," he corrected himself, "because my home is yours too, you know."

"Oh," she said gravely, and then, taking in a breath, she asked bravely, "When?"

"Yesterday," he said, and then relenting, he laughed, before he grew as grave as she did. "Soon as we can. I have to be there before I can be there."

"You will," she assured him, for she knew he could do anything.

There had been trouble from the first. To begin with, it was raining. Rain was not unexpected in this part of the world this early in the spring, but this was an especially annoying mizzle: damp, chill, and clinging, and from the way it had started, before dawn, and the way the wind blew, it would likely continue all morning, and on into the reception, and ruin any roseate plans that had managed to survive intact until this wedding day. Not many had. But the bride's mother had a last lingering hope for at least a wedding breakfast with the sun shining down upon rose-decked tables.

For it was clear that the sun might shine until it charred the roses and it still would not illuminate a smiling, blushing bride. No, for here she stood at the very altar, and every time the minister paused for breath, the congregation could clearly hear her sniveling. The bride's mama forced an insincere and rictus smile upon her tightened lips. The wretched chit was doing it on purpose, of course; she didn't know her very well, but rebellion had been part of her nature since girlhood, or so all her nurses and governesses had said. And so it would be necessary afterward to inform every guest at the reception that her dear daughter suffered from a catarrh, so as to explain away her swollen eyes and tear-streaked cheeks and constant snuffling. But that would hardly explain why the bride had dragged herself to the altar like a woman approaching the Newgate hangman, or why every sniffle was followed by a long, lingering, loudly audible broken sigh. No one had ever suffered such tragedy with a head cold, or even a persistent catarrh.

The groom, of course, was red-faced, sullen, and swollen with outrage. But he'd been that long before the ceremony, and to those who didn't know him it could be passed off as an unfortunate and characteristic pose. A gentleman of volatile spirit and apoplectic bent, it could be claimed; it was possible to cover his attitude with the veil of social reason. Still, that would scarcely account for the venomous looks he bent upon his soon-to-be bride as she subsided into muted hiccuping sobs at his side as the minister came to the integral part of the service. The bride's mother tightened her jaw. Someone, she vowed, would pay for this display, and she, who had always pitied anyone on earth who was not fortunate enough to be herself, found for the first time in her life that she wanted to be other than who she was. She discovered herself heartily wishing she were her daughter's groom today, so that she might beat the miserable chit black and deeper shades of blue for treating them all to this remarkable wedding day.

The congregation was lively enough. They were all whispers and shifting heads and craning necks. The sounds of the patter of the rain upon the high stained-glass windows were obscured by their hushed murmurs and their creaking and shifting in their seats in their restlessness. It was a handsome enough group of persons that filled the old church to overflowing, for the cream of London society outnumbered the native population this morning. Those in the chapel who were not squirming to get a better look at the way the bride was carrying on were peering about to get a better look at their well-dressed, well-known, temporary neighbors.

Dukes and duchesses sat side by side with the local gentry, and here and there a marquess sat beside a grocer, and a lady alongside a farmer, for although the bride's mama would gladly have shunned every one of her neighbors here on the Isle of Wight, where her husband's principal home existed, the groom's family were longtime islanders, and they had, unfortunately, an equal say in the makeup of the invited guests. All of those present were got up in their best new clothes. The local gentry looked uncomfortable and stiff in them, because that was the case, while the London guests managed to make clothes straight from their tailors look both appropriate and comfortable, and they all looked fine as fivepence.

Banks of fragile first spring flowers surrounded the chancel, the dim watery light softened the dying martyrs in the stained glass to pastel miseries, and the organist poised above his instrument awaited the nod to let the music swell and release the guests from their pretense of pious observation to full-throated gossip. Clearly they yearned to comment to each other. For when the minister asked the happy couple to kneel, and the bride, all enveloped in creamy lace, faltered and seemed about to fall flat instead, as her harassed groom clutched her arm and helped her to her knees, the collective gasp from the spectators drowned out whatever uplifting thing he snarled into her ear. It was also lucky, her mama thought, and deuced unfair, a young blade complained loudly to his companions, that the bride's face was obscured by a heavy veiling of antique lace, for it might have been that her sufferings would make the stained-glass martyrdom above her pale by comparison.

"High theater. I'm impressed," a lean, elegant, long-nosed gentleman murmured to the gentleman next to him as that huge fellow stirred uneasily in his seat. "It will be a pleasure to add to it, as I've promised, though likely I'll never live it down."

"You need not," his large companion replied in a low whisper, which, because of the size of the instrument it issued from, sounded more like a low chord struck from the mighty church organ than a confidential aside. "I've given my word I'll do the honors, Duke."

The elegant fellow seemed about to argue, but a nudge and a look from his beautiful fair-haired lady silenced him, just as a tweak and a frown from the dark lady with speaking eyes who sat next to the colossus caused that large gentleman to capture her hand in his great one, and he too fell silent as he carried that little hand to his lips instead of speaking again. But although obedient to their ladies' wishes for silence, neither gentleman took his eyes from the drama going on before him.

On the other side of the aisle, a magnificent young dark-haired lady who had attracted a great deal of attention just by sitting up straight and paying attention to the service, and so letting all the gentlemen get a good look at her pure and famous profile, also shifted with a hiss of her silken skirts and allowed the slightest frown to cross her perfect features. "Blasted chit," she breathed into her chaperone's ear, leaning her dusky lips so close to that aged lady's wrinkled cheek that several observant gentlemen were shocked to find themselves envying an ancient dame. "It looks as if I shall have to act, after all," she mused.

"Constance! You must not!" the white-haired lady replied, trembling, so shocked and terrified at the idea that she spoke almost audibly. "Think of the scandal!"

"Oh, nonsense," the exquisite young woman said, though a smile played about her perfect lips as she did think of exactly that, and never loath to take the center stage at any affair, she sat back and relaxed. This reassured her chaperone, because she never looked again to see how closely her charge watched the ceremony go forth now, nor noticed how her gentle smile was one of calculated expectation and never gentle resignation.

A few rows of pews in back of the magnificent young lady, another young woman fidgeted and fretted and shifted her position and frowned. But no one watched her discomfort. She was pretty enough, with her rounded cheeks and silken brown hair, and fashionably dressed as well, but in an audience of Incomparables, one more pretty lady was no more singularly noticeable than one single, however perfect, daffodil might be in one of the great massed bouquets that adorned the old church. Especially when such a spectacle was going forth before the audience.

For now the minister asked the groom if he took the young woman at his side as his bride, and he barked, "Yes!" The vicar's next words were drowned out by the moan that issued either from a stray dog that had got into the church or from the gloomy young bride herself. But no cur had crept into that holy place after all, for when the nervous clergyman asked the same question of the bride, a similar strangled howl of misery issuing from behind the lacy veil was taken as a "yes" from her. The minister hurried on with the service as the murmurous comment from the congregation rose, just as the groom's color did.

Then the audience quietened, as the spectators at a bullfight do when the matador's sword rises high in the air and points directly between the sullen bull's horns, for the minister, looking almost as tremulous as the bridegroom looked aggrieved, stared out at the congregation and asked the question so many had been waiting for.

"If there is anyone present who can show just cause why these two should not be wed, let him speak now, or forever hold his peace," the minister quavered.

He looked down to his book again, as he always did, so as to be able to hurry on, and make the thing look solemn, and so didn't notice anything amiss until he heard the hiss of a hundred-odd breaths being drawn in sharply. He'd never expected an answer, after all, for no one had ever objected to the wedding ceremony, save for an occasional bride or groom, and no one ever listened to them, in all the years of his ministry. But now he looked up from his book to see one . . . no, two . . . no, three—good heavens, the minister thought, shocked into wondering if he would soon awake and find that it was only that the cat had fallen asleep on his face again and caused this panicky dream—four persons slowly rising from their seats among the congregation.

One was a beautifully dressed ginger-haired gentleman so tall and broad and wide-shouldered that the eye went immediately to him, but then, two seats from him, another exquisite gentleman, this one lean as a greyhound and with that same sort of aristocracy bred into his long bones and long nose, uncoiled from his seat to stand and look quizzically at the large gentleman before he stared pointedly right back at the minister. But by then the vicar was gaping at a wondrously lovely young woman, black-haired and camellia-skinned and standing so tall and composed that he should have known her for a famous beauty even if she hadn't looked vaguely familiar. And then, a few rows behind her, unsure, and red-cheeked with overwhelming embarrassment, but staunch, another young woman, comely and neat, and with a very determined expression on her flushed face, also stood and waited politely to be acknowledged.

The minister gawked. The silence grew. The four persons had time to look around and discover each other, and smile or shrug or wonder before they then looked back to the clergyman. The bride turned round and stared, or at least it seemed she did, for nothing issued from behind her veil, not even so much as a breath to disarrange her lacy cage.

The minister honestly did not know quite what to do, for although he decided he had to acknowledge one of the protesters, he was now stricken with the dilemma of what order to do it in. Ladies before gentlemen? But which lady? For which was more closely related, or older, or more titled or prestigious? Or did the gentlemen precede the ladies in this, as they did in all else but the file in which they walked into the church? He cleared his throat as he waited for inspiration, as he always did during his sermons. But no one had ever listened so attentively for what he might say then, and so he only cleared his throat once more, and being a proper clergyman, prayed.

The groom was not feeling very religiously inclined.

"Get on with it!" he shouted.

"Ah, but there's an objection," the minister equivocated.

"Who dares?" the groom challenged, growing redder and clenching his fists as he turned from threatening the vicar to menacing the congregation.

The two gentlemen opened their lips at almost exactly the same moment as the beautiful young woman took in her breath and the rosy-cheeked one opened her mouth. But none got the chances to do more than breathe out.

For "I do!" cried a gentleman as he entered the church with a gust of cold air and strode down the aisle.

The doors to the old church still swung closed behind him and so they all knew he could not have come down from the great rose glass window above, but as he passed among them, not a few in the church would have sworn he had materialized there amidst them, rather than walked in, as human men must do. For he looked, even dewed with mists of weather and mortal stress as he was, still more like an angel than any man most of them had ever seen.

He was lithe and broad of shoulder, but narrow of waist and supple of limb, and although he wore a many-tiered greatcoat, it swung open with each forward step to reveal a fashionable gentleman's dress of white neckcloth and snug vest over his shirt, blue jacket and tight gray inexpressibles that were encased to the knee in high Hessian boots. He might as well have been wearing celestial robes. For his brow was high and noble, his eyes were long and blindingly pure gray, his nose was shapely, and his mouth soft as a girl's, yet hard and beautiful as any heathen statue of a god's might be. His chin was determined, yet with a light cleft gracing it, while over all, his thick overlong hair glowed old gold and flax as it curled at his neck and tumbled over his high brow, which, like the rest of his amazing countenance, was lightly gilded by the sun. It was Apollo himself among them, or an angel, they thought, depending upon their religious convictions, but in any case he was never so handsome as he was literally beautiful, and he took their breath away as surely as his unexpected entrance had done.

He strode to the chancel and went directly up to the furious groom.

"I object," he said then in a melodious but human tenor, pausing, staring down into the amazed young bride-groom's eyes, "and strenuously. For she doesn't love you, as you well know. She is being forced to wed you against her will, and moreover," he said, as the congregation grew still as stone, no one breathing for fear of missing a word, "she is promised to me."

Then he turned his back on the frustrated groom and tenderly reached down one gloved hand to the bride, who knelt frozen still, at his feet. He drew her up to a stand. She was not very large, and so, even when standing, came to no higher than his heart. He smiled then, so sweetly that even the minister forgot the circumstances, and began to beam upon them. And then the beautiful stranger raised his gloved hand and gently, lightly, almost reverently drew the web of creamy lace up and away from the bride's face. He stared down at her wordlessly.

Great topaz-colored eyes looked back at him, long-lashed eyes of so light a brown they shone amber in the wash of their recent tears. Her skin was whiter than the lace that he had brushed away, and finely grained and unblemished, though here and there upon the bridge of her small nose, and at the top of her high cheekbones, a tiny freckle glowed. Her mouth was tender and full, her chin small and defined; it was the face of a lovely mischievous elfin child, but as she gazed at him in wonder, her expression softened and it became the countenance of an unusually styled but lovely woman. And woman she was, for another glance showed white shoulders rising above a shapely high bosom, and beneath its high waist, her fashionable cream-colored gown tapered and clung, more than subtly hinting at a trim slender figure that, for all its diminutive size, was completely, exceedingly well-developed. Framing all these graces, her dark auburn hair curled about her cheeks, and though drawn up in back, still tumbled down to lie in careful disarray upon those smooth shoulders.

The golden gentleman stared down at her. He swallowed hard, and then he blinked. This could never be the girl he remembered.

"Ah," he said softly.

Then he drew in a deep breath, and wrenching his startled gaze from her, he looked to the minister, and squaring his impressive shoulders and jaw, said more clearly and quite contritely:

"I'm terribly sorry. My mistake. Wrong bride," he explained in an aside to the groom. "Wrong wedding," he confessed apologetically to the vicar.

"Oh, Julian," the bride sighed, enchanted, delivered, delighted.

2

THERE WAS SCARCELY enough room in the minister's study for everyone who wanted to be there. There was barely enough space in the small chamber for all those who needed to be there. Even after most of the chaff of those pressing for entrance for the conference among the minister, the would-be groom, the twice-claimed bride, the handsome interloper, and the four other aspirant protesters had been separated from those genuinely concerned, there were still some of the insistent vulgarly curious and marginally involved to be dissuaded.

When the vicar seemed at a loss for a means to restore order, the two gentlemen who had risen when the call for impediments had been given took over. The large gentleman saw to the larger number of expulsions, simplifying matters beautifully by merely crossing his arms over his enormous chest and looking down at those attempting to crowd in, clearing his throat and smiling, before nodding to the direction in which he wished them to leave. In every case, they did, and immediately. Even though his smile held the gentlest reason, his size spoke of a better argument.

It was the tall, elegant gentleman who whisked the bride's mama from the room, with a smile and only a few well-placed words.

"My dear Mrs. Merriman," the gentleman said, placing his lean, lofty person between the outraged lady and the daughter she was clearly about to tear limb from limb, "wouldn't it be far better to allow the young people to work this thing out between them?"

Just as Mrs. Merriman turned, obviously about to tear a few strips from the gentleman as well, he added dulcetly, "I'm sure the viscount has a difficult enough row to hoe right now and would appreciate your forbearance until things are nicely settled."

The word "viscount" had acted like the slap across the face that the lady was about to deliver to her daughter. She paused and looked up at the gentleman.

"Oh, yes," he went on blithely. "Doubtless you didn't recognize him at first, of course, as it's been years since he was in the country. Five, actually. But Viscount Hazelton has only lately returned from a tour of his estates in the Americas and the tropics. That tanned skin quite disguises him, doesn't it? Not at all the thing, I know. But give him time in dear Mother England, and it will fade to a nice drawing-room pallor again. But how rude of me, I've quite forgotten myself in all this clamor," he went on, gently taking the lady's elbow as she hung on his every syllable, as she had since the word "estates" had fallen sweetly on her ear, and as he walked her from the room, he added, "I know you only by sight, I'm sorry to say we've never met, but what an opportune moment to remedy that terrible oversight! Since everyone here is so involved"—he laughed lightly—"allow me to introduce myself, I'm Peterstow . . . Warwick Jones, Duke of Peterstow, an old, dear friend of the viscount's, as I'm sure you know."

She didn't, any more than she'd recognized the viscount or his name. But she'd rather have admitted to high treason than that. For she did know the name Peterstow. And once her eyes had cleared of their killing rage, she recognized him, which was more than he'd ever done for her whenever she'd sighted him at any public occasion in London. For he was very high *ton* indeed. Eccentric as he could hold together, of course, but he could well afford to be, being wellborn, titled, clever, and wealthy almost beyond her own dreams of avarice. He numbered among his intimates peers and poets and any number of infamous persons, but had little to do with society, although society would have dearly loved to have anything to do with him. Mrs. Merriman had a place in the *ton*, but it was several rungs below his.

Clearly, she thought quickly, her wretched daughter had something interesting going forth. Even if her reputation were ruined by the events of this day, they might well have made her mother's.

She looked up at the duke, schooling her thin face to a terrible vivacity, but before she could say something charming or witty, he'd reunited her with her husband—who was morosely sobering up enough to worry about whether he'd missed anything important—and had left her, disappearing with miraculous grace and speed behind the now-closed door to the minister's study.

"Quiet," the large gentleman said loudly, clearly, and simply, and all the confusing cross-talk stopped instantly, for the gentleman could speak very loudly.

"Thank you," the minister breathed as they all fell still. Obviously it was up to someone to sort matters out, he thought, and as a member of the clergy, that person was himself, but he had no taste for it, or skill in such matters. If he had, he thought miserably, he'd have read for politics and not for religion when he'd gone to university, matters of the nice points of justice and morality and honor being far more pleasant to discuss when they happened a few thousand years ago rather than right before his aghast eyes.

And so as he could think of nothing to say in that moment of silence the large gentleman had won him, it wasn't long before the assembled parties—the four witnesses who'd been about to testify against the wedding, the one who did, and the almost-bride and groom—all began to talk at once again.

"Quiet," the large fellow said once more, and this time, when they grew still, he added impatiently, "Here. Julian, you said she's promised to you, but then denied it. Please, make up your mind so that the wedding can go on, or out upon it, will you? I woke at dawn and dressed to an inch, and was about to make an even greater fool of myself on your behalf if you hadn't arrived in time, and all on your express request in your letter, and all for the sake of our friendship, and now you've doubts. Will you please resolve them so we can go on with our lives? Is she or isn't she the bride you've come to rescue from a fate worse than death?"

"Oh, this is wonderful," the would-be groom said savagely. "I behave like a gentleman and you put it about that I'm some sort of monster. Thank you, I'm sure, Liza."

"Like a gentleman *and* a monster, Hugh," the bride said with some agitation, "for you weren't doing me any favor, and you know it."

The groom, his fair face suffusing with high color again, took a step to the bride, about to continue the discussion, when the Duke of Peterstow cut across his opening words and ordered peremptorily, "Clarify, Julian, and let's have done with it."

"She's the right girl, and it is the wrong wedding, and the only reason I'd doubts is that she's changed so completely. Eliza, you little wretch," the viscount said, smiling as he walked up to her and took her hand, "how comes it you never told me?"

"I told you I grew up," she said, her eyes shining as she looked up at him, before she glanced away from his frankly admiring stare, a light blush adding amazingly to her loveliness.

"There, she's doing it again," the angry bridegroom said in disgust. "That's how I got caught."

"As I understand it," the tall, darkly beautiful lady interposed, with much amusement coloring her velvety voice, "you were doing rather a bit more—that's how you got caught, Hugh."

"He only kissed me!" the bride blurted. "And I didn't ask him to, either!"

"If you don't call all that blushing and eyelash business, and walking out into a dark garden with me alone asking me to, Liza, I don't know what is," the young man shouted back, stung to high anger.

"A kiss?" the viscount asked with interest, arching one dark gold brow at the bride. "You didn't mention the kissing part in the letter."

"Because it didn't signify," she said seriously, and before the outraged groom could say another thing, she added, "It's not fair, it's beyond gothic, that I should have to spend the rest of my life with Hugh, who don't even like me, not really, just because he kissed me."

"That much, then, is true," the viscount said on a sigh, "but it does go beyond gothic. I didn't know parents in modern-day England could be such high sticklers."

"They are if their daughter's one-and-twenty and getting older every hour with no serious suitors in view," the young groom declared, shoving his fists deep into his pockets as he saw the look of annoyance on the largest gentleman's face when he heard his retort.

"That's true," the bride said somberly, her eyes searching the viscount's face so that she could read his reactions there, "and now I've sunk myself for the future too, I know it. But still, even if I'll be a spinster forevermore, I told him I'd never marry him, and so I won't. I thank you for coming, Julian, but if you hadn't, my cousin Constance or my friend Anthea would have spoken up for me. I might have had to come to the altar, because I had nowhere to run to, but I would never have left it as your wife, Hugh," she vowed, turning to him then, "and so I told you, and told you. And don't claim you were marrying me for your honor, either, for there's that little matter of our fathers' estates matching on the northwest boundary too, isn't there?"

The stocky, fair-skinned young man grew an even more truculent expression, but although he spoke up grudgingly, he spoke fairly enough. "Oh, there's richer chits I could've leg-shackled, Liza, I really did think we'd a chance."

"Thank you," she said a little sadly, "but no thank you, and anyway, I've ruined all my chances now, I think."

"What? But why aren't there a dozen other suitors vying for your hand, Eliza?" the viscount asked gently.

"Because everyone knows she's a Jill-flirt and a jilt," Hugh commented darkly. "Just look at me."

"Because she didn't care to marry, and the gentlemen can't understand a female not wishing to leap into wedlock with any man that deigns ask it of them," the rosy-cheeked young woman who'd remained silent all the while said heatedly, before she saw them all looking at her and subsided, even rosier than before.

"Because anyone can see you're worthy of them," the viscount continued, ignoring the spiteful outburst from the young man he'd supplanted, as well as the young woman's spirited defense of her friend. "You were . . . an unformed child, only a little girl, the last time we met, not at all the beauty I see before me. 'Grown-up' indeed," he chided her teasingly to make her smile again, just as though she were the little girl he spoke of. "How was I to know you'd done it up so amazingly well?"

"I was a rotund little party, Julian," she answered, giggling now, only her laughter childish again, for the sparkling look she flashed to him was not, "however nicely you put it. 'Unformed' indeed," she mocked him merrily. "I was plump as a pouter pigeon, you can't deny it. But I told you the ladies on my father's side were late bloomers, and so it was with me. And as for telling you—fine letters they'd have been if I'd gone on about my charms for pages . . . wouldn't they have been enthralling, All full of brag about my wondrous beauty? —come, Julian, you'd have been bored to bits, and I'd have been laughing too hard to set a word down straight. Why, you'd have crumpled them up and used them for . . . kindling," she said slyly, hesitating before skipping over the naughtiness she'd clearly intended as he laughed, "if I'd done, wouldn't you have?"

"I don't understand," the minister said unhappily. "How could you have proposed marriage to the lady if you last saw her so many years ago?"

"I didn't," the gentleman replied, still smiling down at the blushing girl. "I proposed friendship, and that I got in full measure."

"But you've stopped the ceremony," the minister persisted, for he'd begun to think of his fee, and was wondering if he could still salvage a ceremony from the confusion, "and spoken up for Miss Merriman, before witnesses, and so I do believe you've gotten yourself a bride now, sir."

The viscount grew still and his face became solemn.

"So I have," he answered thoughtfully, as though realizing the full extent of the matter for the first time, as he looked steadily at the girl whose hand he still held. "So I have done, then, haven't I?"

"We must talk," Miss Merriman said anxiously.

"Aye," the big gentleman agreed from where he stood, his broad back against the door as if he were holding out wild barbarian invaders, and not wildly curious wedding guests, "and soon. But if you put your noses out this door, it will be hours until you have privacy again. Tell you what, Julian—either we all troop out and stand in the rain while you settle accounts, or you two nip out those long doors and have a talk under the eaves, while we wait for you."

"Well put, Arden," the duke agreed, "and I think that you two children stand a better chance of going in secret than the herd of us would if we went thundering out. It's rather difficult," he mused, "for a legion to move stealthily, don't you agree?"

"You just don't want to get your new slippers wet, Warwick," the viscount said on a laugh. "Fop," he mocked with affection. "You haven't changed at all. But it's a splendid idea. Sir, if I may ask only one favor?" he said, turning to the minister, who'd been nodding agreeably, causing the clergyman to stop and grow a hunted look, for things seemed to be working out without any need for him to interfere until that moment. But his apprehension turned to relief when all the viscount did was to ask, "If you've an old coat or an oilskin for the lady, please?"

The rain had turned on an easterly wind to a light mist, and so after they slipped out the long doors, Julian Dylan, Viscount Hazelton, and the bride he'd just claimed walked from the back of the church out into the churchyard, and then roamed further as they talked, so as to escape notice of anyone in the church itself. It wasn't likely that any one of the guests would have consented to be dragged from the church until the dramatic events there were done, but the further they strayed, the freer they spoke, and so they strolled on, heedless of the mist above and the mud beneath them.

"Yes, I'd certainly have got here sooner and avoided

all the theatrics, which I didn't plan, Eliza, my word on it," the viscount continued explaining as they walked, "because I left on the instant I got your letter and read your plea. But the spring weather was bad, and even after the tides calmed enough for a passage, there was a storm at sea, we were blown off course and arrived in England much later than I'd hoped. Then, of course, as always when speed is of the essence, there was the usual pelter of unforeseen emergencies with broken axles and lamed horses. Why, I took over the reins and drove the coach myself for the better part of the journey. I think I set a record on the Plymouth road," he said, shaking his head in amazed rememberance. "And then, of course," he sighed, "for all my racing, since every guest here today had spoken for every available vessel on the mainland, I had to haggle and threaten and beg for a boat to get to the island this morning. I'm surprised you didn't take me for a haddock when I appeared, since it was a fishing sloop I finally commandeered. I'm as heady as I'm late," he said ruefully, "but if it's hard for you, consider how it is for me. I can't get upwind of myself, you know."

She gazed up at him. His scent was that of lemon and sandalwood, she'd noted it immediately when he'd stood next to her in the church, it was exactly as she'd remembered, for his scent was an integral part of the picture she'd held of him all these years. Even his letters had been lightly reminiscent of that delicious aroma she'd detected about him that warm summer day they'd met, or so she'd fancied, down all these long years, each time she'd held the pages to her lips and breathed them in.

"I consoled myself with the fact that I'd the fore-thought to write to my two best friends." He went on when she didn't answer, "You remember, I've told you about them often enough. The elegant one's Warwick—ah, I'll never remember, he came into his title so late, you know—the Duke of Peterstow, and the little fellow is Arden Lyons, my mighty lion of a friend. They were prepared to act in my behalf if I failed to show up on time. And outrageous as that request was, they are nonetheless here today, are they not? I never doubted them. Lord! For all the nonsense today—it's beyond good to see them again," he said. "Five years!" he wondered aloud. "It never seems so long now, and still it never seemed like less than an eternity from the moment I left these shores. But it is an eternity, isn't it, Eliza? Just look at you! Where is the little girl I wrote to, where has she got to?"

She did look very like a child again, he thought as he stopped and looked down at her. For though she'd grown, it hadn't been much in height, and the vicar's oilskin dragged through the mud for all she tried to lift it in her hands. It was so outsize it completely concealed her newly acquired shape, and as she'd also put on the minister's floppy hat, it too hung, thoroughly dampened with mist, all about her face. He suppressed a smile; she looked an infant dressed for a masquerade.

But then she stopped as well and looked up at him, and even in the shadows of the hat's brim, her eyes were large and filled with sorrow, and he wondered yet again at how lovely that face had become from what he'd remembered it to have been. The infantile plumpness was gone, there were all new contours, and when she spoke, it was strange to hear that impudent little voice issuing from an entirely different face. Whenever he met people who'd grown old since he'd last seen them, it was simple enough to deceive himself by superimposing their youthful faces on what he saw; erasing wrinkles and forgetting lines had become automatic as his mind's eye compensated for the loss of more familiar, pleasing images. But he'd never met a child so quickly grown to adulthood, and so it was rather an addition than a subtraction he had to do to recapture that round and childish visage he'd always pictured when he read her letters and wrote his replies to her. Now what he saw was so enchanting that he soon gave up the effort, accepting what his eyes, not his memory, showed him.

"Julian," she said, that newly lovely face extremely troubled, "we're in for it. Truly. What's to do?"

He laughed.

"What?" he asked lightly, seductively, touching her cheek with one finger. "Don't want me for a husband, love?"

She startled, stared into his mist-gray eyes and saw the devil of mischief there, and then cast down her gaze and laughed as well before she said gruffly, "Lud! There would be fair play for you, wouldn't it? To be tricked into marriage forever by doing a favor for a friend you haven't seen for years!" She waited the space of a breath to see if he was as aggrieved about it as she was, but before he could be gentleman enough to deny what he obviously agreed with, she hastily added, "Yes. And you never mentioned to the vicar that 'when last we met' was when first we met, did you? I'm glad of it, for he's an old fellow and it's bad luck to turn a wedding into a funeral."

But then she shivered, and looking about her, saw that they were standing in the center of the graveyard.

"Cold?" he asked as she shuddered again. When she didn't reply, he looked at her closely, and then around where they'd paused. Then he understood. And as she collected herself and hurried on, he followed close so as to catch her words, so as to forget where they stood.

For they'd met near this same churchyard five years before, both grieving for losses they found hard to bear, and both had found that comforting the other helped comfort themselves. The child had been on the brink of adulthood, and had been mourning for the loss of her best friend—her dog—as well as the approaching loss of her childhood home, for she was about to be sent off to school. The man had grieved because he couldn't mourn the loss of a woman who had wanted him, a woman he'd just seen decently interred, and guilt-stricken and empty, had been on the brink of leaving his homeland so that he could wander the world to seek his fate and leave sorrow buried behind him.

Yet even though they'd not set eyes on each other since that day, they'd begun speaking today, five years after those few hours they'd passed together, just exactly as if they'd left off talking just the other week. Of all the startling things that had happened this day, that was a thing that neither of them had troubled to wonder at.

For, in a sense, they'd never stopped talking. Because they'd been writing to each other regularly, just as they'd promised to do when they'd parted on that odd day all those years before.

At first, the man had written to the child because he'd given his word to do so, in order to dry her tears, and he was a man of his word. Then he'd replied to her answer because her questions were so amusing. He'd written again because there were times in his new life in new lands that made him long for that curious, sane, confidential little voice that kept replying to him from home, for all that he told himself it was because she expected his letters. And then he'd continued writing out of habit and custom, offering her his advice, recounting his adventures. At the last, never realizing the change, he'd written because he had no wish to break off his conversation with his friend.

And friend she'd become over the past five years. He knew all about her school, her tutors, her family, and all her triumphs, alarms, and shames—from her award for composition, to her tooth extraction, to her disastrous come-out. But, he thought now, gazing down at her, finding her wholly adorable even in her dampened state, there was obviously a great deal she hadn't told him as well. Turn about was fair play, he realized on a wry smile; he'd done his own editing too.

She was thinking much the same as they walked on in unaccustomed silence. His concerned, clear voice had sustained her in her initial loneliness after leaving home, and then had advised her cleverly through the difficult times of her growing up and on beyond that, even when she hadn't written to tell him her problems. And how he'd amused and entertained her! For she felt as though she too had traveled through America—from Vermont to Virginia—and then onward to the tropical islands off that wild coast. But now, stealing yet another quick look at him, as she'd done since he'd arrived, the way a chilled person cannot bear to leave the fire for too long, she realized that obviously there'd been a great deal he hadn't told her as well.

She knew all about America's Indians and animals, foods and fads, plant life and sea coasts, and stagecoach lines and inns. But nothing at all about its women. And, she decided, it was simply not possible that he was not now an expert on that subject. He was even more handsome than he'd been before, and she hadn't thought that possible. She'd sometimes wondered, as the years passed, if she hadn't gilded his appearance with her knowledge of the man, allowing memory to be enhanced by fondness, as always with friends. But no, if anything, he was more beautiful now than he'd seemed to her dazzled eyes then, when she'd taken him for an angel come to life from a carving on a tombstone, come to earth to comfort her in her grief.

Now he was more grown man than angel, and so even more wonderful to see. His shoulders had more breadth, his limbs, in his tight-fitting fashionable clothes, could be seen to be more muscular, even his face was subtly harder than it had been. His hair was burnished white yellow on gold from the breath of the sun, and that tropical sun had turned his white skin gold as well, making his light gray eyes clear as ice by contrast. But then, there was a sharp edge to all his features now. She knew hard labor had shaped his body, and could only guess what had firmed and framed his face to its present cold perfection. It might have been the result of both his work and his trials, whatever they'd been, that had written themselves into his very lineaments, but now, curiously, it was his very humanity that made him seem less mortal. He was no longer like a statue of a fallible human young Adonis, but rather had become the image of a grown, remote, amused Apollo.

She'd been a child then, and he a man, and there'd seemed a world between them. For she'd been almost sixteen and he nine-and-twenty. Now she was grown to her majority and yet there was still a distance, for all there was a closeness they'd established by their letters that she had with no one else in this world. Amazing, she thought, how it was that she felt such a bond with this beautiful, fashionable gentleman . . . fashionable . . .

"Your boots!" she remembered, horrified, turning to

him, stopped in her tracks by the sucking of mud beneath her feet as well as by the sudden thought, as she led him beyond the churchyard and climbed the muddy track through the bracken above it.

". . . were fashioned for walking," he answered, grinning at the way she froze, staring at them. "I've been out of London for a long time, remember? My boots are for function, not fashion. But your slippers!" he exclaimed, frowning, looking down to the mud-encrusted footwear that might have once been any color, any material.

". . . were not what I wanted, and will not be used again anyway. I never want to see them again, so it's as well that I likely won't be able to," she said impatiently, moving onward even as he was about to pick her up and bear her in his arms above the muck, as though she'd been a lady.

When she stopped at last, and looked back at him, triumphant, he remembered.

They stood on a rise overlooking the omnipresent sea, and though it was still mizzling slightly, and it was mud beneath their feet and not sweet grass, and the sea was as gray and expressionless as his eyes and not the bottle glass dappled blue and green it had been then, he remembered. How could he not? This was the exact spot where they'd stood then. His eyes lightened to seafoam, and he smiled.

"A long while ago," he agreed, looking out over the water, "and for all we've changed, you and I, Eliza, we haven't, not really, for all I didn't recognize you."

"Ah well," she said, smiling up at him. "But I couldn't forget you, you know. Don't be so vain, I could scarcely help it. Look, remember?" she asked, and reaching into the oilskin wrapper she wore, she drew out an oval miniature at the end of a chain that she wore about her neck.

He put out a hand, and reached down to the painted bit of ivory, and grew very cold, and very still. There was nothing so frightening to see, it was only an idealized face of a blond god, or a man, and not very well-executed, at that, for the face was as lifeless as it was insipidly beautiful. His gloved hand closed hard about it, and he released it only when he heard her indrawn breath and recalled she wore it still about her neck.

The woman who had given it to him before he gave it to Eliza, so as to forget it all those years ago, lay silent, not far from where they stood. And remembering her, and the young man he'd been who'd been no more thoughtful or wise than the lifeless painted face he gazed at, he loosed his hold and let the pendant swing back down, feeling old and weary, as exhausted with his trip and the distance he'd come as he was with his entire life.

She grew grave and big-eyed, and looked down at the pendant that lay on the oilskin as it blurred with dew. He recalled himself then; she'd made him aware of himself again. He'd frightened her, he'd clearly upset his young friend as he'd never meant to do. And so he smiled, and picked up the pendant in one hand, while the other lightly plucked the drenched oilcloth away from her shoulders, and he dropped the miniature carefully back to safety beneath the coat again.

"Lucky thing Hugh never got to call you wife," he said lightly. "He'd have had every reason to beat you soundly. It's not fair to wear another man to your wedding day, you know."

"But I always wear it. I said it was my lucky piece," she answered, "and as he always carries a rabbit's foot, he never complained. And," she said defensively, anticipating a comment from his telltale eyebrow as it rose, "you can see for yourself it's on a very long chain, and so was clearly visible with any gown I wore . . . well, most gowns," she said, looking up at him from under a sudden dropped fringe of lowered lashes.

"Was I your talisman?" he asked, amused. "I'm glad of it, then. The more so if it helped you through bad times."

He looked about himself then, and sighed again, and let the past drop back as well.

"But this is still a beautiful place. We forged a mighty friendship here, Eliza, my love," he said, shaking his head, "and I'm still glad of it."

"A friendship, precisely," she said with satisfaction, in

more natural tones, craning her head to look up at him, for he was a great deal taller than she, and stood on the top of the rise, besides. "That's my point. I'm happy you came, Julian, and I thank you from the bottom of my heart for making a scene and ending that charade I was going through, but I won't—I refuse—to let you be held to anything because of it. Because you *are* my friend," she said emphatically, "and *not* my lover, and there's no further use your pretending to it. Fine friend I'd be if I let this nonsense go on," she said gruffly, "and I saw the look in Mama's eye, even if you didn't. And I know her better than you do, and if Hugh's been turned out, she'll be only too happy to let you be caught in his stead, depend on it," she brooded. "And I won't have it, do you hear?"

She looked very fierce, and entirely adorable, standing with her head thrown back, her fine eyes glinting with martial fervor, and he laughed before he answered, which made her eyes flare like a cat's caught in lantern light.

"Lord! You do talk. But it was your friend—the dark-haired one from Leeds, the chief gossip of the second form—she was the one that was called 'Babbling Bess,' wasn't she? I'd hate to hear her out if she got the title and not you," he said as she looked embarrassed, before she began to grin, remembering that girl she hadn't thought of in years.

"And so far as knowing your mama," he said more grimly, "I do believe I know her just as well as you do, love, for I think I've seen her about as often as you have, haven't I? No, Eliza," he said, entirely serious now, holding up a hand to silence her before she could interrupt. For she'd begun to murmur about how it was always so for children who came along so late in life after all the others were grown, in order to excuse her mama and her family and all those who'd forgotten her for so many years—forgetting, as he did not, that he'd helped her invent many of those same rationalizations for the sake of her family honor, and for her own peace of mind.

"No," he insisted, "I pitched myself into the bumblebath fully aware, I assure you, because I *am* your friend.

Hugh's been routed, and society, not just your mama, is slavering for a substitute. And so I am he."

"But Constance or Anthea would have spoke up if you hadn't come, they promised!" she protested.

Privately he wondered about that, having heard some little about those two ladies in her letters over the years. Her lovely cousin Constance, the Incomparable Miss Merriman, was an acclaimed beauty and an ornament of society. He couldn't see her doing more than amusing herself by voicing some faint objections. And the pretty blushing mouse, Miss Anthea Baker, was Eliza's former schoolmistress, a radical thinker, to be sure, but not, he feared, a clearheaded one if she thought her objections would have achieved a thing except mockery.

But, "Certainly, they might have," he replied carefully, "and made laughingstocks of themselves, thereby. For what could they have said? That you were unwilling? And so . . .?"

He waited as she remembered how many times she'd said the same without effect, and then added, "And so the wedding would have gone forth." As she looked down and bit her lower lip, he said gently, "Since no one would really have cared, and your Constance and Anthea's objections could have been written off as jealousy or spite. Or even their own hidden passion for dear Hugh."

She grinned at that, before he continued, "But it would have made no matter. For neither of them could have offered herself in exchange. And like funerals, once a wedding ceremony's begun, the feelings of the featured players are unimportant."

"But your friends—they were standing! They would have spoken!" she persisted.

"Of course—to say that you were promised to me. I'm sorry, Eliza," he said, and he was, and it showed in his softened eyes and voice, "but we're stuck fast. For now. There's the point, dunderhead," he said, touching her cheek and making her look up and then down, in disarray, before she tried to meet his eyes again, "because it's only for now. We'll play at being lovers, for your mama, unless you'd rather not just play?"

He was amazed at how ruddily she flushed. Seeing her

flustered reaction to his automatic, unthinking flirtatious comment, he immediately wished it unsaid—he didn't want her to think he was actually casting out lures. He felt the pride of a father and the affection of a brother for her, and so wouldn't offer her false coin, meaning to or not. He knew, without vanity or particular pride, exactly what his appearance did to females, from the oldest to the youngest of them, willy-nilly, whatever their real feelings about him. And his seductiveness had never failed him. But he didn't wish to succeed in anything like, here. He'd never deceive his little friend, or play games with her, for all that now and then she tried her own newly acquired wiles on him, as she did, he'd realized, indiscriminately, on all men, like a child with a new game she'd just learned to play. So he teased her to elicit honest merriment and banish that painful hectic stain from her cheeks.

"What, you haven't conceived a passion for me as well as for Hugh?" he asked, as if amazed. "Poor Eliza! What will you ever do when you finally do find love, if you keep getting engaged to marry men you don't fancy? You'll have to divorce the poor fellow to show you're head over heels for him, I think!"

She blinked and then after a second's pause laughed just as loudly as he did, before he continued, "But first things first, agreed? We'll be properly engaged and not-too-demonstrative lovers then, while we'll be looking sharp for someone for you to really wed. Someone," he said on a deeper, sadder note as he gazed into her eyes without actually seeing the longing sorrow mirrored there, "that you want so much that you'll whip out a pistol and dispose of anyone daring to object when the vicar asks for impediments.

"Because we're off to London, missy. And we'll survey the crop of likely lads there. I've friends, and your friends are mine. You'll stay with them, not your dear mama or any of your delightful relatives this time. Don't make faces, they'll stick, don't you know anything?" he lectured as she began to protest, before he added more kindly, remembering her past experiences of London, since he could scarcely forget them after all the doleful letters that had inundated him when she'd been there. "It's been ages since that dreadful come-out ball of yours, petite, and you've no rashes or wheezes or sneezes this time, either. But most of all, you've got me, and I'll see you through it all. I promise. All right?"

"And if I don't care to wed?' she asked rebelliously, "and you find the lady of your dreams in the meanwhile?"

"I'll drug you and wed you to a footman or jilt you and meet your papa at dawn with pistols drawn. Dear humbug, I'll find the answer to a maiden's prayer for you to wed, never fear. And I'll make the world a safer place for maidens by marrying one out of hand after I see you popped off. Because you see, puss, I've met the lady of my dreams," he said with a twisted smile, "any number of times.

"But that's no topic to discus with a lady, however young, however much she's my friend. Now. Your answer please?" he asked, and as she hesitated, he added wickedly, "I doubt you find the program entirely without merit. Because I doubt you're entirely averse to my gender. I seem to have heard something about kisses, and those even with the detestable Hugh. Hmm? Now, why didn't you write to tell me about them? All I heard of was how you disliked him. Not a whisper about kisses. And don't try to cozen me," he said, enjoying her discomfort hugely.

"Ah well, that," she said, and opened her eyes so widely that they became unfocused in her attempt to seem innocence personified. 'I wondered. That is to say, he asked me to marry him and I wondered what his kiss would be like. Well, you wouldn't expect me to wed a fellow I hadn't kissed, would you?" she asked in some annoyance, her mask of innocence forgotten when he didn't reply, but only stared at her gravely.

"Certainly not. But poor Hugh. It was hardly fair to him. How could you judge it rightly if it was your first kiss?" he asked, even more innocent than she'd been.

"Not precisely the first," she said, lowering her eyes, before she raised her head, and he could see how they flashed in sudden anger. "Julian, you're the humbug! No one expects a girl to go unkissed until my great age

anymore! I'm one-and-twenty now! Or will be sooner
than it takes to tell. It's true I've kissed a few gentlemen,
no more than that, I assure you, and it wasn't any great
thing either, I can tell you. Oh, monster!" she cried as he
couldn't contain himself any longer and roared with laughter. She joined in despite herself, for he was just the
same as he'd always been and she couldn't deceive him
any better in person than she'd done by letter.

"Now," he said when they had done except for brief
chuckles, and he noted how damp he was getting and
how the vicar's hat drooped even lower about her ears
while the front of it dripped down over her face in a thin,
steady stream like the eaves of a house in a thaw, "we
must return, and of a single mind. We're betrothed for
the moment and in love for the public and off to London
as soon as the tide turns. Now. All agreed?"

She hesitated. But then she thought that London was a
far way away from here and all the scandal. And then
there'd be time enough to tell him that she'd no wish to
wed at all. Not yet. And perhaps not ever. But there was
time for that later too. For really, she thought, there'd
been enough to-do already today.

She nodded, and gave him a grin.

He saw the impish look and then the innocent-seeming
concurrence as clearly as he'd watched all the plots and
schemes she'd thought secret as they flashed across her
winsome face.

"Lord!" He sighed as he scooped her up and lifted her
high in his arms, this dear little friend and almost-sister,
and began to march back to the church with her as she
wriggled and complained that she didn't have a broken
leg, and what would people think? "I don't know why
you haven't said yes to any of those fellows who didn't
kiss any better than poor Hugh, Eliza. The men of England must have changed since I left. And stop squirming, you don't weigh much more than a feather, but it's a
very wet feather today. It's faster this way and you're all
over mud and a little semblance of affection is expected
between the betrothed, and you want them to believe us,
don't you?"

She stilled, and let him carry her, and wrapped her

arms around his neck as well, for the show of it, as well as to make his burden lighter in actuality. She'd agreed to his plan and so now had no idea of where she was going next or what she'd do when she got there. But he was here and so she knew everything would be all right now.

For she felt lighter too. Freer, purer, and much better all around. She'd told him everything, even about the kisses that she'd never dared to write about. Everything, just as she'd always done. Except for the greatest truth. She'd never married any of them, of course, because they none of them had been him.

3

CONVERSATION STOPPED ENTIRELY when the Viscount Hazelton stepped over the doorsill with his soggy burden. And when the sodden young lady was released from his arms, to stand by his side dripping rain all over the carpet, but with a smile like the sun rising of a spring morning, it was only the giant gentleman named Arden that Hugh had been speaking with who prevented the abandoned bridegroom from attempting to do the viscount an injury.

So it was that the former would-be groom shouted, "Never!" just as soon as the viscount finished announcing, "Ladies and gentlemen, my prospective bride!" as he whisked the drenched oilskin from her with a flourish and delivered it back to the vicar. But then, no one in the room, save for the blushing bride-to-be and the amused new prospective groom, seemed very elated at the announcement.

The minister looked thoughtful, whether at his armful of drowned clothing or at the turn of events, no one could say. But Hugh was outraged and fairly dancing with rage, and Arden Lyons, who was effectively taming him by capturing both his arms beneath his one, and wrapping that great arm around the furious young man's waist, seemed pensive himself, his rough-hewn face no more jovial than a boulder's at hearing the news. The elegant Duke of Peterstow was, for once, entirely silent, bemused, not amused. The Incomparable Miss Merriman lifted a sleek, perfect tracery of a black eyebrow and wore a contemplative look. And Miss Anthea Baker looked almost as chagrined as the excitable Hugh, and at the brink of tears, besides.

But no further attempt was made to smooth troubled waters. Because after taking another look at the results of his pronouncement, the viscount strode to the door to the anteroom, flung it open, and addressed the startled crowd of persons outside in the same fashion. Order was really never restored at the church after that. The only way the company quieted at last was when it was moved bodily away, and that only when someone mentioned that there was good food to be had at the Merrimans' house—the wedding party was to be transformed into an engagement feast—and the promise of sustenance produced results reason had not.

The new fiancé and his friends did not attend those festivities, but there was a such a crush, scarcely anyone noticed. The bride-to-be wasn't there either, and those few who were not stuffing themselves with food or gossip imagined the newly reunited pair were together at last. It was really a rather touching story, after all: how the pair had been secretly in love and pledged to each other since Adam was a pup, and how the groom, after braving adversity of several exaggerated and various sorts, finally won his way back to his love at the eleventh hour and fifty-ninth second. The exact nature of those adversities and trials varied wildly, depending upon who was relating them, but that only added luster to them.

It was a lovely story, whoever told it; it would be repeated in a hundred drawing rooms in the best houses in London, as well as by the firesides of every house on the coast here in Ventnor until the end of time. It charmed those of the *ton* that they'd witnessed such historic proceedings; it delighted those from Wight because they'd been host to history. Clearly the aborted wedding was a raging success, and all were enchanted with it and themselves. Except for all those most directly concerned, of course.

The erstwhile groom had tracked his once-promised bride to her rooms and was shouting the rooftop down, while those downstairs heard not a word of it above their own happy babble. Eliza listened to his loud arguments with amazing sangfroid, so both her cousin Constance and her friend Anthea thought. Although they were there to see that he didn't do her harm, they were far more worried about their success in that than she seemed to be. Hugh—stocky, amiable, fun-loving local lad that he'd seemed to be the day before the wedding—now looked more like a prizefighter than a squire's son as he stood red-faced and shouting at Eliza, occasionally thumping the wall with his fist to make a particular point. And Eliza, still in her damp and clinging ruined wedding dress, stood leaning on that vibrating doorsill, looking bored to flinders, and nodded as she listened to him.

He stopped at last. For breath, or for her reaction. The quiet was enormous after his display of anger.

"Quite done?" Eliza asked sweetly. "Well, then," she said, straightening to her not very considerable height from where she'd lounged against the doorsill with exaggerated languor, "I'm not. How dare you, Hugh?" she asked with real annoyance, but with a quiet insistence that seemed to startle him just as much as a shout would have done. "Everything you've said is just not so, and you know it!

"One—I never agreed to the wedding. Two—it was you and your father that said I'd 'come round to it in time.' Three—I told you about Julian time after time and you just laughed. And mostly," she said with exactly such a look of half-conviction and half-entreaty that had won his interest from the start, "oh, Hugh, I never meant to lead you on, I vow I didn't. I just was playing, I suppose that much is true. But, Hugh, if a girl had to marry every chap she threw a wicked glance at, she'd be a bigamist, sure as I'm standing here, wouldn't she? Why, what if you had to marry every girl you flirted with, eh, my friend?"

"But a gentleman does have to marry every girl he kisses," Hugh replied with a grieved air of vindication.

"Every 'good' girl he kisses," she corrected him acidly.

"That's not something you're supposed to know about—" he began, before she cut him off wearily, "But I do, and there's an end to it. Look you, Hugh," she said at last, after a long breath, looking him directly in the wide, blue, and hurt-looking eye, "I'm sorry. Truly. But it was all a mistake and you're luckier admitting it now than later. I like you very well, and you're a good sort of a fellow and can and will do much better for yourself. Have done, then, eh? And you won't look a 'laughing-stock' if you act as if you know it's best, in fact you'll get yards of sympathy from all the ladies. You're far better off this way, believe me," she said, and thrust out a hand. "Friends?" she asked.

He'd stood listening quietly, and now the fire went out of his eyes and the stiffness from his shoulders, and, "Oh, aye, always, fool that I am," he said at last, sighing, and took up that little hand, and in a manner very unlike himself raised it to his lips and kissed it rather than shaking it, as she expected him to have done.

"If things don't work out, Liza," he said, "you know where I'll be," and then he shrugged, and left her there, to go belowstairs and face the company with the lie that she'd suggested he tell, which was that he'd decided it was all for the best, after all.

"Astonishing," Constance said as Eliza came into the room and closed the door behind her. "I thought we'd have to call in troops to pry him away."

"I thought he'd do you an injury," Anthea breathed as she slumped down into a seat.

"Hugh? Ah, no," Eliza said sadly. "Poor lad, I did him an injury, rather, I think. Oh, blast," she said, and there were real tears in her eyes. "I never thought a bit of a flirt would end up in all this."

"Your papa was very keen on consolidating the properties, and your mama wanted a wedding," Constance commented reasonably as she watched Eliza struggling with her row of tiny slippery pearl buttons, since she'd dispensed with the services of her maid for privacy's sake.

"Not that," Eliza said, her voice muffled as her head lowered over the fastenings she worked at, as Anthea rose and came over to help her. "I mean really attaching Hugh's affection. He does deserve better, you know. And I feel like a . . . a beast, I do." She subsided, whether from the effort she was expending, or real emotion, as Anthea helped her raise the wet gown up and over her head.

She stood before them in her dampened shift, her hair all undone and hanging in desultory curls about her shoulders. Both other women observed her silently for a moment, and she thought they were searching for the right words to say. But both were summing up her appearance, for they already knew her mind, and yet, for all they were her friends, neither had ever seen her in her dishabille.

Eliza had always been properly attired at school, of course, Anthea thought, and as she'd been her schoolmistress, she'd never seen her in less than her demure night rails. But the dampened shift clearly showed Eliza's figure to be as delightful as her face, Anthea thought with a pang of hastily suppressed jealousy. The girl was all of a piece in her artless, gamine charm, for her breasts were full, but high and pointed, her waist was slender, yet defined, and yet her hips were scarcely rounder than a lad's might be. A sprite, Anthea thought, an enchanting sprite, and withal, unaware of her charms. And she, only five years her former student's senior, felt ancient and hagged just looking at her. For her own form, although hardly obese, was fuller and larger in all its dimensions. But then, she thought, quickly burying her suddenly sprung envy, she was a full-grown woman, after all, and Eliza only newly come to that estate.

Good lines, Constance mused, eyeing her cousin as she took up the towel Anthea gave her and turned her back to march into the dressing room to dry and change, thus giving them a brief view of a slender back and saucy derriere. Her little cousin was built to a smaller scale than herself, but she was all in proportion, and would display well in fashions cut to suit her style. The clothes she'd been wearing since they'd met as adults in these past days here on the island were as boring as they were likely considered proper in the girls' school she'd just emerged from, for they were styled in the same fashionless fashion of garment her friend Anthea wore.

The vogue in London was no longer to go lightly draped in material, as though one were a Grecian statue come to life. That style was passing. But the newest craze was just as demanding, for the high-waisted dresses still clung to the body and now fitted even more tightly to the figure, at least until the nipped-in waist, before the skirts belled out more fully at the ankles. Eliza would show to advantage in them. Still, Constance thought with a sigh of relief, as well as her cousin might dress up, she'd never be a great society beauty, for she lacked the inches. But, she decided, remembering the curving grace she'd seen, the gentlemen didn't give a hang for fashion's dictates in certain matters, at least the more interesting of them never did. The chit would do, then, and very nicely too, but she'd never outshine her. And that, Constance thought, with slightly guilty relief, was as well, for she liked her very well, and shouldn't like to have to sever such a promising, newly begun friendship.

Because for all there were only four years between them, Eliza had been considered a child when Constance first came out, her plump fourteen years being nothing like her radiant cousin's eighteen had been. And yet London being what it was, and life being what it was, since they were both single and wellborn and female, they were now rivals, after all.

"I'll be going to London," Eliza announced as she came from the dressing room, as though she'd made her mind as well as her toilette there. She'd wrapped the towel pasha-style about her hair, and was enveloping her body in a heavy gray cotton robe, old and shapeless enough to make Constance shudder, as she asked, "Are you coming?"

"There's no chance of my not," Constance said with amusement, "unless you think me enraptured enough with your island, or your Hugh, to stay here forever. It's my home, Eliza, and my life."

"I'd forgot," Eliza said, sitting and drawing her feet up under her, hugging her newfound warmth and comfort to herself as she huddled there. "You fit in so nicely here," she went on, and as Constance made a face, she laughed. "Or at least you pretended to so well. Wonderful, then. And you, Anthea?"

"I'm afraid I won't be coming with you," Anthea said softly, looking everywhere but at her young friend, for she would dearly have loved to say yes, but would never let the girl know it, for that would be begging. "I've my position, you know.'

"Indeed, you have!" Eliza said happily. "Remember Miss Martin gave you the time to 'escort and accompany Miss Merriman until her nuptuals,' " she imitated in a strident voice, and as Anthea laughed despite herself at the mockery of her employer, she went on earnestly, "And that, dear Anthea, will not be for a while yet, and so I hold you to it, and her too. Mama will take up your salary if Miss Martin won't, but I think Miss Martin will never mind, for it would never do to get Mama vexed, she's very influential, you know, and could discourage new students from coming to Miss Martin's if she were crossed, and I need a companion, and you are she, so there!" she concluded triumphantly in a rush, before Anthea could speak. "And we'll see to getting you some new clothes to prance about in, and it might be that you'll make such a splash, you'll never have to go back. Well, you never know," she added crossly when both ladies laughed at her.

"And where will I live? I don't think there's room for two in that lovely castle in the air you've built, Eliza," Anthea answered, as Constance studied her seriously for the first time and decided that the schoolmistress might actually dress up rather nicely, at that. She'd a neat form and a pleasant face and a dignified demeanor, and so might very well do for a naval officer or a young solicitor or even some elder widower peer with a vacancy to be filled for a new wife or stepmother for his brood.

"Julian said I'm to stay with friends of his," Eliza said comfortably. "I'd never go to London if it meant staying with Mama. Indeed, she don't expect it. She's probably downstairs thinking of whom she can land me on even now, and likely already buttering them up to bring it about," she went on without a trace of sorrow, for she was used to her Mama not wanting her about. It was a thing she'd accepted as a fact of her life long before, as natural to her as the color of her hair and her skin.

She'd been, after all, a late-life surprise, gotten at the last possible moment, when her four sisters had been grown and wed and gone from the house, leaving her mama in peace for the first time since she'd wed as a girl. And newly relishing her privacy, for her husband had already found his best friend in the bottle and his favorite lodgings in his club, Mama had not been about to give it all up for another bout of motherhood. Maybe, if she'd been the long-sought boy her parents had never got, Eliza had often thought, but that was an old fancy too. No, she'd grown up in peace and by herself, here on the island, tended by servants as comfortable and old as the robe she'd unearthed from her wardrobe, and had only been rediscovered by her mama when she'd been nearly sixteen. Then she'd been shipped off, protesting volubly, to school

That had been when her life had begun to change in every way, when she'd met Julian, and then Anthea. Only two years later, Eliza had the privilege of admiring her magnificent cousin Constance from afar, when she'd come to London for her own come-out. So for all she'd feared them, those turbulent years had brought about her wonderful new life, she thought now, smugly, thinking of the future. For now she was going to have her cousin and her friend and Julian too. She pushed those lovely thoughts away, fearful that gloating might attract vengeful spirits.

"Oh, and I'm to be taken on by the viscount's friends too, I assume?" Anthea asked with a forced laugh, because it sounded so lovely that she feared contemplating it as a real possibility.

"Of course," Eliza said on a yawn. "Excuse me, but it has been *such* a day. But of course you will, Anthea, because they expect a lady to have a companion. I haven't asked Julian, but I'm not a flat. He'll agree because he's knowledgeable, as well as wise. But even I know that much about society, though I know I didn't *take*." She grinned, flashing such a devilish look to Constance as to make her wonder for a moment if ragged old robes and turban headdresses might be the coming thing, because she'd never seen anything more attractive.

"Lud, Eliza," Constance sighed then, in the drawling and lightly amused tones that Eliza would have killed to have got right, "more about the miracle of Julian Dylan?"

"I've not been wrong yet, have I?" Eliza said at once, sitting up straighter. "He's everything I promised, isn't he?" she went on, warming to her subject as Constance had hoped she would, for she'd only listened with half an ear before she'd set eyes on the viscount this morning, and it had been a doubting half-ear at that, each time her cousin had begun to expand on her favorite subject outside of literature, food, and the beauties of the Isle of Wight. "Have you ever seen anything handsomer?" Eliza crowed. "Confess, you both thought I'd dreamed him, didn't you?"

"Indeed," Anthea answered, smiling, "all those years, whenever you went on about him, Eliza, we all of us at school thought he was a particularly lovely myth you'd invented to go along with that pendant you'd found."

"But you read his letters!" Eliza protested, stung. "I always read you the good bits."

"Oh, yes," Anthea answered softly, also remembering how she'd been able to contrive to read the rest of each one of them as well, "but I never truly believed that such an admirably well-versed gentleman could have such a face as you showed us on the locket."

"Well-versed, well-bred, well-tempered and clever and adventuresome and kind and good and wholly beautiful." Eliza laughed. "Get the whole text right, please. But he doesn't. I mean he doesn't look like the portrait, does he? He's much better-looking, and so I always told you too."

"He is very well-looking," Anthea said, ducking her head and smiling as though she were amused at Eliza, to conceal the blush she began to display.

"He's a magnificent-looking creature," Constance declared, and as Eliza grinned, she added, "but I've never read his letters, and so take leave to take the rest of his superiority with a dish of salt, thank you."

"You'll see," Eliza promised.

"Doubtless," Constance answered. "And now, cousin, if you don't mind, I'll leave you, because if you don't wish to come down and entertain the company, I certainly am anxious to hear every bit of gossip."

"I'd love to hear it all," Eliza admitted, "but only if I

were a fly on the wall. Imagine if I dared show my face belowstairs tonight! Why, would you have me stand shoulder to shoulder with Hugh and thank everyone for coming to our interrupted wedding? Oh, poor Hugh," she said, growing misty-eyed again. "And however are we to sort out those wedding gifts and whatever shall I say in the notes I return them with?"

" 'Thank you, and I believe I'll just hold on to these until I need them again,' might do," Constance laughed. "I'm off, then. I don't believe I can take another round of sympathy for Hugh, thank you. Good night, little cousin. I'll sob on the poor fellow's shoulder for you, if you like, but I don't doubt he's got a bevy of cooing females comforting him even as we speak." She paused at the door to watch for her cousin's reaction to that parting shot.

"Oh, good," Eliza sighed. And so then Constance knew that much at least was true, the girl had not more than a fondness and some guilt for her stalwart local suitor.

"Are you coming, Anthea?" Constance asked, startling her, for she'd never been called anything but "Miss Baker," and not frequently at that, by the Incomparable Miss Merriman. But that distinction alone heartened her, and she began to think it might be true that she would go with Eliza, after all, and go on to London, and live among interesting people, and perhaps never have to go back to Miss Martin's school for young ladies again, as well.

And so Anthea wore sparkling eyes to go with her rosy blush when she bent to kiss Eliza on the forehead, after hearing her assurances that she wanted to be alone now, and smiled very honestly when Eliza whispered that she didn't want to be spared a smidge of the best gossip when she saw her again the next day. Then she fairly floated from the room after Constance Merriman, after she said good night to her charge. She went down the stair to join the scandalized company, side by side with the Incomparable Miss Merriman, as though she herself were a lady and belonged there.

But she did, Miss Anthea Baker thought with a dollop

of rare hope to temper her usual rebelliousness when she accepted a cup of punch from a tipsy gentleman. She was a lady too. And she was also a rebel at heart, though very few knew it. For a wise rebel could conceal it. And a poor rebel, who was female besides, had to be wise, which meant being prudent.

Prudence was a thing she'd learned from the cradle. She'd been born to a good family, but a genteelly impoverished one. For if her father had been fortunate enough to have been the son of a baronet, it seemed his luck had run out at the moment after he drew in his first breath. For he was the fifth son to have done so, and unlucky enough to be of healthy stock, and so hadn't a prayer of inheriting anything but his manners and wits. He used his prayers to get a decent religious education, and must have used them up entirely, for he never had either the push or influence enough to secure a snug living for himself. Instead, he remained at the school where he'd gotten his education, passing it on to subsequent generations of aspiring ministers for a meager fee and a roof over his bowed head.

He wed another schoolmaster's daughter, from similar circumstances, and prudence being their watchword, they had exactly one child, due to a combination of lack of effort and a rare run of good luck. For they'd scarcely enough funds to see her through a decent girls' school. She had not enough money or connections for anything other than an education, though she'd both looks and wit that must have skipped some several generations to get to her.

She grew up to acquire commendations from school and compliments from the few gentlemen she met, but no chance at a future even so limited as her parents had enjoyed. Silky brown hair, and a smooth round face with clear blue eyes and a straight nose over a demurely bee-stung little mouth, were enough to exact a second glance from gentlemen, and her full figure sometimes earned her a third one, but if the clothes she wore didn't discourage them from a more comprehensive look, her attitude did.

Because the other thing she learned was the meaning

of inequality. She realized early on that lesser girls with fewer gifts had far more opportunity because they'd superior funds, or family. But that was nothing so startling as the other, slower realization, gotten after reading pamphlets given to her by an older disgruntled gentlewoman turned tutor, as well as from watching the progress of her friends as they went out into life. And that was that her only hope for advancement was to wed well. All her cleverness and erudition and skill could be used to best effect only in snaring a husband. Then, for the use of her body in bed, and childbed, and her services there and in running the fellow's home, she might be recompensed with security. Anything more would depend upon his better nature, and anything less could be expected, as well. It was insupportable. But it was true.

There was nothing she could do about it, not even protest. Although she read the bluestockings' pamphlets, she was wise enough to see that even the best of them, from Mary Wollstonecraft to Hannah Moore, had the funds or family to afford to be rebels. Every female successful at anything but pleasing gentlemen did. Even poor, doomed Miss Austen had had a competence to feed and clothe her while she wrote her charming books. Even the seamstress in town had a mother to take her into the family trade. Miss Anthea Baker could only seethe. And because she was young, dream.

She'd been courted. She was, after all, six-and-twenty, and had not lived in a bottle. Widowers and schoolmasters, vicars and merchants, brothers of friends or friends of their husbands, all men of small ability and large opinions of themselves—they were the sort who saw Anthea Baker, and saw there was a bargain to be got cheap there. Or so she thought. For she'd come to distrust them all; having never really known a man as a friend, nor ever having had a brother, they were all mysteries to her. Mysterious, inferior creatures with all the advantages. This was always in her voice when she spoke with them, and in her eyes when she was introduced to them, and so it was not really such a wonder as many people believed when they thought it amazing that such a pretty piece was a spinster still.

But there was another sort of gentleman she dreamed of, even though she knew it was a dream. The sort who came from all the high romances she'd read—not apothecaries or teachers of Latin, but the men from myth and fiction and the fiction of the myths she'd invented when she read their poetry, or poetry about them—the Galahads and corsairs, the gentlemen of breeding and intelligence and sensitivity. And they all looked very like that portrait that little Eliza Merriman always wore about her neck. What they did sounded very like that gentleman's exploits that Eliza always related, as well. And the letters that Anthea eventually devoured that came to Eliza so regularly seemed to have been written by one of them too. That was why she'd been drawn to Eliza, for all the girl was charming. Because his letters—so erudite, witty, sensitive, and warm—had warmed her too. As the years passed, she'd fallen half in love with a dream. But it was safe and hopeless, a comfortable sort of idyll, never taken seriously—before.

Now she'd met him, and he seemed even more than Eliza had claimed. And, she thought, smiling so warmly at the tipsy gentleman who offered her a second cup of punch that he drew all the wrong conclusions and wondered if this damned mess of a wedding hadn't been a great stroke of luck for him, she'd be in London, near to the Viscount Hazelton, and she'd be able to speak with him often. If he were the man she'd thought she'd read in his letters, it wouldn't matter that she was of mundane family and had no dowry. Because for all his beauty and position, if he were what she'd dreamed, she knew that even if their fortunes and places in society didn't match, their minds certainly would. And she believed with all her heart that no female on earth could compete with a true meeting of the minds.

And Eliza? Eliza was a charming child, and Anthea was very grateful to her, because although she would not, could not, show it, she hadn't been so excited in years. She could scarcely wait to get to London. But she knew only too well how to wait. For she was, with all her prudence, a very determined young woman, and from necessity, a patient one.

Miss Baker was doing well for herself, Constance Merriman thought, glancing over to where the shy school-mistress was being stalked by the lecherous Lord Bascombe. Georgie Bascombe had better look sharp, Constance thought on a smile that had nothing to do with any of the gentlemen surrounding her; it was the quiet, virtuous-looking ones that nobbled husbands up like the prawns he was trying to press on her. One stolen kiss and they'd be altar-bound, and she doubted Miss Baker was so air-headed as Eliza, to throw away a rich and legally caught husband. No, she thought, smiling to herself with the sphinxlike turning up of her perfect lips that had inspired not a few feverishly scrawled imperfect sonnets, it was the meek and mild articles of virtue to look out for. She'd remember that. She wouldn't let Miss Anthea Baker within six yards of Julian Dylan, alone.

The gentlemen crowded around Constance so that she lost sight of Anthea, but it didn't matter anymore. She wasn't thinking of her any longer, no more than she was of any of the fellows who thought they were the reason the Incomparable was smiling. She'd learned the first lesson of social success years before; the ability to be in one place in body and another in mind was second nature to her. Gentlemen had swarmed about her since her debut. She'd been hailed "The Incomparable" on that day, and never relinquished the title, although other girls with superior looks might have come by and taken it up as well since then. Because, even she had to admit, most of them had retired from the lists after their first triumphant Season, and she had gone on through so many more of them.

She was five-and-twenty and had been on the town for seven years. Any other female might be considered on the shelf, or be called an "ape-leader" by now. Any other might have been pitied for her single state. But she wasn't, no more than she pitied herself. For she was the Incomparable. Still sought, still admired, still envied.

Her beauty hadn't faded. It was true that tall, slender, black-haired ladies with huge dark eyes and classically straight noses and full cherry-red lips had been the thing that first Season. But her beauty had ripened and flourished through all the seasons, as fashions changed, nodding yes to blond beauties one year, and tossing them over the next for brown-haired ones, before taking them up again. Yet fashion always honored her, for she remained constant, and her adoring court the same size. It was only that the composition of it changed.

Season after Season, she'd noted her admirers, each of them in his prime, each in his time: the clever Lord Leith, the charming Baron Daventry, the wicked Marquess Kidd, the mysterious Marquess Bessacarr, the roguish Lord Barnabas Deal, the fascinating new Earl of Clune, the old Duke of This and the new Lord of That—a thrilling roster of the finest catches on the Marriage Mart, each in his Season. And they'd noted her too, of course. But by the time the year turned, she'd seen them eventually go to other young women in wedlock. Because each time she'd lost interest at a crucial moment. Because always, she knew, she'd get a glimpse of someone—some elusive, half-spied one, just over the current one's shoulder—the one she'd always dreamed upon, the one she'd not yet seen. She'd never seen him close, because once she'd met him, he was never the one.

But time was running out; she'd become aware of that of late. It was not that she noted any diminution in the looking glass or in her admirers' eyes. It was that one year had melted into another and now for all that she loved every detail of the social season, it was beginning to take on a certain sameness, a certain dullness. It was time perhaps to let one gentleman win for a change. If only she could find one that deserved her.

She had a nightmare not unlike the wedding scene she'd witnessed this morning. In it, she exchanged vows with a gentleman, and then, rising from her knees to take his kiss, she'd turn and see the face she'd been seeking all her life staring at her from the gallery of witnesses. But when she awoke, she never remembered just what that face looked like.

She wasn't foolish. She had fully as much intelligence as countenance, and sometimes wondered if her elusive bridegroom really existed, or if it were not the hope of him that she wanted more than the reality. She'd been born to everything she desired. Her father had called her his star, his Treasure, his clever puss; her mother had never got in her way. She'd no sisters, only a brother to take the title, and praise her higher than his own reluctantly accepted prearranged bride. It might just be that she could never desire whatever she won.

But since she wasn't a fool, she wasn't willing to give up the search yet. And so London this year should be very interesting, she considered, with a thrill at the thought of the chase she hadn't felt in years. Because the gentleman in the gallery in her dream couldn't possibly be more handsome than Eliza's Viscount Hazelton.

Amazing, really, though, she thought, that this sort of excitement and opportunity should come from such an unlikely source as little cousin Eliza. She'd been such a dreary little girl—unfortunate in looks, uncomfortable in attitude; those few times they'd met, she'd ignored the child when she didn't actively avoid her. Yet now she seemed quite clever and had grown into a little beauty. Not beautiful enough, of course, to compete with her successfully, yet amusing enough so that her company was enjoyable, and intelligent enough to contribute to any conversation, and so, in all, more than acceptable as a friend. Constance was very glad she'd come to the island for the wedding as a favor to her aunt, and had met the girl and heard her tale, though she'd discounted half of it, when she hadn't disbelieved the whole of it. Until she'd seen Julian Dylan this morning. Then it had all made more than sense. She must have been very preoccupied that brief season he'd graced in London years ago. But it wasn't too late.

She'd go to London with Eliza, and keep her constant company there. It might just be that her search for an eligible *parti* was over at last. For if it should come to pass that she decided she wanted the magnificent-looking viscount for her husband—if, that was, it transpired that he were half so clever as he was handsome, and a fraction as noble as Eliza claimed—she didn't doubt for a moment that she could have him. There was time enough for that decision.

At any rate, the Incomparable Miss Merriman thought, on a glittering smile that made several gentlemen wish there was dancing so that at least they could have a reason to hold so much as her hand without being challenged to a duel, the future was bright again, and she was honestly grateful, and very eager for it all to begin again.

Eliza was eager for sleep to come, and was afraid it might take another noxious cup of warm milk to bring it. She generally fell asleep the way she did most things she set her mind to do, which was to say: at once. This evening, of course, she was too excited. It might be that she could have slept if she could stay in one position for over a minute, and didn't twist and turn and plump up her pillow and rise to look out the window and lie back and chuckle to herself and keep reliving the morning over and again. Because he'd come, he'd saved her; she had never doubted that he would, but was, withal, very glad, because she'd been so afraid he wouldn't.

It wasn't all joy that kept her wakeful. Sometimes she grew very still and felt terrible for Hugh's sake, although she knew he was only deceiving himself and would be grateful for this morning's work someday. Because for all she liked him very well, and they'd been friends forever, and he had after all, been the one to teach her how to fish, and had been the one who dried her tears when she'd wept for the poor fish she'd caught, if he'd insisted on marrying her, she'd have hated him forever too.

But that kiss they'd exchanged had turned his wits, for all that it had only disappointed her. She was honest enough to admit they'd exchanged it, he'd never stolen a thing in his life, poor Hugh, and hadn't started that night at the party Mama had given, for all Mama had been so quick to claim his larceny to drag him to the altar. It was just that she knew Mama promoted the marriage, and she had after all, liked Hugh enormously when they'd been young, and now that she was grown and back home for a visit, his attentions had been so flattering . . . well, she admitted sullenly to an attentive pillow, she had wondered what it would feel like to kiss him, anyway. It was an enthralling subject she'd never been able to research properly, although she'd begun her lessons when she'd been in school.

Caro's brother William had had wet lips, and so the

first kiss she'd gotten was remarkably disgusting. The next one she'd sneaked on visiting day, with freckle-faced young Lord Howard, Mary's brother, was better in that it wasn't wet, but it was rather foolish and dry and she remembered wondering if there was something they'd left out when it was done. The Italian language master had showed her what that was, and she was very glad she'd bitten him, too. But tongues, the girls afterward had all agreed when they'd met in secret conference about it, had no business being included in kisses, after all. Hands did. Thomas Fuller had convinced her of that at one of her first parties in London, when he'd got her alone in an anteroom. Of course, she didn't like him, but both his kisses were a revelation, and there might have been more if the touch of his hands hadn't been so thrilling. Nothing that felt that good was proper; she'd known that much at once. She wanted to learn more from Thomas, but it was difficult to be alone with a young man, and he really was too much of a complete ass for her to stick it out long enough to get another opportunity to test his skills.

And skills they were, she'd decided. All of it, the whole business of males and females and everything that transpired between them. She remembered the moment when she'd first really observed cousin Constance at a party, and seen how the gentlemen all became besotted, but instead of watching them, she'd concentrated on watching Constance. A flutter of an eyelash here, a dip of one white shoulder there, a widened eye, a pouting mouth, any one of a dozen discreet gestures could bring her suitors to their knees.

When she'd been to London for her own come-out, she'd been a disaster. But she hadn't been done with growing then, and so she'd looked a fright that Season, all outsize feet and hands and round as an orange and blessed with a lingering head cold to boot. If she had practiced such arts then, they'd have thought she'd run stark mad and no doubt would have had her in Bedlam, convinced she was having fits if she as much as fluttered an eyelash in a gentleman's direction.

But now she had her own repetoire of coquettishness

and it was amazing, really, how well it all worked. Too well, she thought gloomily. For hadn't she caught Hugh immediately, with just a few pouts and sighs?

She hadn't learned that much more about the actual arts of love, either. For all that she was a month lacking one-and-twenty years, she hadn't had much more experience with the world than she did the world of gentlemen. Because after her disastrous try at society, Mama had forgotten her again. And so she'd stayed on in school long after she ought to have left, feeling very like a girl who had to stay on at a ball because no one had bothered to pick her up after it, left to sit, uneasy and pretending she didn't care, after everyone else had gone except for servants and the host and hostess, who pretended they didn't notice anything irregular. That had actually happened once that disastrous Season, she recalled, and promptly decided not to remember it, because she did want to eventually get to sleep tonight.

She'd been very glad of Anthea's friendship during those unnecessary last years at school, glad of anyone's friendship then, actually, she realized, since she was so much older than the other students and younger than the schoolmistresses. Julian's letters, of course, became her whole life.

It wasn't just that they were the one thing she possessed that no one else at school did, for no other girl—or teacher, for that matter—had a gloriously handsome young nobleman who ranged the wide world writing to her to tell of his adventures. Nor was it even the glimpse of the exciting life he led. It was the bits and pieces that weren't about scenery and geography that meant the most to her. It was the offerings of solutions to problems, the discussions of them, and sometimes, rarely, the wonderful glimpses of himself he allowed as he puzzled over events in his life or hers.

She knew his taste in books, music, food, and wines, she even knew his favorite color, and had taken to wearing the most disastrous hue for her—red—in his honor. She knew he was noble and kind, considerate and good. After five years of emptiness save for him, she knew him a great deal better than she did herself. And, of course, loved him more. She loved him entirely. Odd, she thought, snuggling down into her pillow, holding that warm thought, that such an enormous fact of her life could be so simply put.

Of course he didn't know it. And would not until the time was right, for she wouldn't have him pity her or feel responsible, or marry her for any reason but that he'd realized he couldn't do without her. She could have held him fast just by accepting the offer he'd made to propriety this morning if she had been willing to settle for that. But that would never be enough, it would be worse than nothing. She'd been in this world too long in her short life without a welcome to agree to let her only love merely tolerate her for the rest of it. And she knew very well that toleration was all he could offer her now, aside from kindness, for all that he'd gone on about the changes in her appearance. It was clear he still considered her an infant. Fair enough, she decided; compared with most females her age, she was.

But that would change, she would change anything at his command, or the hint of his wish. She'd wait to see what he desired, and she'd become that thing for him. He'd come to love her too. And it would be precisely right. Because he needed her as much as she did him. For all he'd led the life of an explorer and a wanderer, seeking new horizons each change of season, roaming the earth so far as ships could carry him, he had kept wandering and so was, she knew, as lonely as she was.

Now he was home, and now he was here, and she never for a moment doubted that he was hers. She thought of him, and counted over all the changes she'd noted in his face and his voice, his form, his clothes, and his demeanor. So it was a very long while until she slept, but it was no longer a trial, and indeed, she was regretful when she lost hold of the thought of his face at last, and drifted away from him to sleep.

4

THE GOLDEN-HAIRED gentleman had walked all the way from the wedding he'd interrupted to the inn near the docks, mulling over a great many things, so thoroughly engaged with his thoughts that he didn't notice his physical discomfort until he reached his destination. Then he shuddered, surprising himself, as the inn door closed behind him. Now he was feeling the chill of the day at last, even as he ought to have felt the warmth of the fire in the room, his reactions inappropriate to the need—again, he thought ruefully. But there was no time to do more than note it, and so he only nodded his mist-bedewed head and went to the private parlor where the innkeeper indicated his friends awaited him.

"Ah," the Duke of Peterstow said at once, breaking off what he was saying to his companion as the door opened, looking up from where he sat in the depths of an old and comfortable chair near to the fire. "Look you, Arden. An angel! Or, if not, an earthly paragon!"

"Indeed," the big man rumbled from his own fireside chair, the first smile he'd worn in hours appearing in tribute to the quote he'd just heard, "but likely not an angel, Duke. I remind you: 'Rarely do great beauty and great virtue go together.'"

"And you rarely napped during your Latin classes either, did you?" the duke replied with pleasure. "But I agree, '. . . Beauty and wisdom are rarely conjoined . . .'— just as they taught us, to be sure."

"I'll leave you two to your poetical pursuits," the golden-haired viscount said on a weary smile, backing out the way he'd come in, not bothering to cap their quotations with a witticism of his own. At that, both men exchanged a quick look and, as one, arose from their chairs to prevent him from leaving as he'd begun to do.

"Good God, man!" Arden Lyons said with shock after he'd put his huge hand on the viscount's shoulder to stay him. "You're wet to the bone and cold as the grave. Here—we've saved you a case of brandy. Drink it down, lad, and don't pause for breath to argue, you're outnumbered."

"It's only to be expected. I've been visiting a great many graves today," the viscount explained simply, but he drank down the contents of the glass he was handed all in a gulp. Yet still his friend could feel long shivers continuing to course along the wide shoulders beneath his hand.

"No, no," he protested when they urged him to sit, "I'm all in my damp and I'll ruin the landlord's chintz, to be sure. Here, my friends, I'll hang over the mantel like a dandy whose pantaloons are too tight to permit sitting, and dry myself out while we talk. We've the night ahead for me to sit with you."

He smiled again as he said it, and moved to the fireside, but there was that in his eyes that the humor never reached, and that in his voice which spoke of a weariness beyond his exertions of the day. His friends remarked it, but neither did more than to shoot a brief look to the other again as if to confirm something they'd been discussing before he'd come in.

He was exhausted, but never slow, and as he noted their reactions, a slow grin appeared on his mouth to relax the tight line of it, and he drawled, "Well met after five years, and all you two can do is to look at each other as though I'd come in war paint like a savage? Come, friends, true friends would rail at me if they saw something they didn't like. Closed mouths and little nods are for strangers, surely?"

"But do we know you anymore, Julian?" the duke asked thoughtfully.

"I'm still your foolish friend Julian Dylan, the lad who puts his hand into the fire and stares to see it burning, I'm still the golden youth whom everyone desires and who desires nothing more than that. Why, here I am, unchanged, didn't you see me this morning? Still making idiotic gestures to honor where there isn't any, and living in a storybook world, as ever. Who else could it be? Never say you don't know me, Warwick, I'm just the same after all these years."

"No," the elegant gentleman said soberly, studying his friend with his clear and disconcertingly unwavering wide sapphire stare. "No, the Julian I knew would do and be all that, for a certainty, but he would never know it."

The viscount only nodded absently and drank down the next glass of brandy he was handed, and as a faint flush of health returned beneath his tanned lean cheek, the duke's gaze softened and he asked, with a quirk curling the side of his long mouth, "Tell me, sir, how did you do it? I mean, toss the Viscount Hazelton overboard and take on his clothes and voice and manner? For you're remarkably like him, you know, except that it's clear you've seen harder work than that fribble ever did, and you've more good sense in your hard head than he had in the whole of his career. I'd be pleased to call you friend, actually, if you can promise me the foolish fellow didn't suffer long in his ending."

"He never saw the end coming," the blond gentleman said solemnly, though at last his expression lightened. "He drowned 'neath a heap of compliments, sir, choking to death on a surfeit of praise, and died of an overdosage of female companionship, even as he was succumbing to a bout of self-pity. That foolish youth is dead four times over, and I'm here to take his place, and . . . Oh, Lord, Warwick, Arden, it is good to see you two brutes again!"

They embraced all around then, as they'd wanted to do but couldn't when they'd first seen each other at the church, and then Julian stepped back and laughed at the traces of wet his jacket arms had left on them, and they stared back at him, ignoring the damp, having felt the tight, muscled lean strength of him that his clothes had only hinted at.

"For all you're thin as a wraith, Julian," Arden said on a shake of his head, "and have been burnt to the bone by work or your travels, it's hard bone to be sure, lad. I'd think twice about going a round with you now."

"Well, you won't have to, my giant friend," Julian laughed, "because I'm smarter than I was and won't take you up on the offer. Why, for all your domesticity—and your letters reeked of husbandly things, my poor toothless Lion, all to do with infants and wives and estate management and annuities—I still believe you could last twenty rounds with Gentleman Jackson himself. Aye, and with the black Molyneaux at his side, at that. Dandling a baby on your knee must be excellent exercise," he laughed as the big man actually looked embarrassed at this reading of his new virtues.

"And you, your grace," Julian went on, as the other gentleman laughed at his friend's discomfort too, "I know the sort of exercise that's kept your middle so lean, and I'd tell you about it too, if I didn't think you'd plant me a facer for it. But *four* children, Warwick! Can't you let Susannah take up other hobbies? Lord, do you think to populate the kingdom all by yourself now?"

He'd seldom seen the urbane gentleman's olive skin grow so ruddy or often seen him so momentarily at a loss for a swift rejoinder, but after a pause, in which Arden laughed at the table-turning, the duke shrugged and said briefly, "Twins, you oaf, explain part of it, it's as if we'd only had three children, really . . ." before he realized how amusing his defensiveness was, and laughed along with his friends.

"Four and one, and yet when last we met there were only the two of you and a pair of twins I hadn't seen . . . gentlemen, I congratulate you and I envy you . . . five years is as nothing to me, but when I consider that you two have brought five new souls into the world in that time . . . Lord! Do you know how old I feel?" the viscount asked, shaking his head in wonder.

"We *four* have brought them into the world. Get your mathematics straight," Warwick said with more of his usual confidence. "Good heavens, Arden," he went on in a great mock whisper, "you've got to take the boy aside for a little talk one of these days to explain these matters to him, you know. And that soon will be six new souls," he added, when Julian laughed, "for though Arden's lady is still slender as a reed, it's not just because she chooses to pass up her breakfasts these days—she does it because there'll be a new little Lyons eager to greet the world in a matter of months that she's presently entertaining . . . that is," he mused, "if there's really such a thing as a 'little' Lyons—his firstborn entered the world of a size ready to walk out and greet his tenants, you know."

Arden began to protest that his son was as clever as he was sizable, but the viscount's next words stilled him completely, for all that they were uttered softly and wonderingly.

"Look at you," he breathed, "family men, all settled as nicely as any town burghers. No more quips about your successes with females and cards, it's all talk of infants and acreage and firesides. I recognize you both, for your faces haven't changed, but you're different men now. And so all this takes on a certain dreamlike unreality, you understand," he said apologetically. 'It will take me a space to become reacquainted with you—your letters didn't prepare me for the half of this. I feel a dozen years older and at the same time two dozen younger than both of you."

Each of his friends began to speak, but then checked. Because he was right. A great deal had happened to them in five short years, and it would take more than a moment to comprehend.

Julian had known Warwick Jones since their school days, when the beautiful youth had been befriended by his brilliant but admittedly eccentric classmate. They had maintained their friendship over the years, and it had been renewed and forged into an even stronger bond when they'd met again as young men. For Julian had found himself suddenly impoverished due to the improvidence of his father and his own disinterest in estate matters. And it had been his friend Warwick who had aided him in those difficult times. Though it was Julian's own hard work as well as Warwick's help that had seen him through, their trials had helped them form an even firmer friendship. And it had been then, when the two of them had made a dangerous enemy, that they'd discovered yet another friend, the then gentleman king of London's underworld: Mr. Arden Lyons. The three had bested their enemy, and found themselves to be odd, mismatched, and perfectly mated friends together—all with the same sense of bizarre humor and absolute honor, albeit of an unusual sort.

Those brief years had wrought amazing changes. Warwick had inherited a title, and succumbed to love, finding in marriage all and more than he'd always sought in the excesses of his bachelorhood. Julian had traveled on with Arden, soldiers of fortune together, after they'd both had to leave the country, one to escape the unexpected humiliation of having been rejected as a husband, the other to escape the inquiries of certain authorities. But their journeys had ended in triumph for Arden, when to his own surprise and his friends' unalloyed delight, the big gentleman had found respectability, along with the lady he'd thought he'd never deserve. Then Julian had taken to the road alone, and this time it was a road that led over the seas to distant lands.

Now he was returned. And everything, from the child he'd befriended the day before he'd left, to the men he'd left who'd been so much like himself, had changed in his absence. They'd all of them grown up. All, he thought, smiling the new cynical smile his friends had never seen, one that made him seem more of a satyr than a saint, as it lent a weary look of corruption to his perfect features, all of them except for himself.

"Good heavens! Arden, lend a hand, please," Warwick moaned, instantly doubling his tall, lithe body into a perfect caricature of decrepitude. "I must sit down, and after the look this handsome lad just shot me, it's clear I'll not be able to dodder to a chair by myself. And then bring me my ear trumpet, will you," he managed in a dry whisper, "in case the boy has anything else to say."

"Eh?" Arden shouted testily. "What's that?" he snapped, cupping his hand over his ear, before he grumbled, as he shuffled back to his own chair, "Oh, fetch it yerself, Duke, whatever 'tis. Can't see m'self cross the floor, much less give ye a hand, I'm some years yer senior, don't y'know?"

Laughter mended the moment, their unified laughter

bound them all again, as always, and it wasn't long before they were talking animatedly, and sipping their brandy, together again at the heart of matters, as they spoke of safe things: England, their joint business ventures, the changes that had occurred in their land. And for the sake of that newly restored amity, they never so much as touched on sensitive topics, not just yet, and didn't speak of those things that had occurred in themselves and their lives or even in the day they'd just passed.

"You don't approve of the match I made this morning, then?" Julian remarked suddenly, unexpectedly, out of the ether, in reply to some question about what he thought would happen now that the old king had died and Prinny was king in all but his official coronation, having already taken over the title as well as the coffers he'd dipped into so deeply when he was Regent all these past years.

But because his friends had been aware from his distraction that he'd been holding two conversations—one with them and one with himself—and because for all the five years that had parted them, they understood each other very well, the slender duke spoke up without a blink of surprise.

"It seemed rather . . . precipitate, Julian. I understand the girl was forced into an unenviable position. It was a noble gesture on your part. I expect, though, that you don't mean to go through with it."

"Think I'm a bounder, then?" the blond gentleman answered, though he smiled into the mug of hot buttered rum punch his friends had bespoke for him to chase his shudders.

"Think you're no fool," Arden said. "Pretty chit, bright as she can hold together no doubt, but you're never a lad to pine away in love by the letter, Julian, don't try to gammon us. More like Hotspur in matters of the heart, I'd think, than any languishing poet—unless you've decided to become fashionable."

"I quite agree," the duke said easily. "Love's always been more a matter of the body than the soul with you, Julian—not to demean your heart, my friend, but as I recall, you never forget that it's firmly placed in a nice warm body. In fact, in truth, I don't understand why some clever party hasn't snared you yet. Those winters you wrote about in that New England you lived in, surely they were cold enough to cause you to seek out some amiable lady who'd help you warm that heart."

"Oh, yes," Julian replied with a charming nostalgic smile, "I did. They did. But they were seldom 'ladies,' you see."

He continued smiling and never mentioned, for he was a gentleman, after all, that some of them had indeed been ladies, just as some of them had not been anything like, and in any case there'd been a great many of both kinds and he'd liked them all, and never loved one for more than the time it took to find another. His heart, he'd discovered, to his own horror and sorrow, for all it dwelt in a warm body as his friend had said, was itself as cold as any icy day he'd sheltered from, frozen fast within his breast in fact, for no little hands that had caressed him there had ever thawed it. That was another reason he'd decided to return now. Because cold or warm, it had been beating for over thirty years, and lately he'd had reason to ponder at how any man could be sure of adding so much as thirty more to his span. And so he'd decided that frozen or melted, it was time for him to think of the time when it ceased to beat at all, and make plans for his succession, so that his name would not vanish from the earth when he did.

But, "Oh, yes, I found her amiable, and her name was 'legion,' I believe," he said, on that new and unpleasant smile, "and I didn't love her, though I found her sportive enough. I haven't been as lucky in love as you two gentlemen, but that doesn't mean I've given up hope of it," he lied, "for I've come home to make a match. And you're right again, O prescient one, her name is not Eliza."

"Oh, but I never said that it was not," Warwick answered on the merest smile, "and so I suppose you're going to leave us in suspense as punishment for our presumption, and never let us know the fortunate lady's name?"

"You'll know as soon as I do," Julian said, shrugging,

"because I haven't found her yet—and it won't be easy, since you two great greedy creatures have already nabbed the two best females in the land for yourselves."

The duke didn't so much as stir at that, though perhaps he did in his singularly private heart. For he remembered, indeed, could scarcely forget, there'd been a time when his friend had fancied himself in love with his own lady, and she, as a part of the miracle that constantly amazed him, even up to this day, had rejected the beautiful viscount and instead had chosen himself as her husband. But Julian had gotten over that years before; for all his arts, he'd never been able to conceal the heart in his eyes from his friend, and his love for Susannah, if indeed it had ever really been that, had long since transmuted to the love of one friend for another, as it had been when they'd first met.

"So you weren't quite lonely in America, and even so, there was no one female on that continent that you wished to bring home and make your own?" Warwick asked musingly.

And at that, a certain silence fell over the cozy parlor, as Arden's blunt face, unreadable, as always when he wished it to be, turned so that he too could watch the viscount as he stood at the mantel, and the big man's keen hazel eyes glinted in the firelight as he studied his newly restored friend closely.

"No. And I suppose that's why you've kept your gems from me tonight," Julian commented idly, searching his mug and finding no more than a sip at the bottom of it, and that so mingled with the dregs of cinnamon and citrus rind that he didn't take it. "Your version of domesticity perhaps don't suit them as well as it does you, and so you don't dare let me near them for fear I'll abscond with the pair of them, I suppose?"

"Something like," Warwick agreed, but there was that in his voice and that in the room that the viscount didn't understand, and so he looked hard at his friends then, his light gray eyes dark with suspicion, and a deeper, darker dread. For if he lost these two, he thought, he would be almost entirely alone. And for all that he'd been alone so long, the illusion, at least, of his friendship with them had sustained him through much.

"Oh, they've been otherwise occupied since we arrived here this afternoon, after the pantomine at the church. I expect," Warwick said idly, too idly, "that they'll be along soon. Odd, though," he continued to muse, "that during all those years, you found no special one female—lady or not. And with your past record, and you such a paragon of manly beauty."

"But I never said they never found me," Julian answered coolly, for there was something here he didn't recognize and could not like.

"Vanity was never one of your sins, for all you'd a fair excuse for it," Warwick commented.

"And lack of clarity was never one of yours," Julian said tightly, "or dishonesty," he said harshly, as the duke's slender hand tightened on his goblet of brandy at the words, and Arden grew still as stone. "What is it, Warwick?" Julian demanded.

Before the duke could answer, there was a commotion at the door and it flung wide. The young and beautiful Duchess of Peterstow, as fair and classically beautiful so as to be almost a twin to Julian, stood there, as did her opposite in loveliness, a study in dark-haired, dark-eyed grace, Francesca Lyons, Arden's lady. But between them there was a stir and a tempest. A small girl with long tan hair, as fair of face as Julian and the young countess, but with the camellia complexion of Francesca Lyons, looking very like a creature created by the three of them together, brushed past the ladies' skirts and gazed in joy at the viscount. A second later she was dismayed, and breaking free, rushed forward to fling herself into the room.

"Oh, Julian!" she cried as she raced to him. "But you're wet and it's so cold, and you'll get sick again!"

"I'm not wet anymore, and I'm warm as toast in here, and healthy as a horse, muffin," he said, grinning and bending so as to scoop her up in his arms. "See?" he asked as she wrapped her arms about his neck. "I wouldn't dare hold you if I were dripping with rain, you'd catch cold, and we couldn't have that. Rest easy," he said gently, "I'm well. But I see you've met the two most beautiful ladies in Britain, haven't you? And so do you know these dreadful gentlemen too, then?"

She nodded, mute from being among strangers, he thought, but then she spoke again, never taking her wide gray eyes from his. "You were out in the rain for hours, and the doctor said that you mustn't take cold again. I was so worried."

"We found her wringing her hands like some miniature Lady Macbeth, so wrought up that her maid couldn't drag her from the window where she was waiting for you," Warwick said, "and so we introduced ourselves. Any friend of yours is obviously a friend of hers. But you trained her well; it took more than Arden's thousand faces and all my mimicry to get a syllable from her, and we couldn't lure her anywhere without her maid in tow. The ladies only got her off to her room with the promise that they'd alert her as soon as you arrived."

"And at that, we couldn't get her to bed, you see," the duchess added.

"Nor get a word from her other than her name and the fact that she awaited you," Arden said, shaking his head in wonder. "I don't know how you did it, Julian. We can't keep our cub from telling his brief life history to anyone who passes within earshot."

"I beat her soundly every day," Julian said, grinning at the child, and only then did she allow herself a small smile. The others in the room looked at the pair of them, the tall, slender blond gentleman with the slender child in his arms. Her complexion was dark cream to his fair one, her long hair was fine and of a dark blond, while his was thick and straight only where it had been recently cut, the rest of its flaxen length curled at its ends, his lashes were thick but blunt and gold, hers long and dark, but both were fine-featured, and gray eyes stared into gray and their affection was as real as it was palpable.

"Now you really must go to bed, Miss Mary," Julian said sternly.

"Did you really save the lady from the dreadful man?" she asked as he put her down.

"Really." He nodded.

She sighed, content. "I knew it," she said, and went

willingly then, after remembering to drop a curtsy to the gentlemen before she left with the ladies, who offered to bear her back to her nurse.

When they'd left, Julian turned round to see his two friends watching him with grave expressions.

"Her name was surely something more than 'legion' then," Warwick said quietly, his dark blue stare both sad and considering.

Julian stood very still, perplexed. And then he threw back his golden head and gave a shout of laughter.

"Oh, Lord!" he crowed. "Yes, it was! It was 'chance' and 'coincidence' and 'happenstance,' and otherwise unknown to me. My dear, charming, marvelously suspicious friends, what must you think of me? She has seven years to her credit, idiots, and I only sojourned in her country for four of them. I'm talented, gentlemen, but even I have human limits. She's my ward, or will be, as soon as I get my man at law on it, and not the child of my body—though I couldn't ask for a better, and had I one like her, I'd be grateful. But so far as I know, I have none, and so there's room and to spare in my house and my heart for her."

"You never mentioned her," Arden began to explain unhappily, but he was already looking very sheepish, and the duke was pouring himself some more brandy, shaking his head, and smiling to himself.

"Did I not?" Julian answered in amazement. "Surely I meant to, but my letters had usually to do with our mutual investments and my itinerary. I must have thought I'd mentioned her. Or else, like the directions I traveled and the dreams I shared, I took it for granted you knew, she's been so much a part of my life since I found her. And find her I did, gentlemen, I did not get her in any construction of the word. It was in the wintertime, the last winter I was in America, in a remote part of Massachusetts. I often worked as a coachman there, you knew that. No man can see a country as it is if he tours with his nose in the air and his hands in his pockets," he explained.

"Cut line, Julian, a man can see a country from any angle he chooses. You love coaching, admit it," Warwick said on a laugh.

"There's that," the blond gentleman agreed readily, "for all I detested doing it to keep body and soul together in those years when my pockets were to let, I liked the sport of it well enough. And I found it exhilarating there, because coaching in America is very like ours, but different in fascinating ways. There's no tipping the guard or the driver, imagine! And no highwaymen to beware of either, the coaches don't carry enough gold to make it worthwhile, I suppose, for the Yankees are no angels. They've even got 'shouldering' there too—I think I wrote to you of it—aye, a few passengers in every trip whose fares go in the guard's pocket to be shared with the coachman, and the company none the wiser, just like here, well, a man has to make a living," he went on with greater animation than he'd shown all evening, as his friends watched him, smiling. "But the roads are well enough, except in winter. Did you know I drove huge sleds in America? When it snows enough, the horses founder with the usual coaches in tow, you see, and—"

"That," Arden finally put in, with some grievance, "we knew. Pages and pages of sleds and roads and inns and coaching ways, we know. But nothing of a child."

Julian turned and stared into the fire, and moved a bit of a burnt log back to the grate with the toe of his boot, careless of its leather. "Ah, well, her father was a coachman, you see. An unlucky fellow. His coach overturned and he got a rib through the lung, and it was a damnably cold winter, after all. He was dying of lung congestion in the back room of an inn I stopped at, and he'd a problem, besides that. We tried to help him. We coachmen are a fraternity, we have a brotherhood," he said, raising his head and looking to his friends, "which transcends rank and spans oceans. The fellow was dying and leaving a wife and three children to fend for themselves. We got up a collection, and we'd a deal of money amassed for the widow and orphans before long.

"But, you see," he said softly, "he'd a conscience too. And so could scarcely leave his other child to his wife—not when she didn't know of her existence. But there was no one else to look after her, since her unwed mama, a tavern wench, had left her to run off with a trapper the year before. He'd been paying the landlord where the drab had worked, to look after the child for him. And as she'd no future, not even in that land of limitless future, or not more than that of a bondwoman or drudge when she grew—if she survived charity school or the innkeepeer's wife, bastard children not being considered proper infants even there—I told him I'd take her. And I did. Nor have I ever regretted it." He paused then, and then said lightly, to cover the deep note of sincerity that had crept into his voice, "Taking care of someone who depends upon me has turned out to be far more entertaining than I'd believed."

"It appears that she takes care of you," Warwick said just as lightly, though concern colored his voice too. "Whatever else we couldn't get out of her, we heard enough of her terror about you falling ill. She said you'd almost died, Julian," the duke said seriously then. "She said she'd almost lost you."

"Almost does not count," Julian said on a smile. "Were you never a child? They take fright at shadows and fancies."

"As well as fevers that last for weeks," Arden said with finality. "Her maid was more forthcoming on that subject, at least."

"I had some plaguey tropical fever," Julian admitted with annoyance, turning his back on his friends, "and was ill. I don't deny it. It was ghastly, actually," he murmured after a pause, his head down so they couldn't see his face, as he stared into the fire, his arms high on the mantel above his bent head. "I froze in the torrid heat and boiled all the cold compresses they put on my brow. And the worst part of it was that at its height, such fevers make a man imagine weird, phantasmagorical things, and see the impossible—like coming home after five years away to find his best and oldest friends chaffing at him and suspecting him of spawning illegitimate children, when they aren't downright accusing him of worse, and nagging at him about his health—all sorts of terrible things like that," he said wonderingly, and would have gone on if they hadn't begun to pummel him so soundly that when the ladies joined them again, they'd have thought their husbands were murdering the hapless, beautiful Viscount Hazelton. That was, if they all hadn't been laughing so loudly.

But later, as he lay alone, motionless in his bed, his gray eyes opened upon nothing, and staring deep into it, Julian Dylan thought about his treacherous body. Lying unclothed as he was in the warm room, as he'd got into the habit of doing in the tropics, he couldn't see anything amiss with that body, even though it ached all over with weariness from his long, harried, and hurried journeying. There in the dark, he even fancied he could hear his body creak and settle like the frame of a great coach cooling down after a day's hard riding on the road.

But his frame showed none of the stress. He never dwelt upon what others called his handsomeness, but he could see no disorder in his form. Driving teams of mettlesome horses on rough and ever-new roads took strength and stamina, and it showed. Unlike so many coachmen who fueled themselves with too much alcohol and food for their chores, he'd always been of a Spartan nature, and so hadn't grown their typical prideful great-bellied swagger, distorting what nature had gifted him with by that sort of excess. There were enough other sorts of excess he preferred, he thought as he brooded. And tonight, he brooded.

He lay in the darkened bed, and the faint moonlight showed the lambent power evident even in his relaxation. He was all virility and vitality suspended, even in the lax line of his sex; he was as the classic Adam a moment after his creation—poised on the brink of awareness even as he seemed to lie at peace in the night. If he saw any of this, it only emphasized to him that in all things, then, his appearances were deceitful. For he was never at peace, and tonight especially he knew too well how badly his body had failed him, in all its seeming health—breeding fevers and pains that he'd thought were the stuff of nightmare during all those long and painful weeks. He'd almost died then. He'd almost wanted to. "Tropical fever," he'd told his friends. They were weeks in hell that he remembered.

But when he'd lived, he'd come that last step needful for adulthood—he'd known at last that he could die. Not that he expected to soon—for all of little Mary's fears, there was no evidence the fever would return. But it might. Or a coach might turn over. Or a bridge give way, or a horse throw him off, or a hundred other things might put paid to his existence. It had always been so, of course, but he'd never before believed it. Now he did, and now he had to live his life according to that truth.

He'd need a wife, and soon, because he wanted a boy child of his own. That much vanity, he had. His parents had left him only himself. He'd worked as a menial, driving coaches for the funds, not the joy of it then, so as to restore his fortune and his estate. He'd done all that and more for his pride in his name, and now he refused to die and leave it all to chance again. That much, he determined, he must have—the knowledge that he'd kept the name alive. He expected little else from a marriage, or his life.

For just as the beautiful body showed no sign of its failure, so too his mind and heart showed no outward sign of their lack. He could not love. There it was, he thought, with the same sad shock he felt each time he thought it. Oh, he could love his fellow man and woman, and did, for he'd friends he loved with all his heart. And children, why, he was enchanted with little Mary, and would have given his life to ensure hers. He could sacrifice himself, he could grieve, and he could yearn, but he could not, he realized, for he had not ever, much as he wished to, loved a woman as he'd always longed to do.

He loved them all too often and all too well in different ways. Pleasures of the flesh were very fine, and he'd gotten the sport of it down to the art of it. Yet, for all his skill, he'd never used it in what the poets called love. Once, he'd thought he loved a lady, but she'd only been a dream he'd invented. Because the actual loving of her had been a brittle thing, worse than the pleasuring of a serving wench in the hour before dinner. Then again, once he'd thought he'd loved a lovely girl, but she'd been only a friend and had enough wisdom to see that when he hadn't. He'd never loved her physically at all, which was as well—he grinned, now vastly entertained at the thought—for if he had, why then no doubt Warwick would have killed him for it, for all that they were friends, since Susannah was his lady and had been from the moment he'd laid eyes upon her.

He stopped smiling at the thought of them. Warwick and Susannah, Arden and Francesca—he'd watched them tonight, and what he'd seen of their love, though they'd not so much as touched hands before him, had hurt him as badly as if they'd stoned him. Because he'd never felt that sympathy and devotion they so clearly did for each other. He'd only ever deceived himself. And others. For it had been his last mistress's grave he'd visited today. His first and last paid mistress, he corrected himself. After her, he'd never hired on a body to suit his own. There were enough given to him. Nor had he let any female deceive herself by imagining his love as she'd done, either. Poor shallow, greedy Roxanne had died, drowned as she'd run off with another man, whether in chagrin at his lack of love for her or as a lure for him to follow, he'd not known and never would now. But he knew what he hadn't felt. And rued it.

Perhaps love had always come to him too easily. Handsome gentlemen become like petted cats, taking pleasure as their due, or so a lady once told him. Perhaps he looked for what didn't exist. No one can be expected to love another person forever, after all, or so a great many married ladies had often told him across their pillows. Too many females had told him too many things across too many pillows, he thought, even though he was slowly becoming aware of the fact that he'd very much like another to tell him something, anything, across his own pillow right now. It had, after all, been a long journey in close proximity to a child, and therefore, he'd not been free to pursue his usual lonely hunt.

But his need did not make him rise from his bed to seek out the barmaid. Nor did it make any part of him stir save for that which was reminding him of the offer she'd made before he'd gone to his room. Because he knew tonight's need was nothing that could be cured by flesh meeting flesh; it was vaster than that, this feverish yearning of his. And as he'd not the energy to arise, he'd also not the heart for even the little moments of delightful oblivion such sport would bring him tonight.

He'd become master of several sorts of oblivion. For he'd discovered that pleasure could only deceive him for a moment, to make him think in that shuddering moment that he'd no need of anything else. Activity could push the emptiness away until he rested again. Imagination could disguise the loneliness for so long as he concentrated. But only sleep could hide him from it entirely, and for hours. Eventually, then, he slept.

The ladies were abed, the Viscount Hazelton had left them, and yet the Duke of Peterstow and Arden Lyons were troubled enough to sit up awhile longer and continue to talk about what had happened this evening, beyond that which had brought them to this tiny island this day.

"She's a taking little thing, little Miss Mary," Arden went on, "isn't she?"

"Oh, yes," Warwick Jones breathed, staring at the fire.

"It was good of him to take her in. He has a heart, he always did, but it's grown larger, I think," Arden said.

"Indeed."

"At least he isn't alone any longer," the big man persisted, as though trying to convince himself of something as he mulled over the events of the day.

"You think not?" the lean gentleman asked, his eyes opening wide.

"No," the other admitted.

"Nor I," his friend answered just as quietly.

"I'd hoped he wasn't," the big man explained.

"Ah, but for all everything else has changed," the duke sighed, "some things, unfortunately, have not."

"Aye," Arden agreed. "Oh, aye, poor lad."

5

THE LADY WAS wild with anger. Her narrow face was pinched, and blanched to a startling deathly white shade. But it might be that she had that shockingly pale complexion naturally, the young woman she confronted thought with some anxiety, or it could be that her pallor was enhanced by powder or paint, for it was, after all, considered attractive to be wan in some circles. She really didn't know the lady well enough to know. But the narrowed eyes and shaking voice seemed sincere enough. So it might well be, Eliza thought guiltily, that her mama was very angry indeed.

"I'm sorry, Mama," she said staunchly, because she was, "but there it is."

"It is ridiculous," her mama countered, chewing each word before she spat it out, "and not to be countenanced."

Eliza didn't know "countenanced" could be spoken with so many syllables in it, and she set herself to admiring the achievement in order to keep from crumbling, as she began to fear she'd do as her mama went on, now progressing to a cold, white-hot fury, "My daughter to stay in London with her aunt and cousin? Whilst her own mama still lives? Unthinkable. Impossible."

There were silent witnesses to the confrontation being enacted in the morning parlor. Constance Merriman stood by quietly, considering, waiting for a chance to interject some soothing, reasonable comments. Anthea Baker remained silent, for that was her place. And Eliza stood tall as she could, and she thought rapidly as her mother raged on, elucidating all the reasons why she couldn't stay in town with her cousin. Because if she had to stay with her mama in London, she thought, her own face growing quite pale, she would not stay on in London at all; it was as simple as that.

Her mama might believe that her daughter's engagement to a member of the nobility would give them the opportunity to play at being fond parent and devoted daughter for all society to see and admire, but it would be nothing like, and impossible for Eliza to playact. She remembered only too well those difficult days when she'd been launched, only to sink, into the London Season, and couldn't forget—though she'd tried—her mother's loudly voiced disappointment and disgust with her then. And at that, those bitter attentions had been the most she'd ever received from the lady. Nothing had changed in their relationship since that time, for they'd seldom seen each other since.

When she'd finally been allowed to leave school and return to the island she loved, her mama had visited once, and that only a few months ago. Her mother had given a party to alleviate her boredom with her visit during that short week, and that was when poor Hugh had been snared. After that they'd seen each other as seldom as before. The only thing that had changed between them in all these years that Eliza could see was that she herself had grown up. That would scarcely ignite this sudden passion for motherly love. So the major reason, she suspected, for this turn was that she'd suddenly acquired a devastatingly handsome, wealthy, and noble fiancé for herself.

It wasn't merely vindictiveness that made her balk at allowing her engagement to make her mama a wild social success, although she had, in all honesty, to allow that the thought of depriving Mama of the treat made her feel a low but nonetheless delicious thrill. But since the whole of it was a farce anyway, she saw no need for the trappings of London's social whirl. No, she was more than willing to forgo the parties and socials, despite Constance's kind offer of hospitality. The theaters and shops had sounded very fine, to be sure, but she'd Julian now, after all, she thought, and so really she needed no one and nothing more. So she wouldn't argue the point with her mama, she'd pass up London if she had to, for Julian was here, and with her, and so she was content.

Constance evidently was not, and Eliza was touched by the way her beautiful cousin began to explain her reasons for wanting to sponsor her in the coming weeks. She listened to Constance's reasonable arguments about the size of her acquaintanceship and reputation in London, as impressed by the lucid tones of the dulcet voice as her mama seemed to be, for that lady had calmed herself and seemed to be listening intently. But even from so short an acquaintance with her mama as she had, Eliza knew better.

As soon as Constance had done, Mrs. Merriman smiled. But it was a terrible smile—and Eliza hugged herself against the reply she knew was coming. But never came.

For Julian and the Duke of Peterstow were announced then. And from the look of suppressed amusement on Julian's face as he was shown in, Eliza knew he'd heard quite a bit of the argument on the way to the morning room. Obviously some kind one in the house had left the door ajar after her new fiancé arrived and before he was announced, so that he could hear all and come to her aid. It might even have been done by the butler who showed Julian in, since that family retainer scarcely knew his employers much better than she did. The butler and the rest of the staff of the house on the Isle of Wight owed their wages to the Merrimans, Senior, but all their allegiance to Eliza. They, after all, had more to do with raising her than the Merrimans ever did.

Mr. and Mrs. Merriman had a more fashionable house just outside of London, where they passed most of the year when they felt like rusticating. They divided the rest of the time they spent together between visits to their other grown children's homes across the length of England, and sojourns at their town house in London. But that time together wasn't frequent, Eliza knew, for Mama delighted in endless games of cards with her friends, and Papa enjoyed himself most in his favorite clubs or taverns, accompanied by a friendly glass or two dozen of spirits. Or so she'd been told, for that amiable gentleman was even more of a stranger to her than her mama. Still, she'd never felt deprived of his company in the least, since her grandfather here on the island, then old Mr. Davis, the butler, and Vicar Pine had all been excellent fathers to her each in his own time, although all their time had run out on them all long since.

After the two gentlemen had greeted everyone in turn, and even Eliza's mama's pallid complexion had turned a hint rosier from their adroit compliments, Julian spoke. He did it so well that had Eliza not been privy to his private thoughts for the past five years, she mightn't have guessed that he had indeed heard every word that had passed before he'd come into the room.

"Dear Mrs. Merriman," he said softly in his rich tenor voice as he held the lady's hand and gazed down at her, "or ought I to call you 'Mama'?" he asked with a lazy smile and admiring look in his mist-gray eyes that clearly said such a notion was ridiculous, since she was so young and fair. "It's been only a day since we met, a delightful day to be sure—except for that first moment, and you know how grieved I am that I caused such a stir then. No, no," he said gently, patting her hand and cutting off any reply she might have made, "as I've said, as I explained last night, I understand entirely, and scarcely would have expected you to have put any faith in what Eliza said about her intended husband over the sea, for it sounds as farfetched as I was far-flung, and she's been known to tell a tale now and again, and don't I know it," he added ruefully, but charmingly, as though he were discussing some naughty little girl rather than his stated intended bride.

"And I'm grateful beyond words," he continued, "that you've accepted my apologies, as well as my offer for Eliza's hand," although from the look on the lady's face, he might well have done better to worry about whether he'd get his own hand back from her again, "and am only sorry that we had to meet in such an unseemly fashion," he went on, although the tone of his voice implied that his regret was more because he'd met Mrs. Merriman herself years too late.

"But here I am, at last," he said, "and that's precisely the problem. For here my friends are too. And they must go—Mrs. Lyons is anticipating, you know, and the duchess left all her children behind and soon must fly away home too. I have to go as well, I've been gone so long, you see, that I've a dozen things to tend to in London."

Before the lady could explain that she understood, and the look in her eyes clearly stated she'd have done so if he'd come to her this morning with an admission of high treason and murder, he went on reflectively:

"But I dislike leaving Eliza alone here again, even for a week. Why, who knows whom she might take it into her head to encourage this time?" he asked, half-joking, but the other half seeming to be so troublesome a thought that his dark gold eyebrows lowered as he mused, "And I can't expect you to trundle on to London so precipitately, especially since your husband gave me to understand your daughter Ann awaits you in Norfolk, as she always does this time of the year."

As his listener drew breath to speak, to assure him that her daughter Ann might await her in Norfolk until the last trumpet if he wished her to go to London, he added, "And Eliza can scarcely stay on with her cousin, though I understand she's kindly offered her house room in town. But how ramshackle that would make you look if you were absent at such an important time, and her aunt her hostess," he sighed, and she stopped and shot Constance a look of triumph before she turned to her prospective son-in-law again with a look of such love and gratitude as she'd never bent upon her husband since the day she'd met him.

"So what shall we do?" he wondered aloud.

"Why, Julian," the duke exclaimed, "foolish fellow! Why didn't you breathe a word of this to me?"

Since she'd seen better charades performed in the nursery at Christmastime, Eliza frankly stared as the duke went on shamelessly in the same wondering tones:

"I've a house in London, you know, you gudgeon, right in the heart of town. And we've a dozen things to do there as well now. I'd be only too pleased to have Eliza stay on with us, we've ten bedrooms, imagine, ten! A great white elephant of a place, ma'am," he confided to Mrs. Merriman, who in her fonder dreams rode on just such white elephants, "but it was part of my legacy. Room and to spare for your lovely daughter, and her companion, and this wicked lad too, if he wishes, for they are affianced, after all. And never fear, even if I must be gone now and again, she'll be well-chaperoned until her wedding day, believe me."

Since the elegant duke said this all in the same cool, languid, half-mocking drawl he affected with her mother, Eliza doubted her parent would swallow a word, and braced herself for the disappointment of her rejection of the scheme. But then, she didn't know her mother very well. The Duke of Peterstow had been a rake, and was still an original, but not a word of scandal had been uttered about him since he'd wed. More important to Mrs. Merriman, even if he had been rumored to be partial to orgies in his library, he was a duke of the realm, and of the highest *ton*. She couldn't refuse him anything. If she wasn't to have the pleasure of flaunting her daughter's match before the eyes of society, she could at least have the joy of saying who was hosting the chit in town. "As a favor to me," she could imagine herself saying, and on that delightful thought she tittered and said, "Oh, how very kind of you, Duke," as her daughter blinked.

His hostess made sure the Duke of Peterstow would always have a full plate before him, a filled glass at his elbow, and an earful of amusing conversation at dinner. She instructed her footmen to see to the matters of his meal, and she was pleased to prepare to take care of his entertainment herself. But since her house on the Isle of Wight was seldom visited by her, it was never fully staffed and tonight's dinner would be served by local people pressed into service. She was beside herself mapping out the table, cautioning the cook, and drilling lessons into the temporary help's thick heads. Or so she said. And so her daughter was delighted to report to her cousin and her companion.

"So she wouldn't notice if you came to the table bare-back . . . and front." Eliza giggled as Anthea frowned at her usage, and then went back to frowning at herself in the looking glass.

"Anyway, you look splendid," Eliza said bracingly, and so she thought her companion did tonight. For she'd lent her a silver comb that sat nicely in her soft brown hair, and showed up far better there than it would ever do in her own, she swore, when she persuaded Anthea she'd never miss it. She'd lent her a shawl, as well, since she needed something to liven up her dove-gray gown, and the lilac paisley was perfect, especially with the pearly pin she also lent to fasten it at her shoulder. And then she'd coaxed her to do her hair in ringlets at the face and one huge curl at the back, for Anthea looked very well with her severe hairstyle softened that way, she persisted, as her cousin Constance looked on in silent wonder, much like someone watching a lamb gamboling merrily to the slaughter.

There was little doubt the schoolmistress looked far better when she'd done, but Constance was astonished at her cousin's determined efforts. Didn't she notice the way Anthea Baker colored up and cast shy glances at Julian Dylan whenever he came into view? she wondered. Even if she didn't, Eliza's generosity was in itself astonishing, for Constance knew few females who'd willingly dress another up so as to better compete for attention. She herself was an acclaimed beauty, and never doubted it, but she'd never knowingly set up her own competition. In fact, she often fished about for hints of what her friends and acquaintances had in mind to wear on important occasions so that she could then plan to wear something to take the shine out of them. And tonight was important, if only because tonight Julian would be there.

But she relaxed when she went to her own room to dress, for although Anthea looked well, she only looked better, and not at all splendid. Eliza's dress was far from fashionable, but it was clinging and sheer enough to show her lovely figure, and the canary color showed up her own unusual coloring magnificently. Jonquil yellow did wonders for her little cousin's rich auburn hair and sherry eyes. Still, good to better to best, Constance thought complacently, gazing at her own image in her looking glass when she'd done dressing. For her deep blue gown was imperial enough to make the wearer of a dove-gray frock look like a Quaker, and its trimming of daffodil-yellow ribbands, hastily sewn on by her maid, would make an entirely yellow gown seem garish by comparison.

It was never malice that impelled Constance, any more than it was malice for a bird to sing, and she'd nothing but kind thoughts for Eliza as she screwed on her sapphire earrings, but when it came to her appearance, she was all business. And Julian Dylan's opinion was very much her business.

But she'd forgotten about the other lady guests, Constance thought in chagrin when the company was announced, and though she stood poised and posed near to a salmon settee that could have been made to complement her gown, she wilted for a moment when she saw the other two ladies enter the salon.

The Duchess of Peterstow was as fair as Julian himself, and in many ways enough like him to have been related, for she was flaxen-haired with alabaster skin, and her fine features were as enchanting as her form was exquisite. But Constance knew that fair can never be compared with dark, no more than apples can be seriously compared with oranges, and so it was the tall, regal, and lovely dark-haired Francesca Lyons, in her larkspur-blue gown, that made Constance's spirits plummet and set her mood to match her dress. The lady was said to be enciente, but it was early days yet, so nothing of it showed. But even if it had, Constance had the uneasy feeling the lady would only be enhanced by the gentle swell of her graceful shape, for it would heighten the look of the Madonna she seemed.

The gentlemen came in after the ladies, and so none of the assembled company had time to note their elegance, because they were so busily gaping at the third female the gentlemen had brought in with them.

"Ladies and gentlemen, I'm pleased to present to you . . ." Julian said gallantly as he walked with his escort to the middle of the room, his handsome face composed, although his eyes brimmed with love and secret laughter, ". . . my dear friend Miss Mary."

The child might have been anxious, it was difficult to tell, for the lamplight was uneven and her smooth face showed neither a smile nor a frown as she concentrated on her curtsy. But none of the guests she'd been introduced to looked any merrier than she, as they stared at her in wonder. Except for Eliza, and she laughed.

"Lud, Julian," she said as she came up to Mary and took her hand, "you ought to have gone on the stage and not the stagecoach for a living, you know. Mary," she said as she sank to her knees and looked at the girl with interest and pleasure, "I'm Eliza, and it's so good to see you at last. Oh, but you're even prettier than Julian said."

"So are you," Mary said softly.

"Well, I should hope so," she answered, looking indignant. "He hadn't seen me for years, you know."

"No," Mary said in even softer accents, "even prettier than he said you were last night, and then he said you were beautiful."

That silenced Eliza so effectively that she didn't even join in as all the explanations for Mary's presence were being given, and she stayed still until they were seated, and her cheeks flamed to match the glow of her hair in the candlelight when Julian whispered, as they went in to dinner, "I don't believe in telling lies to children, you know."

The company was so splendid that the hastily trained servants made a dozen mistakes each hour, but the company was so merry that no one noticed. When the time came for another toast, and the subject of the engaged couple's health, wealth, and future was exhausted, Mrs. Merriman herself rose to the occasion. It was a country dinner, after all, and her husband had drunk himself beyond the stage of reciting three words together by then, anyhow.

"To London, and your success there," she said, thinking of her daughter's future and how brightly it shone a path for herself to climb now.

"To London," they all agreed.

"But first," the elegant Duke of Peterstow said on a

low laugh as he bowed Eliza into the carriage himself on an early morning a few days later, "we'll stop off at Greenwood Hall in Sussex, although it's London that's dazzled your ears, and my principal seat is near to Gloucestershire. I'm sorry, but we must make a stop at my heart's home, our humble country house, to see how the children are doing, before we're off to the great city at last. We're disgustingly fond parents, I know," and before Eliza could deny any of the things he said, he gave a real laugh and bent to whisper for her ear only, "and don't fret, Constance knows and won't call for Bow Street when we don't arrive in London at the same time she does. *If* we arrive anywhere at all, with young Phoebus driving, that is," he added, gesturing with his head to the coachman's seat, where Julian sat. That made her grin, but with pride, because she was thrilled that Julian had taken up the whip, and would trust him to drive her across the very sky itself, just at the god the duke mentioned was supposed to have done, if he so chose.

The company all waved farewell to them: the Merrimans, the left-over wedding guests, and the left-over groom as well, for he'd come for this good-bye, and he alone looked sulky as the company all merrily saw the two coaches off on the first leg of their journey, as they drove to the dockside.

Arden Lyons and his wife had left a day earlier, for they traveled at a slower pace due to the lady's condition. Constance went back to London on the same tide, to permit her to set events in motion in town, for she was determined to give a ball for her cousin and her fiancé, and had begged that if it couldn't be at her own house, at least the duke and duchess might allow her to assist in drawing up a guest list. She'd been delighted when they'd instantly agreed to leave it all to her.

She'd have been less pleased if she'd heard what that nobleman had commented to one of the guests of honor when she'd gone. For, Warwick had said on a shrug to Julian, so far as his duchess and he could see, if the guests were to be members of the *bon ton*, they were none of them any worse than the others. She might as well have the naming of them; he'd feed them and shelter them for the proper number of hours and then be done with them all, he hoped, until his own daughter reached such a foolish age as to want to have anything to do with them. If, he added, she weren't wise enough to run off with a likely coachman first. And, Julian thought, he might well have meant it too.

"You mean to drive all the way, I expect," Warwick said on a sigh now as he took his place on the high coachman's seat beside his friend.

"Naturally," Julian answered as he flicked the whip lightly against the left wheeler's ear so the lazy brute would keep his mind on his job and not the left leader's tail, "and I suppose you've every intention of sitting next to me so you can nag at me and criticize all the way, as well?"

"Naturally," his friend said.

"Good," Julian replied on a grin.

"She's very taken with you, you know," the duke commented idly as they drove down the long gravel drive to the road that would take them to the sea.

"Who?" Julian asked, half-attending, deciding he'd change that left wheeler first opportunity, the beast had notions unbefitting his station.

"All of them, actually," the duke replied. "The Incomparable, of course—she has the reputation for never resisting a pretty face; the pretty little schoolmistress-companion too—for all her shy ways, she never leaves off watching you, and it's never a standard anatomy lesson I believe she's thinking on; and Eliza, especially, of course. She's the one I was speaking of."

"That's good, then, they're interesting ladies, don't you think?" Julian asked on a smile. "The Incomparable is deucedly handsome. If you'd ever lift your eyes from your fair lady you'd notice that. And the pretty little schoolmistress is not mean-looking at all either, and charming too. And before you go on about wicked seducers, as you're itching to do, I remind you I'm in the marriage market at last, with money in my pocket and a ring at the ready. I really do intend to make some lucky girl my legal wife before the year is out. It's time, you know."

"Ah. But it was Eliza, remember, that I was speaking of," the duke answered slowly.

"Oh, Eliza," Julian laughed, thinking about his charming little correspondent. "But she's my friend."

"And all grown-up now, I remind you," Warwick commented.

"Is she? I wonder," Julian answered thoughtfully, before he grinned and added, "But where's the sport in that? We're already engaged, remember?"

"Have you any apprehensions about coming with us?" Susannah, Duchess of Peterstow, asked as the coach rolled on toward the coast.

When Eliza looked to see Mary's answer, she saw the child looking at her, just as the duchess and Anthea were, and then realized she'd been asked the question.

"I mean, about leaving your home and visiting London. I know when I first went there years ago, I had some trepidation," Susannah explained, because Eliza had been quiet, only sitting upright, expectant, as they'd driven away. From what she'd observed about the young woman, Susannah thought, even from the few days she'd known her, this silence wasn't very like her.

"Oh, no," Eliza answered, turning so that the young duchess could see how her eyes glowed and her face shone with eagerness. "No trepidation. Only expectations."

His friend Warwick's home was all he remembered and his family everything Julian expected, and it delighted him so much he could scarcely bear it and yearned to be away. But there was no way anyone could have guessed that, for he admired the house and praised the children, and indeed passed as much time with them as he could, as though he truly enjoyed their company. He did. That was part of the pain of it, because they were the sort of children any man would have been proud to have produced. It was only that he could scarcely comprehend how it was that his friend, who was of an age and temperament to match himself and who had shared so much history with him, could have acquired such a wife, produced children, and established such a completely different life in the same number of years that he himself had acquired nothing but pleasures and funds. It seemed to him that Warwick was a man of an entirely different order from himself now. He didn't know if they could even remain close friends, and this troubled him, for he'd not that many friends of his heart that he could afford to lay aside any—and especially not this one.

"Such abundance, it must be something to do with the air of Sussex," he commented now as he strolled with Warwick through his gardens and watched the pack of children playing on the long lawn. It was a rare clement early-spring morning and the occupants of Greenwood Hall, as all good Englishmen, were out taking advantage of the weather in the hour before it changed. There was a wan sun and a hint of warmth on the breath of wind, but Julian shivered slightly, still unused to the temperatures that passed for comfortable in his homeland.

"A fertile land, yes," Warwick answered with the hint of a smile lightening his long face.

"I've just come from the tropics, where things grow with amazing speed and the nights are long enough for any purpose, and yet I never saw more children even there," Julian said with wonder. "Just look! You've your three eldest cavorting here, but there are at least a dozen more with them, and all from the estate. The gardeners, the gatekeepers, the stewards and grooms, all have children the way other townsfolk have mice. And the gatekeeper's wife looked at me to be on the brink of antiquity!"

"Don't let her hear you say that," the duke answered with suppressed mirth. "She wields a mighty broom, ask anyone who's tried to snare her cooling gingerbread."

"Fingers still smarting, are they?" Julian laughed, thinking of how the duke's tenants and workers adored him. "It might be the water—" he went on, before his friend interrupted him.

"You'll find out soon enough," Warwick said with great and secret amusement, and was surprised to hear the note of disquiet in Julian's answer of, "Perhaps, perhaps I shall, and it can't be soon enough."

"Julian," the duke said seriously then, stopping in his tracks to turn and look hard at his old friend, "that isn't what I meant. That might be true enough too—for what a determined man sets out to find, he does. But I don't think a man ought to determine to set out to find himself a wife. It's never like picking a new suit of clothes or acquiring a property. The need must be there—yes. But other needs must be met. It's not so much a matter of convenience as coincidence. Look for a wife, if you feel you must. But don't choose one until you know you have no other choice. It ought to be a great love, for you've a great heart, my friend. Lord, I sound as prosy as old Peters—our philosophy master, remember? Or were you ever awake long enough to hear him?"

But then his smile slid and his dark blue eyes became intent as he spoke again. "I'm only cautioning you because marriage is for a very long time, and closer than any other friendship. When you find a wife, she should be someone you know you can't live without—not someone you decide you can live with. You worry me, Julian, for not only is its capacity great, but you've a hasty heart, I think."

"Oh, very hasty." His friend laughed bitterly. "About to be four-and thirty and as much a bachelor as the day I was born. With such haste Rome was built, I think."

He was about to go on to mock himself by enumerating a great many foolish things he had to show for his great age, when a small figure detached itself from the mass of children playing before them, and spying him, sped to his side. He reached down to pluck her up in his arms, and it was only at the last moment that he remembered not to say aloud that *this* was the one real thing of value that he had acquired in all his years.

"Miss Mary," he said with pleasure, picking the husk of a newly burst catkin from out of her long smooth tan hair, "how goes it with you?"

"I've been playing tag," she said, and as he nodded, she continued breathlessly, and seriously, for she seldom smiled, "and Jeremy is wonderfully good at it, and Buck is even better, but Pippa says he cheats, but he does not, even John admits that."

The other children joined them, and Julian looked down to see two sets of intent blue eyes looking up at him, so like his friend Warwick's that he felt a pang as the thin dark-faced boy said defiantly, "Pippa says I cheat 'cause she can never find me," and his twin, her eyes just as sapphire blue, but her hair as light as the sunshine, grew truculent and began murmuring darkly something to the effect that some people hid in forbidden places so that decent law-abiding children could never find them. Or so he thought she said, but her lisp confused the issue further. A great many other childish voices joined in the accusations and counterclaims and it was only when the duke said "Quiet!" in a severe tone that they all fell still.

They all of them then, all the children of assorted sizes and shapes, gazed up at the duke as he ordered them to get on with their games before the wind changed, or get back to the house and on with their schoolwork before his patience ran out. They were gone from his side in a twinkling, and a sudden stir in his arms showed Julian that Mary was all haste to be away with them too. He let her down and watched, bemused, as she ran after the others.

"No wonder you've gotten so prosy," he laughed, "when your word is taken as holy writ here."

"Which is as it should be," Warwick said complacently before he added, "and shall be for about another two years—that's when they're all due to decide I'm an antiquated humbug, I believe."

They were still laughing when Eliza joined them. She wore a worn brown pelisse, and not for the first time Julian thought of how he'd have to get her to see a fashionable modiste when she reached London, for she must have amazing good looks if he could consider her charming-looking in the sorts of clothes she usually wore.

"Oh, good," she said happily. "Live people with nothing to do! You've no idea how useless I feel," she confided. "Susannah is hovering over little Timon and shooing me away, for she thinks he's coming down with the chickenpox, and though I've had them, she frets it might be worse or I might be wrong—whatever—she won't let me within yards of her. And Anthea is preparing a lesson for all the children. She wants to be useful, you see. But so do I."

"Splendid," Warwick said. "I've a fence needs mending. Come," he said as she looked up at him, wondering whether to change her clothes for the chore, or laugh with him, "let's stroll on, we two have been boring each other to pieces, we've need of you. Julian says you've an enthralling way with a story. Entertain us!" he commanded.

She did. They were all laughing together when they finally got back to the house, for even though her only experiences had mostly to do with life on the little island she came from and the little school she'd attended, she might have been a traveler returned to regale them with her adventures garnered from the four corners of the world, she told her stories so well. And all the while, the duke noted, she kept her eyes on Julian's face, and gauged his reaction so as to know how to pace her narrative, for it was clear his smile was her ambition and his laughter her reward.

"Now do you see how my little Scheherazade kept me writing to her for all those years?" Julian asked as they entered Greenwood Hall again, just as the first drops of rain began to fall.

His friend agreed, although he saw far more. And even more when Anthea greeted them, wondering if they'd been caught out in the wet, wondering where they'd been so long, her great blue eyes searching Julian's face for an answer, before she immediately fell to studying her fingertips when he looked to her and replied.

The subject of their leaving was brought up at dinner that night. Julian broached it himself, but no one was offended. Although he was eager to leave for his own reasons, they'd stayed a week, and a week was all that was obligatory. More and they'd be more than passing houseguests, less and they'd be considered less than mannerly. It was time for it to be resolved.

Eliza was discomfited by the subject. For all that London sounded exciting, she'd been happy here. But Julian seemed ready to leave, and so it was time to go. Anthea nodded to herself agreeably. London would be very good, for here she felt she ought to contribute something for her keep, and though she never minded, there were a great many children to see to and the work often kept her from the adults. London had no children for her to volunteer to teach, save for little Mary, and wherever Mary might be, Julian would be sure to appear sooner or later.

But it was the duchess who spoke of Mary.

"She's happy here," she went on when Julian fell silent after her first comments, "although you'd never know it from her smiles, for she doesn't laugh much, you know."

"She'd little cause to get into the habit," Julian explained quietly, keeping his dark gray gaze on his wineglass as he drained it.

"And she'll be cared for here, and has already made friends. My goodness, Julian, what will she do in London? Even if you hire the finest nursemaid and governess, here she has other children and a world to explore on her own. She's not a city child, you know." the fair-haired lady continued, as her husband once again wished that custom didn't demand his wife must sit all the way at the other end of the table, but this time he wished it didn't only so he could put his foot on hers so that she'd hold her tongue. For though she didn't see it, he noted how each reasonable word she spoke lacerated Julian.

"And if our youngest looks to be developing the chickenpox, she might come down with it too—you don't know anything about that part of her history, do you? And what shall you do with a child confined to the sickroom, all alone in London, I should like to know?" she asked triumphantly.

But Julian was thinking a shout of "She won't be alone, I'll be there, dammit!" as she went on, "At least here she'd soon have ample company," and she groaned at the thought, which made them all laugh and Julian pretend to do so.

But she was right, or might be, and so he only said, on a shrug, momentarily hating the lady he'd once thought he loved for her wit and kindness for just that wit and kindness, "Very well. It will be all right with me—*if* it is for her. Because for all I love you, Susannah, and she does too, she hasn't known you for very long, and she's very young. Children have odd fancies, and I'll not force her to anything."

"Of course," the duchess said, amazed and even offended that he might think her so insensitive, in that moment looking more like a duchess than he'd ever seen her, as her husband remarked so as to get them all to laugh and let Julian order his thoughts.

"Certainly. We're not so tyrannical as that, I hope," the duke said reasonably, "But, of course, if she doesn't agree, you must leave within the hour, and at once, you understand."

Mary was almost asleep when Julian came in to bid her good night, and though he'd thought to broach the subject in the morning when she was fully awake, a small selfish impulse made him bring it up at once. The night was the time for homesickness and sentiment—it was so for himself, he'd seen it to be so for her in those first weeks they'd traveled together. Now, then, was the time to bring up the possibility of separation, now when she was least likely to accept it.

She sat up in bed, her eyes very wide, all in a huddle of bedclothes, looking so small and defenseless he hated himself for his decision to bring the matter up to her. Because abandonment was a terrifying thought, and that was what it amounted to, no matter how nicely it was dressed up. He did try very hard to dress it up as best he could, and so stressed that it was only a possibility he mentioned, and whatever possibilities it held, it would always be her choice.

Her face remained so still as he spoke that his spirits soared. He even tried to make the projected stay seem more pleasant now that he knew she'd have none of it, adding on bits he hadn't thought to before in order to make the idea more attractive, embroidering it with reassurances about how near he'd be if she needed him, only a day's ride by coach—with him driving, of course—and how they'd meet up again soon enough when they and the duke's litter went to visit with his friend Arden in the north, in the summer. But a cold March wind whined at the windows and summer was far away, and they both knew it.

She remained still when he'd done, for she wasn't a talkative child any more than she was a jolly one; unwanted bastard children learned early on how to keep to themselves and attract the least attention. He was thinking of the best way to put a good face on her rejection of Susannah's offer of hospitality when she spoke.

"I'd like that," she said.

"But I must go on to London," he answered, startled into thinking she'd misunderstood.

"But I'll see you in the summertime," she replied, as though he hadn't understood. "We're going to build a house in a tree. John's father will help. I can serve tea in it. Meg's mama has an old set we can use. Jim has a toad named Eleanora," she explained further, as she yawned.

"Summer will be soon," she said at last as he brushed her forehead with his lips and settled her back to sleep, and he didn't know, or care to know, if she thought to comfort herself or him with that.

Susannah insisted on remaining home near the nursery, to watch the progress of her toddler's spots if they formed. Warwick declared he'd miss the treat, although he promised to come home at once if they appeared. But he knew he must at least open his London town house for his guests, if only for the look of it, and so he sat beside Julian on the driver's seat again as their carriage, containing the reduced party of Eliza and her companion, Anthea, headed toward London, followed by the coach filled with luggage and servants.

"Miss Mary will be well off with us, I promise you," Warwick said offhandedly after they'd driven their first mile together.

"Oh, well I know it," Julian answered lightly, and he appeared to concentrate on the horses, though he'd a pair of well-trained teams in hand. He got over the hurt of it soon enough, having realized it was beyond foolish for a grown man to feel rejected by a child. After all, he'd told himself, he was the one leaving her behind; it wasn't as if she were running away from him. And she was only a child, after all.

But all the way to London he kept patting his pockets and searching in his waistcoat for something, as if he'd lost something, or misplaced it. He kept doing it until Warwick asked if he were doing an imitation of Bonaparte, and then he laughed, and stopped, realizing what he was doing and remembering what it was he sought. It was only that he'd grown so used to traveling with her, of course, that his new freedom made him feel as though he'd forgotten something. He withdrew his hand from his waistcoat, shaking his head for his folly—as though such a responsibility were something that would fit into his pocket—and he'd a smile for his foolishness as he paid new attention to his driving.

And yet, soon after, again, without thinking, he began to search himself absently for something he seemed to have lost.

6

THE LADY LOOKED up at the gentleman sideways from beneath a fringe of lowered eyelashes. A little smile quirked the corners of her pink lips and she flushed before she cast her lashes down over the look of pleasure in her light-filled brown eyes, and she paused, as though to fully savor the flavor of the gentleman's delicious compliment before she spoke to him again. He was as thoroughly enchanted with her performance as he knew he was supposed to be.

It was getting more difficult by the day for Julian to remember that this coquettish creature was his quaint little Eliza. It was not only the new wardrobe she'd acquired during this stay in London that transformed her, it was all the other arts and graces she'd taken on since she'd arrived here as well. But the new clothes helped amazingly. Today she wore a striped white and rose concoction that personified the essence of feminine contradictions. The sleeves were dramatically slashed, but after that initial puffy extravagance at the shoulder, they clung to her arms down to her delicate wrists, just as the snugly fitted dark rose velvet bodice showed every contour of her high bosom before the fabric was permitted to relax at the top of her trim waist and then fall away loosely until it belled over the tips of her rose satin slippers. Her hairdresser had conspired with her maid to continue the artful, artless effect, for her smooth, shining auburn hair was pulled up high in back, only to collapse into ringlets all about her face. And even the bonnet she wore was flirtatious, permitting him only peeks at the charming face it did not quite enclose. As she turned her head, he saw only a blushing paper rose blooming beside her piquant profile, before she looked up again to show him a blushing cheek.

And then she spoke, and tiring of the game, was again the Eliza he knew, as well as the one he was daily becoming more delighted to know.

"Lud, Julian, if you continue to compliment me I won't be able to speak with you at all," she answered crossly. "It was so much easier writing to you, because then we could speak of real things without me forever having to wonder if you're teasing me about my appearance . . ." she complained, before she stopped and suddenly looked straight at him without a hint of artifice and seemed to be just as worried as she sounded. "Or if you aren't teasing, then having me wonder if you're listening at all, or only just looking."

"Shall I close my eyes, then, when we meet?" he asked in the new drawling voice he used with her, not teasing her as he used to do when he thought she was a child those weeks ago when they'd first met again. At least not teasing in the old way, she thought, because he sounded provocative nonetheless.

"But if I don't look while we're walking," he explained, "then I'll fall even harder than if I do. If that's possible," he said, smiling in such a way as to make her lower her eyes again. This new Julian, she thought, breathless again, this Julian she'd only just begun to know, was so much everything she'd dreamed upon that she was as thrilled as she was sometimes terrified.

"There! That's just it!" she said triumphantly, determined to be honest while she could still think straight. "I said something very real, and you've turned it into a compliment that's made me forget what I was going to say. And for all I like to be told I'm pleasing to look at, Julian," she said, studying her slipper tips as they strolled along the avenue, "it seems we end up speaking of *me* all the time, but not the 'me' I wanted to talk about. And so when I get home again, after you've gone I'll find I want to sit down and write Julian a letter to tell him what I did and what I saw and thought that day, just as I've done for all these years."

"So I was your diary, eh?" he asked. "But that's odd,

for I don't remember any entries about a gentleman named Hugh or any kisses exchanged, and so I wonder if you're so jaded by being courted and told of your beauty that you don't think such trifles as kisses are worthy of even mentioning in passing in your own daily diary."

She stopped walking. "There again!" she said, and crossed her arms and tapped her toe tip until he laughed aloud.

"All right," he capitulated, taking her hand and putting it on his sleeve again, "I'm done for the moment. No more about your eyes or hair or the way you use your lips, my dear Eliza, although," he said, putting his golden head to the side as he seemed to contemplate something, "you might try to turn the tables and compliment me, you know. I've spent a fortune outfitting myself in new togs since Warwick told me everything I owned was antiquated, five years out of style being a century outmoded in London now, it seems, for even Arden snickered at my cuffless sleeves, and he's never a monster of fashion. Now here I am—a veritable Bond Street Beau. But all you've ever said is, 'Lud, Julian, you look fine.' "

He was an amazingly good mimic, and so she could only laugh, as Anthea, walking slightly behind them, looked up as he spoke, wondering if Eliza had interrupted him.

Both women gazed at him then: tall and straight in his good new dark blue jacket and buff pantaloons, with his new brown half-boots on his well-muscled legs, and a new beaver hat set rakishly on his overlong streaked gold hair. And both women sighed, as all women who saw him did, for he could never be out of fashion in whatever he wore, any more than any of those marble fellows clad in stone tunics had been in the museum they'd just come from. But that particular truth would never do, Eliza thought, any more than coals to Newcastle would, and so she only said as lightly as she was able:

"Lud, Julian, you want a chorus of praise every time you appear? I'll add my voice to it if you like, but I thought it might get tiresome. Now I wonder why you bothered to read my letters, for there was never a word in them about your wondrous beauty."

"I noted that," he answered, nodding agreeably, "don't think I didn't. But I forgave you because it had been so long since you'd seen me. And as for choruses—who ever gets weary with hearing his favorite song?"

"Very well," she sighed, before she went on in higher, more excited accents, "Oh, Julian, that coat is exquisite, you know, for it frames your shoulders, it does, my goodness—where did you ever find a tailor with so much material to spare for such great big shoulders as you have? And yet, see how nicely he's fitted your breeches to your wand-slim—"

But Anthea's gasp cut off her words and Julian's laughter drowned out any other indiscreet thing she might have said about his hips or any other aspect of his nether regions. Her face grew more than becomingly pink as she suddenly recalled what a lady was not supposed to compliment, although obviously supposed to notice, for otherwise gentlemen's unmentionables would not be tailored so tight, or their coats and waistcoats cut so high so as to put such areas constantly on view.

"Hush," he said, placing a long finger to her cheek as she looked down, "and never mind. I never named you 'friend' because of your compliments, and my favorite song is, like my favorite people, rare and difficult."

She looked completely captivated, before she collected herself and wailed, "Again?"

"But this time it was your wits and not your winsome face I was extolling," he protested as she cried, "Again!" and then they all laughed, Eliza to cover her pleasure, Anthea to hide her disappointment that he hadn't flattered her, and Julian genuinely at Eliza's wit and at his own pleasure in it.

"Now, then," he said as they continued on down the fashionable street this balmy morning, "tell me about what you might have written to me about, and I swear I won't say a word about how delightful it is to see the words on your lips rather than on paper. I promise, I swear it," he laughed as she began speaking, only to stop as his deft compliment finally occurred to her. Then she grew so nettled it looked as though she might forget the surroundings and actually use her parasol on his back to more effect than the way she'd been twirling it over her own slight shoulders.

But she calmed herself and began to talk about the art exhibition they'd just seen, and since he agreed and could follow her without effort, he allowed himself to follow his own thoughts as he nodded agreement with hers. And though he didn't speak his mind, despite all his promises he looked at her and very much enjoyed what he saw.

These last weeks, as she'd come to know London and prepare for the ball that would reintroduce her to society, even as it set the seal on their false engagement, he'd come to know her again, this time as a grown woman. And as the season had grown to spring, his hopes had grown as well. He'd been invited to stay at Warwick's house too, but had taken rooms at his club instead, so that constant exposure to her wouldn't bring the usual disillusion to him. But he'd seen a new facet of her every day, and each day he'd managed to find another excuse to see her for a bit longer, visiting with increasing frequency even as the days themselves grew longer. And nothing he found displeased him.

She was clever and kind, literate and sweet-natured, with just a touch of temper to keep her from being insipid, for she was sharp and observant and shrewd withal. But these things, he'd known. He'd known her mind, after all, these past five years. But now she was grown so lovely, and even more, and even better, she was as comfortable with him as he was with her. Or at least she had been before he'd begun circling her slowly, and slowly moving closer as he focused on those other things he did not know before, those vital things he yearned to discover. Because she had the whitest skin and softest contours, and now he found he sought more than wisdom from her lips, and far more than the pleasure of her conversation in her company.

He would not leap to love again. But having discovered his little friend grown to a beautiful woman, he was at least ready to allow himself to fall. She laughed at something she was telling him and he marveled again at the changes age had wrought in her. That, at least, he no longer commented on. Because the last time he'd mentioned her age they'd been in the company of her cousin and her friend. She'd grown angry and Anthea embarrassed, and even the usually suave Constance had grown a trifle vexed with him for it. And all of them, he owned, with some justification.

She'd said something cynical and amusing that day, he'd replied with a jest twitting her about her "vast experience with the world."

"Lud, Julian," she'd answered, exasperated, "I may not have been *out* in the world very long, but I remind you I've been *on* it for more than a score of years—almost exactly one-and-twenty, to be precise—and that, I remind you, is considered to be on the shelf," she'd said. He'd grown silent as the two older women looked distinctly displeased, for it was true, and so then even truer for them. For all he'd always thought of her as an infant, for all he supposed she was, compared with himself, she was three years overdue at the altar in the eyes of society and not likely to forget it. But neither did he, and he rejoiced in it.

Bright enough, beyond beautiful enough, and at last old enough for him, he thought gleefully. But, steady, lad—steady, and quietly, he cautioned himself. For if he'd had a hasty heart in the distant past—and Warwick hadn't been entirely wrong about that, he admitted—he'd a cautious one now too. Once, he'd believed himself in love with a lady who was society's own self reflected, a paragon in the *ton*—an empty shell in his arms. And again, he'd thought he'd loved an innocent girl, more for her innocence, it transpired, than for herself—she'd been right in that when she'd refused him. After that he'd shuttered his heart, put it in a box of golden, and fastened it off with a silver pin, just as the old song said he should. Or at least he'd hidden it away. But now, discovering his friend grown to such a womanhood . . .

He hesitated. And yet . . . and yet, watching her, how his heart soared even as he tried to disregard it, remembering things he'd long forgotten. But he didn't believe in such serendipity, to find a love when he most needed one. No, this time he'd bide his time, for time would bear proof; he'd force himself to wait, for the waiting was better than the losing. Whatever his friend Arden's favorite poet said, it was better to lack love than to lose it. Or at least less painful. And pain was a thing he'd had enough of.

"No," he said, not missing a word, because her voice had changed to interrogative and so he'd begun attending to her just in time, "I don't mind showing you about London every day, and that's not another compliment either. Because I'm selfish and I'm showing myself about just as much as I'm touring the city with you. I don't know why it is that the best cities always think the way to improve themselves is to change themselves. If I tell you I adore your nose, you'd not rush off to have it flattened, I think . . . Oh aye, I'm sorry," he laughed, "I dislike your nose entirely—is that better? But here's London, surely the most wonderful city in the world, and here I am returned after five years to find it tearing itself down and building itself up again as though there'd been something wrong with it to begin with.

"I feel the veriest yokel—my favorite club gone from its corner, my new one is on a street that didn't even exist when I left," he complained, "Watier's closed, my apothecary sold out to a greengrocer . . . Thank God the holiest places, Tattersall's and Astley's, remain untouched," he said fervently, as the ladies giggled.

"Not to mention the human attrition I discover," he continued darkly. "My tailor dead, inconsiderate fellow, and my friends all home each night cooing at their wives and babies . . ." And then, from the utter silence realizing the deep water he'd got into, he went on at once, "So you see, Eliza, if I didn't know you, lass, I'd have to invent you, I think."

"Do you like your new club?" Anthea put in hurriedly, remembering, from his look to Eliza and his voice as he reassured her, that she was supposed to be a chaperone, after all. And from her own reaction to that look, wanting it trained on her if only just for a moment.

"Oh, the Travelers?" he answered, diverted. "It's fashionable, so I suppose I must," he said on a shrug. "But we're quite close. Should you like to see it?" he asked.

"Oh, no, not from within," he laughed, "you'd never be allowed, and I'd be tossed out for smuggling you in. But at least you may have a peek at its lobby. It's the last word, all the crack, I assure you, and you'll be the envy of anyone who has never actually lived there. Because the talk is all true—neither family nor funds will get you in, you know. No, the rules clearly state that all members must be gentlemen who've traveled at least five hundred miles in a straight line out from London, or they can't rest their weary heads there. Foreigners abound, as much as we peripatetic Englishmen clog its salons, and so it's not a bit like England, but rather more . . ." He paused.

Because he'd been about to say how disappointed in it he was for that very reason. He was sick for the feel and taste of home, and yet felt as though he were still on some alien shore. But instead, not wanting sympathy, he rhymed the word before it was uttered and so said, ". . . a bore, for all that, it's a bore. But worth a look, if only for the conversation you'll get from it. Come, then, it's only round the corner and down the new Regent Street."

They accompanied him readily, and he was relieved. Because he couldn't think of any other place to take them today, and for all that they were due to meet for dinner, that would be tonight, and for all that it was close to teatime, he didn't want their day to end yet.

"Of course there were other clubs," he went on casually as they strolled. "I'm not such an exile that I dropped all my memberships, no, White's and Boodle's still have my name in good order, but if I were planning to stay, I'd be more active with the Four-in-Hand Club fellows, since they're all as coaching-mad as I am, so I suppose—"

"You're not staying on?" Eliza gasped, cutting across whatever he was about to say.

"Once upon a time I wasn't sure of anything," he said gently, "except that I had been summoned home to rescue a fair maiden. And I did. And now," he said, bending to breathe the word close to the artful artificial rose on the hat he longed to pluck from her hair so he could rest his lips against her listening ear, "I am sure I must stay. But not here," he added, straightening, even more when he caught the reproving look in Anthea's eye.

"I'm sorry it's not more interesting at this hour," he said. "The chap with the elephant is off buying up wives at Almack's, and all the fellows wielding scimitars are taking their afternoon naps . . . no," he laughed, "we've some exotics here, but not so many as all that, but I had to say something to liven the place up for you," he said, indicating the large bare and largely uninhabited foyer to his club.

There were a few gentlemen reading, a few looking at magazines, and a great many more somber-looking ones grouped together, standing in agitated whispered conversation near to the windows.

"No one exotic, that is, except for the Frenchmen, and they only to me, I suppose," Julian explained softly, inclining his head toward the group. "We've packs of them presently. You're used to it, but when I was last in London we'd just ended the war and they weren't in such good odor here. They're still not, actually." He grinned. "Seems to be a constitutional oddity, their distrust of water. I think they don't know they can drink it, and believe scent replaces it entirely for other purposes."

"Dreadful!" Eliza said, stifling her laughter. "But I remember your taking a rather long look at the French singer at the opera the other night," she said slyly.

"Of course," he answered, low. "I never said I ever held anything against Frenchwomen, did I? Except . . ." He paused as he remembered just in time that for all his casualness with Eliza, she was a lady, and he'd been about to say, ". . . for myself, and as often as I possibly could," so instead he hastily thought to intercept a passing footman and ask, "What's got the French guests so stirred up, do you know?" as though he cared.

"Haven't you heard, sir?" the fellow answered with the excited pleasure of someone who's got something stirring on his mind, but something he's sure everyone knows too well for him to repeat. "Why, we've word that Boney's dead, the word's just in from the docks, it came in with the tides, sir, Napoleon's dead, a week now, they say."

"A week and he's not risen again? Then dead enough," Julian said slowly. "And of what?"

"Whatever. Dead, though, sir, gone, and good riddance, I say. Oh, but excuse me, sir," the footman said, remembering his own place and hopes for gratuities, and not knowing the viscount's political sentiments, he hastened away.

"But surely you don't mourn him?" Eliza asked, seeing Julian's face suddenly grown grave, his eyes bleak and still.

He looked down at her with a strangely tender expression. "Bloodthirsty wench. But yes, I do. But only for my own sake. He's been my enemy since I could toddle. And now he's gone. You're too young to know," he said sadly, "but losing an old enemy is not unlike losing an old friend. Because it leaves a hole, you know. And now the world's changed again. We oldsters resent change, you see."

Her smile wavered. Because from his gravity, she didn't know if he jested. But then, neither did he.

"You must do him proud, and you'll see, you will," Constance said emphatically. "Now, turn around, and yet again, and—"

"I won't do him proud if I reel in so dizzily they all think I've been tippling in my rooms. Here, Constance, walk round me this time, I'm done with turn, turn, turn all night," Eliza said testily.

"You'll do," Constance said with satisfaction, ignoring her cousin's outburst as she walked around her, studying her. "You'll do."

"I should hope so!" Eliza said with feeling. "Because I'm done. To a turn. If they don't like me now, after your hairdresser and dressmaker and maids are done with me, they never shall!"

"They? But it's the viscount we're thinking of, Eliza," Anthea chided her. "You do want to please him, don't you?"

"Exactly so," Constance agreed. "After that dramatic engagement of yours, tonight the world must be made to see that he's lost his heart to a lovely chit, and not his mind, entirely."

Eliza fell silent and fidgeted with a bow on her waist. She'd not given a thought to Julian's reaction to her transformation tonight at all. Now that she did, she realized it was because she was confident he'd be pleased. He'd liked how she'd looked every day he'd seen her so far, and so she'd taken it for granted that he knew her too well to be swayed by how well all of Constance's cohorts had gotten her up in style. It was the reaction of the *crème de la crème* of the *ton* that she'd be meeting tonight that had worried her. They—all the peers and wellborn, the sophisticated and clever social lights of London, the elegant gentlemen and brittle ladies with their penetrating eyes and wounding tongues—they'd been the ones that had almost killed her with their cool amusement and disinterest three years before, when she'd come out on the town that first, and last, disastrous time.

This spurious engagement ball was given for them, and never for herself or for Julian. All her hopes that Julian would turn their secretly false betrothal into a true one were based on his daily and growing knowledge of her, and his getting to see the new woman she'd become. This pretty, trumped-up doll that Constance had helped create that stared back at her from her mirror was nothing to do with that. She'd consented to become this prettified creature only so that those clever, idle, and cruelly knowing persons Constance had invited to her ball tonight would not turn and rend her sensibilities as they'd done so well those years ago.

But nothing she'd become was anything like she'd been, and so she nodded, smiling. Her cousin and her companion thought she was thinking of Julian's delight and praise, but she was only imagining the possibility of the *ton*'s accepting her, or at least their allowing her to pass among them unscathed. She couldn't expect Constance or Anthea to understand that—they knew neither the real situation between herself and Julian nor the way the thought of the social world still terrified her. The one because it was not just her own secret, and so she couldn't in honor unfold it to anyone, even her closest friend; the other because it was still too demoralizing to contemplate, much less to attempt to relive with anyone.

But no, she looked nothing like that scorned and ignored child of eighteen that she'd been. Not this elegant
little lady she saw in the glass. This cool beauty wore a
daringly cut black-and-gold-checked satin dress of the
latest mode, not a conventional white and girlish gown
that pointed out the pallor of terror she'd shown as she
made her first trembling bows. And the figure it graced
was that of a voluptuous woman, and not an unformed,
late-growing child. Her dark auburn hair was dressed
high and enlivened with sparkling bits of gold-petaled
flowers, like stars trapped in a shining mahogany firmament, and looked nothing like the tangled red locks that
had been tortured into temporary submission and foolish
frizzled sausage curls that ill-fated night. Her complexion
was pale and interesting, not blotched by nose-blowing
from the streaming cold she'd had then, and her eyes
sparkled with the secret knowledge of the sham engagement they were all come to envy her for, because the
idea of those cool, clever social dictators being out-witted
quite disarmed her. She held her head high with a confidence born of the knowledge that she would have Julian
by her side this time, and with the thought of Julian to
beguile her, she needed nothing more to enhance her
looks. Oh, yes, she thought as she turned to go belowstairs,
she'd do, all right, or at least she'd do tonight if she ever
would.

Constance was well-pleased by the image that appeared
high over her little cousin's reflection in the glass. Eliza
looked very well, in her fashion. But what fashion could
touch the one that set all the others? The tall, slender
dark-haired lady with the famous half-smile wore a dis-
armingly simple cloth-of-gold gown tonight, just as she'd
planned to do when she'd selected her cousin's gown for
her. For it quite outshone the black-and-gold confection
Eliza wore, pretty as it was. But pretty, she thought,
gazing with pleasure at herself in the glass before she
turned to accompany her cousin belowstairs, was never
perfect. The gentlemen would all see that, and Julian
Dylan had eyes that functioned as well as fascinated. An
engagement ball, after all, was not a wedding ceremony.
And remembering what had happened at the last one of

those she'd attended, with almost all the same principals involved, she picked up her fan and on a tide of rising good humor followed her cousin out the door.

Anthea had one look in the glass at herself before she turned away with a small smile of guilty pleasure. For her new lilac gown was demure, yet candid about the charms it did not quite conceal, as all the gowns she wore usually did. She looked just as she'd always dreamed she could: modest, yet feminine; stylish, yet sensible. The golden girls could go before her, Anthea thought, head held high as she followed them, yet still, she would not go unseen. She'd see to it.

There were several handsome persons awaiting the trio of ladies. There was only one they all saw at once. Their host, the Duke of Peterstow, was elegance personified; that trim giant Arden Lyons was excellence itself in his meticulous tailoring; his lady was charmingly gowned and meltingly lovely; but it was the Viscount Hazelton who was simply magnificent.

He wore nothing more than the standard and correct clothes a gentleman must of a formal evening: black satin jacket, black satin knee breeches, white shirt, stock and stockings, black slippers, with only a flash and a glint of the gold thread of the design of his richly embroidered waistcoat to be glimpsed now and again. But his hair shone like the sun itself, and his eyes were soft and gray as clouds at dawn, and his calm, handsome face bore a look of rare delight as he moved to take his fiancée's hand as she stepped to him, and the other two ladies at her side held themselves back only with the greatest effort.

"Eliza," he said, only that, though his tone of voice spoke volumes more.

"You like it?" she asked, beside herself now with delight as she twirled, all memory of turning before others forgotten as she spun before him, "You approve? Oh, Julian?"

"Oh, yes," he breathed, for he did, and more, and more again for the look on her face as she looked to him for his approval.

"If you two chatterboxes will accompany me," the

duke said as he began to smile as foolishly as a fond uncle before he caught himself at it and was appalled, "we will greet your guests and begin to amaze and delight the *ton* in all its splendor. Our guests, children," he said, "arrive."

But at that, Eliza's hands grew cold, and Julian could feel the chill of them through her gloves as he took her hand in his, and he smiled warmly enough to thaw the marrow of her bones as he led her into the anteroom to face the arriving guests. To face, she thought, unable to swallow, even if there were anything in her parched mouth to swallow, the company come to judge her again, and she walked as a woman would to a firing squad.

But "enchanting," they said, and "delightful" they breathed, and "lucky fellow" they congratulated Julian, and "where did you find her?" they demanded in chagrin, as they came, one by one, to be introduced to her. Not the ladies, of course. They only murmured the correct things as they gaped at Julian, before they looked hard and searchingly at her, pricing her gown and evaluating her charms with cool, envious calculation. No, it was the gentlemen who breathed the incessant compliments, and when she'd the courage to look up to judge their faces as she had their voices, she found nothing but honesty in their shock and envy of Julian. And that, although she looked as hard for humor, malice, and irony in their praise as she did for honesty.

"You're a wild success," Julian whispered as he led her to the dance floor to open the dancing at last. "I wonder, little jilt, are you going to make ours the briefest betrothal on record? Take care," he said, half in jest, "too brief, and your mother and dear Hugh will become suspicious. Or," he asked, before the pattern of the dance pulled him briefly away, "will it make no difference, since you intend to find another lucky fellow to replace me this very night?"

She was going to laugh and say something foolish in reply, something light enough to let him know she jested, something weighty enough to let him begin to know how she cared. But her new partner told her how his heart ached to let her go to her next partner, and that next gentleman vowed his love eternal, before the next gentleman who handed her back to Julian asked her to please smile once for him before he did, just once, he begged, so he could die a happy man. And so she danced back to Julian and had nothing but laughter to reply to him.

It seemed the world had become a dance, it seemed there was only one female in it, and that was herself, and the rest of the world was a blur of handsome gentlemen's faces, all with smiles for her, all saying things they seemed to believe, and all of it sounded like psalms of praise, and all of it for her—for Eliza Merriman, the newest and most wonderfully enchanting female to grace London's social scene. She'd never even had dreams of such glory.

If she chanced to look across the room now and again, she saw Constance holding court as well. For the Merriman ladies, as the *ton* would whisper the next day, between them, held the reins tonight, and not the Viscount Coachman, and made, a wit said and the fashionable world repeated, a great many merry men. To ensure that it wouldn't end just yet, Eliza now had the courage to do as Constance did and had always done. She threw back her head and laughed at every witticism, and giggled at the warmer compliments, and fended off the warmest ones with a flick of her fan or a flash of her eyes, and though she vowed she began it all only to show Julian and herself and the world this new Eliza, she soon found she reveled in her newfound power.

Only to think—the tilt of a smile could bring a gentleman scurrying from clear across the room to her side, the tilt of her head could cause a gentleman to add yet more praise to his lavish praise of her, and a tilt of her brow could make another vow he spoke in earnest even as he swore his poor heart was breaking for her. She could make dignified gentlemen say foolish things with the tone of her laughter, old ones act like the merest cubs in their eagerness to win her giggles, and intelligent ones grow cow-eyed as fools with a new closed-mouth smile she'd only just perfected. It wasn't that she was so beautiful as it was that she was so successful, and that in itself bred her success. In some part of her mind, perhaps she knew that. But it was heady to suddenly have such power.

There was simply no time to consider it while she lived it, any more than anyone could dissect pleasure while in the throes of it. She flirted, she dazzled, she triumphed. She was amazed.

Nor was she the only one.

For when she looked up, at last, from encouraging more gentlemen than she could count to fight for the privilege to take her to her fiancé to take her in to dinner, she remembered Julian again. He stood across the room looking at her. And when he saw her look up, guilty and surprised, he smiled. It was a warm and loving smile and in it she saw, even from across the room, the exact size of its regret.

"She's never been so popular, she's unused to our London beaux, she is . . ." Warwick began, before he left off, veering away, seeing the trap he'd unwittingly laid and planning a *bon mot* to replace it, unwilling to utter what Julian then cut in to say.

". . . very young, after all," Julian said in a low, bleak voice, although his face belied it. Because noting the young fellows she'd been speaking with, he smiled again, as though he were restored, and spoke the cliché that was, he felt, almost as old as he felt tonight. "And youth calls to youth," he said.

And he accepted it. As well as the end of his brief bright fancy, for all it pained him, for he was old enough, he decided, to know better, after all.

7

THE BEST THING about hosting a ball for the truly fashionable, the Duke of Peterstow confided to his friends, was that it was an inexpensive undertaking. The shining stars of the *ton*, he explained, were experts on fashions and gossip and so were unrelentingly critical of a mistaken dance step, a poorly tied neckcloth, or a badly run affair of the heart. They were, however, he explained, totally ignorant about everything else. And so one could confidently hire the worst musicians and put out food rodents might reject, but so long as there were enough interesting persons also subjected to the awful tunes and swallowing down the ghastly victuals, they were happy as they could hold together. The worst part of entertaining them, however economical it might be, he said darkly, was that one had to have them in one's home for a certain number of hours before the doors could be flung open, and them out.

But since the duke would no more fling a guest out-of-doors than he would serve inferior food or listen to discordant music, his friends were too busily eating to do more than nod their agreement with him.

The dinner served after the first part of the dancing at a ball was usually an afterthought, but in the duke's house it was almost worth the price of admission, Julian allowed, when he came up from his plate of cold beef and relishes with a sigh and a satisfied smile. But since the price of admission in his case had been his engagement to marry, no one at his table offered him more than another smile in response to his jest. It was too near to a truth they'd all begun to wonder about.

Because since the gentleman had come in to dinner,

he'd had scarcely a word or so much as a lingering smile for his beautiful fiancée. He sat at a companionable table that was set up for only the closest friends and family of the happy couple, and maintained in that exclusivity by the quelling eye of their host. And so the Viscount Hazelton sat with his intended bride, her cousin, and her companion, as well as with his host and friend Warwick Jones, Duke of Peterstow, and Arden and Francesca Lyons. And he had a word for them all—all, save for his lady.

It seemed that she didn't mind. Although, in truth, she hadn't noticed. For she'd been too busily waving and smiling and mouthing responses to compliments from her new court of admirers at other tables to note anything or anyone at her own, until half the food was gone from everyone else's plate but hers. Then she looked up and around, looking so deliciously guilty and confused, her hand at her O of a mouth and her eyes wide with surprise, that she was instantly forgiven for her inattention by all her tablemates.

"Best eat up that bit of lobster, Eliza, love," her fiancé laughed, "before Arden and I come to blows over it. That is," he added gently, "unless fame has filled you up so much you haven't room for another bite of mortal stuff."

"Ah, but as our friend Byron says, 'fame's the thirst of youth,' so leave the poor girl her lobster and hold back on the champagne and you'll have it right," Warwick said, and then wished he hadn't when Julian's bright face grew a closed expression he knew too well, and he answered on a laugh that had no laughter in it:

"But don't you remember, Warwick? When you're young you don't need food or drink, so long as there's plenty of company and laughter. We old fellows are the ones who need our meals and bottles and pillows by nightfall."

"And gout medicine too, I'd think, if you go on that way. So kindly omit me from your 'we' category, Julian," Francesca Lyons spoke up crossly.

Her husband agreed and then immediately observed how he'd noted his ancient friend Julian to be spry enough on the dance floor, and Constance Merriman began to complain loudly that it seemed to be so, but alas, not with her, even as Warwick began to jest and ask Julian if he'd prefer to soak his bread in some nice warm milk so as to save his teeth the ordeal. Soon they all were laughing at the subject of the viscount's antiquity. All except for the viscount himself, as he made a great show of having difficulty hearing them without his ear trumpet. And all except for him, because he might have not been so very amused as they all were.

"And if you remember, 'our friend Byron' was actually more your friend, Warwick, than mine. How does he go on, by the by?" Julian asked as though it were an idle thought when they'd all done laughing for a space, because he had no wish to hear the subject of age brought up again, even in jest.

"He would have been your friend if you hadn't been so nervous about the way he kept staring at you in class," the duke answered, smiling reminiscently. "He only ever said that it was because your face staggered him, he was a poet after all, and that Greek master was blindingly boring, if you'll recall. At any rate, he left England at almost the same time you did, only he went in the other direction. He's been happily scandalizing himself across the face of the Continent and now's he's busily cuckolding half of Italy. But now you're back and so perhaps we'll soon have all our prodigal sons returned . . . though from his letters of late, and his recent damning poetry about the crown, I doubt it."

"Two children now, isn't it?" Arden asked.

"Oh, yes, two that he'll acknowledge," Warwick began, until Anthea's blush reminded him that all females were not so liberal as his own lady. And then, remembering that lady again—as though he ever forgot her—as well as his own children, he fell silent, wondering if it were an opportune time to mention that now that the ball had been given, he'd soon be off home again.

But the topic of children having been brought up made the Lyonses homesick themselves, and they grew reflective and quiet, and exchanged glances, wondering when they could decently leave for their home in the north.

Anthea and Constance, finding the table grown still, applied themselves to their cakes and ices. Eliza, seeing the sad and distant look in Julian's darkening eyes, wondered if he were missing little Mary just then. And Julian thought that age and children and change were the only subjects left in the blasted world, because that was all that he seemed to be hearing about since he'd returned to London, since he'd come to see how the world had changed, even if he had not.

Then the music struck up again, and at that, a dozen gentlemen hopped up from their tables and looked eagerly toward the new star in their social firmament, that daring young lady who'd been so delightfully and scandalously snatched from the altar, at the brink of an unhappy marriage, to be restored to their ranks again. That she hadn't been in their ranks to begin with didn't fadge, as one fellow commented, for anyone could see she was a stunner. That she was nominally engaged didn't matter beans, either, as young Lord Gribbons remarked to a friend, for she'd been saved from wedlock at the very last minute once before, and the inhumanly handsome fellow who'd done it didn't look like he was best pleased about what he'd done anymore. Which left the door wide open, his friend thought cagily, as did all the other young blades, for some other fellow to pull the deed off again and so make himself the subject of all the envious gossip this time.

Julian had another dance with his lady, and then a waltz; they were engaged, after all, so he could have three, four, or all with her now if he chose. The penalty for more than two dances in an evening with a proper young female was wedlock, and he'd already paid the price for his pleasure in her company on the dance floor, or at least he'd promised to. She was reminded of this when she stepped into his arms for the waltz. She reminded herself of her great good fortune so far, even if it was still yet a ruse. Because from the moment she found herself within his circling arms, close enough to the lemon-and-sandalwood scent of him to have it fill her senses, close enough to his gravely beautiful face to read every nuance in it if she dared raise her eyes long enough, she forgot all else, even the outsize praise and plaudits of her former partners. But he did not.

It wasn't words of love he bent to fill her ears with as they waltzed, as all the onlookers thought. Or if it was, it was not his love he spoke of.

"So, Mischief," he said, his breath a warm thrilling presence on her neck, a distraction and a joy that had to be coped with before the sense of his words could be taken in, "which of them is it to be? Take care, my heart, I won't march down the aisle to save you again, so choose carefully this time.

"Lord Greyville's a handsome fellow, I'll admit," he mused, his tenor voice vibrating in her ear, "but he and his friend Harry Fabian have been on the town forever, I remember their flirts from my youth, they're as long in the tooth as I am, and no bargain either of them. The others are babes—after my time, at least, but Constance says John Archer's pockets are to let for all he's dressed so marvelously, and the Baron Whiteside's after less than marriage, or more, depending," he said, smiling as she gazed up at him, amazed, "on your interpretation of that happy state. Beware of yon Captain Barstow, puss—for all his airs and graces, she says he's very wicked. But Vincent St. Clair has a fortune and an easygoing temperament, and those unfortunate ears of his could be covered over if he'd a better barber, I'd wager. And Jamie Conklin's a good lad, she says, with the advantage of an ailing father, so he'll be an earl before the year is out.

"But you don't have to decide right away," he assured her as she gazed up at him in surprise. "Warwick may have to run back home soon to guard his fireside, but you and I can stay on in London until the Season's out. No, no," he said again, looking down into her worried eyes, "no need to jump to judgment yet, enjoy yourself tonight, child, and let your decision come to you as naturally as the steps of the dance do now. You do dance well," he said. "Lord, no"—he shook his head in amazement—"you do dance *beautifully*, you know."

As they danced on, he complimented her on her dress and her grace, her success and her popularity, and although he was all smiles and flattery, she felt as though this handsome gentleman was only impersonating her Julian, for he was so polite and charming it was as if they'd never met before tonight, as if she hadn't shared her thoughts with him for the past five years of her life. There was suddenly a distance opened up between them, so that even as he held her and she moved with him, she felt his thoughts were on something else.

And then there was a polka, so she was spared his preoccupation. And then he relinquished her to another gentleman, so he was spared the feeling of her in his arms.

As she danced away, he smiled again, and stifled every natural impulse he had. For, "youth to youth," he thought once more as he took Constance's hand for his promised dance with her, and never looked back to see Eliza again. Because he didn't wish to see her now, he was too old to be a languishing boy, too young to carry off self-sacrifice as well as he wished to do. Too young in spirit only, he reminded himself, determined not to spare himself anything tonight.

Constance was a charming lady, lovely and clever, and her laughter made him feel wittier than he knew he was. The only fault he found with her through two dances and an idle moment of chat before she was claimed by her coterie of admirers again was that she couldn't stop talking about Eliza's success and rating her chances with various eligible gentlemen. But she thrived on such tattle; she was, after all, a totally social animal. Still, she was amusing with it, and it was pleasing, being entertained by a creature in her own element; dancing with Constance, he thought, was like swimming with a mermaid. This was her world, and she led him through it deftly. For she was facile and beautiful—yes, very beautiful, he thought as he watched her led away.

It wasn't poor Anthea's world, he thought when he waltzed with her and watched the top of her head as she watched the floor they danced over. But then, her hesitancy and shyness and air of apology and the fierce but hastily suppressed flash of despair he caught in her eyes before she could hide it—when no one had come to her side before he did—reached out to him and found a corresponding chord tonight. So it wasn't only pity that caused him to give her two dances, nor was it mere politeness that made him hold her in conversation until his singular attentions made her interesting to other gentlemen and she was asked away from him and taken into the dance again. No, he thought, for she was bright and kind, as well as pretty, and deserved far better than she had or seemed likely to get.

But then, he'd enough of ladies and music, and with only one last look back to see Eliza—or at least to see where he supposed she stood, surrounded by her newfound court—he sought out his friends for talk.

He found them in the study, and was delighted to find them alone, and so wasted no time in berating them for it.

"Excuse me," he said as he came upon Warwick and Arden deep in conversation. Francesca sat back in a chair as her husband, on an ottoman before her, absently massaged her feet, which disappeared entirely in his huge hands as he held them while he debated something with Warwick, standing in front of the fire before them.

"Excuse me," Julian went on with a great show of false meekness as they all looked up, "don't take alarm, but I thought someone ought to tell you—there's a roaring party raging out there."

"Precisely"—Warwick nodded—"which is why I don't intend to show so much as my lovely nose out there again until it's time to extinguish it. I'll have to put it out sooner or later, I imagine, for it's so successful I doubt it will burn out for hours. But as it's an engagement party, and not a debut or a dinner dance, it needn't last the night. I'll hint them away an hour into the new day. Francesca and her little friend need their sleep, you know. And so does the baby they'll be having.

"And so do I," he added over all their laughter. "But why isn't our prospective groom out there causing all the gentlemen to expire from envy?" he asked accusingly, to pay his friend back. He realized he'd paid him far more than he'd earned when Julian only lifted a shoulder and said too lightly, "Because no one noticed me gone. And it's no more a thrilling event for me than you, Warwick. Social events were the one thing I didn't miss when I was gone from England, you know. And becoming engaged don't make a fellow lose his mind, only his freedom, remember?" he asked.

Exactly how much he was really engaged was his own business, he thought, for though he shared most things with his friends, the whole truth of this betrothal of his was a thing he'd never fully gone into with them. They knew he'd had to save Eliza from an unwanted match, he'd denied serious intentions of wedding her, and never thought to bother explaining further. After he'd passed some time with her, he'd been glad of that omission, and was even more so now. Because if it would have been embarrassing to let them know he'd changed his mind and decided to see if falsity became truth in time, it would be doubly so now that it had not. But he hadn't an ounce of foreknowledge to credit himself with; they were clever, he'd thought then—no need explaining.

They were cleverer than that. For they dropped the subject of the engagement and the party entirely, and soon were earnestly discussing the various investments they'd made together, catching up in conversation that which they'd left only to letters before. They were business partners as well as friends, after all, each bringing his own talents to their joint endeavor.

Arden advised them on speculative matters—he could scent a scheme or a bubble or bamboozle a mile away. And they needed such advice, for Warwick had a nose for odd but promising new fields in an age of scientific marvels. If Arden agreed the scheme was clean, they trusted Warwick on the venture, however bizarre. If any other man had suggested buying up land for the eventual use of those new coaches that would ride on rails, they'd have hooted him down. But since his suggestions for shares in the gas company and other marvelously foolish-sounding flights had already paid off, they were already dutifully purchasing the acres for his smoking faradiddles of the future, as they were pleased to call them. After all, they'd funds enough for such speculation and could afford to buy dreams of a steam-driven future, since they could ride to their banks on the stagecoaching line they'd already established, the one Julian advised them how to run and improve. He was, of course, also their expert on investments in America and the tropical islands near its shores.

Shareholders in ships and mines, collieries and manufactories; importers of sugar and coffee, livestock and plants, they were as successful at business as they were at their friendship, their three disparate personalities forming one huge profitable enterprise. A duke, a viscount, and the illegitimate son of an earl—the only stink of the shop they worried about was the stench of poverty. The earl's son had known grinding poverty too intimately, the viscount's son had lost all his money once upon a time, and the duke was an original. They'd none of them any concern about what the *ton* thought of them engaging in trade, simply because they'd no concern about what the *ton* thought of anything. And so the *ton*, of course, loved them for it and accepted that business was their pleasure as well as their business. After all, as Warwick often said, inheritance was good fortune, but great fortunes came from good investments.

At length, when Francesca's eyes began to close from weariness, not just from the pleasure of their close company and her husband's easing of the cramps from her feet, and the fire needed replenishment, Warwick arose to put out the music, and then his guests.

And when they reentered the ballroom, they saw Eliza Merriman, dancing and laughing, her head spinning from the praise she was getting, even as her body twirled to the music. She was so caught up with the gaiety and the attentions she was receiving from the male guests that Warwick was very glad he'd come to end the revels. For though he saw his friend Julian come to a stand at his side and smile and watch her patiently, pleased as her father might be, he knew he was not. Not her father, nor patient, nor pleased. But benevolent—oh, yes, that, Warwick thought with disgust, for if Julian played the kindly old gentleman any more to the hilt tonight, he'd soon take to passing new pennies to the children, rather than smiling on them all, even those older than himself, as though he were about to toddle off this mortal coil and not just the dance floor.

"Fudge!" Eliza giggled as Lord Kinnock smiled down at her. "They're the color of fudge in the kettle, sir, not 'light shining on tea.' "

"Just so—a sweet treat," the young gentleman sighed, and as Eliza giggled again, another young gentleman in the circle around her, jealous of the adorable look of mock censure Lord Kinnock had earned for his fervent nonsense, added, "Never tea! Nothing so paltry. Your eyes are like brown silk, Miss Merriman, gleaming and rich."

"Never! Honey—sheer honey," Mr. Russell vowed, using his deep voice to best effect to drown out Captain Barstow's clever comment about how he hadn't noted the color of her eyes, he'd been so blinded by their shine.

Even as the several other gentlemen in the circle around Miss Merriman racked their brains for something outrageous and clever to say to capture the new beauty's interest, her eyes shone even brighter and she fell still, gazing at the tall fair-haired gentleman who came toward her. Unfair, they most of them thought then, stepping back, the Viscount Hazelton didn't have to stretch his imagination to the limit conjuring up something interesting to say. He'd only to show that devilish handsome phiz of his to get her attention. And then they'd another thing to grudge him for when he said, lightly and cleverly, "You may bestow your brilliant gaze anywhere you wish, Eliza, if you'll only give me your hand . . . for this last dance, please."

She went into his arms on a laugh of pleasure and looked up at him, her eyes nothing like fudge or tea or silk, he thought as he gazed back, dazzled, but rather like stars. And then was glad he hadn't said that, for half the gentlemen around her could have done better and probably had done. But he meant it. She glowed. She blossomed: her face, her form, her grace, even her scent delighted him as much as her wit and imagination had done in all her letters. It wasn't only that he found her beautiful; he knew her to be beautiful.

He wondered if she'd scold him for his desertion; he

thought she might really be angry, and recognized she'd good cause. He ought not to have left her alone, after all, no matter if they'd agreed that she ought to meet the available gentlemen in the *ton*. He could have seen to that even while with her, for any gentleman could remain a gentleman while flirting lightly with an engaged lady, after all. He'd left because her success had defeated him, and could only hope she'd be easy to jolly out of her vexation with him now. Yet still, he'd a lingering hope that she wouldn't be that easily pacified, that she'd demand his total surrender, for then he might be able to admit that truth to her as he explained his actions, and that might lead to other admissions. Wise enough to let her begin, wary enough to wait, he said nothing as they began to step to the music.

"Lud! But it's been fun," she sighed then.

"Hasn't it?" he answered.

London at night had changed less than London by day. There was a certain familiarity in the darkness. He walked down the long clean streets to his new club, and then the Viscount Hazelton veered and walked away from it. It was late, but it was too soon for him to go to bed. And far too soon for him to go to it alone. It had, after all, been many long weeks since he'd had a female in his bed, or hers, or anyone's. There was no reason now to exercise caution, he'd no child's trust to fear damaging; he'd no woman's trust to fear betraying any longer, either. And he needed some pleasure this night, he decided.

But for all the town was familiar, as he walked on he realized that the persons in it no longer were. His old flirts would be wed by now, and if they weren't, he could scarcely come calling at this early hour of the morning anyway. The married ones had been in society, poor men being more attached to their wives and therefore less obliging in matters of their personal freedom than those who'd wed their wives for their portions or their families' wishes. The single ones who worked at various trades, including those of lovemaking, were also undoubtedly abed, and perhaps not alone, by now. Even if they might be, he realized he hesitated to revisit them after a lapse of five years—he wouldn't want simple lust confused with endless devotion, after all.

But there was this simple lust, which was becoming more complex every moment, to contend with. He sought his body's ease, of course, but he didn't want to face the night alone, either. He thought of his options as he walked. As he wandered, he never worried about those who might lurk in the shadows watching him as the streets he passed grew narrower and nastier. This was a land with laws that decreed death for any of a hundred crimes: from taking a man's life to stealing his watch fob. But life was beyond hard in parts of this city, and he knew there were many who'd let fate decide whether it would be hunger or the hangman that got them first. Still, he never picked up his head or his pace as he went on into the dwindling night.

He'd traveled through many foreign lands, he'd learned a thing or two—it showed in his musculature, it was hinted at by the way he carried himself. He had wit, and if both brain and brawn failed him, he'd a pocket pistol in his waistcoat ever at his side now. He didn't stroll through the deadliest slums, because he was no fool. But then, he didn't trouble to remain in only the most elegant areas, either. He was often observed, as he expected. Those who watched had learned to read their victims well. He went unmolested. By thieves.

For whatever district he roamed through, now and again, some secret creature of the night appeared from out of the shadows to whisper her price and her talents to him. Few were surprised when he shook his fair head in polite refusal. Not after they'd got a clear look at him. But there was one who was stunned by his quick look, gentle smile, and whispered "No, thank you."

She was newly come to town, with an old and drearily familiar tale of seduction and desertion to have brought her from the country, and she had as yet little experience in the streets of the city or she'd not have seriously thought he'd buy her. Because comely as she was, and she was young and robust and fresh-faced, and popular with the lads as she'd been at home, that had been at home. She was only common street-ware now, though she hadn't realized the extent of it yet. Any of her sisterhood could have told her such handsome gents as she'd just accosted seldom had to buy their pleasures in the gutters. And so for all his gentleness as he refused her, he left her standing staring after him, as disturbed as if she'd been repudiated by the last god she'd believed in.

But her question made him think. He didn't like to buy pleasure, but it was doubtful he could find it freely given tonight. For tonight, then, to lose the feel of rejection, to forget the feel of another in his arms, he determined to find someone who'd sell him a pair of welcoming arms and a welcome in her warm body. Not at a house where female bodies were rented by the hour—that, like sexual commerce passed in the streets, had always been as distasteful as it had been unnecessary for him to seek.

Then he recalled an odd bit of gossip he'd heard from a huddle of gentlemen at the party tonight. There were still courtesans. Although their favors were for sale, they were clever enough to be subtle about it, and subtle enough to find favor with kings. The best he'd known of, Harriet Wilson, was gone from favor, along with Julia Johnson and Lucille LaPoire and those of that circle— Lord, he thought, they'd be almost as old as he was now! But this new bit of muslin—he could do worse than try his luck. She might have a friend if she were spoken for. It was, of course, sordid. In the mood he was in, that lent the business extra savor. He remembered the district— not far. And her name was familiar to the watchman he asked. She was, in her own way, famous.

The street was a good one, the house well-maintained. He had second thoughts when he applied the door knocker. And almost lost all his resolve when the maid bade him wait in a parlor that would not have disgraced any proud family he knew. When the lady came into the room, he could scarcely believe she was a demirep, and would have reached for his hat if he hadn't realized that no lady would receive a strange gentleman in her peignoir, covered over by a robe or not. Still, he made desultory talk, naming a gentleman who'd named her, never saying why he'd come. For he felt crass as well as foolish—until she smiled to end his conversational efforts and placed a light hand over his, to begin something more.

Her maid had told her it was an archangel at the door. And when she rose from her bed where she'd been boring herself to sleep with a book and came belowstairs to see, so she too thought it was.

She was delighted with him and fully as anxious to further their acquaintance as he immediately found himself to be. Because she was petite and small-waisted, and yet full-breasted; sweet-scented, as well, and full of smiles. If it weren't for her deep brown hair and heavier features, he might almost be able to pretend . . . But then, they would be in the dark, after all, he thought, and so he might.

She wasn't employed tonight. Her chiefest protector was home with his wife in the country. Her lover was at his diversion's childbed in the city. And her toy was home with a streaming cold. She'd marked the night for refurbishing her body with beauty treatments and sleep. But she was a restive creature and was ever uncomfortable alone with herself. Then, too, she knew no better mirror than a man's eyes, and sleep could come later, and it came easier when she wasn't alone.

He didn't have to explain. Or wait very long. Nor did he then have to be gentle, romantic, or even kind, for she wanted none of that and he always took his method from his partner's desires. She was easily as avid as he was. For he was beautiful and clean and strong and she saw little of that sort of male in the usual way of her trade. Her business was seldom a pleasure, although she was adept in providing it, as well as conversation and consolation and all the other things a wealthy gentleman would pay for. Providing sex alone, after all, would never make any female as rich as she was becoming. But tonight she wouldn't have to work.

There was no meeting of anything save flesh between them, although there was a great deal of that. She was as expert as he was, but tonight they met as equals, both seeking their own release, and in so doing, providing the other's. But when he was done at last, and she was finally sated, he realized at last that he'd needed more than that.

He thanked her as he disentangled himself from her arms and her bed, when he felt enough time had passed for it not to be an insult. There'd been pleasure, after all, if only of a distant sort, and he was always polite. Polite enough to oblige her again, when she insisted, though nothing of himself but his flesh was involved in it, and he was already growing weary. It was only when he attempted to pay her that she grew angry. She had, it seemed, her own tallies to keep, and her pleasures were her own rewards.

He mused about that after he'd left her, as he walked home down the long dark streets again. It was while he was distracted that the figure came out of the lessening shadows of the night to stand before him and confront him directly.

Strangely enough, for all he'd only had a glimpse of her on his way to the courtesan's house, he remembered her. Or at least he remembered the streetwalker's look of astonishment when he'd not taken her offer, for it had been as unusual as she herself hadn't been. Now she faced him directly, and that too was odd. Because they knew their place, these streetwalkers of London. Omnipresent and far more numerous than the streetlamps, they were also an integral part of the night scene, and they'd fade away at dawn or a negative word, shrinking back into the shadows that seemed to breed them. But not this one, at least not tonight.

For she'd taken no trade this night. His refusal had cut her to the quick. She'd offered herself and he'd refused. She'd offered herself to no other one after that. Because it was staggering to her. And her pride was such, and her newness to this city and the trade that would soon destroy her body and mind were such, that she'd been deeply hurt by his refusal. She'd stood brooding in the night waiting for morning and an excuse to return alone to the room she called home, when she'd seen him once again. Now he stood in front of her, as beautiful and implacable as an angel, as he waited for her to speak.

"I ain't dirty!" she cried, all her inchoate anger and

fear in the tone of her voice. "You hear, Mr. High and Mighty? I ain't dirty! An' I only offered 'cause I wanted to! I ain't sick neither, and I ain't just nothin', no I ain't," she cried, before she was shocked to find she could still cry, and was, and bitterly, as she stood there facing him down.

"No, no, you're not, of course you're not," he murmured as he held her close to him, and comforted her, lifting his head so that the feathers she wore in her hair didn't tickle, and never seeming to mind that she was ruining his shirtfront as the paint she'd applied ran with her tears down his chest.

Her room was small, and the bed so narrow it had only room for them both, the way they employed it. Her body was large, wide-boned and full-fleshed, and could have supported him better than the poor thin mattress did, but he turned her round and held her against himself and gave her himself until she stopped weeping, at last, and then only wept for the pleasure he gave her. He took none for himself even as he took her.

But there was pity in this, and the comfort of giving comfort, even if her great breasts and heaving hips brought only his body's automatic salute, and nothing more. For in pity there was a sort of love, and that, he discovered, was what he'd wanted all along, for all of his adept little courtesan's tricks, this poor girl's need suited him far better. So there was more of a mating in this exchange than there'd been in the hours before, and it was recognition of that need, he thought, that gave him the ability to please her. Although he'd never studied her face well enough to recognize it again if they ever met—for all he'd come to understand the simple demands of her body soon enough, in some strange fashion—tonight, then, he'd loved her.

He rose with the sun at last, sleepless and tired unto death. His body decently clad again, his emotions entirely numbed, he withdrew a large sum from his wallet to leave her in his stead, so that she'd continue to feel of value. But she grew angry at that, and refused it, for she'd wanted to give him pleasure only for his own reward.

As he let himself out into the new day, his money back

in his pocket once again, he thought of how cheaply he'd bought his pleasures tonight, this signal night of his betrothal ball. But though he'd paid nothing, as he wandered into the dawn he began to understand just how dearly it was costing him each time he sought love and found, always, only mere pleasure instead.

As the blond gentleman with the exhausted face of a saint that had undergone his earthly test left the perennially dark district he'd passed the night in, walking toward his club to wash and change his twice-doffed garments, the man who'd been watching him all night noted his direction with relief, and slipped away. They were both gone back to their proper haunts, then. One to rest and to recover his spirits. The other to give in his report to his superior and be grateful he hadn't had to take on the pretty viscount tonight, after all. For murder was never an easy business—not when it was a gentry cove who had to be turned off—not even for him, who'd done it so many times before.

8

" 'E's 'OME. I left 'im on 'is way back to 'is club, at least.
'E'll be sleeping by now, snug as a bug, never you doubt,"
the thin man reported, his words a hollow echo from the
depths of his cup.

"Then he breathes?" the other, thicker-bodied man
who sat by his side at the table in the dreary taproom
asked, though he knew the answer and merely wanted to
see his companion as defensive as he immediately became.

"Eh, you dint expect me to turn him off for no reason,
did you?" the thin man asked in a hiss of a whisper as he
laid down his fortifying gin and looked up in amazement.
"I said I'd do 'im if 'e looked to be makin' trouble, but
he dint, so I dint. It's what you wanted, i'nit?"

"Just so, Jacko, my lad. Don't fret. I was just making
sure you knew the game."

The thin man frowned into his cup. It was a bad
business he was into this time, and he knew it. None of
his business could be termed good, but if there was
enough of it and it paid well enough, he'd consider it so.
Killing men for a fee was nothing to him. But killing a
nobleman was new, and he was anxious about it, and he
could have done without his employer putting on airs
with him, it troubled him and took some of the edge off
his confidence.

His employer had survived the same doss-house nurs-
eries he had; they'd filched handkerchiefs and fobs together as infants and played the thousand confidence
games children must in order to grow in their low slum;
as much friends as such youths could afford to be, they'd
been. They'd sold their first girls on the same street
corners, and stolen side by side. But as they'd grown

they'd each focused on his own special skills, and adulthood had brought them to different occupations. Will Peep had a gift for leadership, and the thin man had the stealth and the hands of a strangler, a flair with the knife, and a way with the garrote. So it was that one now worked for the other.

But he, the thin man thought, knew himself for what he was. And Will was putting on airs with his new affluence and looking further afield than the mean streets from whence they'd sprung. This was dangerous. Still, a man might look anywhere, and Will had been amazingly successful so far, disposing of his powerful employer, Sam Towers, with a flourish that had been the whisper of the dark side of town for days—it was over a year ago, but it might have been a century, for gossip had become legend and the body hadn't been found yet.

So it wasn't the game, it was the new clothes and new airs and the new voice with the perfect diction that raised the thin man's hackles; it reminded him of risks. Like so many of his kind, he understood ambition but distrusted anything outside his ken. His friend had plans too big for his grasp, but so long as he played by the rules and paid by them, he'd no real complaint. Only unease. But then, he lived with that daily, after all.

"I know the game, all right," he said sullenly now, " 'n know 'tis my neck that'll be on the stretch if I'm caught wif a finger on the 'andsome viscount's corpse."

"It's not a finger I want on him," Will Peep said patiently, "it's a knife, Jacko. But only if he gets too close or gets wind of our doings, because if he does, it's the rope, and for all of us, not just you. It's bad luck," he said, frowning, "that he's come back to England just now. In a few months I'll be able to sort things out and move the game. But the stagecoach line that carries our goods now is his, and he's the only one that knows enough about that trade to smell something rotten."

" 'Tis Lion's too," the thin man said in a whisper, although the spoken name hurt his mouth as he uttered it, and made Will Peep's eyes shift to the door where his men stood guard, as his florid face grew red about the ears. Then Will laughed, as though to dispel the dread from the name he'd heard, but when he spoke again he'd forgotten some of his newly learned enunciation.

"The Lion's toothless now," he scoffed, "out of the game now that he's wed proper. And a proper country gent he is, too— *Mr.* Arden Lyons, if you please—never guess 'e was once the great Lion who ran our lousy world. No, nothing to fear from him, Jacko, not no more, nor from the duke who's a partner neither. It's only the viscount knows coaching ways—he's the one been away long enough for the mice to play; and it's the cat who comes back into the room that sees the cheese has been moved, and not the fat ones sleeping by the fire. Remember that. There's profit in his line he never sees, and I mean to see he don't. I just need time, I'll find another way to move the merchandise from the ships that come by night, as well as what we take to them."

He fell silent. It was a profitable trade he was in now—the common trade of bringing in goods without tax stamps, as well as the less common traffic in goods that could never get a stamp, for human flesh was not considered salable by their government. But it was, in parts of the Eastern and Western worlds. And so some of the passengers on the coaching line rode drugged, with the luggage, and not all of them paid coin for their fare, for some delivered up their souls to get passage. Those who delivered up even more were still salable—if one knew which medical students to approach. And this one did.

"So keep an eye on him, Jacko. You've the night watch," Will cautioned. "I've another lad on the day-side. And relax. It may be that the viscount will copy his friend Mr. Lyons, and we'll have no more to worry about from him. After all, I don't care who owns the line we use. What he don't know won't hurt him. But what he does discover will kill him. So see he don't—if you're feeling that kindhearted."

They both laughed at that. Then the thin man smiled his small smile and shook his head.

"I shoulda took the day watch, for all the sun gets in my eyes. 'Cause the viscount's got a mite of sleepin' to do now. Gawd, 'e's as randy as a goat, that one, for all 'e looks like an angel. First, 'e's in Delia Bradford's bed 'alf the night, and for all she's 'igh-tone enough for a king, she likes 'er sport, they say. Then, on 'is way 'ome again, 'e picks up a street whore and takes 'is ease wif 'er 'til dawn! I left 'im on the way to 'is club, 'e'll prolly sleep the day away. Aye, cushy job your day watch got today, all right."

"Indeed . . ." Will Peep said, holding up one hand to interrupt himself. Then he sat back and inclined his head to catch the words his man whispered into his reddening ears, before he spoke again. "Then why," he asked coldly, leaning forward and staring into his old friend's eyes, his own eyes blazing, "do you think the viscount's at the Bull and Mouth, checking out his carriages and his horses in the stagecoach yard, right now?"

The dawn was rising and all proper gentlemen were sleeping or creeping home to do so. But halfway back to the Traveler's Club, Julian thought of his destination and stopped in his traces. He'd been at the brink of sleep twice tonight, and now had gone past sleepiness to that stage of exhaustion where he was almost more awake than he could ever remember being before. But he did remember, and so knew he'd have to stay on his feet now until he fell down at last. He'd no desire to pace his room alone thinking of all sorts of lost chances until that moment of oblivion.

London was a city of delight for the rich. Yet there weren't many occupations considered worthy of a *ton*-ish gentleman to be found at daybreak. All to the good, then, that he never styled himself as such, for he suddenly recalled that there was sport available at this hour that never failed to delight him. He headed toward the Bull and Mouth Inn.

Over a thousand coaches a day left London now, and the nightly procession of mail coaches leaving St. Martin-le-Grand was in itself something of a tourist attraction. But few tourists wished to rise at dawn to watch the coaches readying to leave the city. Still, most of them had to do just that, if they'd booked passage, because that was when the stagecoaches left on their journeys across the length and breadth of the Kingdom. But it was no tourist that was standing in the courtyard of the busiest inn, chatting with guards and coachmen, bright-eyed and alert, and clearly having the time of his life. Or so the man waiting in the diminishing shadows thought the blond viscount was doing, even as he put a fist to his own mouth to stifle his yawns, and continued to watch as he was paid to do.

The dawn rose from a bleary wash across the sky to a glow, to a fuller burgeoning light, and as it increased, the line of coaches waiting to leave decreased. One by one, the coachmen ended their conversation and climbed up on their high seats and saluted each other and the blond nobleman with their whips. The guards in turn stepped up on the backs of the carriages and raised their tins to play their stirring notes as their coaches drove off into the new day, one after the other, leaving the city in file like some mighty clattering earthbound Armada.

The line prospered, Julian thought as he raised his hand to yet another departing coach. His company wasn't a patch on Chaplin's famous red-and-black line, of course, nor had he a fraction of the number of Sherman's yellow-and-black wheeled beauties plying the roads. But it was his—and so eleven gold-and-black coaches on this morning's runs to Brighton, Southampton, and Portsmouth were his own, and he was as pleased as a boy who owns his own candy shop. Even managed from abroad as they'd been, they were in good order; his horses were sound (he'd countenance no mad, sick, or starved beasts on his line), his coachmen seemed competent, and the coaches themselves were brightly painted as well as well-equipped. As he watched the last of the day-departing carriages take leave of the city, he forgot the hard, pounding miles and swallowed dust, the aching buttocks and strained arms and hands that were the lot of the stagecoachman. Instead, he remembered the open road and the freshening wind blowing past his ears, and the feel of the team's power held in his own two hands as the miles dwindled away on the blurring road far beneath his feet, and he envied his employees with all of his heart.

For now he stood alone in the courtyard, and it was full morning, and they were off and down the road to freedom, and he was pent in the city and left to himself. He dropped his hand from his last salute, and went into the dim recesses of the Bull and Mouth to forget the hour and ignore the day. There were always some coaching men there to chat with: those too old to take the road, those too young to try their hand at it, and those temporarily out of service due to some other cruelty of fate.

It was rising noon when Julian emerged, blinking as he remembered the day again, and at last he began to feel some tiredness. But he knew that giving in to sleep now would only buy him a lonely wakening in the small hours of the morning and would make it the devil of a task to get himself back into the schedule of his world again. He'd walk back to the club, he decided, and then, after running his hand along his jaw as he thought, he grinned and remembered that he'd better keep to the less-affluent sections of town as he did. A gent in evening dress at noon with a day's growth of beard to go with his wrinkled splendor might not be remarkable in the lower depths of the city, but wouldn't be at all the thing in the better parts of it.

By day even Spitalfields and Shoreditch looked safe, although they never were. In full light, they seemed even bearable too, made so by the thrusting crowds of people, the whooping masses of children, the vendors and the buyers of every imaginable thing under the sun that managed to climb over the tops of the derelict buildings. Julian meandered, and bought himself a meat pasty and a drink of lemonade to wash it down and a sweet to make himself thirsty enough to buy another swallow of lemonade. He wandered on, getting glimpses of those arts that thrive in crowds: Punch and Judy shows, pie men and oyster women, hawkers of sheet music and dead men's confessions and every sort of ware; as well as those that thrived on crowds: pickpockets and cutpurses, whores and all those sleight of hand and foot. So he felt enough unease along with his amusement to watch his wallet and his step as he walked onward through the stews.

He refused to review his past night, and only thought that there were worse ways to bring forgetfulness than this, and that he'd tried most of them in his time, and many of them last night. It was as he was wending his way around a mess so vile that no one thought to see if he could retrieve it to sell to someone else, that he saw the man across the street and stared.

It would have been difficult not to see the man across from him, even though he was a man trained to see things others might not notice. For the fellow was tall as a door, and almost as wide about the shoulders as one too. So it was not the sight of him that made Julian pause, but the fact that it was the man across the street who had trained him in those same observant arts. He'd been at loose ends, bored and regretful and edgy, and that was what had brought him to this stroll through London's cesspits, where few gentlemen ventured by day, even if some took their baser pleasures here by night. But what in the fiend's name was Arden Lyons doing in this vile district today?

Once Arden had prospered in these slums. He'd been king of this underworld. But he'd repudiated all of it even before he'd met his Francesca. And had never returned, for he turned his great hands only to honest labor now, and the most of that was in the paperwork of investments, or in the cleaner dirt of his beloved flowerbeds in his home in the north. Or so he said, Julian thought uneasily. Arden was his friend and partner in a dozen ventures. But it had been, after all, five years since he'd been in England, five years since he'd set foot in London, and a great many things had changed in that time. For all he could swear he knew his friend as well as himself, he'd begun to see that he didn't know himself too well any longer now either.

Mistrust of his own judgment was never distrust of a friend, he told himself as he faded back into the crowd and determined to follow Arden Lyons in his rounds today, unobserved. It was an art, this tracking of a man as a predator must do, treading smoothly and secretly in his wake, always keeping him under one's eye, and out of it at the same time. As the hunter stalking in a forest must learn to fade into the quietude and small sounds of the wild, Julian disguised himself by becoming part of the rowdy, pushing mass of humanity. Once, Arden raised his mighty head as though he'd gotten the scent, but just as he'd never be able to actually detect any stray scents in this noisome slum, with all the other ripe human odors around him, he'd never have heard or seen an unusual thing in the noisy, colorful crowd even if he, a master of deception, had not himself trained Julian to his skills.

So it was, then, that Julian was stunned when he turned a corner to keep Arden in sight, and came face-to-face with him, and Arden, pointing a huge finger at his chest, said sadly, "Bang!"

The big man shook his head.

"Dead, mourned, and planted proper . . . if I'd have been of a mind to do you in. Julian, my pet, doubtless you were as a shadow stealing across my path, but damnation, man, even though your finery's wrinkled and you've a day's growth of fuzz on your glorious face now, it still is a glorious face. Will you never learn you've got to cover it over entirely with a scarf or a mask or a tilted hat? I saw you reflected in every lass's eyes, I saw you in every widened stare of every female of a sporting age, and every female down here is of that age. You'd be an excellent shadow if you didn't cast such a glow. No matter. I'm not out for your blood. And I'm pleased to explain that damned prickling I had at the back of my neck. But by the by, dear friend, why were you trailing me?"

Julian thought of a dozen amusing answers and several more believable ones. But Arden was his friend, and he couldn't lie to him, or at least wouldn't, if only because if he did, he scarcely could call him "friend" again.

"I wanted to know what you were doing here. And I was, I suppose, wary of asking you. I've been gone a long while, you see."

"Ah. I do see," Arden said as he stood and contemplated the matter. "Very well, then, I hadn't thought to show you yet, but it's as well. I'm here, just as I used to be, to recruit for my own purposes. Yes," he said as Julian's face grew grave and they began walking, "I'm returned to my old haunts and habits and am seeking poor unfortunates to use for my benefit again. Come along, then, and see."

They walked rapidly, in silence, as they passed along streets that grew darker and danker, even in the afternoon sunlight. When they came to a cracked and swinging sign that spelled out "The Hole in the Wall" and ducked their heads to enter the filthy taproom, Julian could see that the place was aptly named, even if the contrast between the bright day and the dark interior blinded him to everything else for a moment, save, of course, for his growing disappointment and sorrow with his friend.

When his eyes adjusted to the lack of light, Julian could see what his nose had told him—which was that the room was crowded, and with a variety of starved and ragged persons. Most of them were young. The man who came forward to take Arden's hand, while taking his companion's measure, was young enough too, but he was handsome, well-groomed, and dressed as a gentleman, and spoke as one as well.

"Good afternoon, Lion," the young man said, and then, extending his hand to Julian, added, "And good day, Viscount, how nice to see you again."

"Very good!" Arden said admiringly. "You impress me, Ben. Julian, make you known again to my friend Ben-Be-Good—you met him once, years ago, when I was ailing and staying with Warwick."

As Julian remembered his one brief meeting with the young, well-spoken, unlikely-looking would-be captain of crime who rose from the same slums Lion had ruled, the young man smiled.

"No credit to me, Lion. I'm observant, sir, but I've all the advantages in this case. I meet few gentlemen, after all, and fewer still that look like the Viscount Hazelton. But then, I suppose there are few enough like him. It's as well, then, that he's here today. He can run an eye over this lot himself. What do you think?"

"Excellent," Lion agreed as he eyed the nervous, silent group in the room.

"Then let's get to it. They've been waiting since first light. Here, then, Peg, up front and forward, please. But only in a matter of speaking, of course, for you're with the gentry now, girl, so mind your manners. Tell the gentlemen what you can do," Ben-Be-Good commanded.

A thin, pale, and none-too-clean young girl stepped forward and folded her hands before her. She could have been any age, but Julian doubted she was above thirteen, for all her ill-fitting worn dress showed her clearly growing to womanhood faster than her budget could allow her to cover.

"I . . . I kin fetch," the girl said softly, " 'n I kin learn quick. 'N I likes children, I do."

"And what have you been doing?" Ben-Be-Good asked sternly.

She grew fearful, and in the quiet room they could hear her swallow before she mumbled, low, "I bin fetching for folks 'ere and there, and doing the odd bits where I could, and I was one of Mother Carey's chicks for a week, and she said bad as I was at the game, it were good, 'cause I could stay on for the gents as liked 'em young and unwilling, but I dint like it. No I dint!" she said with a brief show of spirit before she foundered, and then murmured, "S'truth, I swear it. Else why would I be here?"

"Why else, indeed?" Ben asked in a soft voice. "Well, my lord," he said, turning to Julian, "there you are. Will you have her?"

"What?" Julian asked, genuinely staggered, as the two men and all the assembled persons stared at him. "Have her, I? What for?" he asked, as comprehensions dawned and he hoped against all hope he was wrong in all of them.

"As under-kitchen-maid, I'd thought," Ben said thoughtfully, "or for general housework, unless she shows an aptitude for something else. Remember that stammering chit we gave the duke, Lion? Clumsy at everything, but a rare talent for the needle, it turned out."

"Oh, yes," Lion answered, so amused his voice was a purr of pleasure as he saw the expressions on Julian's face. "And remember that scrubby youth I gave to the blacksmith? Well, he's with the vicar now, seems the boy has a golden voice, and he's being trained up for the choir."

"Damn you, Lion!" Julian said, but then he began to laugh with purest relief before he even fully appreciated the joke played on him. "You run an employment bureau now!"

"Of course, how else do you think we get these poor creatures out of here and into some proper job of work? Religion is all very good, and I'm pleased to give the missions money, but Ben and I know that a man needs work for his hands as well as food in his belly. A man, and a woman, for poverty's even crueler to the girls. Some fail, that's true. And no one," Arden said as much to his listening audience as to Julian, "gets a second chance, for we don't tolerate fools. So much as a penny piece missing, or another servant mistreated, and they're home again, home again, jiggity jig. But if they work fair, they're treated square and they get a chance to leave this vile place and start a new life."

"No wonder I felt so ancient at Warwick's," Julian managed to say even with his laughter. "Half the help there was adolescent! I wondered why the ancient gatekeeper had such young children. Why, you've repopulated half of Sussex, haven't you?"

"And Hants and the Midlands, and we're working on Surrey and the North Country. It keeps the oldsters young, having the new ones to teach. And of course, it profits us, having such cheap labor," Arden said blithely, as Julian sobered, thinking of how much it probably cost these children's employers in time and effort before they were worthy of their dinners, much less their hire.

"Yes," Julian said with the straightest face he could assume, "I believe you're right, the girl will do for an apprentice kitchen maid."

As the girl sighed with relief and stepped back, Ben-Be-Good cautioned her, "And mind, the viscount's engaged to be wed, so no calf's-eyes at the master, hear? Not that it would do you any good, for his fiancée is as beautiful as she can stare. Mind, whatever she looked like, we don't tolerate to-do betwixt the help and the quality, not ever. And so," he said, turning to Julian, "Peg is on. Is she to be for the London house or the country estate, Viscount?"

Julian looked at him in surprise, as Arden prompted, "You are going to have to at least rent a house in

London after the wedding, I believe. And of course, open Elmwood Court at last, aren't you, Julian? You and Eliza aren't just going to live in London, are you?"

"No. Yes. That is . . ." Julian said, but then he realized a man would return to his country seat to begin his marriage. "Yes. So," he said, now deciding that as his hand was being forced where his will wanted to go, whether or not Eliza would be his bride, he would indeed have a bride—and soon, "I'll need many servants, I think." And as he saw, even in the darkness, a great many eyes shining, he added with pleasure, "A great many servants, indeed."

He hired on almost all of the assembled children. And as he shared a glass with Arden and Ben-Be-Good after his new servants had left to be taken in hand by Arden's helpers, he was given to understand that he'd have to hire on many more. He'd need a number of them in any case, and some of the children would leave at once, and some would fade away after a few weeks, for not all of them were willing or able to walk the straitened path.

"And, never fear," Arden assured him, "I'll gather some experienced and capable servants as well, to train the youngsters, and incidentally, to actually serve you."

"All of them indigent pensioners down on their luck, except for those who are reformed gamesters, sots, and pardoned murderers, of course," Julian commented.

"Of course," he was assured with an enormous smile when he finally took leave of his friend and Ben-Be-Good.

For he no more wanted to go back to Warwick's house with Arden than he wished to return to his club as yet. Eliza was likely holding court today too, and facing his fiancée at the height of her newfound social success was a thought that didn't appeal to him any more now than it had the night before. But he'd no intention of trying to forget the matter the way he'd done the previous night. He'd had quite enough of females for a while. And so it was that he remembered with pleasure one place where he'd find no females, but a great deal of stimulation nontheless.

The young blades of the Four-in-Hand Club that were gathered in the common room of The Black Dog were arguing. One fresh-faced youth was protesting volubly as Julian entered the tavern.

"But I was lucky to get off with only scrapes to show, for there I was, skidding, trying to edge the bite so we didn't tumble, our speed was such that I had a care—"

"Ho! You'd a care! You was fanning the nags, Jeremy," another well-dressed youth scoffed.

"Fanning? Toweling, more like," another gent put in, as the first young lord, growing red with embarrassment lest anyone should really think he was such a no-account sawyer as to whip his horses like the veriest ham-handed amateur, protested, in his defense reverting to his class, and losing all his hard-learned slang, "No, no. It was that steep a hill, sir, I vow it. I could have been driving tortoises and I would've come a cropper on such a sudden incline. And it overlooked the sea, sir, for it was on the Portsmouth Road near to Gosport."

"I mark it well," Julian said kindly, agreeing aloud because he remembered the twists on that bit of road, but more because judging from the young man's friends' half-hidden grins, and his vehement protests of his caution, the poor fellow probably usually drove like a tortoise himself and was being teased. "It's devilish narrow there."

They all turned to see who'd spoken, and all of them fell still then. There couldn't be two such wondrous-looking chaps in all the land who knew the road. Incredibly enough, it seemed they were face to actual face with that celebrated legendary whip Julian Dylan, Viscount Hazelton, at last. Even their elders, practiced whipsters all, fell silent. They'd known he'd reemerged in London, but were agog to find him in their midst. Fanatics of the sport, these wealthy gentlemen amateur coachmen soon had Julian regaling them with stories of his coaching days in America, and were hanging on every word of his adventures when he'd actually driven on the Brighton Line.

He returned to his club that night only to change his clothes and shave himself (securing a valet, he decided, and one that was *not* a pardoned murderer, would be his next order of business) before he returned to dine with some of his newfound fellow charioteers.

He drove out with a procession of the Four-in-Hand Club the very next day on one of their tri-weekly excursions out from Piccadilly. And what with being invited to try Lord Bristow's team of grays on Monday, and dining with the club on Tuesday, and having a go with young Pritchard's mettlesome chestnuts on Wednesday, and going off to Tat's to help John Whitcombe with his selection of a matched pair on Thursday, the days began to drift by him. Now and again he thought of Eliza, when he heard her name taken in exultation by one of the younger clubmen; she was rapidly becoming as fashionable as a young woman could be, so that even the coaching-mad bucks of the exclusive Four-in-Hand sang her praises. More often, he tried not to think of her. The fact that he, as her fiancé, never visited with her, was not remarked upon. She was engaged, and so was he, and in the *ton*, marriages of convenience were understood well enough, and had never interfered with anyone's pleasure.

And he was having enormous pleasure as he passed her by almost two weeks later. So much so that he never saw her at all, for all she'd stopped in her walking and stood and stared at him. But so, then, did everyone else who was strolling the perimeters of the park that day. For he drove a high light phaeton, a sporting carriage all airy fretwork picked out in gold, drawn by cream-colored horses, and his gold hair was blown in the wind and his eyes shimmered with pleasure and light as he flew past, and more than one spectator thought of Apollo and looked to see if he dragged the reluctant sun itself behind him as he coursed across fashionable London's sky. Or so, at least, one caricaturist portrayed him the very next week in Humphries' print-shop window. Or so, at least, Eliza thought as she stopped and stared, pierced to the heart by the sight of him, as the sight of him diminished all the gentlemen she was with to their true and trivial, merely mortal size again.

"I say," Lord Cabot said, squinting, "ain't that Hazelton?"

Lord Young, Fred Coombs, and the Baron Burgess stopped bickering over who would buy Eliza an ice to have a look, while Captain Barstow, Lord Greyville,

Harry Fabian, and a few of the other older fellows in her train silently cursed the fellow for bringing the matter up to her. It hadn't looked like a love match to them so far. Some of them had hopes of dissuading the adorable little lady from taking the final fatal step, and some of the more realistic of them had plans for her after she'd taken the final, not necessarily fatal step, and in either case, a good look at what she was either going to give up or give up on was not beneficial to any of their plans.

But one look at the lady's face as she saw Hazelton flying by made them all sigh. For if ever a female looked at them like that, especially such a charmer as Eliza Merriman, why, then, they thought as one for once, they'd never ask for more. For her look went from shocked surprise to sheerest, purest, most transparent love. And then, to their delight, the look changed, even as Hazelton was gone around a corner from their sight. Because then, clearly, Miss Eliza Merriman was purely enraged. They all might have been a good deal less merry afterward if they'd realized that all that anger was solely with herself.

"It's too bad of him not to have called in all this time," Constance agreed as Eliza flung her gloves to the table-top after they'd left the gentlemen and come back to Warwick's house.

It was too bad for Eliza, she thought, and so perhaps for herself as well. If Julian avoided her cousin, he perforce avoided her as well, whether he wished to or not. The only way she could attract his attention at this stage was to divert it from Eliza. There was no way she could, or would, lure him to a meeting without his fiancée, at least, not at this point. So she was as vexed with him for his long absence as she saw that Eliza was.

"I am surprised at him," Anthea commented softly, but she was not. A gentleman like Julian Dylan would detest the foolishness of the London Season fully as much as she did. He too would see the inanity of it, the hollowness of fashion, and the heartlessness of the inhabitants of its world. He was far too sensitive, of course, and too good to indulge in it. Still, she regretted his long absence, for she couldn't see him unless he visited with

Eliza, and the more he saw how childish Eliza's pleasures
were, the more he would eventually appreciate a woman
of sensibility and reason. She sighed, fully in accord with
Eliza's evident displeasure with Julian.

But Eliza, aflame with fury, didn't wish to share it with
anyone, and so on the most abrupt and graceless of
transparently false excuses, she begged their pardon, and
pleading the headache, took herself off to her rooms.
Where she lay on her bed with a cool wet cloth over her
forehead, for her head did throb abominably, and wept.

The sight of him today had struck her to her heart. It
had been like a window opened on a dark room, where
her foolish fancies were revealed for what they were, as
if by a sudden shaft of clean clear light. She must have
been enchanted by her success in society in the truest
meaning of the word, for nothing she'd delighted in, she
saw now, had any basis in reality. No sport, no diversion,
and certainly no gentleman. All the fawning young men
and the clever, calculating older ones were as dross when
compared with Julian. She saw that clearly now.

It wasn't just the look of him. It was the reality of him,
well-remembered from his letters, well-beloved from his
conversation. She was, she thought, weeping silently now,
like a girl who'd been given a diamond and had thrown it
away for a handful of colored stones that sparkled in the
lamplight. Because surely he'd grown as disgusted with
her pleasure in her foolish fame that last time he'd seen
her, as she was with herself now.

For all her popularity, she thought on a dry sob, because her tears were too bitter to shed any longer, the
moment she'd seen him again she'd realized how lonely
she was. She'd dined on air, she'd talked of nothing,
she'd laughed at nonsense, and so she was, in some deep
part of her soul, starving. She'd flirted, jested, and fluttered her lashes, devouring praise like sweetmeats, nour-
ishing herself on the insubstantiality of it—in vain—for
the best of it had only given her a craving for more. Most
of all, she missed her Julian of the letters, and wondered
if he, her closest confidant and friend, was gone from her
forever now that he had come to her in person.

She snuffled and used the wet cloth for her eyes and

then her nose, instead of her forehead, for the tears had vented her misery and lessened her head's aching. She was left with only a numbness . . . and a longing. Then she remembered what she used to do whenever she was so wretched, and thought that if she'd lost one Julian, she might at least see if she could recover the other. She sat up, and sighed, making a terrible face at the rumpled, dreadful-looking girl in the mirror before she rose to go to her desk. She would, she thought, chewing on the end of her pen until some ink dripped down on her chin, write him a letter. And tell him of his old friend's latest folly. Of how she was like the girl stolen by the fairies, who danced all night and drank faery wine, and woke one morning to find a hundred years had flown by. Or what seemed like a hundred years, she thought on a last sniff as she wrote, a century that had earned her nothing but a memory of music and laughter and bright lights.

Eliza came down the stair before dinner to find Constance and Anthea chatting with Arden and Francesca. Now that their duke had returned to his country home, it was only the large gentleman and his lady who remained in the town house with Anthea and herself and the dozens of servants, and the Lyonses, she knew, had plans to leave in a matter of days.

"I feel much better, thank you," she said when they asked, although from her unnaturally white face and swollen eyes, her audience took leave to doubt it.

"Oh, a letter!" Constance said brightly. "Never say it's from Julian?"

"I never shall," Eliza replied on a ghost of a smile, "for it isn't. It's *to* him, you see. Well," she said defensively as they all stared at her, "it's habit, I suppose. We wrote to each other constantly for five years, after all. I suppose I quite forgot he was in London . . . that is," she added, seeing from their expressions that she'd phrased it wrong, and refusing to have them pitying her, "I'm used to seeing him on paper, not in person."

And not even on that anymore, Arden thought, looking to his wife, and, seeing her slight nod, decided to get on to the matter they'd discussed last night over their pillow.

"We're leaving for our country home within days," he said as the other ladies made appropriate noises of sorrow for their departure, "and not only because we miss that rogue of a boy of ours and Francesca wants to increase in peace, far from the city lights. But it's very lovely in the Lake District. So much so, in fact, that Warwick and Susannah and their clan regularly visit with us each summer. They're due to come within a month, if the chickenpox has abated. We've boats to sail over our bit of lake in, and mountains to clamber over, and long country walks through fern-filled forests carpeted with bluebells at this time of the year—and I'm a dandy gardener," he added when he grew aware that he was about to wax lyrical and slight his point, "fish ponds and fountains and the like, overflowing with flowers as well as water. In short, although it's still fairly cool and the summer people haven't arrived yet, so it's devoid of company, except for those in our overflowing house . . . should you like to come along with us now, Eliza?"

"Oh, yes, we'd love to have you," Francesca Lyons urged. "If you paint, you'll have acres of inspiration. But if you can only admire nature, like me, why, then, you'll still find it a tonic. And, of course, I'd love the company," she said, purely for the sake of politeness, or so most of her listeners thought, for no one seriously believed she ever needed more than her huge husband at her side. "You might find it a welcome change of pace," she added.

Constance hid her smiles. Change the pace to a crawl, she thought. For of course the "summer people" hadn't left London yet. The ending of spring signaled the coming end of the Season, and like a spectacular fireworks display, society saved the best for last. Eliza had invitations to the lavish ball next week at the Swansons' house. Not to mention the many minor fetes, and the musicale at the Rigbys' Monday, the dinner date they'd all made for a party at Vauxhall next Thursday night, and the masquerade that everyone in the *ton* would kill to get invitations to at the Duke of Austell's town house. Then, too, this year a good many of the *ton* would be staying on in London longer than usual, awaiting the coronation and all the subsequent festivities that would offer. Of what use would all of Eliza's new frocks be in a fern-filled forest? Perhaps Arden was only jesting again; it was difficult to tell from his impassive expression. Francesca couldn't seriously expect Eliza to come with them either. At least Constance hoped that was the case, for they were, however unusual, a charming couple, and seeing Eliza already beginning to smile, she disliked to think of their being wounded by her cousin's thoughtless ready laughter.

Anthea turned so that her face wouldn't give away her amusement. Eliza was promised to a poetry reading at Mrs. Surcliff's house on Wednesday afternoon, a tea at the dowager Duchess of Fen's on Thursday, and had in her room, propped on her glass, an engraved invitation to a dinner on Saturday night, where it was promised that Mr. Southey himself would be guest. She'd spoken of little else for days. For she was taking to the world like a duck to the water the large gentleman had just been going on about. In all fairness, Eliza had been secluded for so many years that her enthusiasm was understandable. Anthea had shared some of those years with her and knew the feeling very well. But the Lyonses' invitation, however kind, was, she thought on a suppressed laugh, like offering a canary a slice of roast beef. It was absurd. Because however tasty, the girl would have no use for it. She only hoped Eliza would be subtle in her refusal of the kind offer.

Eliza looked up to Arden. Her eyes sparkled, color returned to her cheeks, and she smiled with transcendent joy.

"Oh, yes!" she cried. "Oh, please! Thank you, I'd love to go with you. I can be ready to leave in the morning!"

9

ANTHEA BAKER knew Latin, French, a great deal of literature in those languages as well as her own, and the name of every flower nodding in the fields and on the banks near to the road she traveled. Eliza had always known Anthea's store of knowledge, but it had never irritated her before. Still, the French and Latin were only a literal conversation piece, and since Julian was up on the driver's seat of the coach they were in, the flowers only got her Arden Lyons' undivided attention. And even his wife didn't give a hang about that. But Arden wasn't the only one Anthea seemed bent on impressing these days, Eliza thought sulkily.

Francesca, after all, could be secure in the knowledge that Anthea might be sitting naked and Arden would have only handed her his greatcoat so she could continue talking horticulture without interruption, Eliza thought as she listened to Anthea go on about rose graftings. Not only that, but this morning Francesca was too busily trying to avoid hanging out the carriage window to be sick, to care even if her husband should go mad and run away entirely with Eliza's clever companion.

And clever she was, Eliza brooded. Last night at dinner at the inn they'd stopped at, Anthea had been in her glory, making herself the centerpiece of their table, with her talk of flowers. Arden had noted her interest in them and asked her something about flowering shrubbery, and then Julian had spoken of the flowers of the tropics and the New World, and then naturally the talk had turned to how Anthea had got to know so much, and she'd been pleased to go on about herself until Eliza had gotten as queasy as poor Francesca's green face showed her to be now. She'd never seen Anthea so animated before, not for years, at least not since one of the more malicious girls from the lower form had put beetles in her teacup, Eliza thought, cheering up enormously at the remembrance.

The worst part of it was, she realized now as Anthea burbled on about hybrids and hyacinths, that there was nothing wrong with Anthea's erudition, nothing unnatural about her blossoming under Julian's interest, and nothing untoward about anything in her manner or morals. It was only that Anthea was clearly interesting Julian, and that was something that wrenched at Eliza's heart. Because she'd only undertaken this trip so that she could begin to repair the damage she'd done to her tenuous engagement to Julian while she'd been playing at being queen of the London social scene. She hadn't expected him to come along, and when he'd immediately seized upon Arden's invitation, she'd been thrilled. Only later had she wondered at why he was as glad to quit London as she'd been.

It might have been because he'd heard about the letter she'd written to him—the letter she'd never sent because she'd been so shamed at how the thing had seemed, as if she were begging for his favor. It might have been that he was weary with town too, for all he'd dazzled the members of the Four-in-Hand Club so thoroughly that they'd driven out from London in elegant parade with him until dark the day they'd left London, just so that they could forever after say they'd ridden alongside him and watched his handling of the ribbons. Or it just might have been that he'd wanted to be with her. Or so she'd dared to hope.

But he'd been nothing but polite to her. And she'd been tiptoeing round him, trying to find things to say that wouldn't have to do with the future of their assumed engagement, her behavior of late, or his, or the fact she tried to hide at every turn: the intensity of her feelings for him. Nothing would put him off more now. She knew too well that she'd seemed a heartless flirt with Hugh and then a feather-headed flirt with half the eligibles in London. No, if she should try to charm him now, he'd only think it was more of the same. And her feelings were such that she wanted him to be entirely sure of her when she at last divulged them. If, she thought gloomily, she ever had the opportunity.

Because now Arden called for the coach to stop, for Francesca's sake. No sooner had the wheels stopped turning than Arden tenderly took his lady out for a revivifying march around the grassy verge. Eliza primed her face with a welcoming smile as Julian handed the reins to Arden's regular coachman. And then Julian came round to the door and helped Anthea down, with a smile and a word about buttercups at the side of the road as he did.

Jealousy was bad for the soul and for the spirit, and moreover, it gave one a pang in the depths of one's stomach, Eliza discovered to her dismay as she took Julian's hand and descended the stair from the coach even as Anthea took up all of his interest. Well, but I know buttercups too, she thought petulantly, and who better? since it was Anthea who taught me. But I know more, she thought rebelliously, deliberately trampling a squat daisy set in the grass deep as a mosaic tile under her toe, and watching it spring up again as she passed by. She didn't know the Latin names, nor the Greek ones, she admitted, for she'd tended to wander during that part of her lessons. But she was proud of her own store of wisdom of things observed during a long country childhood of wandering alone.

She heard Anthea prosing on prettily about buttercups and frowned. But does she know how to sip the honey from honeysuckle? she silently challenged, remembering how carefully one had to pull out the long stamen to lick at the one sweet drop of nectar each blossom held. Does she know how rhododendron leaves curl up tighter than Captain Barstow's cigarillos when the north winds blow sharp? Or how foxgloves slip off their cylindrical bells when they've done with them so that they can be picked up by children and blown as pretended faery horns? And does he care? she thought sadly, pacing on in Julian's wake as he smiled down upon Anthea.

But she was a remarkably pretty lady, Julian thought,

noting how the sun made the light brown hair that escaped from Anthea's bonnet take on a slight blond glow, and wondering why he'd never properly appreciated it until now. She is herself a meadow flower, he thought, delicate but needful of close inspection, for such shy loveliness might be overwhelmed by the blatant hothouse beauties of town. Or so he thought until he took a look at the wild and flaming color of Eliza's hair in the open light, and saw the bright sharp glance she shot to him, and remembered that not only violets bloomed in the country, for the wild rose prospered there too. No, Anthea was a pretty lady, but Eliza was, or would be, a wondrously beautiful one. But well she knew it, he thought on a rueful sigh, just as she'd made sure half the gentlemen of London did.

He eyed the two ladies and thought that Eliza was like a beautiful kitten, or colt, or other young and heedless thing, whose whole attraction lay specifically in her freshness. But Anthea was a woman: rich and warm and deep and fully developed in all her mind and body. Or so he tried to tell himself as he avoided Eliza's eyes—which wasn't difficult. For she stared down so fixedly at the bindweed Anthea was lecturing on that her round bonnet hid all of her face save for the merest tip of her impudent nose—which, Julian discovered, with horror, he suddenly longed to touch with his lips. But she was dressed adorably today, in a dark violet promenade dress covered over with a paisley shawl, and was herself bonnier than any of the blooms they dutifully inspected while trying to ignore poor Francesca's discomfort behind a budding hawthorn hedge.

There was only so much one could say about wildflowers, or at least only just so much even an attentive gentleman could pretend to listen to with animation, and they all were as relieved as Arden was when he signaled that they might enter the coach and start up again—only slowly and carefully, he cautioned, as though Julian could help how many ruts there were in the road before them.

"They might like some more room, at that. Care to ride up with the big bad coachman, Eliza?" Julian asked carelessly as he escorted the ladies back to the coach.

"Oh, but can I, really?" she answered excitedly, completely forgetting how vexed she was with him at the thought of such a treat, for she'd longed to see the world from his vantage point from the first time that he'd written about his coaching days.

As he helped her up to the high hard seat with as much tender affection as if she'd been a portmanteau he had to hoist there, she'd second and third thoughts. Anthea had not been asked to ride with him because he thought Anthea a lady, and herself a child. Or because he felt sorry for her. Or because he'd something dreadful to say to her that he wanted no one else to hear. She grew very still as he positioned himself, took up the reins, nodded Arden's coachman to the side to ride postilion, and raised up his whip to start off again as slowly and carefully as Arden might wish.

Julian minded his tongue as well as his off leader, because all of Eliza's speculations were right. She'd looked dismally depressed, and he knew she'd take a child's pleasure in what a fully mature female might find boring or terrifying; he felt sorry for her being cooped up with a bilious lady, and he decided it was time to ask whether she'd like to call off their sham engagement when they got back to town after their stay at Arden's estate.

But it was difficult to broach any subject to a girl who sat still as a stone and looked straight ahead, so that all he could read in her face was woven straw, since it was her bonnet and not her expression he could see from his seat. Still, he could see the profile of her body as the wind shaped her soft muslin dress to her sharper curves, and he became aware of all that he'd tried not to notice when he'd lifted her to his high perch. He wrenched his gaze back to the road and shook his head before he spoke, for he'd thought he was sated with one aspect of females for a space and was disturbed to discover he was decidedly, emphatically not.

"You're distressed. Out with it, then, it's something I said, or did, or is it something you think I'll do?" he asked more bluntly than he intended, but he was having difficulty reminding himself that his fiancée was not for him.

"It's something *I* said, and did, but by God," she said straightly, turning to look fully at him, "nothing I'll do again, I promise."

Then she looked down, as surprised at herself as he was, but not before he saw the flash of anger in her eyes and forgot his lust in his care for her.

"You can't just forget you said it, you know," he said when they'd driven on for a silent half-mile. "I'd stop right here and have it out with you, but then Arden and Francesca and Anthea would come boiling out of the coach to see what the matter was. And I can't shake it out of you by driving to an inch, out of concern for Francesca. But I can nag at you for the next fifty miles, and I promise it will grow tedious. Let's hear it, please. Or would you rather write me a letter?" he asked, gentling his voice as he saw the beginnings of a grin appear in the fraction of her cheek her bonnet let him spy.

"I did write you a letter," she admitted, "last week. But I never sent it because it seemed foolish when I could speak with you. And now," she said, turning so that he could see her full shamefaced smile, "I find I can't speak with you."

But she had to, she knew, and so though she couldn't tell him the whole truth, she could tell him a particle of it and save face, so she seized on the simplest version of all her troubles.

"I made rather a cake of myself back in town," she said sadly.

"What?" he asked in amazement. "But you were a raging success."

"Just so," she replied, and at his curious look, she added, "I didn't mean to be." At his smile, she saw she'd given him the wrong idea and went on, "You see, I know I was wildly popular, but it was because I gave the gentlemen the wrong impression, I think."

He grew very still, his face suddenly cold and set.

"Which gentleman in particular?" he asked, and then added, just as carefully, but in accents that were a fraction more kindly, "I am your friend, Eliza, and I hope you know you may always count on me. Have I not been as a brother to you for all these years?" he asked as she stared back at him, stricken with the truth of that, and she almost wept as she gathered her wits so she could answer. And when she did, it was in that high, bright voice that had so enchanted all the gentlemen of London.

"Lud, Julian! What do you take me for? You don't have to polish up your sword or your pistol, Father dear. And if you're that keen to see oaks at dawn, you can go with Anthea, because I'm sure she'd be delighted to lecture to you about them until the duel begins—which will be never. Because I wasn't compromised by any gentleman. Though I could have been. It's just that I was so wildly successful that they all thought me a foolish fribble of a society belle, which I never meant to be, or am."

He grew cold as soon as she mentioned Anthea so mockingly. He didn't care to hear a lady rip an absent friend up the back—that was the sort of thing females did that gentlemen never cared for. It reminded him of what his little friend Eliza had become, no matter what she'd been, or looked like now. Her new artificial drawing-room accents set his teeth on edge as well, so he said a bit too pointedly:

"But Constance is a society belle and I never thought her a fribble."

"Well," she answered, too quickly for thought, stung by the censure in his voice, "but then, a gentleman wouldn't, would he?" And cursed herself silently as he stiffened, and so admitted immediately, in vexation, in her own voice, "Oh, Lud, Julian, that's never what I meant. I've just been turned around since I got to London is what it is."

"Of course," he said then.

But there was a world of patient elderly understanding in those two words, and she read it correctly. It had all to do with his sympathy for her youth, sex, and condition, and she might have hit him for it, if she hadn't been of a pacific nature. And it might have been better if she had, for then he would have shaken her until her teeth rattled, and they would have been appalled at each other and themselves before they laughed and spoke together as the friends they both so badly needed, instead of riding on in peace and perfect misunderstanding.

Arden Lyons' country home was reached after the long landscaped drive to it gave the visitors a hint of the even more splendid gardens to come. There were walls of riotously blooming rhododendrons and mountain laurels, banks of tulips and fritillarias, and avenues of beech and linden through which, in the distance, glittering glimpses of canals and ponds and spillways to the great lake that lay beyond the house could be seen. If they couldn't be, then Arden, his head poked out the window, could be counted on to shout his guests' prompt attention to them.

So, for once, Julian and Eliza were giggling together when he finally drew the coach to a halt in front of a handsome manor house. After their temporary artificial pact of peace, they had another day on the road and night at an inn. They'd ignored each other beautifully at dinner in the inn the previous night, where Anthea, Eliza was pleased to note, finally told Julian so much about night-blooming cereus that he began to look vaguely hunted. Until he saw Eliza's knowing smile and immediately became so enraptured with the subject that one would have thought he was planning to open a succession of greenhouses as soon as he got home, Eliza had thought wretchedly when she'd stumped off to bed with an ungracious complaint about the rigors of riding all day in jolting coaches.

As Arden handed his lady out, a number of young people came pouring out of the great house. A dark-haired stocky square of a little boy, the general shape of a shire horse colt, came barreling out of the crowd to throw himself into Arden's arms.

"Father!" he cried ecstatically. "Mama!" he sang out as Francesca also embraced him. "You're home!"

"Observant lad," Arden commented with a great show of ironic humor that never hid his enormous pride as he lifted the lad in his arms.

"I never doubted you, Papa," the boy said seriously, looking back at his father with a matching pair of hazel eyes. "It's only that I missed you. Not that I didn't have a hundred things to do. For I did. I was splendidly entertained. I discovered an ouzel's nest, or so Mr. Jameson said I did. But he teases so, one can never tell. And he's from London, isn't he, so one can't be sure he really knows. At least I think it is one. It's really extraordinary—"

Arden put a large hand over the boy's mouth.

"This," he said, grinning ear to ear, "is my son, Randolph Graham Sebastian Lyons, ladies and gentleman. He only stops talking to eat and sleep. And these, young fiend," he said to his wide-eyed son, "are my friends Miss Eliza Merriman, Miss Anthea Baker, and Julian Dylan, the Viscount Hazelton."

As soon as his father's hand was removed, the boy cried out, "Julian? Your friend Julian, the famous coachman? Oh, sir," he said, leaning forward in his father's arms, "how I have wanted to meet you. I've heard so many things . . . Is it true? About the Brighton Coach, I mean? And your stay in America? Are the Indians fierce? And red as apples? I thought they might be light red, rather than bright red, but then—"

His father bottled him up again with one free hand.

"He's a lovely youth," he explained, "but very young, you understand."

"But I thought," Julian said, confused, "that you said your son was an infant—not above four years."

"Just so," Arden said, as Francesca began laughing. "His brain seems to have grown at the same rate as his body. And his tongue, unfortunately."

"Prodigious," Julian said wonderingly as father and son looked back at him with quiet pride at the compliment to both of them.

Then the company was introduced to the throng of people standing in front of the house. Although Eliza knew enough of society to know that one's visitors were not ordinarily introduced to one's servants, she soon perceived that Arden Lyons never did things in the ordinary way, and that his servants were more his devoted slaves than household help. There were a great many children among them, or belonging to them, and she wondered at it, until Francesca bent to whisper the explanation. It had been a year until she knew she'd be bearing her husband a child, she confided, so he'd stocked the house with children so that she wouldn't worry about it.

"He didn't wish for me to feel that I must breed or be a disappointment to him," she said on a reminiscent smile, "and brought homeless children here so I could see that even if I could never produce one, he could always pick an heir with ease. He might be the one who was unable, he said, insisting it made no matter which of us it was. Because he vowed it was the getting of a good wife that was difficult for a man," Francesca murmured, the joy of what her husband had said still in her eyes, "and not the begetting of an heir, which any fool could do—or else why would there be so many abandoned children?

"But I still believe it was because he knew I could never have all the children he needed about him," she said on a laugh, to bury sentiment, before she sobered and whispered softly, "The places these children came from! Someone has to see to them. Maybe when you and Julian are wed, you might consider taking on some of Arden's children? They're good workers, and it's so rewarding . . . But oh, I've become like Randolph in my nattering on. You haven't even had your honeymoon yet. Never mind me, Eliza," she said, completely mistaking the reason for her guest's hectic flush. "I'll show you to your rooms."

Eliza's room was light and airy and well-supplied with everything she'd need, and oversupplied with maids of work. For one poured out her bath, and another laid out her clothes, and yet another, she swore, was about to do the same for her own maid. When they'd all left, she lay back in her hip-bath and sighed as she soaped herself, thinking of the beauty of the house she was in, the kindness and care of her hosts, and the impossible and complete muddle she'd gotten herself into.

Anthea sank back into her own bath in her own guest room and thought that this was the way a lady must feel. She had no social ambitions—indeed, she was contemptuous of the entire social world. But she'd her own dreams, and now they seemed closer to waking. She'd had the best of treatment at Eliza's house, of course, and was well-cared-for at the Duke of Peterstow's town house. But her experiences so far with the Lyonses and in their household made her forget her place entirely. In these past few hours she'd been waited on as a lady, and spoken to as an equal and looked at, oh, unmistakably viewed as an eligible female by the one man she'd ever wanted to see her as such.

Of course, her friend Eliza was infatuated with the same gentleman, and nominally engaged to be wed to him. But however punctilious Anthea was in such matters (and she believed that in this cruel world females owed it to each other to support each other), still she knew it was no betrayal of that friendship to fancy the same gentleman. For Eliza had flirted with every man who'd flirted with her in London, and had kissed and heaven knew what more with the stolid Hugh, who could not be less like her supposed ideal, Julian. No, Anthea thought, relaxing in the warmth of her bath and the comfort she found everywhere around her now, Eliza was still an infant in matters of the heart. It might even be that she'd never grow up in some things, fidelity might be an inborn virtue, since she herself had never been so fickle and couldn't imagine being so. If she'd corresponded with such a gentleman for five years of her life and he'd come to her at last, she'd never look at another, not for a thousand years. If she'd secured his promise to marry her (and though Eliza had never confided the whole of it to her, Anthea had a shrewd idea of how that had occurred), however such a miracle had happened, she'd never let him go.

Julian deserved better. Indeed, it might be that he knew it, for it didn't appear that he regarded Eliza as more than a charming friend. And for all they were engaged, there seemed to be no real plans for a forthcoming wedding, any more than there were any signs of devotion between them. Love was not necessary for society matings, but surely such a man merited more than mere liking for or from his bride.

Now they were in a place where a man might have

time to think, away from the distractions of London, far from the lure of other females. Not only were there no opera dancers or demireps in the countryside to entice a gentleman, but such modish beauties as the Honorable Constance Merriman were absent as well. Although invited to join them, Eliza's fashionable cousin had elected to stay on in town until the Season ended. By then, with luck and effort to make her own luck, something else might have begun for herself, Anthea thought. Luck and wit, even more, courage, and perhaps some cunning, she decided daringly, gazing down her naked form and for once evaluating it with neither shame nor regret, but only with pride and rising expectation. Now at last, she decided, she had a fair chance at what destiny seemed determined to have deprived her of before.

But she'd little chance to try anything but her dinner when she sat down to dine that night. The adults at the long table hadn't much to say to each other and less to do to entertain each other. Because the Lyonses were eccentrics in every particular and so had their son in to dine with them. The guests' reactions were as varied as their own experience.

Julian was at first amused, and then enchanted, and wasn't hesitant to say so. His reaction gave Anthea time to recover herself. She soon reasoned that the Lyonses were wealthy enough to be eccentric as they chose. After all, the Duchess of York was said to give her ninety-nine dogs free run of her house, and the Lyonses only tolerated one infant where no civilized household would permit one. But Eliza was instantly delighted with the boy's presence at the table. Remembering her own lonely infancy, she determined on the spot to allow each of her children the same freedom with the family. But then, thinking of the chain of events that must lead to the possibility of ever having any of her own at all, she fell to brooding again. This made the other company at the table believe she was scandalized—that was, when they took the time to notice her at all, for young Randolph kept them alight with merriment from their soup to the Duke of Cumberland pudding that precocious young man rejoiced in.

That dessert, however tasty, was the least successful part of the meal. For though his son could talk the ear off a brass elephant, the mechanics of his dining, especially concerning foodstuffs he was enthusiastic about, left much to be desired. Or so his father said as he unceremoniously hoisted his somewhat sticky heir in his arms, mid-mouthful, to bear him off to bed with his plate, where they could make merry, unseen by discriminating eyes.

Francesca took her leave of her guests at the same time, but didn't promise to return as Arden did, explaining that she'd seek her bed too because her condition made her sleepy as a dormouse at this stage of forthcoming events.

"Did you dislike young Randolph dining with us?" Julian asked Eliza after their hosts left, as he led her to the salon after dinner.

Anthea turned from bidding her hostess good night at the sound of his words, just in time to see Julian's fair head ducking low to hear Eliza's answer. In the soft lamplight Anthea could see his wistful expression as well as Eliza's sudden bright wakening from her gloomy reveries. The well-shaped flaxenstreaked head so near to the glowing auburn one, the picture the two delicately featured faces made as they neared to each other, caused Anthea to step quickly and softly across the thick Turkey carpets to where Eliza was in such close conversation with her fiancé. She'd an excuse, Anthea thought fiercely, fighting down the small shocked part of herself that was aghast at such a maneuver and appalled at both her own terror and temerity. Eliza was her charge, after all. Eavesdropping was her task.

"Dislike? Lud, no! I enjoyed him as much as the duckling, that is . . . Oh, hush, Julian, anyone can missay something," Eliza complained as Julian laughed at her reply. "Because it's nothing new to me. I always ate every meal with adults, as far back as I can remember," she explained. "But then, they don't stand on much ceremony in the countryside. Or at least the servants I grew up with didn't," she mused without a trace of self-pity, "and they were the only ones in the house with me, so we always dined together."

"You're still very liberal about that, Eliza," Anthea put in softly as she came up to the couple.

"Oh," Eliza said on a laugh, "but I assure you I don't dine with servants now."

"But you do," Anthea persisted gently, "for you've always insisted on my sitting at the table with you since I've joined you."

"Oh, but no, you're never a servant!" Eliza protested.

"But I am," Anthea reproved her. "Your parents do pay me my wages, I am employed by them. I cannot forget that, nor should you."

"But we have," Julian put in, as she'd hoped he would, as he offered her his arm as well, as she'd not dared dream he would, and led them both into the salon, one on each arm, as he added, "We'll set new precedents in society. We'll dine with servants, and we'll dance with them and walk with them and talk with them, until for all the world, no one will be able to tell the difference between us any more than we can or do, I promise you that, Anthea."

He was as good as his fair words, and by the time Arden descended the stairs to rejoin them, Julian was sitting beside Anthea on a settee, listening with more than polite interest as she held forth on the subject of her home and childhood. Arden noted that, as well as the fact that Eliza, whose home and childhood were as known to Julian as his own, sat by herself near to them, lively as a tombstone, wondering what to add to the conversation. She was watching her pretty honey-haired governess enchant her fiancé with all the grace and aplomb of a child whose dessert has just been snatched away, and with considerably less than Randolph had recently shown.

Anthea smiled at Julian's replies, and showed her little white teeth in shy smiles, and laughed in a way that Eliza had never heard before, and she heard every note in that unfamiliar laughter, for all that Arden was so kindly chatting with her to divert her from it. Anthea had never cocked her head to the side just so, nor listened so long to anything she'd had to say, Eliza thought as enviously

as she had whenever another girl had captured her friend
and schoolmistress's attention in the past, before her heart
picked up an erratic beat as she realized she was a long
way from school now. Her jealousy was directed elsewhere and it was never Anthea's friendship she was
afraid of losing now.

And so she was more than relieved, she was delighted,
when there was an unexpected interruption. There was a
clamor at the door, and Arden himself was momentarily
at a loss when the butler had a private word with him.
For it was late in the evening and deep in the countryside, and yet there was a visitor announced.

"Oh, Constance!" Eliza cried gaily when she heard
who it was, although at first she felt odd to be greeting
her relative with such feeling, as though her cousin, only
lately befriended, was come to save her from her own
best friend. But she was too relieved to care about the
peculiar specifics of it just yet. She knew only purest
gratitude as she arose and rushed to embrace her travel-
weary cousin, who was being shown into the salon.

"I changed my mind, I hope you don't mind, I found
the thought of town quite flat without my cousin and
decided I was in need of rustification, and Mama agreed,"
Constance said, as though her mama had any say in the
matter, and she was all smiles as Arden, much amused,
assured her of her welcome.

But her look was one of triumph as she gazed to where
her eyes had seldom strayed since she'd come into the
room. Because they'd narrowed when she'd seen Anthea
and Julian so deep in intimate conversation, and they
widened now as Julian rose to welcome her, as she'd
decided he should.

Town was fine, but it would be empty without him;
she'd realized that the day he'd left. She'd known it even
as she'd waved good-bye, and suddenly understood that
it might be much more she was so blithely saying farewell
to. So she'd decided to sacrifice a bit of the Season lest
she sacrifice something far more important, and for the
first time in her life, she admitted that something might
be. Because the fashions might change and the tunes she
danced to might alter, and the gentlemen she waltzed

with and flirted with might subtly change as well, but
season after season had begun to bear a sameness and
the only truly new things she'd discovered in the past
year were how increasingly young her rivals were becoming, and how desirable Julian Dylan was.

The fair-haired viscount bowed over her hand. When
he gave her over to her cousin's excited queries, his eyes
met those of his old friend Arden, and for one terrible
moment, as they gazed at each other over the heads of
the three reunited ladies, he was afraid he might actually
laugh out loud, he so agreed with his friend's vast unspoken mirth. But he subdued his amusement as he studied
the three lovely females in the room with him: Constance
so triumphant, Anthea so shocked, and Eliza so suddenly
animated.

He was flattered, for he wasn't a fool and understood
more of their reactions to each other than many another
gentleman might. He was accustomed to inspiring such
emotions, and more amused than flattered. Because often in such cases it turned out to be not so much the
ladies' feelings for him that mattered after a while, as
their contests with each other. He was now the centerpiece of an improvised game among them; that much was
clear. He'd have to be careful, he'd be sure to be discreet, he'd be deft where he could and definite where he
could not, and whatever happened, he'd make sure to
hurt not one of the three pretty females' feelings—more
than he had to. Because it could become unavoidable. It
just might be that he'd make a final decision this time.

What better chance would he have to decide his future
and choose a fitting wife, after all? He was weary with
searching, his friends' content made his wandering seem
even harder. What better choice would he ever have?
Eliza was a delightful child in a woman's lovely body,
Constance was a clever and justly famous beautiful woman
of fashion, and Anthea was warm, mature, and wise.
Eliza clearly needed a man to guide her, Constance a
gentleman to accompany her, and Anthea a man to protect her. Any one of them would make him a good wife.
What more was he looking for, after all?

Did he still seek passion that defied the senses and

made a fellow sacrifice all reason? But that was the stuff of Minerva Press novels, and, he admitted, his own foolish youth. Both passion and sensuality could be things apart from what he sought now; sexual delight could be found elsewhere than in wedlock, at any rate it was easy enough for him to find anywhere, he thought on a hastily suppressed flicker of self-dislike. He was ready to settle for companionship and mutual fondness. What Arden and Warwick had mightn't be possible for him to achieve. He was willing to see if in the dispassionate peace of rational choice he could eventually discover that which he'd never found in any of his passionate desires.

If he wondered suddenly whether seeking "a wife" for his pleasure would likely result in just as sweet an experience as seeking "a woman" had done in the past, he just as quickly stifled that notion on a shudder. He chose to believe that intellect might be the seat of real love, as the drier philosophies held, and so cold reason might bring him the warmth he'd never experienced. And pigs might fly, he thought ruefully.

But it was all a matter of belief, wasn't it? As always, when reality failed, faith could hold sway. Faith? The way his thoughts were running, he realized with growing amusement, he might as well act soon, before he was moved to become a monk, not a husband. Very well. He'd try it. He'd tried all else. He'd honestly attempt to pick a wife, since he couldn't imagine a better time or choice, and it appeared he had no other rational choice. So be it. He smiled down upon the lovely ladies who would vie for him, content.

Still, lest his large, knowledgeable friend think him a conceited fop for the way he accepted the situation rather than trying to change it, he changed his smile from one of pleasure to wry acknowledgment of the situation, and shook his golden head slightly so that Arden would see that such flattering attentions hadn't caused him to lose it entirely.

But then there was a more terrible moment.

Because that slight sideways motion of his head caused a ripple in his line of vision for a second, and he felt a chill ripple along his spine with it, even as a slow dull ache began to thud between his eyes. He shook his head again, this time to clear it, hoping it was only fear of the dreadful thought he now entertained that caused the sweating prickles he began to feel beneath his faultless evening clothes—and prayed it was only his troublesome thoughts that had caused all his shudders before, even as he shivered again. For in that moment, he thought he recognized what was coming, and he'd never wanted to inconvenience his friend or shock any of the pretty ladies by dying among them just now.

10

THE TWO GENTLEMEN strolled along the garden paths, speaking in murmurous voices so low that even if there'd been anyone near them, the sounds of the breeze in the newly leaved trees and the tumbling of the various playing fountains they passed would have drowned out any possibility of their being overheard.

"You've known him longer than I have, Warwick," Arden said as he walked with his head down in thought, "although we lived close for two years, remember. But still I don't recall his ever behaving this way. He was always a likely lad, ready for laughter, even when his heart was breaking. He might become distracted, but never despondent. Not a Hamlet, our Julian. But perhaps the years abroad changed him beyond my recognition. At any rate, he isn't the Julian I remember now, that's certain."

"No, it certainly doesn't sound like him," the slender duke agreed. "Even in school, his bad moods were as much cause for hilarity as his low ones, for he was always ready to make sport of himself and his problems. No, I agree, he's never been the melancholic type, to brood in his rooms, and I doubt even five years could alter a man so. I'm glad you wrote to tell me of it, Arden. I've a care for the lad too. It wasn't only the chance to bankrupt you by lumbering you with my household earlier than usual this year that caused me to fly up here with such alacrity, you know. I think I've brought a specific for him. Or at least, if not an antidote for whatever is poisoning his spirit, then a shrewd diagnostician to discover just where the problem lies. What? My all-observant Lion didn't note one particular bright-eyed little person in the enormous party I've landed upon him?"

"One particular little person?" Arden laughed. "You've got so many miniature humans in your luggage, Duke, both those you've caused and those you care for, that I'd have to be Argus-eyed to spy out just one of them."

"Then that's very well," Warwick answered approvingly, "because when I first took her into my care, she was so singularly solemn that we always noted her. No, I've brought Julian his cherished little Miss Mary, and if she can't cheer the fellow, we'll call in the undertaker and be done with it."

Then the duke frowned, and paused beneath a budding bower of roses. "Do you think it's an illness, perhaps even the one he suffered in the tropics, returned?"

"I don't know," Arden said consideringly, "he never acts ill so much as he behaves differently. He stays alone in his room, or takes long solitary walks, or fiddles with the food on his plate and neglects to answer questions any of the ladies put to him from time to time. But he doesn't cough or sneeze or complain, and brushes off all inquiries into the state of his health. Yet at first he was all delight to be here and to be fought over by the three ladies, as though he was actually pleased to be the juicy bone of contention among them. But the past week or more he's been distant and glum. Maybe it's simply a surfeit of temptresses that's put him off his feed."

"Three ladies a surfeit for *Julian*?" Warwick hooted.

"Well, he is older," Arden reminded him on a grin.

"But he's not dead," Warwick laughed.

"But they are three *ladies*, and so he can take only one. And only to wive, at that. He's engaged to one of them, true—the best of them, or any, for him for my money, though I'll never be asked to put my penny's worth in. But I increasingly doubt she's the one he plans to wive. He acts as though he's considering all three, and she don't seem surprised, although she's not exactly ecstatic about it. And taking a wife is never an easy decision, you know."

"It ought to be," Warwick said soberly, "it ought to be

the simplest choice in a man's life, if the right person happens along."

"Oh, aye," his friend agreed as they both fell silent, thinking of Julian's regrettably bachelor heart, before Arden directed his friend back to his house.

"At any rate," the large man said, "you're here and I'm glad to have you, and better still that we had this chance to speak before Julian knew you were here. I'm interested in seeing what you make of the matter."

"I'll have a month to tell you," Warwick said, clapping his friend on the back, though the huge man seemed to note it no more than he would a fly landing on his shoulder, "because then I have to remove to London to do the pretty for Prinny before I can return to pass the rest of my summer here. I'll likely take our brooding friend along with me then. Well, Prinny does expect all his noblemen to decorate his coronation, and though I don't care for such rigmarole, the poor fellow's suffered so much with this nonsense of trying to rid himself of his wife before she becomes his queen that I think he deserves me now. And Julian, as well," he added as Arden laughed, "for he adores pretty personages, and our Adonis is a viscount, after all. See if he don't get a front seat, despite the fact I outrank him," he grumbled.

His friend chuckled, for he knew Warwick Jones, now Duke of Peterstow, would prefer to sit clear across town from the ceremonies. He was only going to the coronation so as to please his wife, since he'd scoffed at being there often enough in his letters until his Susannah had hinted wistfully that she'd like very much to attend. Because, the Duchess of Peterstow had said, being born the commonest of commoners, a merchant's daughter, or a "fishmonger's daughter" as she liked to proclaim herself, being an honored guest at the king's coronation would seem so ironic as to be delightful.

Although Warwick appreciated matters of court about as much as he did a month of rain, and though he claimed grumpily that irony was fine but it had all been done before when Charles had come back to the throne and dragged all his ragtag band with him, still now he was going to attend the affair. He must have guessed how Arden's thoughts were running, for as they approached the manor house he looked at his friend and said on a smile:

"Yes. Just so. When Susannah says do this, it is performed. I think I'll advise Julian to pick a good gundog as a life's companion and have done with the idea of matrimony."

They were laughing when they came to the door of the manor and were greeted by the sight of an assortment of children from both households excitedly renewing their acquaintance. They were still smiling when they reentered the house, and only stopped when they saw Julian.

He stood, tall and impeccable, at the entrance to the hall, among five lovely young women. The fair Duchess of Peterstow, the dark Francesca Lyons, the proudly beautiful Incomparable Miss Merriman, comely Anthea Baker, and the fiery-haired Eliza Merriman were all arranged as if in tableau around him. Julian held up his hands as if in surrender and shook his pale head and laughed, and protested, over all their questions and concern, that he'd only caught the heel of his boot in a runner on the stair, and clumsy oaf that he was, had been lucky enough to make a recover before he'd hurtled down the stairs before them. But for all he made sport of his gracelessness and for all he smiled and soothed them, his newly arrived friends noted he was pale as ice and had that same sort of transparency about his fair skin now.

"Oh, just in time," he said as he sighted Arden and Warwick over the tops of the heads of his concerned retinue, "tell these angels of mercy, please, that *almost* tumbling down is not the same as breaking my crown. I tripped," he said on a shrug, "and see the audience it's gotten me."

"He walks in beauty but he staggers in it too—he's only human, you know," Arden said dryly, though his hazel eyes held as much concern as any of the ladies' did, for he knew Julian too well, and knew he scarcely ever lost his step even when he was deep in his cups, and he was entirely sober now.

The women laughed and let the matter rest. Francesca

and Susannah, Duchess of Peterstow, went on with their
animated conversation to do with Francesca's condition
and Susannah's children. Anthea and Constance stood
by and listened as politely as they had done before they'd
seen Julian stumble and then catch hold of the banister
rail on his way down the stair to join them. But Eliza
stayed still and continued to stare at Julian with as much
speculation as concern in her grave eyes.

It was never his boot heel catching in a runner; she
knew it. He'd lost more than his step in that instant, and
moreover, he'd been concentrating too hard on the mere
act of descending the stair when he'd done so, for she'd
been watching closely every moment. She'd never stopped
watching him since they'd come to the Lyonses', waiting
and wondering when she could broach the matter of the
length of their engagement and when she could summon
the courage to explain her own flighty behavior in London. She was desperately anxious for more than his approval and understanding. She was lonely. She missed his
company and his conversation more since he'd returned
to her than in all those years when he'd been physically
apart from her.

Now that he was here, she knew she'd both found and
then lost her best friend. And as she'd watched him,
waiting for her moment, she reacquainted herself with
the little things about his form and face in many small
ways: the tilt of his broad shoulders when he bent to
listen to another lady's prattle, the easy grace with which
he moved across the room to go to another's lady's side;
noting, when he turned to chat with another at table, the
shape of each curling frond of the overlong gilt hair that
covered the back of his neck; appreciating, when he gave
his hand to another, the sensitivity in the long fingers
that belied the strength in them.

Then she began to know how much she desired him as
more than her best friend. If she'd loved him reasonably
before, because of his written words and the memory of
him from the look of his painted picture, she was as
stricken with the actuality of him now as she might be
with a raging fever.

And so she knew that in these last days there'd been

something terribly amiss with him, and not just with his attitude toward her. For he was absent even when he was present, and silent when he should have been participant, and distracted, always. His near-accident on the stair was only more of what had lately distressed her. Her eyes were full of that disturbance as she watched him go to meet his friends, though her heart was full of far more when she realized she no longer seemed to count as one of them to him.

"Warwick! Not a word of your coming, and then you appear like a rabbit out of a hat? You almost outfoxed yourself," Julian said as he took his friend's hand, "because I was thinking of paying a call on you. We would have passed as two carriages in the night," he said, laughing lightly as he thought furiously, for he had actually been going to use the excuse of a purported visit to Warwick in order to leave this house this very day. He knew he didn't have much time left now, and he very much wanted another plausible excuse to go, and quickly. So he seemed more distracted as he tried to assemble his thoughts and find a reason to leave now that his friend was come.

"And I know why," Warwick said, grinning, his smile slipping when he saw the momentary confusion and then the guilty look of startlement spring to life in Julian's fogged gray eyes. "So I've saved you the trouble—look here."

He went to the door, and the parcel of small persons who'd been surrounding young Randolph Lyons stopped chattering and looked up at him at once. "Children!" he commanded. "Come along," he said as he returned to the hall, and they followed in his footsteps immediately.

Julian recognized his friend's children at once. They were unmistakable. The twins, Buck and Philippa, because the boy was a replica of his papa, and the girl the miniature of her mama, and Roderick, because the flaxen-haired, long-nosed toddler could be no other than a child formed by his parents' cooperation. Their youngest drowsed in their nurses' arms, and so the other milling young people would have to be various of Arden's waifs, adopted by members of both households. So he only smiled absently as a freckled, round-cheeked, smiling little girl stepped forward. And was surprised when she laughed aloud before she raced toward him and flung herself at him. He caught her just in time, though he scarcely believed his eyes or ears as she cried:

"Julian!"

He was glad his cheek was against hers so she couldn't see his face as he held her, because he was shocked at the sight of her and couldn't yet sort out his feelings. His sober, serious, camellia-complexioned little Miss Mary was gone. In her stead was this sturdy, merry-faced little girl. Her long straight tan tresses were replaced by a myriad of bouncing sun-touched sausage curls, as though even her hair was less serious now.

Now he realized that her quaint and stately air of maturity had been only a figment of her sorrow, now he saw that sunshine and happiness had transformed his somber little pilgrim into a real child again. He was both happy for her and grieved at the loss of her, for her sorrow had given her an odd and special beauty that joy robbed her of. Or was it, he thought, as he finally let her go and listened absently to her excited telling of her new-made curls, that it was himself he grieved for now that she had so obviously found herself and her childhood again?

"And so Jennie wrapped my hair in rags wound about bottles! Can you imagine that, Julian? And in the morning I looked just like a French doll! Don't I, Julian, don't I? Even Buck says so, though Jim said I look like a French something that his father trounced him for saying." She giggled. "Do you like it, do you?"

"I do, love, I surely do," he lied. "It becomes you entirely." Or becomes, he thought, whoever you've become.

As she went on about her new curls and friends, and sports and amusements, interrupting herself only to assure herself of his approval, he gazed down at her, vexed with himself for his deep disappointment in her. For he saw that it was her sadness that had made her unique, and now she seemed as no more or less than an ordinary child to him. And though he still loved her, of course, he saw how little she needed him, and so perhaps, he admitted on a disturbing flash of insight, that was why he had already wisely begun to love her less.

Very wisely, he had reason to think when Warwick and Arden stiffened as she said, at the end of her recital, "And the duchess says I may stay on. There's room in the great house. But Jennie's new parents, Mr. and Mrs. Calicut, the gatekeepers, have asked me to stay on with them too. So may I, Julian? Nurse has already gone home to the islands, she didn't even wait to come here with us. She was homesick, I think, and so if I stay on you won't have to hire on another for me," she confided, before she added eagerly, "Jennie's my very best friend, and Mrs. Calicut is teaching me to bake, and Mr. Calicut to garden, and they say when you've set up a home and if you send for me then, of course I can go to you if you want me to."

"Of course, puss, that's fine, muffin," he said, hugging her to reassure her, thinking that only the pure heart of a child would give up a viscount's protection for the comforts of a gatekeeper's cottage, and loving her again for it. And thinking only a child would know enough to value love over everything, even as something inside of himself turned over and curled up tightly upon itself for it.

When he stood up again, his head spun, and so he could only hear her laughter, and it was a moment before he could make sense of the words spoken around him. When he readjusted his balance and his senses at last, she was gone in a flurry of laughter and children as they all raced up the stairs to the nursery wing together.

The ladies were moving on toward the drawing room, and yet Warwick and Arden still stood gazing at him as he tried to focus again. Eliza, he finally noted, stood rooted to the spot, staring at him as well. To take the discomfort from the moment, to rid their minds of pity, or suspicion, he thought as quickly as he could, seeking a light word for diversion.

"Ah, well," he said, to cover himself, as he essayed a smile for Eliza, "if I've lost one little girl child, at least I've still another, eh, my Eliza dear?"

She froze. And then shot him such a look of furious despair that his heart stumbled and his breath caught in his throat.

"Eliza, I'm sorry, I truly am," he began haltingly, for he felt as badly as he said he did, in every way. True or not, he'd offended her dignity, and there was no worse offense he could have offered her. As he sought the right words to mend matters, he thought with that clarity that comes with pain that perhaps he'd struck out at her because he couldn't at little Mary, and for the same reasons—they'd both hurt him by not being what he'd wanted them to be.

But she was turned on her heel and gone down the hall before he fully comprehended that, and long before he could finish his apology.

It grieved him. Arden and Warwick thought that was the reason for his prolonged silence with them, and so at least he was grateful for the incident for that. But not for very long. Because when he went to his room to change for dinner, he couldn't dismiss the misunderstanding from his mind as easily as he dismissed his valet from his presence. He sank to his bed and held his heavy head in his hands and thought, in those last moments when he could think with any clarity, of the hurt he'd dealt Eliza, and wished he could undo it even more than the pain that began to slice through his body. And so he remembered her face as it looked in that moment, for as long as he could remember anything.

Because when Arden came into his room to see why he'd not come to dinner or answered his summons, he no longer thought of anything but himself. And Arden, who had prided himself on supplying his friend with a fine bed made from an oak as old as the kingdom, grew numb as he saw the stout bed quaking like a willow in the wind, rocking and dancing from the force of the shaking of the shivering body upon it.

"Dear God, Julian," he said as he held his friend close and felt the heat rising from the strong frame shuddering uncontrollably in his arms, and he sat a moment in silence before he called hoarsely for his friends, his servants, and all the physicians in the kingdom.

* * *

"The child wants to give him this filthy ground-up *tree bark* he had in his luggage," Arden hissed in an angry whisper at the physician, "and it's all we can do to keep her from trying to rouse him to get it to him—that's why we're not letting her near his room, and why she's wailing like a banshee now," he explained as they stood in the hall outside Julian's room with all the company, and the physician eyed the red-eyed and furiously howling little girl struggling in a maidservant's arms.

The physician took the packet from the large, aggrieved gentleman who'd summoned him to the stricken viscount's bedside and poured some of the dusty brown lumps into his palm. He sniffed at it.

"Ah. Cinchona bark," he said, nodding. "He got this from his doctor in Jamaica, did he?" he asked, ignoring Arden as he went over to the child.

"He did!" she shouted, and then, remembering her manners from the reproving look she got from the pretty lady who was wife to the great monster who was keeping her from Julian's side, she added in a quieter voice, "And it helped him last time. So the doctor gave it to him in case he should ever get sick with swamp fever again."

"Very good," the doctor said. "It's fresher, no doubt, than any I can lay hands on here up in the north—we don't see much of his complaint hereabouts, I promise you, but I studied in London and saw strange things newly come off the docks there, I can tell you. So we'll start to give it to him at once. It's a specific for malarial fever," he said to the duke, ignoring Arden, who looked dumbfounded, "and the best medication for him at the moment.

"Continue the sponge baths and keep him wrapped in blankets to avoid a chill," he added, taking pity on Arden when he noted that the big man's eyes were as suspiciously red-rimmed as the child's, "for the danger lies in his weakening condition as much as in the fever. It's a bad business," he said, shaking his head. "I'm surprised he managed to conceal the matter from you for so long as he did. Brave fellow. And a strong one. Or at least I assume he was," he said ruefully. "The point is that it usually worsens before it betters—that's why I'd rather not bleed him just yet, however impure his blood may be, whatever custom says. There's nothing to do but wait for it to pass, but we shouldn't like him to get something more on top of it. It's most important that you keep all the children away from him," he warned, "and that includes you, little missy," he said, wagging a finger at Mary, who began to puff up in rage again.

"It's not catching, not a bit of it," she protested at once.

"Of course not," the doctor replied, "but you are. Regular little pest houses, children are," he mused, "always coming down with colds and spots, coughs and measles and chickenpox and the like. We don't want him contracting something nasty on top of his miseries in his condition, do we?" he asked sternly as the child deflated and looked abashed. "No," he continued, nodding to Francesca, whose hand had gone automatically to her abdomen in a protective gesture when he'd warned the children away, "rest easy, he'll give no one in the house anything but worry—it's the miasmas and bad air from the swamps that cause the illness, and he's only a danger to himself now, poor fellow."

"How much of a danger?" Warwick asked quietly, drawing the doctor aside, as Eliza silently stepped closer to try to hear the answer.

"From what I understand of the disease, it will depend on how long this episode lingers. The sooner he recovers, the better the possibility that he'll recover completely. He could tell us better himself, for he knows how long the last bout took to run its course and what its severity was. For some, the further they get from the source, the more the fever relaxes its hold, and there comes a day when they're free of it for life. For others . . ." He spoke very softly now, lowering his gaze as he absently took out his watch and wound it. "Others are not so lucky. We shall see."

They waited to see.

But some of them couldn't bear to see while they waited, and so Constance, after one glance at the pale and shivering figure beneath the high-heaped blankets, retreated to the door and never came to Julian's door again after that. Warwick and Arden stayed hours each day, taking turns watching over their friend, instructing the valets who took turns tending him as though they suspected them of trying to murder their friend, not nurse him. Susannah and Francesca came only to sigh, but they came frequently, and left only when their duties to their children called them or their concerned husbands ordered them away. Anthea came often, and was a great help. She was calm, cool, and collected with Julian in his illness as she wasn't with him in his hardihood, for manners in a sickroom were matters of perseverance, and that she excelled in. And Eliza came, and was so aghast that they had to order her out lest Julian should wake to his right mind in that moment and see her face and believe he had passed away.

But the next time she came, and it was an hour later, she was calmer. And the next time, she was more composed, and soon they allowed her to sit in her cloak of silence and watch over him. For it seemed she sat the same way when she wasn't with him, so they decided they might as well allow her in, since, little as it seemed to ease her mind, nothing else would comfort her at all.

It was in those hours that her love for him was set as a seal upon her heart forever. For in those hours she realized how easy it was to lose love forever. And as he couldn't speak to humor her, or smile to charm her, and wasn't at all attractive as he lay shivering until she feared his very bones would fracture from the force of it, she understood that it was never his beauty or charm that she loved. For even his beauty became a matter of bone and essence as the fever burned away his flesh and wit and he murmured and tossed, as no romantic hero she'd ever envisioned did, so bedewed with sweat he seemed newly bathed. It made no matter.

She loved Julian Dylan, she had always done, whatever he looked like, however he behaved, and always would, and there it was; she believed that if she left his side he'd slip away from her. And so she sat and silently warred against whatever it was that threatened him, as though there were really a reason for her to stay, as though she could somehow magically hold him together in this world so long as she sat there. Anthea might do a dozen little errands and make herself useful to the gentlemen and the servants. But although Eliza was too frozen with terror to be of any use that anyone else could see, she knew she must stay. And so she did, rising only to eat, or relieve herself, for she'd learned how to doze while sitting up, and was hard at work at learning how to subdue those other trivial physical matters that distracted her from her vigil.

Julian shivered in the grip of the chills he had contracted in the tropics he had gone to in order to escape the cold he had felt in his bones that last long New England winter. The bitter humor of that was always with him, even when nothing else was in those long days as he lay locked in combat with the fever. Then at other times he got his wish and burned from the heat he had sought, until he yearned for the chills again. And they came.

At times the fever would lift from him, and unseen hands would wipe his brow and he'd smile up at Arden or Warwick or Anthea or Eliza—there were times he swore he saw Eliza, but he'd never seen her so grim, so he could never be sure—and he'd return to them only long enough to try to smile, and warn them, on a shake of his head that cost all his energy, that he was sorry he couldn't speak but knew he must rest, for he knew the waves of burning cold would come again, and he must be ready. And they did, time and again.

Arden cursed aloud that first time, when all his joy turned to shock as the fever returned moments after it had broken, for he was used to the reasonable illnesses of the Old World, and had thought that when a fever broke, the back of the disease was broken as well. The days taught him the patience Julian had learned. Warwick had grown up with patience and now grew holloweyed and silent. Anthea grew confident as she grew more useful. And Eliza sat perfectly still and fought.

She was sitting near to his bed in the early hours of dawn, deep within the solid gray numbness she had built, when she heard his voice, so scratchy and thin that she knew it was real this time.

"Good Lord, Eliza," Julian said shakily, "you must have learned to sleep with your eyes open. Like a fish. Is it morning or evening, little fish?"

"Morning," she said softly, wonderingly, for his eyes were steady if his voice was not, and no sweat dotted his high white brow.

"How many days?" he asked, as Warwick turned round from the window and looked at him, his thin face still, his watchful indigo eyes wide.

"A week and a day," Anthea said gently as she laid a cool hand on his brow, for Eliza couldn't answer now, she was so busily forcing down her sudden joy, as fearful of it as she'd been of his fate.

"A week and a day," he mused, actually smiling up at Anthea, as Eliza, watching him, thought how amazing it was that unshaven, yellow-bearded, hollow-cheeked, and tousle-haired as he was, his smile was still like the sun rising.

"Excellent," he said on a sigh, and closed his eyes, and they feared he was leaving his senses again, until he opened them and grinned, actually grinned. "A week and a day is excellent," Julian continued, "since it lasted almost three weeks last time. And a month the first. It diminishes, just as the doctor promised, and I . . ." He looked up as his host came rushing into the room from the dressing room where he'd slept, fumbling his belt about his robe, having woken at a touch from his valet. "I am devilish sharp-set, Arden," Julian complained, a certain unmistakable merriment rising in his eyes that could clearly be seen as the sunlight increased in his room. "Don't you have any food about your house, man?"

They didn't know whether they ought to hold a ball or a gala picnic, or hold their invalid down forcibly as the days went on. Because, Warwick complained in his loftiest accents, Julian was recovering like the rudest weed in nature, and not at all as a delicately bred person ought. And a fellow just out of his sickbed ought not to be larking about the grounds like a spring lamb, Arden nagged.

Seeing him strolling slowly along with the children on a warm morning a week after his recovery, Arden threatened that he'd forbid his going to the coronation if he didn't slow himself down. This only caused the invalid to immediately scramble up a nearby tree and dangle upside down shouting insults. But when he righted himself, he was glad of the children's laughter, for, he admitted if only to himself, he'd come close to landing on his head. He'd seen the world through a thin red mist as well as the golden veil of his own overturned hair, and it sobered him. So he was good after that—for at least a few hours. But he was so glad to be whole and healthy again that he felt just like the spring lamb Arden had named him.

He was still not so whole and healthy as he'd wish, although the horror of the chills and fever was gone. But he'd been left with a damnable weakness that turned his teacup into a ten-pound turnip when he picked it up in his hand, and made the pulling on of his hose in the morning into a major effort. No one would know it, not even his valet. He kept his hands by his sides or at rest on his lap or any other surface when he wasn't using them, so that no one could see how they trembled after any exertion; he strolled as though he'd no idea of striding; he ambled so that they'd never know how he yearned to run. They'd had enough to bear with him during his illness; he'd not lean on them now if he could prop himself upright in any way. It was vexing, but he'd dealt with it before, after all, and knew it was only a matter of time until he was a healthy man again in truth as well as in his friends' eyes. Whenever he saw them he walked a little faster or held his head higher, or even defiantly pulled a caper or two, lest they realized his astonishingly prompt recovery had been made the prompter so as to lighten their cares. It was as well, he reasoned, as he found each day a little easier to walk through, because the longer a fellow pretended to a thing, the simpler it became to forget the pretense.

He was so involved with his recovery and so in charity with the world that he only briefly noted that Constance was newly uncomfortable with him, and Anthea newly comfortable, while Eliza was strangely silent. He noted, and then disregarded it. For they were all beautiful to him now, and all perfect. In his new gratitude for life he was at ease with the entire world again, and even though he knew his problems were never solved, the very fact that he walked and talked and breathed brought him a contentment that bordered on rapture. He was wise enough to know, of course, that this wild joy was as transitory as his weakness was, and that such gladness for no reason could never last. Nor did he expect it to. But he never expected it to end in quite the way it did.

It was a glowing day and Julian was being kind to his hosts by sitting and resting in an invalid chair in the sunlight on Arden's long lawn, behaving, he thought with languorous amusement, like a gentleman and a sundial. He'd made several drowsy decisions as he watched the children at play. He'd decided to ask Constance what the matter was, because he'd decided it was time to act upon the realities of his life. He'd also planned to tease Eliza out of her sullens and make some real plans for the end of their spurious engagement at the same time. Because the weeks were flying on toward summer, his illness had extended matters beyond his plans, and he'd never wished to leave things unresolved for as long as they'd been hanging.

He'd just been passing the time of day with Anthea in easy conversation, as aimlessly as a drifting bumblebee, for she was the most undemanding of the three ladies he'd been graced with, when he saw a dusty coach and four lathered horses pull up in the long drive in the front of Arden's house. A well-dressed dark-haired gentleman hastily alighted from it, but he was too far away for Julian to make out his features. His curiosity stirred him from his invalidish reflections, but he tried for courtesy's sake to ignore it.

He was pleased and relieved when Anthea, ever attentive to his slightest, unvoiced wishes, noted the time and clapped her hands to call the children to lessons. She was constantly useful, he thought, smiling slightly as he saw her duck her neat head to answer a question one of the children posed as she led them back to the manor. She insisted on making herself as useful in the house as she'd been in his sickroom, and was pleased to give the children lessons each day, so that, she'd said shyly, dimpling when he'd asked her just yesterday how she could be so cruel to them in the spring, their wits would not have worn away by summer.

Constance had only gazed at Anthea thoughtfully at that, and then smiled sweetly, and praised her, and drawled that she was uncommonly impressed by Miss Baker's endless patience. For in truth, she vowed, she'd have offered her own chaperone's services as schoolmistress if she hadn't felt the dear old party deserved a rest now that she herself had grown. Which statement had caused the "dear old party," who'd been dragged along to Arden's for the show, as always, to gape at her mistress in astonishment. And Eliza, Julian thought, frowning as he made his way back to the house, had only said bluntly, after he'd asked if she spent much time with the youngsters too, "I don't get on with children so well as you think I do, my lord," and vanished from his sight. And had stayed invisible to him since.

He sighed, but then his attention was diverted by the sight of Arden coming out of the house to put an arm around his new visitor's shoulder as he welcomed him, and then hurried him into the house. Julian squinted against the brightness of the day, and hurried forward in as leisurely a style as he could assume, his curiosity killing his annoyance at the memory of Eliza's unexpected gracelessness.

"Ben, my boy," Arden said happily as he led the handsome young man into his study, "it's good to see you. I'm pleased you finally took me up on my offer, but I can hardly believe you actually left London town. I thought you felt the end of the earth yawned at your feet two steps beyond the city limits. Warwick, look whom we've here."

"Ah, Mr. Be-Good," Warwick said, smiling as he held out his hand to stop the young gentleman from bowing, "it is good to see you again. Have you brought another two dozen children or so for us this time?"

"No, I've two thousand or so anytime you want them, your grace," Ben-Be-Good said as he took the duke's hand, "but I've brought none but my own servants with me now. And closemouthed ones at that. I've news that I didn't trust to paper, and cautions that I dared not put in ink," he said seriously.

"Out with it, then," Arden said, losing his joviality, and looking again as dangerous as those who knew him well knew he could both look and be.

"I've real fears for the Viscount Hazelton's life," Ben said simply.

"But he's recovered," Arden began, as the slender young gentleman's even-featured face grew pale and he asked, in despair, "Never say they've got to him already?"

"My hosts," Julian said from the doorway, "are vigilant, but they haven't tried to do me in yet. It was a fever I had, my friend, and not a knife in the back. Is that what you feared?"

"Oh, yes, or worse," Ben-Be-Good said.

11

THE GENTLEMEN REMAINED within the study for a long while and so it wasn't long before the ladies in the house were consumed with curiosity as to who their handsome young caller might be. They hadn't seen him, they'd only the butler's word as to his presence—his, and the more interesting unofficial report of Miss Merriman's pretty new maid from London. She'd been hanging out the window flirting with a gardener when he'd arrived. But she was an expert on the subject of gentlemen as well as common men. For although good as her word to her employer in that she never had any traffic with the gentry, she was as bad as she could be within her limits and so was a Circe of the servants' hall and the Cleopatra of the stables. For she'd a keen eye for masculine charms as well as a deep appreciation of them. She'd also an excellent memory.

"It's Mr. Be-Good," she sighed to her attentive audience, "from Lunnon. As if I'd ever forget 'im, although I only saw him the onct. 'E's as fine as 'e can hold together . . . both mind and matter, miss'," she added saucily, because she knew how to make the most of the merest scrap of information, before she left the wondering ladies she'd reported to and took herself off on her appointed rounds belowstairs to tempt the chef and fluster the footmen.

The one thing both the butler's and the maid's reports agreed upon was the unknown caller's air of distraction and his hurried entrance. But that was all the three unwed young women could gracefully discover. Sometime before his arrival, Francesca and Susannah had linked arms and gone for a walk to catch up on all the things they'd dared not put in their letters to each other, and so were off in the gardens somewhere pretending to admire Arden's handiwork while they gossiped and giggled together like the girls they lately were. It was unthinkable to break into their privacy for the sake of mere vulgar curiosity, and impossible to subdue that curiosity, however vulgar. So Eliza found an engrossing book to pretend to read in the salon opposite the study, while Constance was moved to try to catch up on her correspondence in the same room, as Anthea sewed a fine seam on a handkerchief there as well. And they waited for the door of the study to open.

Behind the door the gentlemen all stared at Ben-Be-Good.

"There's news of something unpleasant for you, Viscount," Ben-Be-Good said seriously. "I don't know what it is, I wish I did. But I'm sure that it *is*. Someone cold and clever is no more— Slippery Jim, Lion—he that knew every whisper. He knew one too many, I suspect. They found him in an alley—what was left to find, that is, but his was a stubborn spirit. Because for all that's all they left him, he clung to it long enough to spill everything he knew before he died so he could revenge himself on whoever had done him. There's many scurrying for cover in Shoreditch and Spitalfields tonight, and more that have gone to ground in Whitechapel and near to Seven Dials, since that was his main ken. But one of the things he said alerted me—and that was that the viscount here is in mortal danger. But for the life of me, Lion, I can't discover more just yet. I decided to come here with what I had in the meanwhile."

Arden nodded. "You've not made a wrong decision yet, Ben," he said. "Go on."

" 'The 'andsome nob, the rangling rattling cove— Viscount 'Azelnut'—it's what he called you," Ben-Be-Good said with an apologetic smile to Julian, "and all he said was: 'They've an eye out for 'im. 'E'll live forever if 'e stays clear of Lunnon. But 'e's a dead man if 'e comes back on the wrong road.' "

Ben shook his head and dropped the perfect slum accents he'd assumed. "It doesn't sound like much, I grant you," he sighed, "but it means someone plans danger for you, Viscount, and danger that Slippery Jim wasted one of his last breaths on is clear and present danger, believe me."

" 'The wrong road,' " Julian pondered, "I take it Slippery Jim wasn't a religious man and so it's a literal warning, is it?"

"God knows . . . and that's literally," Ben said with a suggestion of a smile, "because he's the only one Slippery Jim can tell about it now."

"Well, I was a 'rattling cove' and so 'road' would have to do with my penchant for coaching then, I suppose," Julian said, "but I can't think of any enemies I made in my days on the road . . . not that I'm a paragon," he explained quickly, "but we coachies tend to stick together. Oh, there are little transgressions committed on the job, but we all know of them and have a bond of silence about them. I'm an owner now, but I still look the other way when it comes to 'shouldering' and 'swallowing' fares—or even putting a bit of cargo on the coach and not the waybill, as a favor to a friend or for an extra bit shared between the coachie and the guard, and the company none the wiser or richer—but it's in the way of a bonus on the job, so unless there's a guard or driver being a foolish pig and taking it all for himself, there's no sin in it. And as to other sins—why, many coachies have a girl here and a wife there, or an inconvenient secret or three, but I've never regarded it, and for all my sins, I can't think of anyone who has particularly regarded me as an enemy."

"No inconvenient husbands, Julian? Or any irate fathers after you?" Warwick asked in a musing tone, but with a grave look to his friend.

"How dare you, sir?" Julian asked with mock outrage, but then he grew thoughtful before he spoke up again. "No, none. Or at least, I doubt it. The fathers would have come to me with ministers in tow rather than pistols in hand, I think, and the husbands with a glove in the face, not a knife in the back. I'm not a good man, precisely," he said on a shrug, "but then, I've been a cautious as well as a lucky one. Or you might say a callous one," he admitted, "since my pastimes are usually less a matter of passion than propinquity for me. My lust generally runs a poor second to my laziness. I suppose convenience is a female's most fatal attraction for me," he said on a half-laugh, before he went on, "In any event, I make it a point not to bother with any females whose husbands or fathers care about whom they bother with, you see.

"And so far as paternity goes—it hasn't. At least I'm not a father that I know of, and because I've amassed a bit of coin, I think I would certainly have been told if I'd been so blessed. No, the ladies have never brought me any danger that I know of," he said on a bitter smile, for he'd begun to believe his spiritual malaise lay in that very fact.

"But I assure you something has brought you danger, you do have an enemy, and I beg you to at least think on it," Ben-Be-Good insisted, "because a dying man is economical of words, sir, and he spent his last breaths on you."

"To be sure," Arden said, putting his arm around his disturbed visitor's shoulder, "we'll all think on it, and our friend won't take a step from this place without we've done some more pondering the matter. But as the poet said, it's good to be merry as well as wise. So have a drink with us, Ben, and as you've hastened here, relax now and stay awhile. I promise you the clean air won't slay you. Ben deeply distrusts anything green, excepting if it's currency," Arden explained to his friends as the young man's face relaxed into a true smile for the first time since he'd arrived.

"So now you've finally come to my country lair, I'll not let you return to the city until I can entertain you. Come, come, don't shake your head. When was your last vacation, lad?" Arden demanded.

"Why, I once took a coach to Brighton, Lion, when I was only a boy, and had a devilish good time there too, come to think on it. I came home with more than thirty purses I'd plucked for myself, and good fat ones at that. I hear there's a beach there, s'truth?" he asked, grinning, before the grin turned to a sourer smile and he shook his head again. "Oh, excellent guest I'd be here among your noble friends, Lion, thanks to you for the thought anyway. I'll be going back to town soon as I can have fresh horses," he promised as he finished drinking the contents of the glass his host had handed him all in a swallow.

"Hold your blasted horses, lad, for you'll be going to the room I'm having prepared for you," Arden declared in a good-natured rumble, but loudly enough to make Ben-Be-Good pause, "for if my noble guests disliked your presence, Ben, they'd not be my friends, and I have no guests who are not."

"Thank you, Arden," the duke said, cocking his head to the side and smiling. "You've never said a fairer word to me, you know."

"Don't preen, Warwick, you haven't heard what he says behind your back," Julian commented, taking pity on his host, for Arden was growing visibly uncomfortable, as always, from praise.

"Not another word on that head," Arden said at once, glaring at Julian dramatically, pleased to change the subject, "or I'll huff and puff and blow you down. Aye," he added, "and I could. There's no need to worry about Viscount 'Azelnut loping off to do battle with dragons now, neither, Ben, since he's recovering from a visit from the worst enemy he knows he has—he'd a bout with some exotic tropical fever just the other week, our home-grown ailments being too common for him, no doubt."

"Just so. Talk about preoccupation with rank—English illnesses are too plebeian for our friend," the duke put in, "so never fear you'll catch it. He's such a fashionable fribble," he complained to an amused Ben-Be-Good in a loud confidential whisper, "that he won't even entertain an ailment he'd have to share with the rest of us."

"Aye, and that's why he's not ready to encounter so much as a hostile fly yet . . . whatever he thinks," Arden announced with some finality, cutting Julian off as he was protesting both his generosity with diseases and his hardihood.

"We've three lovely unmarried females visiting with us too," Arden added, "and so it's well that you've arrived."

"It's providential," the duke agreed.

"Yes," Arden explained, smiling at Julian before he turned his full attention to Ben-Be-Good and prepared to open the door and introduce the impeccably dressed young fellow to the ladies, "the viscount needs *some* rest, you know."

If only, Eliza thought, he'd look at her like that, she'd be content. Beyond content. She sighed so heavily she heard the soughing sound above the polite conversation and so had to quickly duck her head and pretend she'd been blowing on her tea to cool it—bad manners before pity for her any day, she decided. Because he never had; in truth, she'd never seen him look at anyone that way. She'd noted Julian when he'd seemed interested in, amused by, or concerned with herself or other females. She could guess how he'd look when no lady was around and he was interested in a female, because she'd seen that sudden look of speculation leap into his eyes when he was being flirted with. She'd seen him bored, alert, and in pain, and had surprised a dozen emotions more as they arose in those speaking gray eyes before he could suppress them. She watched him that closely. She knew his face now as she used to know his thoughts when they were so far apart. But she'd never seen him absolutely stunned and utterly fascinated. Or hanging on a lady's every word, or registering her every expression, or being encompassed by her presence to the point that it illuminated him so that a person could tell when she entered a room by the sudden subtle quickened tension of the bones in his very frame. No, she'd never seen Julian so taken by any female as Mr. Be-Good was by her cousin Constance.

But it was a good thing to dream upon.

Which was, she thought in annoyance, all that she seemed to be able to do in relation to Julian these days. Forget that I am your fiancée, she wanted to shout as she swallowed her tea down instead and watched him, I am your friend. Or was. For since he'd been taken ill, and during his recuperation, and all through these past three days since Mr. Be-Good had joined them, she'd walked and talked and sat with all the company and never had a separate word with the person she missed so much he might have been across an ocean from her again, rather than just across the table.

Something had gone badly wrong. She knew it had begun in London when she'd been so taken up with her success that she'd ignored him. But he was never so vain as to never forgive her for that. And indeed, it didn't seem that he was so much angry at her as indifferent. Yet though he gazed at Constance admiringly as any normal gentleman would, still he never looked at her as Mr. Be-Good did, as a man infatuated would. And though he liked to chat with Anthea, he never seemed to more than like it, or her. No, his heart was whole, or so she thought, and then thought that so she knew. For she'd written to him for five years, and he to her, and she knew him entirely. Or had done. But if she did, she thought so suddenly, so unexpectedly that she put her teacup down and sat astonished at the revelation, why was she so afraid of simply asking him what had happened between them?

She'd shared house room with him for weeks, and as polite guests might do, they'd shared all but the most essential things: their intimate thoughts. As they were used to do, on paper at least. Instead, she'd watched his every expression, had been aware of where he was at every moment, begrudged every moment away from him and every second she saw him pass with any other females, even her best friends. And yet she'd done nothing more than watch and wait and hope.

While all the while she'd thought: Are we still friends? How long shall we remain engaged to wed? Why are you so distant with me, Julian?

But the most important question of all was why she couldn't bring herself to ask him these things. Why her greatest friend had become the coolest stranger. And why she had allowed the estrangement to go on so long. She wondered at it, gazing at him now as he was saying something that made the young Duchess of Peterstow laugh.

"Cowards die many times before their deaths," Warwick Jones, Duke of Peterstow, quoted softly from where he sat at Eliza's side. And when she turned to stare at him in horror, wondering at how that astute gentleman had got inside her head, he smiled his sad half-smile at her as if he knew just what she was thinking even as he spoke of something else entirely.

"A clean social death is preferable to dithering, my dear, don't you agree?" he asked more loudly. "Never fear, I'll remain your friend, whatever the verdict, whatever my lady duchess decides in her o'erweening pride. You have to bite into the thing," he advised, motioning to the bit of fruitcake she'd forgotten she held, as though he knew very well she'd forgotten it, "and then tell us what you think of it. Come now, Eliza, we're all waiting for yours, the last judgment. I credited you with more courage. I know she hedged her bet as ever, by prefacing the offering with a tale of how long the recipe had been in her family, but that never discouraged me from giving my honest opinion of her hobby of cakecrafting. Of course," he added thoughtfully as his duchess tried to fix him with a baleful stare, "I always say I admire whatever it is, even as I store it up under my tongue for discreet removal later. But then, I'd a governess who firmly believed calf's liver was essential for a child's growth, so I've plenty of practice in culinary deceit."

"I've none," Eliza said with some spirit, rousing herself, squaring her shoulders, and deciding that she was done with all roundabout. "It's delicious, Susannah," she said around the bite she popped into her mouth and scarcely tasted, "and tasty and buttery and light and absolutely marvelous and I want the recipe!"

And sat back, resolved to be brave, and so felt just as triumphant as the eighth Duchess of Peterstow looked as she stuck her tongue out at her noble husband and the company roared with laughter.

"Julian," Eliza was able to say then, later, when they'd all gotten up after tea, "Julian," she said very softly so as not to be overheard, touching her hand to his sleeve to get his attention as they walked to the door, before Anthea could finish speaking with Francesca and interrupt them as usual, "I must speak with you—alone."

When he looked down at her, entirely at her, she

hesitated. Flustered by his undivided concern, she said, dredging up a hasty truth, for bravery does not banish embarrassment, "Mama has written that she's coming for a visit soon, and so I must know how we are to go on. And," she added very softly, so that he had to bend his golden head frighteningly, deliciously near to her lips, "we've not had much time to speak before."

"And here I thought it was inclination we'd not had much of," he answered teasingly. "Yes, of course. I tell you what . . . let's meet for a walk and a breath of air in the herb garden after dinner—it will still be twilight. The others should be amusing themselves in the house then, and no one ever roams there anyway but Arden, and he's the soul of discretion. Especially if I order him away."

"Ought we to?" she asked consideringly, looking up at him with concern.

"There's not much mischief I can get up to in an herb garden," he said, "unless you insist."

"I meant," she said, grinning, delighted at his easy, merry mood, "ought you to walk?"

"I'll be passing the day in enforced resting, as usual," he complained. "I should hope I can walk by evening. Unless," he countered lazily, low, touching a finger to the tip of her nose, "you'd rather spare me the walking, and come to my room tonight?"

"Wicked, evil creature," she laughed.

"Well, I try," he explained.

And then Anthea came and asked him if he were going to tell the children about the flowers of the Caribbean as promised during her lessons today, and he said he would, and they moved off, out of the salon and into the soft late spring afternoon.

He liked grammar no more now than he'd done decades before, and so after he'd told the children something of the flora of Jamaica, he cut their question period short (they cared for the forthcoming grammar lesson no more than he, he thought) and bowed his way from their schoolroom and made his escape. Indefatigable woman, Julian thought on a sigh as he lay back on a grassy slope far from the house to stare upward and watch the long afternoon ease into sunset from beneath the tangled leafy arches of surrounding trees—a valiant, admirable, charming, but definitely indefatigable woman. He was glad she was his friend, but gladder still that she wasn't his schoolmistress. Because after tea, after the daily botany lesson there'd be a spell of outdoor play, and then, before dinner, grammar and a wee drop of foreign languages. For all she broke the day up into easily digested bits of schooling, it was schooling. And it was springtime, and so for all he was a grown man, he felt delightfully truant as well as relaxed now. He lay back on the grass despite the risk to his biscuit-colored jacket and gray pantaloons, and felt the weight of all the sun-warmed earth beneath him pulling at him, and thought he might just drowse, at that, since he felt a little dizzy from his long walk from the house and had nowhere else to fall from where he lay.

And so at first he thought the voices came from a dream. But as he listened to them he realized he'd never be able to congratulate himself on such an amusing dream. It was a sort of an early midsummer's enchantment, he thought, his lips quirked into a smile. And he laid his head back again, keeping still, scarcely daring to breathe lest he give away his presence and interrupt the delightful conference going forth just a few feet from where he lay, beyond a hedge on the downslope of the crest of the bank he rested upon.

There were at least six of them, he decided. Six fellow truants from Anthea's improvised schoolroom. And of course, their leader, Anthea's secret competitor. For as he listened he realized that this was never the first lesson she'd led, and as he attended to them, the only disturbing note was that she'd denied having anything to do with the children when he'd asked her about it that once. But he soon forgot that as he lay back, shamelessly and luxuriously eavesdropping, his only difficulty suppressing one stray impulse to sneeze and a few dozen more almost overwhelming urges to laugh aloud.

"Tell one about a printh," one excited voice urged. That was Warwick's girl, Philippa, Julian thought, picturing the fair-haired child, as another imperative voice overrode her to say, "No, no, 'Nuff of noble princes, let's have something to do with a great battle, please, Miss Eliza." And that, Julian decided, was the authoritative voice of Philippa's twin, Buck, his accents already those of command, as befitted the heir to a dukedom.

"Oh, no, a princess, surely," the familiar, loved voice of his own Miss Mary pleaded, even as a scornful cry of "Ugh, poor stuff, kisses 'n cryin'," followed by a very rude sound made by sneering lips—and that, Julian thought on a grin, was surely the masterful young Fleet Fred and his fast friend George, two infants Arden had rescued from some London cesspit, bright as a pair of night stars and come from an equally infinite darkness.

"I think Miss 'Liza should say, she'll be telling the story," Warwick's precocious middle son, Roderick, offered in his reasonable fashion, but there was an immediate outcry of childish argument as to who had the ultimate choice, until the loudest voice was raised, and that was the voice of decision.

"It is my house. And my meadow, for that matter. And Miss Eliza is my father's guest, so it really seems right that it be my decision, and that is that Roderick is quite right, and that it is Miss Eliza's choice, for she will be doing the telling, there's no doubt of the fairness of that. And if you don't agree, you may leave. Miss Eliza?" Arden's son, Randolph, asked politely.

The subsequent pause, Julian was sure, was because Miss Eliza was having as much difficulty controlling her amusement with this high-handed logic as he was.

"I tell you what"—Eliza's voice came cool and sweet and clear to his ears—"I'll tell you a tale of princes and princesses, gods and goddesses, love and war and battle too. Miss Baker will be teaching it to you next week, but in a . . . different fashion. It's all about the great war between men and gods and Greece and Troy. But don't worry," she said quickly, "there's something for everyone in it. Because it begins with a contest.

"Now," she said, and Julian pictured her sitting on the bank with all the children about her, but didn't dare sit up himself lest he be seen and spoil sport. Instead, he carefully rolled over on his stomach, lifted his head, and propping it on his arm, inclined it in their direction so as not to miss a word. He needn't have worried; the children were amazingly still and her voice carried.

"One day," Eliza said in a thrilling, low-pitched voice, "three goddesses—Hera, Aphrodite, and Athena—were having an argument about which of them was the most beautiful."

"An argument? But how could that be?" Philippa asked at once. "Mith Baker told uth that Aphro . . . Aphrodite ith goddeth of beauty—ithn't she?"

There was a pause, in which Julian nearly choked, until Eliza, after a moment, said wonderingly, "Just so! Do you know, I never thought of that! But so, I imagine, the goddesses didn't either. I mean," she said as she felt her audience's doubt, "after all, you told me that Tom Cribb won the championship in that famous boxing match with the black, Molyneaux, didn't he? But even so, I doubt Molyneaux considered him the best at milling, did he? I'll wager he challenged him again. Others likely did too, am I right? They tried to beat him because titles that are awarded really don't mean much, someone's always trying to win them over."

After a moment as this was being taken in, and obviously swallowed whole, Eliza went on, "Anyway, they were arguing about it and they decided to ask this handsome young mortal that they saw—a youth named Paris—to judge them;. And he agreed."

There was a babble of voices.

"Wot?" young Fred hooted. "Was 'e jinglebrained? Didn't 'e remember wot Athena done to that girl wot spun better'n 'er? Turned 'er into a spider, she did, you said."

"Hera kilt Apollo's mama, didn't she, Miss Eliza?" tenderhearted Miss Mary asked worriedly.

"And Aphrodite wath jealouth ath a cat too," Philippa put in nervously, as some of the others shouted out similar incidences of godlike atrocities that they remembered having been told.

"He oughtn't to have agreed to judge such a contest, truly, didn't he know any better?" Randolph asked.

"I imagine he was flattered that they asked him," Eliza

began, but as several groans went up, she added, "And they each offered him a gift if he'd only choose her."

"Oh, a bribe," Fred said, approval and understanding clear in his voice, and they all fell respectfully silent again.

"I never thought of that," Eliza admitted in a stifled voice, but had no time to reflect upon it, as a few of the girls asked her to fill in some details about Paris.

"He was amazingly handsome," she said. "That's why they noticed him, I expect."

"Fair? Like Apollo and Julian?" Miss Mary asked.

"Not at all," Eliza said briskly, refusing to be lured into that particularly seductive fiction just now. "He was dark-haired and dark-complexioned, like . . . like Buck, here."

There was a great deal of pushing and giggling as the young heir to a dukedom turned more scarlet than dark, until Eliza went on, "And he was given a golden apple and told to award it to the fairest of them."

"Shoulda scarpered wif the apple, and had done wif it," Fred mused darkly. "People ort never to have any truck wif the gods."

"They was always mixin' in wif folks, dint they have nuffin better to do?" George asked.

"I suppose not," Eliza said consideringly. "I expect it gets rather boring being a god, unless you do mix in with mortals. But to continue: before the contest they each took him aside and offered him a gift if he'd choose her as the most beautiful. Hera offered him success in the hunt, Athena offered him wisdom, and Aphrodite offered him the most beautiful woman in the world."

Now there was pandemonium. Most of the boys thought Hera's offer best, the girls were divided between Hera's and Athena's. Julian was enchanted because none of them thought a beautiful woman any sort of a prize at all. Buck's heavy-hearted pronouncement seemed to carry the day.

"If he had wisdom he wouldn't of been there, so I s'pose he was too foolish to want more. And I guess he thought he was a good 'nuff hunter. I s'pose you wouldn't be telling the story at all if he'd any sense. He must of picked Aphrodite, then."

"Gentlemen in stories always want the beautiful women," Miss Mary sighed.

It seemed Eliza sighed just as heavily.

"You've guessed it," she said. "Paris chose Aphrodite. And she told him who the most beautiful woman was and where he could find her. Yes, yes," she replied to their moans, "I agree, it wasn't quite the same as giving her to him, but the gods aren't always fair, as you know. Her name was Helen of Troy. And she was already married to the King of Greece. So Paris had to kidnap her, and he did. And that started the Trojan War. Which Miss Baker will teach next week, and I'll help you with it," she tried to add over the sudden noise, as the children were loudly protesting Paris' decision and groaning over his stupidity.

"He wasn't stupid," Eliza said firmly, rising to her feet and dusting off her skirts, "he was mortal. That's the point."

"But didn't he know enough not to bother with Gods?" Randolph persisted.

"He might have," Eliza said sadly, "but it's very hard to remember that when you're with the gods, I imagine. Anyway, it's growing late and you have to get ready for dinner. Next time I'll tell you about the Trojan Horse, which was a very clever, mean, and entirely mortal trick the King of Greece played on Paris' family for revenge. You'll love it."

The children arose and streamed back toward the house. Julian counted a full eight of them as they raced each other down the grassy slope. Young Randolph remained with Eliza, acting as a proper host if it killed him, but he looked longingly after the rest until Eliza noticed and shooed him away, letting him go free as a leaf blown on the wind as he tore after the other children. Eliza wore such a wistful look as she watched them that it seemed to Julian that she might raise up her skirts and try to run too.

He stood and stepped around a break in the low hedge and strolled the few steps down the slope to where she was standing, gazing after them.

"I don't doubt you'll catch up to Miss Mary and Philippa

if you run off right now," he commented, "because they're gossiping rather than racing, and there—Roderick's stopped to gather a flower that's caught his eye, but you'll never beat Fred and George, or Buck either, I'm afraid," he said as she swung around and stared at him, as amazed as if he'd popped out of a bottle and not out from behind a hedge.

"But tell me," he went on, smiling. "That was pretty high stepping, and neatly done, but why *did* they have that contest if we all know Aphrodite was the goddess of beauty?"

"I don't know," she confessed, laughing. "That's why I love to tell them stories—they see things I never did, or forgot I did. Anthea teaches them, you see, the proper way—the way we were taught in school; she teaches them to listen and remember. I like to have them question me. It's all for my own amusement, you see," she said very quickly. "I'm not competing with Anthea, truly," she protested. "Well, I couldn't. I'd be a very poor teacher, and I know it. I probably got half the story wrong at that. But even if I did, I did get them interested and they'll be overjoyed if they can correct me. But they'll only catch me out if they listen very carefully to Anthea, and they know it. So I haven't done any real harm," she reasoned, "even if I haven't done anyone but myself a great deal of good. Because I do so enjoy myself with them during these impromptu storytelling times."

"But you said you didn't get on with children," he said quietly, watching her carefully.

"Oh, that. I was vexed with you," she said at once, before she could think to give him a polite lie, her color rising. "That's why I said it. Oh, dear, their honesty is catching," she gasped, before she started to walk down the hill with him, head down, avoiding his eye. "But I was. And it is true, for I said I don't get on with them as well as 'you think'—I remember the text—and so I don't. You seemed to think I was one of them," she explained, wincing slightly, as if the thought still pained her. "You see," she said hastily, "I truly don't get on with *all* children, just *some* of them."

"Ah," he said, "then you regard them as real people.

What a pity. The fashionable answer for a female to give is to simper and say that she 'loves children,' the way she might love flowers or artwork or any other thing society thinks females ought to admire. It's demeaning to children, of course, but it's the correct reply. I wonder you were such a social success in London, or is it only me that you're so candid with?"

They were speaking of a great many things they were not speaking of, she thought with a panicky sense of delight, but she went on in her conversation as she did on her feet as they stepped down the hill, quickly and naturally, lest she take care, lose the momentum, and stumble.

"They didn't listen to what I said in London," she said, "which was only fair because I didn't really pay attention to their questions. It was just so pleasant to be admired for no reason, like a flower or a picture, as you say. But it grew tedious, you see, because I'm not a flower or a picture. You ought to understand," she said anxiously, at last daring to meet his blindingly light stare, for the sun turned the gray of his eyes to the color of the surface of bright water, "for all that I imagine you take it for granted, because all you've ever had to do was to show your face to be admired. I had to grow into it, and indeed, I think in some way I still believe it all to be a hoax, and always will."

But it wasn't, he thought. The sun did lovely things to her hair, showing it never so red as it was when they'd first met, when he'd seen a fiery-haired child, but instead setting the tips of it afire and causing the heavy mass of it to glow. Her eyes were glinting too, echoing the same russet tones, and her skin was matte, white and pure. He neglected to look at the slim body next to him, not only because he was so enrapt in studying the purity of her profile as she bit her lip and looked away, but also because he didn't want to remember just now that she was not at all a child. She was still young; he'd been burned by this glowing girl before. He was pleased at her renewed friendship with him, but wary of it as well.

But he didn't consciously think of that just now. Instead he thought that she was quite beautiful, she was his friend, and she also was, he realized, very worried about his reply.

"It's no hoax," he said, and carefully chose a very few select words to say slowly so as to give them weight. "You are grown very lovely, Eliza."

"I wasn't looking for a compliment," she said gruffly.

"I know. That's why I gave it," he answered, taking her arm now, because he was growing weary, both with their estrangement and in physical fact.

"Peace?" he asked as he felt her body stiffen as he walked so close to her. "I don't know what we fought about, Eliza," he said thoughtfully as they strolled on and he realized in her close company that he'd not had that company for some time, and he'd missed it, "or for that matter when we did, but it seems you've not been as kind to me lately as you've been to the children. Some of the children," he corrected himself, to hear her giggle and feel her relax, "and I accept that you don't like all men either, just some. Can I be one of them? Please?"

There were a dozen witty answers she could have tried for. There was still an important question to ask him. But she was too glad, too lately come from the honesty of children, and too pleased with what he'd said to seek a clever retort, too thrilled at their newfound amity to pose a thorny question.

"Yes," she said.

And they walked on to the manor without speaking more, but they were both so satisfied with her answer that neither of them noticed they were silent.

But everyone noted that Julian was absent from the dinner table that night.

12

"A LITTLE RELAPSE," Eliza said breathlessly, "is like a *little* murder. It cannot be. Please be more specific, sir."

There was a silence about the long table as Eliza stood clutching her dinner napery and twisting it in her shaking hands, standing as rigidly as if she faced a hangman's noose and not her host at all.

"No," Arden said seriously, although his tawny eyes glittered with pure admiration and not the anger his inquisitor thought he showed, "there *is* actually, according to the good physician, such a thing as a 'little' relapse. A big one, I imagine, would mean our Julian would be abed for months, and sick as a dog besides. No, what he's done is overdone, and merely that. And so he's weak as a kitten, if we're to stay with beastly comparisons, and will be better if we can get him to stay abed for a few days until he's righted himself again."

"Oh, nicely put, Arden," Warwick said happily. "The animal analogies were especially fine. Don't you agree, Eliza? You won't kill him now, will you, my dear?" he asked gently, looking to her. "I did so want to get to my soup, you see. Well, it is lobster soup," he explained to his duchess as she pinched him to stop him teasing the distraught girl, "my favorite. And that hurts," he complained moodily, rubbing at his long thigh that she'd attacked under the table. And then, as the duchess blushed because her husband, under cover of attending to his discomfort, sought sweet retaliation by stroking the more shapely limb directly next to his own, Eliza colored up as well, if for a different reason.

"I'm sorry," she said, her voice sinking even as she did

into her chair. "I was concerned. I was rude. Forgive me."

"Only," Arden said sternly, "if you promise to go up and entertain him after dinner. Because if you ladies don't," he added to the company, "I'll have to hire help to keep him buckled to his bed. You ought to have heard the unearthly plaints this evening, you'd think we were torturing him there rather than just not letting him down here. For all he says it's no exertion toddling to the dinner table, it's too much for him just now. I want to keep this little relapse from becoming what Eliza feared. And the chucklehead is protesting even now that it was only a momentary weakness. People have been buried from such moments," he said broodingly.

"I'll go right up, as soon as I'm done with dessert," Randolph announced, "and I'll bring along some others too, we'll have lovely games, he can guess at charades and such, and then when my friends have to go to bed, we'll play at naughts and crosses together, the two of us, and chess, if, that is, you think that's not too tiring. Papa?" he asked his father when he paused for breath.

"You, imp, are too tiring for a healthy man. I'd never visit you on a sick one. Julian's illness is no excuse for a later bedtime," his father commanded.

Randolph began to explain, with a great show of wounded feelings, that such was not at all the case, his act was purest charity. But his father cut off all protests by musing about how curious it was, then, for his tender-hearted son to deprive his closest friends of his company each night because he chose to grace the adults' dinner table. While the boy searched his youthful vocabulary to find a way of explaining that at his age privilege took precedence over comradeship, the adults at the table vowed to take turns entertaining their absent friend.

"We'll go up one by one," Anthea said softly, "and hold quiet conversations."

"Surely two by two—even Dr. Noah permitted that," Constance said on a rippling laugh, and as Ben-Be-Good looked away so as to conceal the naked longing in his eyes as he watched her toss her black hair back, she added flirtatiously, noting the sudden view of his averted profile, "Will you accompany me, Ben? We'll make a fine pair."

"By twos?" Warwick asked. "I wonder. Knowing our man, I think that if we treat him as an invalid, we'll play a large part in creating one. Surely it would be better if we turned his bedchamber into a salon for the meanwhile. Unless," he said seriously, looking to Arden, for the big man had been the last to consult with the physician, "there is the need for more solitude, of course."

"No, no, I agree, solitude would bring him to the edge of sanity, if not the grave. He's not in bad case at all," Arden assured him. "Merely, he is to rest, but adequately this time."

"Well, then . . ." Warwick said, rising, "if you don't mind, I'll fill my pockets with fruit and have a go at amusing him right now. Save me a bite of that caramel-colored thing, Sukey, will you?"

The fair-haired lady rose with him and linked her arm in his. "It's all yours. Any more dessert and you'll have to roll me upstairs like a hoop, Warwick. I'm coming with you."

"Very well," Arden sighed after taking a look at his guests' faces, and accepting the inevitable as he invented the equitable, he announced in deep portentious tones, "The mountain shall go to Mahomet. Along with all the other company. I surrender. Dessert will be served in the Viscount Hazelton's rooms tonight."

Dessert, and breakfast, and tea the next day were held there as well. And though Julian soon complained that his bedchamber was beginning to resemble a coaching inn, not a salon, he was content to remain at rest, and conceded, at least to himself, that because of it, as the days went on he really did feel much stronger when he took the forbidden exercise he did whenever he was left alone.

It was a secret discipline as well as a prohibited one. But increasingly, he'd more chance to experiment with his health as the days went on, because increasingly, as the novelty of his bedridden state wore off, his friends settled into their own comfortable, predictable visiting schedules with him. He soon realized that he could depend upon seeing Arden and Warwick with breakfast; various assortments of children, always accompanied by Anthea, just before his light luncheon; and Susannah and Francesca immediately afterward. Constance and Ben would appear along with Eliza and any adults who were not otherwise engaged at teatime. And then Eliza would stay on for a good long gossip before dinner, at which time anyone who fancied, but usually just one, would stay to dine with him. After dinner, of course, the entire household would descend upon him, as he delighted in grumbling.

The company was welcome, but their attitude was decidedly not. For all he tried to make them understand that he was not at the brink of the grave, he soon came to realize that their conversation was as carefully chosen and flavored as his invalid diet was. He felt honored, but it was obvious that he was being humored, and he missed the bite and challenge of his friends' arguments as much as he did his normal energetic days. The lovely young women who visited cosseted rather than teased him. And for all his company, his company was limited.

He'd been looking forward to visiting with some of his host's neighbors, especially the devilishly clever Viscount North he'd met years ago at Arden's wedding. That nobleman, famous for his astonishingly good looks, had once been much remarked as a rake but had become a stable gentleman after he'd wed. Now he was as known for his wit and charity as he used to be for his wildness. There might have been as much to learn from him as there was amusement to be had in his company. But if Julian's first bout with sickness had delayed their renewed acquaintance, the second had disabled it. Because when the viscount and his lady had finally come to call, it had been for the briefest time and they had, for all their suavity, behaved as if they'd been at Julian's bier, not his bedside.

His reputation as an invalid had grown all out of proportion. It had become so profound that even his offhand light flirtatious comments didn't cause the maids to giggle, but rather only brought a tear to their gentle eyes. It was insupportable. Despite his lingering weakness, he resolved to be up and about as soon as he safely could manage it. Yet for all their indulgence, it wasn't possible to get his friends to help him in that.

But he'd a lovely corruptible valet in charge of him, and so there was, even so, guarded as he was, prisoner of his friends' love that he'd become, much free time for his secret exercise. For like all crafty prisoners, he'd gotten very adept at solitary, improvised self-improvement. He learned, then tested, then expanded his limits within the limits of his chamber. Having suffered the embarrassment of overdoing once, he was determined to do well this time.

He became proficient at chinning himself on his dressing-room door, hanging by his fingertips from the high ledge above it, inching upward until his head almost touched the ceiling, until the day his chin did touch the high sill. And then he did it again. He took deep breaths at the open windows and did exercises on the floor. Before long he was trotting, on tiptoe to absorb the noise, around the perimeter of the room until he got dizzy, from the circular route, if not from the sport of it, as he grew more sound. And he did grow sound, and bided, patient as a spider, nourished on secret hilarity, thinking of the day when he'd leap from bed entirely whole. He could scarcely wait—for then, demonstrating he was even more hale than most men, he planned a theatrical effort to astonish and irritate his concerned jailers and absolutely boggle his fair, considerate warders. The mere thought of it gave him an extra effortless inch up to the doorsill and another easy lap around the room each day.

He was resting from a particularly invigorating run around the room when Constance came to his chamber alone almost two weeks to the day after he'd been sequestered there, only a day away from his planned exhibition of ultimate fitness. The exercise had made his complexion rise to its highest hue, and so it glowed a subtle peach tone. He breathed irregularly but his light eyes sparkled. He gleamed entirely, he looked, Constance thought sadly, as she was shown in, magnificent. She didn't know the reason for his high good looks, she only regretted them.

"I've come to say good-bye, Julian," she said without preamble when his valet left them to find another of the nonexistent pressing errands his master always rewarded him for pretending to whenever the ladies came calling.

"Oh. Really? But I assure you, I *am* getting better," he said, sitting back in bed and grinning at her.

He wore a colorful robe over a shirt and pantaloons, he even had on a pair of slippers, so there could be nothing said about the immorality of his dishabille. But reclining atop his coverlets, his golden hair disarranged, his muscular arms behind his head, he lazed against his banked pillows, spectacularly masculine, and was everything distracting and undeniably seductive despite his proper attire. Society's whims of conventional behavior in a lady's presence may have been bowed to, but they were also undeniably mocked.

But Constance had been on the town for many Seasons, and was no green girl, at least never in conversation, and seldom in this sort of dueling. Not for nothing was she termed an Incomparable. No, Miss Merriman was up to all the rigs.

"Oh," she echoed him, her dark head high, her best clever accents carefully in place, "I can see that clearly enough, sir," and she smiled, though it never reached her eyes or voice. "No, *I* am leaving," she said.

"Why?" he asked, nothing more, but the way that he looked at her as he said it, as though he was really seeing her, made her turn her head and fidget with a bit of ribbon at her waist, for all her experience with flirtatious gentlemen. But then, his look was enough to make even masters of the art pause. Then she recovered herself and gave him a warmer smile. And since she thought very well on her feet, made a decision.

As all her artfulness had for once won her nothing, she threw it all away and decided to take a last chance on artlessness. In any event, she thought wryly, it could hurt nothing at this point. It might even be entertaining, this novelty: honesty with a gentleman. She paced a little turn about the side of his bed, then paused at the foot of it and looked at him steadily at last, nothing but truth in her famous dark eyes, nothing less on her lips at last.

"I'm unaccustomed to being ignored," she said.

He said nothing, realizing there was more to be said. She answered his listening, and her smile was a lovely, unselfconscious thing as she did so, for she seemed to be listening to herself and learning something as she spoke.

"I don't believe I knew it until Ben came to visit. I missed something so entirely I only knew what it was by its absence and so only recognized it when I saw it again. But I was feeling neglected here, Julian, and unimportant, and for all I do love rivalry, I do not enjoy losing. I have never done, or if I have," she said, obviously remembering as she spoke, since a small crease appeared on her pristine forehead, "I was able to explain it away, or lose the notion altogether with a new interest immediately. Here, there was no other interest for me to take up until Ben came. I do not encourage footmen or dally with stableboys, and although the other gentlemen here have shown no obvious interest in me, I couldn't even amuse myself by pretending to a flirt with them—married men do not exist as men for me, you see."

"I didn't mean to neglect you, Constance—" he began to answer, but she cut him off.

"No, no. You misunderstand. You did not. It's only that you shared your interest in me with others. There were three of us, it cannot have been easy to be so even-handed. But you were entirely fair in your attentions. Completely fair. I am unused to that. I do not like it."

He was very facile with females. He'd always been. He enjoyed their company very much and it was always important that they also enjoyed him. But now, he found he could say nothing. To deny what she said was to commit himself to something he'd neither inclination nor intention to do. She was very beautiful, amusing, and socially adept. But for all he'd weighed her in his mind and even seriously considered taking her to wive at some future date, he'd never done more, or, more important, felt more as yet. That was the point, he thought; the future simply hadn't come yet. Perhaps it was his illness that had retarded things. Yes, he decided, likely that, and so he said at once, adding:

"I've not been able to do or say or even think half the things I intended to when I came here, believe me, but I will not be bound to this bed forever . . . indeed"—he grinned—"I know I'm better now since I haven't been able to leave off thinking of it as a bed since you've come in the room. It was merely a place to rest, before," he said, invitation and apology intermingled in his voice, invitation only in his eyes.

She was not immune to it. But she was up to all the rigs, and knew it, and sighed as she answered him.

"It's never a matter of time. And I believe it never can be. I am accustomed to instant results, even as you are, Julian."

Now, knowing it was over, understanding that it had never really begun, she spoke with complete candor, and discovered it to be interesting, but not half so satisfying as the interminable, challenging games that went forth between a man and a woman—the games she played so well.

"Ben looked at me, you see," she said, "and his heart was immediately in his eyes. He's besotted. I like that very well. If you'd have ignored Eliza and Anthea and followed me with your eyes and waited on my every word and had seen no one but me even when there were others before you, it never would have mattered that illness took you away from me. For you'd have been involved with me still. I came here without an invitation from you. That was irregular enough," she mused. "I ought to have known.

"Ah, face it, Julian, we are too like, you and I. We both attract. Maybe," she said, her head slightly to the side, pondering the matter, "like mismatched magnets placed end to end, having the same force of attraction, we repel each other. I don't know. I'm unused to such heavy thinking," she confessed. "I'm leaving now because I don't like it. I'm accustomed to admiration and I'm leaving precisely because I do like that."

He was very still. "Hardly fair," he said at last, realizing he'd never done more than playfully fence with her, astounded by her honesty and perception, and chagrined because he'd never looked for it beneath all her facile conversation, "since it appears I never knew you at all, you know."

"Oh, I do know that," she agreed, "but then, I begin to think I didn't either. And it makes me very nervous, Julian dear. I don't think I'd care for this sort of honesty as a steady diet. Too exhausting. Far too dangerous. Odd, isn't it, that I've succeeded in interesting you even as I give you up? Odd, but as well, I think. Because it's too late. You're as clever as you're handsome, my friend. That's why I suppose I only got your full attention with my full confession. You've depth, Julian. And I'm not looking for that. I think now that if I thought I still had a chance with you, I'd never have been so honest."

She didn't fully understand what she'd confessed to, he thought, and if she were ever to remember him with any kindness, he'd have to lighten the moment and pretend he'd never understood either.

"Lud," he said, sighing deeply, running a hand through his hair, "if I weren't still so weak, I'd leap from this bed and haul you to it, and show you depth, my lady, that I would."

She laughed. Her eyes rekindled and she lost her drawn expression. Here was the world she knew again, here were the games she excelled in. Wit and parry, thrust and giggle, words and fan-play, subtle smiles and clever innuendo. She almost went back on her word about giving up on him when he spoke like that, for she found his bantering attitude far more erotic than his handsome appearance. But then he ruined it again, and again she was glad of her decision. He became thoughtful and concerned even as she was still laughing and thinking up a wickedly funny naughty rejoinder.

"You're not planning to encourage Ben beyond the limits of this house, are you, Constance?" he asked.

She stopped laughing and drew herself up. Tall and slender, but full-bosomed and long-necked, she would grace a ballroom or a picture frame with equal ease. But now her great dark eyes narrowed, the better to stare down her straight nose at him. She looked every inch the grande dame she would doubtless one day become.

"I do not see where that is any concern of yours, Julian," she said, biting off each word.

"Ah, but I thought we were friends," he answered carefully, "and so for all I've presumed, Majesty, I take leave to presume a bit further on that friendship—in the last seconds of its life, I suppose," he added, and despite herself she grinned—charming rogue, she thought, even as she resented what he said.

"I'm Ben's friend too," he said, lying back against his pillows and gazing at the ceiling instead of at her, "and so for all I was going to say things about unequal stations, and ask if you knew enough about his background, and suggest that for all I'm pleased to call him my friend, you would do well to bring that background into the foreground before you flutter another eyelash at him, I wonder if I'm not being wrongheaded again."

"You realize he'd never hurt me," she said, assuming an air of boredom while watching him closely.

"Of course. But more to the point, I think you might kill him, my dear," he answered, tilting his head to look at her.

"You think I wouldn't take him seriously?" she asked, as though she'd been challenged.

"Have you ever taken any of us so?" he asked, and then again he changed directions, for though she was very beautiful in her usual polished elegant fashion, in her honesty she was at last very vulnerable. "And who can blame you?" he asked merrily. "You've a delightful sense of humor, and no female with any sense of the ridiculous can ever take anyone from my gender seriously. Arden holds that Eve laughed so hard when she first saw Adam that he didn't realize she was a human and could actually speak to him for at least another week. That's why," he invented rapidly, seeing her smile dawn again, "they had an extra week in Paradise, you know."

They parted friends, they left each other in laughter, but so soon as they'd parted from each other neither smiled again for several moments. He liked her very well, Julian thought, sorry now that he hadn't liked her more. She might have loved him, Constance thought, had she not loved admiration more. But as she came down the stairs, she shook her head to dispel the thought. Then when she met most of the company in the salon, she announced, too brightly, that she'd remembered the coronation was almost upon them, and so she'd just said her good-byes to Julian, for she would soon be gone to London to make ready for all the celebrations there would be.

Then she smiled at Ben so warmly his heart sank, for all he immediately offered her his arm into the salon, his escort back to London, and might have offered her his heart on the spot if he didn't know he'd as much as done so already—if he didn't realize such a lady would never accept such an inferior gift. So all he did was tell her his carriage was as good as hers whenever she decided to leave.

She thanked him prettily and accepted with a smile several shades more than gracious. But her announcement started up conversation, as the Duke and Duchess of Peterstow decided to leave for London soon as well, and Eliza, repressing shudders at the thought of entering society again and leaving Julian so soon, thought of a thousand reasons to refuse everyone's kind invitation to stay with them for the affair, and gave out at least fourteen of them each time it was suggested to her. Her own mama was coming to visit soon to try to lure her there, and if she'd the slightest inclination to attend, she'd certainly accept one now before that lady arrived, she thought. In any event, here she would stay until Julian left, leaving her to get on with her depleted life as best she could without him again.

"I thank you very kindly, Arden," Constance said as she paused outside the coach where her maid, her patient chaperone, and Mr. Ben-Be-Good awaited her, before taking her leave of her host.

"Francesca would be here to say farewell too, but it is morning, you understand," the big man said with a hint of a grin, wondering if the lady, being unwed and being a staple of society, would allow herself to let him know she understood his reference. Unwed females of repute, he was given to understand, might coo over babes and adore little children, but were not supposed to ever refer to anything that was at all to do with the way they'd arrived upon the planet. He knew this extended to their recognition of the more delightful aspects of that process; he wondered if it also included the less-charming subsequent details, such as morning sickness.

He'd misjudged her. The Incomparable might be a lady, but she was, he saw again, also an original.

"Unfeeling brute," she said, tapping him with her fan. "See how many infants you'd want if you spent half the time before their arrival regretting you'd ever clapped eyes on your eggs in the morning, much less your husband of a night!"

"You're a sheer delight, my lady," he answered humbly, "and welcome back anytime, no matter how you berate me. But if I may have one word with you before you leave?"

She raised an eyebrow, but put one gloved hand on his arm, and he walked her well away from the coach and stood looking out over his grounds as though he were showing them off to her, as usual.

"Mr. Be-Good is an old friend of mine, none better. He is smitten, a bit, with you. Which is," he chuckled, "very like speaking of the 'little murder' Eliza was complaining of. He's far gone in admiration for you, my lady," he said, suddenly more serious. "Please have a care. He isn't used to the games of high society."

"Is this warning, of him? Or for him? Julian has already told me how fearful he is for Ben's sake."

"Both," Arden answered.

"I know," Constance replied with ice in her eyes, "for I asked, that his mama was a laundress, his papa a sot, and that he lived in the gutters for most of his life, and made his coin from them until only recently. Self-taught, self-made, and self-reliant—that is, I believe, a fair reading of him, is it not?"

Arden nodded. "And you are a lady, sprung from a long line of them," he said.

"The first of which was Eve," she answered coolly, "who was Ben's ancestress too, I believe. Don't worry,

Arden, I know who Ben is, and I am learning who I am."

"I only suggest that society doesn't take to children of the streets, commoners, or former criminals, for some reason, however they've elevated themselves to money or manners. And that if you don't mean the lad mischief, you'd soon discover just that—if you were bold enough to fly in the face of everything you know. That is all," he said in rough, warm tones.

"Francesca was bold enough," she countered.

"Ah, well," he said, a genuine smile upon his lips, "Francesca is unique."

"No. She is extraordinarily lucky," Constance said firmly, "and I have not made up my mind to anything yet. Credit me with some sense, sir, I've even made sure to be gone before my aunt arrives. I've no difficulties with my own mama," she said in such a voice that Arden knew that she told her mama when to breathe in and out, "but Aunt is another matter entirely. Eliza's mama is not to be trifled with. I want no troubles until I do make up my mind, you see. So don't worry for either Ben or me. And as for your lovely wife, I only wish," she said softly, as they strolled back to the coach, where Ben awaited them, "I had such friends as she and Ben do."

"Ah," Arden said, "but you do."

He shook hands with Ben, and when that dapper young gentleman grew grave and leaned close to confide in a low voice as he said good-bye, "Don't worry, as soon as I discover the danger, I'll let you know," it was a measure of Arden's state of mind that it was several moments after the coach left before he realized it was danger to Julian that Ben had meant.

"Don't sulk," Warwick said, seeing him as he came back into the house. "I don't leave until tomorrow."

"So soon? Then why am I sulking?" Arden asked with a fine display of excessive relief, before, seeing his friend's eyebrow quirked, he relented and admitted, "Ah, no, actually, Duke, I was only just thinking that Julian turns away females other men would give their limbs to meet, and I wondered, for all I love him, if he has any heart left in him at all."

"Oh, but he does," Warwick answered, his eyes growing dark. "It's only that he doesn't listen to it anymore."

"Which is the same thing," Arden sighed.

"Which is, yes, sadly, near enough the same," his friend agreed. "But not quite. And worlds can be built on 'not quite.' 'Not quite' dead would be good enough for me, you know. Perhaps if he's left alone long enough, he'll hear it. But he seldom is let alone. The fellow more than invites distraction, you know," he said thoughtfully. "Shall we bar his door?"

"If we did, they'd come through the windows," his host sighed again.

He was exactly right. For finding it open, Anthea came in through his door within the very next hour.

13

JULIAN LAY BACK and watched the afternoon light slant across his bed, illuminating the pages of the book he'd opened but never read, his own thoughts having been more interesting. Constance had left, and as at a dinner party when the leave-taking of one guest reminds the others of the lateness of the hour and causes them to plan the moment of their own departure, Julian thought about his own exit. A long way past time for his, really, he thought.

Oh, he'd miss Warwick and Arden, and their wives as well, for Susannah was a good friend, as was Francesca. Or, he thought, smiling slightly, as had been Francesca, before her condition had absorbed her so utterly, poor lady. Constant queasiness must be a trial, he mused, even more so than his own weakness had been. And then too, he'd never had to face the ordeal of bloating like a bladder as the weeks went on. All he'd been was fatigued, and they'd sent him to bed and practically sat upon him to keep him there. But Francesca, with all her plaints, was supposed to stay afoot, and carry on as though it were normal to look at food with loathing and yet still swell up like an excursion balloon. Women were remarkably fine creatures, he thought idly—and then sat up straighter, discomposed, because for all he admired females and thought of them often, he'd never passed his time contemplating the wonders of their breeding processes. This enforced visit was turning him around entirely, and he'd do well to be gone, he decided, before he became as domestic as a parlor tabby, as tamed as any capon.

Because he knew he'd miss the children too. And then

he realized he'd miss seeing Eliza as well. She was perhaps, in a strange fashion, his very closest friend, or had
been—but then, after all, he decided, her letters were
the basis of that friendship, and when he left, he'd have
those again. Mostly, he'd have his freedom again, and
the opportunity to get on with his life. His eyes became
bleak when he thought for a moment that he scarcely
knew what to do with that freedom, and had little idea of
what he'd make of that opportunity. Turned around and
around, he thought bitterly, like a corkscrew, until he
burrowed deep into his own skin—oh, yes, he needed to
be gone from this bed, from this forced march into his
own soul.

He'd exercised for hours this morning to be sure he
was ready to give his display of hardihood this very day,
and because of that didn't wish to waste any energy and
so couldn't race his body in order to subdue his thoughts
just now. And so he picked up the book again, determined to read it through, if only to drown out his own
words that echoed, unsaid, in his head.

And then Anthea came into the room and saved him.

He put down the book and looked up to her with a
welcoming smile of real gratitude.

"The children," she said at once, after inquiring as to
his health and begging pardon for the interruption of his
reading, "aren't with me, as you can see. Are you sure
my visit is . . . seemly?"

He smiled the wider. Only Anthea would ask that.
Constance had always sailed into his bedchambers, totally at ease with the situation; Eliza was in the habit of
waltzing in like any of the children, and seating herself
wherever there was room, even on his bed itself, without
giving a rap for the conventions. Of course, Constance
would be confident in a heavenly court or at an orgy, she
was that sure of herself. And Eliza was not only a spon-
taneous soul, she was nominally his fiancée, and thus
entitled to several bendings of the social rules. And he
was, after all, supposedly too ill a man to be anything but
a gentleman. But Anthea—gentle, unworldly, and sincere Anthea—she would worry about the proprieties.
But then, he thought with the new insight his enforced

inactivity had discovered in him, she had the most cause to worry, poor girl, since she was an employee and was entirely dependent upon the goodwill of others.

Now she hesitated, as unsure of her welcome without the children as she was of the propriety of her visit, as if she felt that somehow she'd overstepped her bounds by simply visiting him with her friendship. He didn't know whether to be amused or saddened by how humble she appeared to be.

He beckoned for her to come closer, gazing at her with pleasure. She was always a handsome female and today she was an especially welcome sight. Her smooth brown hair was shining clean and neatly drawn into a coronet of braids. It was better than fashionable because it was so classic. Her soft gray muslin dress showed a handsome form, she was all that was wholesome and healthy, and her eyes showed her wisdom as well as her concern for him. Her company, though never stimulating, was already comforting. She'd been like a soothing balm to him in his illness, and was still so now, he thought wryly, with her obvious admiration coming so soon after Constance's defection. He welcomed her for several reasons, then, and sought to put her at her ease.

He'd miss her when he left, but then wondered idly if he'd have to miss her, after all. Because when he was free he'd be free to seek out the company of whomever he chose. And he might do well to review old acquaintance, for as he'd so lately come to see, he might not really know the ladies he knew as well as he'd thought he did.

"It was such a beautiful day," she explained anxiously, still standing so far from his bed he had to lean forward to catch her words, "I'd not the heart to keep the children close, especially since the gardener said it was his opinion we'd have rain before teatime."

All the gardener had said was "good morning," but Julian had neither the opportunity nor the inclination to question that, she thought, as he smiled and beckoned her closer. And she'd never taken the beauty of any day into account as an excuse to let the children out of their lessons. But he'd no reason to doubt that either. Just as he'd no way to know the pleasure she felt as she stepped nearer to him, any more than he could guess at the wild elation she'd felt when Constance had left. Because the Incomparable Miss Merriman had left in defeat, for all she'd gone with all her banners flying. None knew that better than Anthea, for Anthea had watched carefully. Now it might just be that she herself could achieve victory, she thought, as she blushed and listened to all of Julian's laughing protests of his delight with her visit, childless or not, as she drifted even closer to him to fluff up his pillows.

She could take such liberties, she told herself firmly, holding her breath at how close his golden head lay to her bosom as she smoothed out his pillow slips, because she was something of a servant. But she might soon take even more—because she was not at all precisely a servant. And at last, she thought, remembering the line from a melodrama the girls had enacted at school, they were alone. Or as good as such. And they would be for a long while now that Constance was gone. Because she knew, because she watched, that he considered Eliza to be as much a child as any of her charges. So much as he was charmed by her, it was obviously in very much the same way that he was entranced by little Miss Mary or any other bright and lovely little girl.

"Do you like the book?" she asked at once, seizing on a handy conversational gambit. "I'll read a bit to you if your eyes are tired, if you like."

In a matter of hours he'd be swinging from the bedposts and prancing over the tabletops, because immediately after dinner he planned to roast them all by leaping from bed to tumble and cavort until they'd all, astonished, have to admit to his complete recovery at last. But for now, because it pleased him, because he wished to please her, he said, "Oh, yes, how kind of you," and, meek as a lamb, he lay back and listened to her soft voice read to him, beginning at the arbitrary passage he'd pointed out where the book fell open when he handed it to her.

Since it was a book she'd brought to him just the day before, he hadn't the heart to mention he'd read it years before when it had first come out. But Mary Shelley's saga was evergreen and so he listened to more of the poor monster's laments against his creator, the arrogant Dr. Frankenstein, until he heard Constance clear her throat and had an excuse to put a hand upon her wrist to stop her.

"Thank you, but that's enough. It's too warm a day for ice floes, don't you think?" he said. "We don't get good weather here so often we can afford to ignore it. Even pent in here I feel it . . . no, no, please don't close the window, dear Miss Baker, I enjoy the breeze, I'm almost mended, you know. Tell me June things, instead—I've had enough winter."

She told him about the gardens he'd missed seeing coming into their full bloom, and about the children's lessons, especially about how Miss Mary was doing, for he doted on her, before she left him to his afternoon nap, promising she'd return at teatime as usual, with roses for his tray.

He was grinning, arms behind his head, musing about how he might just move his athletic spectacle up to teatime, just so he could see her drop her armful of roses when she saw him capering, when Eliza came in. He eyed her with appreciation before he spoke, for if ever a person could chase away his boredom, it was Eliza. To-day she suited his springtime mood in more ways than that, for she was dressed like a rose from out of the garden herself. Her auburn hair was dressed high and left to depend in a frivolous cascade of tangled curls that caressed the back of her white neck, her dress was a deep old-rose color enlivened with a pattern of burnished gold florets. In all, she looked young and tempting, fresh and fine. He was grinning so expectantly that it took him a few moments for him to see she was newly hesitant and unexpectedly fidgety with him. For she strolled from his bedside to his window to look out for a soundless second before she paced back again, her hands behind her back. Then she stopped and asked where his valet was.

"Sorry, too late, my girl," he said, wondering what rig she was up to, "he's smitten with a dairy maid, you missed your chance. He's off courting. I gave him leave, since there's little he can do for me after I've been shaved. One doesn't have to dress too fine to drape oneself across a bed and languish, you know, and I'm feeling very fragile, thank you so much for asking," he said in what he hoped were the pitiable accents of a dying swan.

"One adorns a bed to *mend* himself, Julian," she answered vaguely, obviously still thinking of whatever was deviling her. "Languishing is purely optional. In fact, I was just languishing myself," she admitted. "Anthea's got the children doing sums again, Warwick and Arden have gone off for a ride to visit some tenant with a boring problem to do with drains, and Francesca and Susannah are talking about babies. They're very good company until they begin with that," she complained, "for there always comes a point when they remember that I'm there, and I can feel them holding back what they'd truly like to say. I explained that at home I was the only child underfoot so I always heard every midwife story," she said on a bubbling laugh that seemed to pop up and surprise even herself, "but I don't think they believe me. Still, it's true, and if I believed every story I overheard," she declared, "I'd have gone off to a nunnery, like Ophelia, years ago. And you look just fine now, to me, at least. But if you really are tired . . . shall I read to you?" she asked suddenly, her mood veering, showing just how distracted she was.

He was about to say that his ears were as tired with being read at as he was with lying in bed, when she added, whipping a leather-bound volume out from behind her back and holding it in two hands before her as though she held up a treat, "This just came from London, it won't be out for the general public until next month, but Warwick got it for me early because I asked. He said you'd appreciate it too, and said you'd explain the bits I mightn't catch. It's by that Mr. Egan you gentlemen all admire," she added. "Bother, that chair's too low," she muttered, and looked about for another more suitable, before accepting that there was none and accepting his hand instead. Then she took a step up, to perch unceremoniously on the side of his bed near to him, so that he could see the book as well as she did. She wriggled into place so she could sit straight among the pliant feathers of his mattress as she placed the book on her lap.

"It's called *Life in London*, and Warwick said bits of it have been issued before, so it's already much-sought-after. It's a trifle naughty," she explained, as he leaned forward to gaze at the book over her shoulder and became aware that her hair was scented like roses too, "and so I wanted to be sure no one else was about when I showed it to you. Anthea, particularly, would have a fit if she found me with it," she added, turning to a brightly colored illustration of a collection of rakish gentlemen ogling scantily clad females in the greenroom backstage at the theater, "but I've been thumbing through it, Julian, and it looks fascinating. I can't quite understand everything, since Warwick says it's written in 'St. Giles' Greek,' and Arden says it's the sort of slang a lady isn't supposed to know, that's the point of it. But I understand enough to know it's amusing. It's all about these fashionable gentlemen: Corinthian Tom, his friends, Jerry and Logic, and their 'Rambles and Sprees,' as it says. It's about the real, the true high jinks you gents get up to in London."

"Yes, so it is, I'm sorry to say," he agreed, taking the book from her and riffling through the pages, "because I've seen chapters of it before."

"What? Sorry? Never say you've got such puritan ideas as Anthea does now?" she said, drawing herself up, putting her hands on her hips, and looking as irate as she could from such close range.

"No, no," he said musingly as he flipped through the pages to see the illustrations of the heroes tormenting the watch by boxing them, carousing in the lowest inns in the East End and dancing with demireps at the Cyprians' Ball, as well as being presented at court and attending Almack's and the opera.

"No," he sighed, "you may look on with me, and I'm even willing to explain what this daring lady is proposing to do with young Jerry here, despite the loss of my immortal soul for so corrupting you, Nuisance, but I'm sorry it's in print anyway. Because it means it's the end of it, you know. For all it's written up in purest street jargon, it will likely soon be translated everywhere and will become sensational.

"Yes," he said wistfully, and he was entirely serious, "once a thing is written up as being daring and unique, it immediately becomes less so. It's true all the young blades of my generation went through this nonsense in just these places—Egan is entirely right. But soon as it's down in print, it'll become the rage for every young man in England to come to London to try to emulate. Once, only a few did these things; soon, it will all become so trite and clichéd they might as well hire on guides and book holidays so that the tourists can watch the young British gentlemen as they come of age. So ends another era," he sighed, putting the book down again, hoping he'd distracted her from it for now.

Damn Warwick, he thought rapidly, there were things in the book he decidedly did not wish to explain to her. But for all that, what he'd said was true, and his regret showed in his eyes and she sighed with him.

"Still, and that's as it may be," she said, taking the book from him, "but I'd like to know about it."

"I thought you would," he muttered.

"Warwick suggested it, Julian," she went on, "and so you needn't feel it's wrong. I am your fiancée, you know . . ." And then she paused, and drew in a breath and blurted out, "And so far as that goes, I've been meaning to ask, it's past time to ask, but there was never the chance, but now I can see you're better and time is passing. Oh, Lord, Julian, how much longer will we be engaged? Mama's been writing me so many letters asking about when we're supposed to get married that I don't dare even so much as open my post anymore."

She paused for breath, seeing from his expression that she'd startled him, and then realized that she'd done all her speaking for now. It was out, and for all she'd been worried about when and how she'd say it through all these days when she'd felt he was too ill to tease with the problem, and although it had been gracelessly done, it was done, and so she felt as much better about it as she felt worse.

She gazed at him openly as she awaited his answer, both because she might be expected to and because he seemed to be thinking so deeply he might not see how her eyes devoured his face. If there were a miracle, he'd take her in his arms and answer her question with one word: "Forever!" and then say, "Engaged, in love, together, for we'll be wed at dawn, my love." But that was only in her groggiest brink-of-sleep fancies. He could say, "That is up to you, my dear," but that was one of the more delicious easy-sleep courting fantasies too. He might say, "For so long as you want to, Eliza," and that was entirely possible and a thing she thought on often, and it would do, for time was always on the side of happy accident. Then too, he could say, 'We'll see," which would suffice. She'd been over many possible responses in her mind, in her solitude.

But he said, slowly and carefully, "I thought we might announce our change of heart together, when your mama arrives in a day or so. You did say she was coming then? Is that all right?"

"Oh, yes," she said, remaining very still, refusing to listen to the "Oh, no" that rang out in her head, for he'd said the very worst thing, just as she'd expected and tried to believe he would not.

She stared at him without so much as a flicker of emotion in her wide brown eyes and so he knew she held some strong emotion in check, and as he'd rather not know of it, but knew he ought, he asked another question.

"Do you mind?"

"Lud, Julian!" she said with great exasperation, for it was an easy emotion to pretend to in order to banish what she really felt. "You were noble and generous and valiant that day. But I promised I'd never hold you to your kind gesture, didn't I? Fine husband a human sacrifice would be," she grumbled as he laughingly denied any sacrifice on his part, but as she heard nothing but laughter in his denials, she was glad she'd stayed with her decision, no matter how it pained her. And it pained her to the point that she asked, despite her every intention not to, "But can we . . . shall we . . . still be friends?" and shut her lips tight together before she could go to say: "for I do not think I could bear to go on if we were not."

"Forever!" he declared, which was the right answer to the wrong question. But she was so grateful for that, at least, that she smiled and never cared if he thought the tears she struggled against were for mere sentimental reasons.

"Well, then," she said heartily as she snatched up the book again, "Let's get on with it. Here," she said, picking a random page and thrusting it beneath his nose. "I can't make head or tail of this, can you?"

He didn't so much as glance down to the page. She was upset, and he scarcely knew how to comfort her. She was no longer the little girl he wished to pretend she was, but he'd no reason to believe she was as grown as he needed her to be. There was still too much he didn't know, too much she might have to learn. She'd disappointed him before; for all she was his friend, he wasn't ready to make her his wife. He'd waited too long to find a mate to make a hasty choice now.

Her face was very white; her eyes, swimming with unshed tears, glinted golden in the light. He'd never noted how they turned up at the corners. But before he could remark it, he noted more that stopped him looking closer. He was so near he could also see the high color on her cheeks had risen elsewhere to give her shoulders and the skin covering the hint of her collarbones a rosy flush. He turned his head quickly to see the page she held out for him, but not before he scented the attar of roses, heated by her emotions as much as the actual blossoms might be by the warmth of the sun, so that it rose to his nostrils, breathing summer and warm womanhood to him.

To turn his thoughts, he turned his attention to read what she held before him at once, not attending to the words he spoke until he'd spoken most of them,

" '. . . "What lovely girls!" exclaimed Hawthorne,' " he read, " ' "I suppose that is the mama, and her three daughters. I declare I was quite struck with their pleasant countenances. You seem an old acquaintance of theirs.''

" 'Logic said, laughing outright, "Yes, yes; they are good-natured enough, if you will furnish the means.''

" 'Hang all the bawds; for where's a greater vice
Than taking in young creatures all so nice?
And yet to them, 'tis merely knitting, spinning—
No more!
Although the innocent is made a wh——.
With just as much sangfroid as at their shops
The butchers sell rump steaks or mutton chops—'

"No more, indeed!" Julian said, snapping the book together and putting it down as though it had burnt his fingers. "Wretch, I suspect you understood that very well. Well, and if you didn't, I won't explain it to you. The devil!" he said, so annoyed with her as well as himself that color rose in his own cheeks as he ran his hand through his hair. "I even think there must be a law against explaining such matters to young chits like you!"

"I am not too young to read or speak about it!" she cried, despite the fact that she'd scarcely listened to what he'd read and so had little idea of what she was or wasn't supposed to understand. There were a great many naughty references in the book, she understood most, and her only sorrow was that she wasn't able to comprehend all the slang so that she'd not miss a trick. But his constant reference to her as a child vexed her, the more because she felt that was the main impediment to their closer relationship now that there was no distance between them at last.

There was so little literal distance between them just now that she had to draw back to stare him in the eye.

"It was that word," she said, catching up the book, opening it, and stabbing a finger at the first unknown bit of jargon she saw, "that I didn't understand. I assure you I can comprehend all else. *All* else. I am one-and-twenty, Julian, a woman grown. An ape-leader, long on the shelf in some circles, if truth be known. Old enough to have cut my wisdom teeth, or have begun cutting them," she added, for she was honest in this, as in most things, "for all that you're so pleased to call me 'child.' "

" 'Chit.' I said 'chit,' " he said, glowering back at her, for he knew she was entirely right, and the more right she was, the more danger he faced.

"Chit, child, it makes no matter, Julian," she argued, "females my age have children! Often several of them!" she said, and seeing how struck he was by this, she went on in a fine rage, "They have children who have children by now!"

But at that she stopped. And at that he paused. And they both laughed. Despite their tangled emotions, they both chortled, finding that their amusement, as ever, glossed over the hurt they'd inflicted on each other. When she stopped laughing, Eliza looked at Julian seriously again.

"In truth, Julian," she said, "I'm all grown by now. I'm sorry I've not got taller," she mused, "for it might be that height would be the only thing to convince you of my maturity, but there it is. Although you met me when I was so very young, I'm not so young anymore. And I do wish you wouldn't treat me so, Julian, so I do wish. When you wrote to me you didn't parse down your words or your opinions, no, I'm sure you didn't. So please don't pass me off as an infant now."

She was, for once, entirely pleased with what she'd said to him, and sat and waited for his reply.

But they'd laughed together, and he felt the danger was past. And he'd been pent in bed for weeks, and it was spring and the imp of mischief was as high in him now as the sap was in the newly leafed trees. It might have been the wicked book he held, or the breath of abandon on the whisper of the breeze that blew in through his window and stirred the tendrils of hair at her neck. It might have been that she challenged him, or simply that he'd lain upon this bed impotently for many days, visited by lovely females who acted as though he'd been either a eunuch or a child himself. It might only have been that Eliza was entirely lovely to him and he'd not let himself look at her as lovely for all these weeks. For whatever reason, he resolved to tease her, only that, but in a new fashion, as she'd insisted she'd wished to be treated. He smiled. But it was a different smile from any he'd ever bent upon her before. This was a game he'd mastered when she'd been yet a child, and one, he knew, she'd only begun to play.

It was odd, she thought as she looked at him, but something had changed in the room. Between one breath and another, Julian had changed in some way she could not quite define. For now, suddenly, he looked different; no, she thought, blinking, it was that he looked at her differently. He focused on her entirely, his light gray eyes gazed at her intently, he seemed to glow, to kindle, to concentrate upon her until she felt as though nothing in the room had reality save for him and herself. She couldn't look away from his bright stare, and tried to think up a hasty jest to dispel this new sensation, but all she could do was to bite her lip before she saw his gaze go to her lips, and then she could scarcely breathe.

"So," he said, his voice different too, smooth and soft and dim and dark for all the bright sunlight that showed his eyes gleaming as he drew nearer, "so, our Eliza wants to be treated like a woman grown, or is it that she wants to be treated like the 'sweet nymph,' the 'little Phillis' she wondered at in the little book? I wonder," he said as he took her in his arms and bent his glowing head and lightly, only slightly brushed his lips against hers.

There had been times before, when she'd walked across a thick carpet on a cold day and then touched a doorknob, that Eliza had felt a shock, more tingling than painful, but startling as much as painful in its unexpectedness. Now, as Julian's lips touched hers, there was just such a jolt of surprise, but the thrill of it passed through her lips to set her senses buzzing with an intensity of pleasure as profound as pain. And so she was aware of nothing but pleasure, so much pleasure that she hardly registered the joy that this was her Julian kissing her, as he gathered her up closer to deepen the kiss.

And he, who'd only meant to tease, he'd have sworn to it, and who had kissed so many females that he thought he knew every sensation such kisses could produce, found himself lost in the warmth of her mouth, wondering at the sweetness he discovered there, and that it was Eliza in his arms never occurred to him either. He did remotely realize that it wasn't unwillingness that kept his kiss so unsatisfactorily chaste when he wanted to explore it further, and further, that it was because this delicious female he held was unused to kisses, for he paused for a moment to murmur instructions so that she might open her mouth against his to permit him more intimacy. But as she did so as soon as he asked it of her, he forgot all else again as he caught her up to bring her body more fully against his.

One of his hands supported her back, the other traced her neck. Finding a slight silken coil of hair beneath his stroking fingers near to the hollow of her shoulder, his lips eventually left hers to seek the pulse he remembered seeing beating at the hollow of her neck, even as his hand went on, smoothing and caressing, finding easeful and exciting shapes and textures. Her hands crept up to his neck to strain his hair through her fingers, and he smiled against her neck as he felt them there. But then he required the warmth of her lips again, and again, and it wasn't long before he needed to discover just what it was that so delighted the touch of his hand. Not many moments passed before he found that the soft gown could be brushed away from his lips with the ease of the sun parting the clouds in the morning, and that the high, pointed breast he uncovered tasted just as he'd hoped and imagined it might. And she could do nothing more than react to him; even if she could think, she could not have done else. His scent was of sandalwood and lemons and it was her air, his touch was fire and it was her world.

There was no way to know how long they'd gone on, no way to predict how long they would have gone on before they stopped, but they would have stopped. Rather, he would have stopped. She could not. He encircled her, he involved her to the point that she could not recall such things as time or place. Yet although he found more than he'd bargained for in her embrace, and far more than he'd wanted to, and although at that moment he never wanted to cease in his voyage of discovery in her arms, still, he would have done. Because he was no stranger to ecstasy, even such as and even more than she provided him. And already he'd begun to pay attention to the little voice in his head that reminded him of who she was, and where he was.

But it was a louder voice that stopped them.

"Perhaps another time," Arden said in a low voice, but his low voice was that of rolling thunder even at its sweetest, and there was a distinct edge to it now.

"Oh, surely not another time!" a shrill voice protested, so familiar that Julian could feel Eliza's hands grown cold even as she snatched them away from his neck as though he was still burning the way he'd done a second before. "*Surely not!* The vows haven't been said, no matter how close to the altar they've come, and surely, Mr. Lyons, you remember Eliza's closer brush with matrimony before—before the very altar. Eee-lie-a-za!" Mrs. Merriman called in a sharp mockery of cheerfulness, saying her daughter's name with more syllables that it had even been written. "Come . . . when you are through, of course, that is, and give your mama a kiss—if you can spare one."

If they would only leave, Eliza thought, her mind scrambling as she tried to scurry into the top of her gown, fumbling with the material, until Julian, suavity itself, wrapped an arm about her again, and keeping her close with her back to the door and her head against his shoulder, readjusted her gown himself with one free hand unseen by the unexpected visitors at his door. As he did so, he spoke in even, amused tones, even as she felt his heartbeat race.

"My dear Mrs. Merriman," he said, "or shall I say Mama? How good to see you, although I'm sure you understand," he said gently, "that I would rather have seen you an hour hence. Still, you've the right of it. But never fear. Our wedding day looms very near, in fact, you have only to name it, since I cannot get this wretch to decide. You witnessed my attempts to speed the day," he said, holding Eliza very firmly still as her head twitched up at that, "and so it well may be that you came betimes for both your purposes and mine."

"Oh, I don't doubt your purposes, Viscount," Mrs. Merriman said as she came all the way into the room and confronted her supposed prospective son-in-law. "I've never done. That's why I've come."

Eliza began to speak, but Julian cut her off with a hard hand on her arm. She fell silent, peering at her mama from the circle of Julian's protective arms, confused and unhappy, feeling like a small child listening to her elders squabble.

"You look very well," her mama said, still ignoring her daughter and gazing steadily at Julian. "More to the point, Viscount, you act very well indeed. All due to the most *tender, intensive,* and *personal* care, no doubt."

"No doubt," Julian agreed. "And I am very well. Well enough to stand before a minister for the requisite minutes, ma'am, you're entirely right in that. Please name the day," he said in accents that Eliza thought gentlemen used to decide the day they would meet to duel to the death.

"Soon. Sooner than that, I think now," Mrs. Merriman said.

"But, Mama—" Eliza began, heedless of Julian's hold on her arm, determined to speak even if he should clutch it hard enough to stop the flow of her blood. But his words did that.

"Next week?" he asked. "My friend the Duke of Peterstow can send to London for a special license, it can be done by next Sunday, I believe. We will, of course, have a limited guest list because the forthcoming coronation will have most of our mutual friends busy in London, and I expect you'd want the wedding here—and now. I assume speed is more essential than ceremony to you this time?"

"I shall be getting a clever son-in-law," Mrs. Merriman agreed, smiling her thinnest smile. "Yes, it will do. I'll speak to you later, Eliza," she said. "When you are *done,*" she added before she marched from the room.

Arden gave his friend a long and searching look before he too left the room, leaving them alone again.

"No, listen, Julian, I can talk her round," Eliza cried at once. "I'll be off to London by daybreak, I promise, you've never got to buckle under to her—she can be hard, but there'll be no wedding if I refuse. I did it before—or at least I was planning to, and so I can do it again, and you're ill, everyone knows you've been ill, they'll never expect me to wed an invalid, we can get out of it that way . . ." she went on, staring at Julian's bleak eyes and babbling in her haste to assure him of his safety from her.

"No, sweet, no, pet," he murmured absently, smiling only with his lips and reaching out to hold her still, at arm's length, until it seemed he heard her and focused his eyes and stopped her protests by giving her shoulders a gentle shake.

"No, Eliza," he said then, very calmly and sadly, "it won't do. I'm healthy as a horse again, you know—or at least so I was planning to let everyone know in a matter of hours. I've done with pretending to weakness. Your mama would have to be a booby to believe it, and she's not. She knows how well I am, believe me. No," he said as he let out a deep breath, "your mama found us in more than a compromising situation." He laughed. "*I* would have been shocked if I'd seen us, Eliza. I was . . . ah, dining on your charms just at that moment, wasn't I? It doesn't matter," he said as she looked away through lowered lashes, "you were in my bed, half-undressed, behaving in a most unprincipled way. We can't get away with that, love. Or—hush—at least, I won't let you. One jilted fiancé doth not a wanton make. Two would be bad enough. But word of this bed-play would escape, never doubt it, it's the sort of thing that does. If the servants didn't tattle, be sure your mama would. It might bar some doors for me in future, but I could live with being thought a sportive gent. Your name would be worse than any you might find in that entertaining book you brought me. You've no reputation left now, Eliza," he said sincerely, gazing at her sadly. "You must marry me, you know."

Because that was only horrible to her because of the sorrow in his eyes, she protested again, "But you don't have to marry me, Julian, you do not!"

"But I am a gentleman, Eliza, and so I do," he said with finality.

That, the coldness and flatness of it, stopped her protests, and her eyes grew wide. It might have been that he saw that; he certainly heard the inadequacy of his own words. But he wouldn't begin their union with a lie, and couldn't think up a better palliative than the truth. He kissed the tip of her nose and smiled sadly at her.

"We're friends, Eliza, the best of friends, are we not? I'll be a good husband to you, never fear. I'll never hurt you, Eliza, my word on it. Now, please, I think you ought to leave, though it breaks my heart to see you go," he jested. "If you don't leave right now, your mama will call a coach and drive us over the border this very night, so as to get us shackled the faster, because of what she'll imagine happening here. Go on, hop it," he said as she crouched on the bed before him and then began backing away, staring at him with confused pain in her brimming eyes.

And then she straightened, and slid off the side of his high bed, and after one last look at him, fled.

He lay back in bed again and closed his eyes.

"Oh, come in," he said wearily after a few minutes. "I haven't died, I only wish I had. Your footsteps are your signature, Arden. Oh, hello, Warwick, in for the kill too? Odd, I didn't hear you stealing in. But then, I've been deaf to all comers today, that's the whole point of your arrival, isn't it?"

His friends gazed down at him with no laughter in their faces, although Warwick drawled, "Do you mean to slip out of this nuptial knot, Julian?"

"Put by your sword and dust off your dancing slippers, my friend, I'm caught and I know it and I will ask only that you pull those strings you can to get the deed done the faster. Well," he said as he sat up and threw back his coverlets so that he could spring out of bed and face them on his feet, "it's you, Arden, after all, who used to go on about: 'If 'twere to be done, 'twere best that it were done quickly,' as the poet said, didn't you?"

"I was talking about a funeral that time, I believe," Arden replied.

"Same thing." Julian shrugged, standing and stepping to the bell pull to ring for his valet so as to dress.

"Are you sure you ought to be out of bed?" Warwick asked.

"I should have been out of it days ago, that's how I got into such trouble in it," Julian snarled from beneath the shirt he pulled over his head. When he emerged from its folds, he added bitterly, "I was planning an exhibition this evening—no, a very different one from the one I gave, I promise you. I was going to demonstrate that I was capable of a different sort of athleticism too. The kind I did show," he muttered as he swung about, looking for a fresh shirt in his wardrobe, "was more fit for display in a bawdy house, more a treat for Mother Carey's establishment than Gentleman Jackson's, wasn't it?"

His friends, noting the breadth of his shoulders and the healthy color of the skin that covered the play of muscles in his lean back as he reached for the shirt, and seeing the surety of his graceful movements, readily believed in his renewed hardihood. But there was that in his voice and words which still caused them concern for him, if not any longer for his physical health.

He knew it. Knew he ought to be more merry, or at least act as a merrier fellow. Caught, embarrassed, and paying up, there could be a jest or two in that. But they were his closest friends and he could summon up no more than japes at the expense of his own realization of the bitter irony of it just now, just yet. He felt like a virginal girl who'd turned down dozens of offers of matrimony, money, and carnal delight, all the while waiting for her perfect vision of love—only to find herself raped in an alley, at the cold whim of chance. Eliza was a lovely chit, a charming girl, and a lively friend. But he had not chosen her for his bride.

It was that loss of choice as much as anything that rankled. He'd waited so long to wed—and now, at last, all the choice was taken away from him, and all for a few moments of sprightly play that had grown out of proportion. But, he thought, after all, he'd get used to it. He'd his life ahead to get used to it in. Like a wild bird trapped in the walls that ceases its frantic, futile struggles and eventually closes its wings about itself and settles down quietly at last to die, he'd get used to it. And she was a charming girl, very suitable for him, just as his friends were now saying. Undoubtedly she was. It might have been far worse. She was his friend, after all.

"And so," Warwick asked softly, "you'll really wed at the end of the week?"

"Why not?" Julian asked, pausing bare-chested, with his shirt in his hand. "Why not?" he said on a shrug. And it may have been that he shook himself then, or it could have been that he shuddered. But then, they couldn't be sure, for he didn't have his shirt on and the window was open, after all.

14

THE CEREMONY was simplicity itself, even if nothing else about the wedding was. The special license had been gotten with great effort; neither the bride nor the groom knew the minister because neither of them came from anywhere remotely near the vicarage; the local church was found to be entirely free that Sunday, only at the last minute, when a christening was postponed due to a baby's bout with colic; the guests were assembled with the haste that the wildflowers plucked for decoration throughout the church had been, and they were just as colorful and eccentric to see.

The locals were there in force; it was their church, after all, and besides, it was such an unusual affair that they wouldn't have missed it for anything. There were hordes of children down from Mr. Lyons' great house, and a horde and a half more from his noble guest, the Duke of Peterstow's household. Aside from that astonishingly elegant nobleman and his duchess, the natives had their own nobility, the Viscount North and his lady, in attendance. There was a scattering of strange but exquisite gentlemen, breathless from their hasty arrival from London, their fancy equipages parked outside the church drawing as many stares as their fashionable London get-ups did. Some few gents who were clearly and obviously no less than professional coachmen, from the cut of their coats and boots, amazed and delighted the local young men, almost as much as the attitudes and appearance of the other members of the wedding party did the other members of the congregation.

On the bride's side, her mama could have cut ice with the merest of her smiles, and her papa was so giddy with drink he had to be pointed to his pew so he could doze there throughout the rest of the morning. The bride's former teacher and companion was as wet-eyed through the ceremony as a sensitive young woman ought to be, but the hurt and reproachful looks she gave to the groom now and again gave new meaning to the reason for young females weeping at weddings.

Otherwise, there was a paucity of nonresident female guests. It was whispered that the affair had been put together too quickly for any more of the bride's family or friends to have been able to be there, and so half the congregation was willing to concede. But many didn't note it. They were so busily keeping their eyes and thoughts upon the high waist of the bride's gown, even though the waistline beneath it appeared to be as straight and slender as the rest of the slim young body was, that they scarcely noticed the absence of her retinue. The rest of the congregation was too busy taking in every other aspect of the scrambling affair to concentrate on trying to discover just one possible telltale reason for it.

It was as attractive as it was an interesting wedding, for the bride and groom were as handsome as they could stare. She wore a gown of white, trimmed with roses as deep pink as the color that came and went in her cheeks, her auburn curls added more rich color, her features were fine as her large, frightened eyes were, and in all she was a perfect little cameo of a girl, and none of the gentlemen present blamed the groom in the least for whatever reason had necessitated the hasty ceremony. A great many females present resented it, though. It wasn't often that such a gentleman came along, and for him to appear only to be shown as he was being taken out of circulation was a hard thing to bear. Even though he stood stiff as a poker, he was amazingly good to look upon, his long golden hair, gilded complexion, and the single fob he wore the only contrast to his stark black-and-white finery.

It was all too brief a shining moment, for it went as smoothly and coldly as a slide along an ice bank. The only interruptions—and those, really, only pauses that threatened, most deliciously, to be more—were when the vicar asked for the plighted couple's responses, and again when he asked for objections to the match. For though the groom spoke up clearly and loudly, and his "I do!" rang like the tolling of a great bell, the bride paused and closed her eyes, and swayed until the groom cleared his throat, and looking up at him, not the vicar, she at least managed a squeak that may well have been "I do." At least it was certainly not "I don't," and that was good enough, for the vicar hurried on.

But it was the vicar who caused the second moment of tension, for it was he who spoke the phrase asking the congregation for objections in a most militant manner, staring hard at the bride's mama as he did so. And then he waited at least a year, as all those in the church looked around, listening to their watches tick and their pulses race, until the profound silence satisfied the minister and he concluded the service. No one else knew, of course, that he extended the time precisely because the bride's mother had ordered him to omit that part of the service, and he, as a man of conscience and a certain pride, decided to show the power of the church. But no one answered his call, and so the thing was done.

"Congratulations, and I do mean that, sincerely, Julian, I do," the Duke of Peterstow said when the groom had done with giving his new wife a chaste salute upon her trembling lips. "I could not approve your wife more, I could not wish you better," he added, putting a hand on his friend's shoulder. But then he whispered, "Courage! This is all for the best. You'll see, the best is yet to come," as he bent to kiss the bride's hectically flushed cheek, before he drawled, "Thank you for wedding him, Eliza, you've relieved our minds greatly," for the general world to hear.

"Welcome to our ranks, Benedict," Arden Lyons said as he swallowed up his friend's hand in his and shook it heartily, but it was, "Welcome to our hearts, Eliza, you're the best thing that's ever happened to him," that he spoke low into the bride's ear as he put his lips to her now pallid cheek.

"So that's that!" the bride's mother said when she offered her powdery cheek to her son-in-law, and she said nothing at all to her daughter, but only gave her one bright, triumphant look. And Anthea Baker pressed a dry flutter of a kiss on Julian's high cheekbone, and held Eliza in a brief shivering embrace, but said nothing at all, because it was clear she could not. And then every gentleman present swarmed over to salute the bride, as every female who could walk unaided came to the groom's side to see if she could get him to regret having made his final choice.

The Duchess of Peterstow and Mrs. Lyons rescued Eliza as soon as they saw all the gentlemen present had gotten their chance to offer their felicitations to her. They bore her away with them as their husbands disengaged the groom from his admirers so that the couple could make their triumphal march to the carriage awaiting them outside.

The coach was decked with flowers, it fairly dripped blossoms onto the cobbles, the children had scoured the woods as well as the flowerbeds, and so it seemed that the happy couple entered into the great round cup of one enormous pied bloom on wheels. Even the horses were wreathed in roses, and petals and rice snowed down upon them as they drove away.

"We're only going so far as to Arden's house again," Julian said, breaking the silence after they'd gone out of sight of the church, "for all their carrying on as if we were off to the Antipodes."

When she didn't answer at once he added, "Of course, after breakfast, we'll be off again, this time for good. Or at least for a while. There wasn't time to make plans for a really grand tour, so until I can get Elmwood Court reopened, we'll stay at a country place of Warwicks' north of London—fellow's inherited more houses than titles, and that's saying a lot."

But as she knew this too, she didn't answer.

When the silence stretched on so long that it occurred to them both how odd it was, she spoke even as he did, and then they laughed a little and then he gestured courteously for her to begin and so she said softly, so softly he had to incline his head to hear her, "I'm sorry, Julian, by God, Julian, I am so sorry."

And then she began weeping, and he held her and tried to quiet her by constantly repeating how pleased he was, it was all for the best, really, all the while wishing it were a longer ride to Arden's so that she wouldn't have to descend from the coach red-eyed and catching her breath. When he succeeded in stemming the flow of tears, but realized she still breathed jaggedly and shed the odd, last lingering tear or two despite all his reassurances, he hammered on the coach roof and called something out the window.

He slipped out the door quickly when the coach rolled to a stop, to have a quick word with young Lord Pritchard, of the Four-in-Hand Club, come all the way from London like several other fellows, but come earlier, for he'd the honor of driving the great whip Viscount Hazelton's wedding coach. And so it was that most of the assembled guests at Arden Lyons' house were wondering if the newlywed couple had got it all wrong and eloped after their wedding instead of before. Because it took a half-hour more than necessary for them to finally appear at their own wedding breakfast.

There was champagne, with slices of early peaches and wild strawberries floating in the punch bowl; there were festive meats and sweets and a great variety of cakes, as well. These had been made expressly for the great variety of children who were present on the long lawn where the wedding breakfast had been set out on several tables. The cakes were a great success with the young gentlemen from London too, for the only time they left off their conversations about wheelers and leaders and off sides and bloodlines was when they stepped out of the tight circles they stood in with each other in order to nip over to a table to get another bit of pastry. The professional coachmen joined in with them, although their favorite treats were sipped, instead of eaten dry. The children played as carefully as they were able in their best clothes, the non-sporting gentlemen talked politics or farming, their wives exchanged local news or gossip, and the other guests roved the grassy lawns, dipping into the many several conversations as well as the many dishes set out for their pleasure. It was generally agreed to be a successful wedding party, for all that was generally noted to have been planned and produced with such unseemly speed.

"At least the sun shines on this wedding," Mrs. Merriman said with satisfaction. But her husband was beyond hearing; he was too occupied with the task of standing up, so she trailed away to seek a sympathetic ear, and not being able to discover her hostess or the vulnerable young Duchess of Peterstow, settled for cornering Anthea Baker instead. The girl had no station, and less conversation, but it was just as well. Meeting with her caused Mrs. Merriman to remember that she still paid her wages, after all, and that was a thing she determined would end this very day, in celebration of her daughter's wedding.

The bride was absent; she'd disappeared shortly after taking her ceremonial sips of champagne and bites of wedding cake. She wasn't hiding, or sporting with her new groom, or feeling sick because it was still morning, or doing any of the things various members of the party imagined. She was sitting on her bed, wide-eyed, as her maid finished packing up her things in her dressing room, and her hostess and the Duchess of Peterstow sought to reassure her as to the forthcoming joys of the married state.

"For," Susannah had told her friend that very morning, indignantly, "with that stick of a mother, I don't doubt the poor girl's quaking."

"But," Francesca had answered, doubt shading her already husky voice, "I don't think . . . I can't believe . . . Sukey, my dear, I don't think it's neccesary for us to advise her . . . only think of *why* she's getting married!"

"Precisely!" Susannah insisted. "I know Julian, and he would never do more than dally lightly with her. She's an innocent and a lady. He was just caught . . . at a difficult time."

Francesca looked at her, and then distinctly giggled. "Not so difficult, I hear," she said.

"Wretch," Susannah said, smiling. "But it's so. And so Warwick says too, so you can be sure. It's for the best they were discovered, of course, because she's perfect for him, you know, and she loves him entirely, and he needs that. But still, I think he deserves a bride who's more than willing."

"Ah," Francesca said, smiling, "you think she wasn't eager enough?"

"Whatever she *was*, she's *been* weeping all week, however she tries to hide it. Have you seen her laugh once?" Susannah asked.

There was a moment of absolute silence.

"We'll speak to her before she leaves on her wedding trip," Francesca agreed.

"Gentlemen are pleased with cooperation, it's surprising how many girls believe their husbands want them to be perfect ladies, when most of the time what they're looking for is *imperfect* ones—at least, when they're at more intimate matters," Susannah said now, speaking altogether too gaily and avoiding Eliza's eye as she strolled about the room, ostensibly looking for anything that had not been packed.

This metaphorical conversation between the two married ladies had been going on brightly and ceaselessly since they'd got Eliza to her room and sat her down. Each lady gave her opinion on some suppositional private marital matter, as the other agreed and then added her bit, and the pair of them seemed to be ignoring their listener, so taken were they with their discussion, and altogether acted as naturally as if they'd been on a stage. While all the while the both of them spoke too quickly and their color ran too high.

"Indeed," Francesca said, "agreeableness is not half so good as enthusiasm is in such matters, and a gentleman who is kind and considerate, such as Julian, for example, would never impose where he felt he was imposing . . . and that might be unfortunate, you know."

They were about to go on with more wifely wisdom when they noted Eliza was positively suffused with color, and stopped, wondering whether they'd gone too far, when they heard a squeak, and then a giggle, and then, for the first time in a week, they saw their young friend alight with laughter.

"Oh, my," Eliza said between whoops, for she was enjoying herself very much now, "you are both so good! And k-kind, and . . . Oh, my," she gasped, " 'considerate gentleman . . . like . . . like, Julian.' . . . 'Why, yes, there's a good example,' " she managed to say in a blithe mockery of their too-enthusiastic tones and stilted conversation, before she subsided into laughter again as they, relieved and a trifle embarrassed, relented and joined in with her.

When they'd done, the two older women smiled down at Eliza.

"We thought," Susannah explained, "that you might be concerned about certain marital matters, you see."

"Oh, I do see," Eliza said, chuckling. "That's what was so funny. But not because I'm not concerned . . . for I assure you I don't . . . we haven't . . ." She paused, truly embarrassed, before she hurried on, "Well, you know. You were trying to be kind, and I thank you, and I oughtn't to be laughing at you, but the thing is, you were so determinedly casual, and tried to be so discreet . . . 'like Julian, for example,' indeed." She grinned again. "Oh, it feels so good to laugh, thank you for that!"

Francesca grinned too, but then she added gently, "It's because we wondered, since we've been married forever and we are your friends, and so if details about those matters were bothering you . . . ?"

"Oh, no . . . or, yes," Eliza answered, sobering, her color fading, "that is to say, I suppose they do, in a way, but that's not what bothers me, truly. I love Julian, you know."

The ladies said nothing, and so she continued, now averting her face and tracing a pattern on the quilt she sat upon with one finger as she spoke. She found it was good to speak to them, however difficult it was, for she'd not been able to speak with Anthea all week, not seriously, for Anthea seemed unhappy and unsure of the wisdom of this hasty wedding. And Julian had been as bright and equally as distant as any night star to her since their true engagement, and she was very lonely and troubled and tired of speaking only to herself about her deepest fear.

"It's that I'm not sure he loves me," she said very quietly, "as a wife, that is. He had to marry me, you know. Well, everyone knows that. And I'm a very imperfect lady, because I'm not content with his acceptance, just as you said about a different matter, I want his enthusiasm too, you see."

They did. And for a moment they couldn't speak, for they were neither of them in the habit of lying. They'd both been courted and wed by ardent gentlemen, men who had known what they wanted and had wanted them more than life itself. They were chilled at the thought of any other sort of mating. And they both knew Julian Dylan well, and yet knew where his heart lay no better than his new bride did. And so she was perhaps right in not fearing the bedding that was to come, so much as she did the reason for his wedding her.

But they were kindly women, not so very much older than Eliza was, and they liked her very well. They looked at the tousle-haired girl sitting so dejectedly on the high bed, and they both spoke up immediately, one after the other, sometimes one at the same time as the other. And all their talk was to do with how independent Julian was, how he'd never wed where he really didn't want, and how good and kind and fine he was. All of which she knew, and none of which was to the point, or answered the question in the way she wanted it resolved. But then, they couldn't do that. And as she was a kindly girl too, she acted very pleased and relieved and happy with their efforts. When they'd done, she was smiling, and so were they, although no one of them believed her or felt very merry either, for that matter.

Julian was in the study with his two friends, and they, in their own way, were trying to advise him, although neither of them had fallen on his head lately and so not a word of it was to do with the sort of marital matters their wives were concerned with. Julian could teach courses on that subject, as Warwick had told his wife, and then pleased her very much by loudly lamenting he'd ever told her that, lest she be tempted to discover the truth for herself.

No, they were practical in their own fashion, and Arden had just done with writing another note in order to staff the house that Warwick had just done with penning another note to ensure being ready for the newlyweds. And now they were merrily squabbling over last details.

"Lion, my friend, you've stocked Willow Manor with so many servants that Julian will have to seek out his bride from the crowd each time he wants a word with her. You've sent to Ben for such an assortment of starveling apprentice footmen and housemaids to wait on them, they'll be forced to steal away to the gardens for a private chat," Warwick complained.

"Not likely to find much privacy there either," Arden answered. "I've a score of apprentice gardeners putting the place to rights as well. Shocking how you let it go down, Duke."

"And how should you know?" the elegant duke replied. "You haven't set toe there since your own honeymoon."

"Do you really think it's too many?" Arden said, suddenly serious. "I wouldn't presume. It's only that I know I become too liberal when I think of how many I can set to honest work."

"It's never too many, my friend, not if you emptied half of Seven Dials," Warwick said, equally seriously, before he added, "although how your Bow Bell babes will be able to tell a shrub from a head of lettuce, I do not know. Alas, woe betide my gardens at Willow Manor. They were very lovely, Julian," he said, noting how still his friend was as he stood looking out a window, "for all that Arden's newly hired minions have likely left nothing but rubble behind them in their enthusiasm by now. But it hardly matters—I'd hope you'd have better things to do than study the flowers when you get there, for you've a fairer bloom in your care now than in any of my gardens," he added, not entirely jesting, when Julian didn't answer at once.

Arden and Warwick exchanged quick glances before Arden said bracingly, "True enough. She's the very one for you, Julian. I believe fate walked in my shoes when I stepped into your chamber that day."

"She's beautiful and clever, kind and charming, and entirely an original, what more could a man want?" Warwick asked, watching his old friend closely.

Julian turned from the window where he'd been gazing steadily at nothing, and smiled at his two concerned friends. They were his oldest, truest companions and yet he couldn't find it in his heart to be utterly honest with them because of his new obligations to another friend, his wife, Eliza. And yet, still, he could not bring himself to lie to them either. He wore a gentle smile but his eyes were light and cool as his voice when he answered the only way he could.

"Indeed, you're right. I could not want more. It is only, I think, that I was still looking for it."

There was a tapping at the door before his friends could think to answer, and they were as glad as they were dismayed at that, for they were wise enough to know there was no answer that they, at least, could give him now.

And then they were gladder still, for when Arden went to the door, Eliza was standing there, looking so adorable they believed no man in his right mind wouldn't be pleased to claim her as wife. She was dressed in her traveling clothes, and her gown of mossy green patterned with gold thread brought out and flattered her distinctive coloring. Her auburn hair was such a mass of curls that it was entirely possible that the only way she could wear her new green bonnet was the way she did—on long ribbons and hanging down on her back. It was a school-girl trick that the cut of the gown on her shapely body cleverly contradicted. She was all consternation, but she aroused little concern, for her outsize excitement made her little woeful face all the more charming. Even Julian left off his musings to smile at her as she stood in the doorway looking for him.

"There you are!" she cried. "Oh, do come, Julian. It's Anthea. Mama has given her walking papers! Well, I should have realized that when I wed she'd have no position left, but I never thought on it, I was far too involved with my own problems . . . ah . . . plans. At any rate, Julian, she's so brave, but she's been weeping. Ah, how can we leave her so? Please come, help me convince her that we still need her and have a place for her and she must come with us now."

If the gentlemen all understood Julian's hesitation far better than his bride did, understanding that however charitable, a gentleman would certainly *not* have a place for his wife's former companion on his honeymoon, they kept it to themselves, just as they kept remarkably straight faces as they gazed at Julian. There had been too much seriousness between them of late, and however real poor Miss Baker's plight, this was vastly amusing. They ambled along behind Julian and Eliza as she led him to Anthea Baker, prepared to step in if they must, but appreciating the situation as enormously as Julian clearly did not.

But the sight of Anthea Baker's face banished their good humor. The young woman had clearly been weeping. Although she'd been overlooked in all the excitement and preparation for her charge's wedding, she had been seen to have been strangely subdued—when she'd been seen at all. Now she incited pity in every masculine breast. For while she wasn't one of those fortunate females who looked better for a tear or two, and, in fact, looked very ill indeed, with her nose red, her eyes swollen, and her cheeks blotched where they weren't pale, her usual calm attitude was so overset that the loss of her natural dignity upset those who gazed at her almost as much as it surely hurt her.

She sat in the anteroom in a small gilt chair, with Susannah and Francesca bending to speak with her. When the others arrived, she tried to turn round, and only seemed like some helpless creature caught in a trap—her would-be protectors all looming over her, looking and feeling as if they menaced her.

"Now. Here's Julian, Anthea," Eliza said at once, "and he'll say the same. You must come with us, and stay with us, and wherever we go, there shall be a home for you!"

Eliza stepped back and stood on tiptoe to breathe in

Julian's ear, "For she hasn't any other. And I wonder if the school can take her back just now—the term's letting out, you know, and she hasn't made any other provision, we did everything so quickly, you see."

As she heard Susannah and Francesca repeat their offers of positions in their own households—as governess, teacher, as companion, or whatever she was pleased to take—Eliza whispered more fiercely, "They're kind, but they're offering charity, Anthea says. And she's right. It is *our* responsibility now, isn't it?"

Eliza's eyes were bright with sympathetic tears. She was pleading with him and wore a look of desperate helplessness such as Julian had never seen in her before, not even when she'd begged him not to acquiesce to her mother's demands, not even when she'd spoken of how she'd planned to escape marrying Hugh. He lifted a hand to her cheek and smiled down at her, very proud of her, almost as proud as he was uneasy with what he knew he must do.

For all he liked Anthea very well, and less than a week before had even seriously been considering her as a candidate for the position Eliza now filled, he was loath to have her live with them now. That was, he thought, before he spoke, as he eyed Anthea, perhaps precisely why he was unwilling to offer her his home, that, and the fact that her presence would be a constant reminder to him of options that he'd had to close out. He didn't think he'd desire her, because she'd never appealed to anything but his intellect, and that, married or not, they could always share without a grain of bad conscience, after all. No, he didn't think she'd tempt him to anything but brooding over the foolishness of the ignominious way he'd finally been captured.

But Eliza was entirely right, he felt responsible for Anthea as well. More than anything else, if it meant so much to Eliza, he could do no less than earnestly entreat her former companion to come to live with them.

"Anthea," he said, going down on one knee before her and trying to get her to look at him, "Eliza wants you to come with us, and so do I. There's no need to be missish about it," he said gently. "The way of the world is that some of us are given more at the start than others, deservedly or not. Then, it's our obligation to share, More, it's our pleasure to share with friends. So, come, my friend, my house in West Sussex, Elmwood Court, has more rooms than a beehive, you won't have to look at us for days on end if you don't wish to. And I've several lively bachelor neighbors," he invented, thinking it might well be true, "and so before long, we'll likely get you popped off in far grander fashion than we ourselves were wed."

She peeped out from beneath her handkerchief. But seeing him in all his handsomeness before her, on one knee, as though he were able and about to offer her something far more than temporary haven, and hearing the word "wed," reminded her of all that she could never have now. All that she had lost when Eliza's mama had found him with Eliza, in that one hour when she'd not thought to keep an eye on the girl. She wept anew and could only hastily improvise a reason for it.

"I cannot take charity, no indeed, there's no reason for it. I can work as a schoolmistress or companion again, and so I should."

"And so you will, if you wish," he said decisively, getting to his feet. He'd heard her agreement in her voice before she knew it was in her mind; there was still some advantage to being as expert as he was in matters of female susceptibility, he thought, as he added, "*When* you wish. In the meanwhile, allow us to give you shelter and friendship."

"I cannot come along with you now!" she gasped.

"You can if you wish," he laughed, never thinking she'd accept. "Warwick tells me he has a room for every day in the week of a leap year in Willow Manor. But I'd think you might prefer to stay on here for the meanwhile, as Francesca asks, or go along with Susannah to London for the coronation as she invites you to do, until we meet you there—or until we settle in at Elmwood Court in a few weeks."

She took a deep breath, and after one sniff that seemed to surprise her, she announced with resolve, "I'll go back to the school, I think," and as Julian stared at her with astonishment, she added, "to collect up all my things before I join you. I'll wait upon your summons there, thank you."

"Your welcome is assured," he said, bowing, and rose to be rewarded with a smile such as he'd not seen on Eliza's face since she'd been the little girl she'd been when he'd first met her.

The wedding coach went off down the twisting gravel drive that led from Arden's house as day itself began to wane. It was true the happy couple had been set to leave much earlier, it was truer still that they'd wanted to do so. But there were so many well-wishers, and so many of them children who didn't know the niceties of letting newlyweds escape when they tried to sneak away, that they'd been delayed until the afternoon shadows had begun to grow.

There was no coachman except for the newlywed groom, high upon the driver's seat, and not a one of his fellow coaching enthusiasts, waving good-bye to him, questioned his decision in driving himself to his new life in the least. But then, they'd never noted the beautiful bride who sat on his left half so jealously as they watched the way he threaded the several reins through his left hand, nor desired any woman, for that matter, the way they lusted for the expertise he showed with the whip he held so lightly in his right. And they could scarcely contain their envy of the trim new traveling chariot he'd just acquired, or the splendid horseflesh his friends had lent to him, as he hadn't had time to set up his own stables as yet. But it was a curious way for gentlepersons to travel, wedding flight or not.

For they'd travel unattended; valet and maid wouldn't meet the newlywed pair until after they'd settled in at Willow Manor. The two days they'd take to arrive there would be passed on the road, and the three nights would be taken alone, at inns on that road. Still, few men knew the road like this bridegroom, and so no gentleman questioned his startling decision to face the rigors of travel alone. And as few females would mind passing the time with him anywhere he chose, so no woman guest doubted the wisdom of his bride's approval of his daring scheme.

But some wondered about other things they faced. For even as they saw the bridal carriage disappear down the long avenue, Francesca and Susannah hoped Julian would dispel all the doubts his young wife entertained, even as their husbands prayed he would vanquish his own.

It was the road itself Julian worried about those first hours. He knew they'd started out late, and he'd booked accommodations at a neat little inn miles away, and preferred to stay in a clean, comfortable place where fresh horses awaited him, to taking his chances with just any room at any chance-found inn as night fell. He wanted to push his horses to more speed than he usually did, but feared Eliza's reaction to a punishing pace. Riding on the high hard driver's seat was taxing, riding at a furious clip of more than ten miles an hour on these country roads was as difficult for a passenger as it was for the horses. He needn't have worried; she agreed at once. And when he picked up the whip to urge the teams onward, her face shone with purest pleasure at her decision not to ride in the coach as she felt the wind in her face and watched the hedgerows fly by, becoming a single blurred green line, from her high viewpoint on the rocking seat next to him. She'd not the slightest doubt of his abilities; such things as broken axles, lamed leaders, and overturned coaches were merely fantastical myths to her with her Julian at the reins.

So they galloped against the setting sun until he felt he'd made up for enough lost time, and then they took a merely decent swift pace toward their goal. The best part was, of course, that with all the speed they were pushing for, and the concentration required to achieve it, conversation was quite impossible.

As a late, lingering light glowed over the top of the inn they'd aimed for, Julian looked down to the last rays of the sun caught in his wife's fiery curls as they lay against his shoulder, and thought that perhaps it might work, after all. Perhaps this lingering feeling of unease that made conversation with his dear little friend so uncomfortable would someday end.

Someday, he thought as he washed in the basin in the small alcove next to the bedchamber he'd booked. Sooner than that, he began to believe, when he sat opposite his new wife and raised a toast to her future happiness as they dined. Someday very soon, indeed, he decided on a smile as he watched her stifle a yawn as night fell deep upon the countryside surrounding them.

But not tonight.

And so he told her when they'd reached their room again and he'd gone in after her and shut the door, and turned around to see her standing, wavering with tiredness, but watching him with a look of trepidation, of wariness, despite her tentative wavering smile. He caught her up in his arms, and held her close, and she leaned against him, rejoicing. For this was Julian, her Julian, and if she raised her head from where she buried it near to his actual steadily beating heart, she'd see that wonderful face as clearly as she felt the security of his arms, and the comfort and excitement of his long, strong form next to her. What she'd dreamed of for what seemed to have been the whole of her life had come true. She was come home. Julian, her bright, beautiful friend Julian, was her husband, and was soon to become her lover.

However it had come about, it would be well, she could believe that now that she was wrapped close in his arms. The touch of his lips and hands had brought her to this moment by too many embarrassing means to think of now, but the memory of that touch had upheld her, it had enabled her to live through the past ghastly, humiliating week. But she'd know more of that wondrous touch now and she'd certainly earned the right to such joy, she thought, if embarrassment were the coin necessary to pay for it.

At any rate, it was done, he was her husband now. She'd bend every effort to ensure he never cursed the day he'd toyed with her; she'd mend all. Because she loved him.

He bent his head and whispered to her, although there was no one else near to hear, but she didn't want him to stop, because it sent delicious shivers along her ear.

"Yes," he said, and there was a smile in his even tenor

tones, "I know, you are exhausted, and who can blame you? I wonder, did you sleep at all this week? I doubt it, Eliza, and I'm expert on you, for as I remember, you were never able to sleep before exams, or parties, or any greatly anticipated event. I doubt you closed an eye an hour in the week before this scrambling wedding we just enacted. Don't worry, love, there's no reason not to sleep tonight."

She rested her head against his chest, staying very still, hoping he never meant that. She wondered just how she could tell him that she'd hoped she'd not sleep much this night either, and feared that for all her sharing of all her thoughts with him for so many years, she could not. But she never had to. For:

"No," he said, his voice vibrating as she heard it from where it began near to his heart, his scent making her both easy and dizzy with longing. "Too soon. It's a delightful thing, this thing I'll show you how to do, Eliza. A whole new palette, an entirely new spectrum. Don't frown so," he said, stepping back and holding her away and peering down into her face. "I promise you, it's great fun."

"Fun?" she asked, wondering what it was he was proposing to teach her, relieved. She must have misunderstood after all; she must be as tired as he'd thought. He was talking about showing her how to drive a carriage and here she thought he was speaking of lovemaking and the reasons why they could not this night. Of course it was too late to drive a carriage. She relaxed and grinned up at him.

"It really is quite wonderful," he said, touching the tip of her nose, grinning back at her. "You'll see. You never imagined the whole, I'll wager, for it's nothing short of miraculous. Delicious, to taste and kiss and touch and give such pleasure to each other. I'll teach you. But not tonight," he said as she stiffened in his arms, at first shocked at the unexpected freedom of his words, nervous of what he meant to do, and then more astonished by what he meant not to do, before, at the last, she was surprised at how quickly he released her and stepped away.

"Because it's far too important to begin with weariness as a third bedfellow," he said, wagging a finger at her, "and we've all of our lives and the world ahead of us. All things in their time, and this is definitely not the time, poor weary little wife. Now, you may wash and clamber into bed with me, and never fear, you may use me as a pillow, but rest easy, I'll not use you in any way tonight."

She was tired, and confused, and had no idea of what else to do in any case, so she obeyed. She went into the little alcove and washed and struggled into a cotton night-dress, so long and long-sleeved that in the lamplight when she emerged from the alcove, it was as if she were a small girl parading in her papa's nightshirt. Or so he said as he kissed her lightly, and lifted her easily to the high mattress, and made sure the coverlets were tucked around her completely before he climbed into bed. To then lie beside her, in his shirtsleeves, wide-awake through a great part of the night.

For he had seen the way the white fabric drifted against her body and knew very well she wasn't a child. And from the way he could not hear her breathing at all, he suspected she was as alert and awake as he was. But she was never, he thought, as confused as he was now.

Because now that it was done and he'd done what a gentleman and a friend ought, he could scarcely believe it was done. After all his travels and turmoil, to end up here, married, even to such a sweet girl, after only one misstep? "Anticlimax" was scarcely the word for it. He was numbed with disbelief at the immensity of the thought and where it led him.

She was his wife but he didn't dare turn to her, lest he take her as his wife. Because for all he thought he would find pleasure in it, he dreaded it. Not because she wasn't lovely, or because he didn't remember, all too well, precisely how pleasurable such things could be, even at their beginnings, with Eliza. But because the act of mak-ing her his wife would seal their bargain forever, and would set incredible things into motion—perhaps even the begetting of his own child, thus ending his own youth, and more, forever.

He knew that by completing this marriage, by consciously and deliberately unstoppering his wife's virginity, he'd let out a thousand things he'd never known before, and at the same time close the door forever on his guiltless, total freedom, and take away his every last option. So long as he did not consummate this union, he was still, however tentatively, in however illusionary a way, free.

He'd played the kind, considerate, and loving husband tonight. She was an innocent, she was exhausted, likely apprehensive, and they did have another long drive ahead of them tomorrow. For reasons of pleasure or prudence, it really wouldn't have been the best time to make love for her. But with all his consideration, he didn't care for himself at all for it, and yet it seemed he couldn't help himself either. There were only two things he knew that could shrivel his desire: scorn and fear. He felt the one for himself, and the other, even as he closed his eyes at last and welcomed sleep, curiously enough, for her.

And she, lying so close to her new husband she could reach out and touch him if she dared, learned something entirely new, just as he'd promised, but on this, her wedding night. And that was that she could weep, entirely soundlessly, in such deep places that it was without tears.

15

SOMEHOW, THEY'D GOT THROUGH two full days on the road and three long nights at inns alone in each other's company. And so it was that the Viscount Hazelton and his newlywed viscountess saw Willow Manor at last as those drowning might see a spit of land, as thirsty travelers might see an oasis. They'd ridden hard and slept little and spoken less since their wedding day, and since they were both convivial spirits, used to laughter and chatter, their unusual silence was felt as a keen deprivation to them both. And now too, they felt, both of them, as though they were being dragged forward and further on some strong tide of inexorable fate.

Their silence had bred silence. In just the same way that an unanswered letter becomes more difficult to reply to as the weeks fly by, so it had become harder for them to speak after the first awkward lull that ought to have been filled by a jest, and explained away with laughter. If the groom did not kiss the bride, neither did the bride any longer bend stolen glances at his lips. He was excessively jovial and avuncular with her. She was suddenly reserved and polite with him. He'd not touched her more than to help her in and out of his carriage since the moment that the vicar had joined them in matrimony, and though they'd driven down various new paths since then, she'd thought of little else but that since. Now their honeymoon retreat lay shining in the sunlight before them, and as it could be clearly seen to have spacious grounds and room enough to spare for a stagecoach full of newlyweds, as well as their well-wishers, they both grew easier in their minds. It was difficult to dissemble when one had to live in another's pocket. With this much space, they could indulge freely in their own thoughts and fears. Newlyweds who now valued their privacy more than penitent monks might, they both sighed when their coach finally drew to a halt.

"I'll wash," the groom announced after the housekeeper had introduced herself and invited her temporary master and mistress to sit and have a bite of something after their long journey.

"Yes, a very good idea," his new wife agreed, and they went up the stairs to their bedchambers side by side in the housekeeper's wake, in sudden concert, both enormously relieved. It was much better when there was another person present to bounce conversations off.

But their relief was short-lived. They'd forgotten that their absent host had an oddly unfashionable romantic turn of mind beneath all his worldly air of boredom. Because it transpired, to their deep shock, that he'd assigned only one chamber to the two of them instead of the usual—the requisite two adjoining bedchambers that most couples in the *ton* shared their marital bliss within. There was an enormous dressing room, and a very modern indoor privy as well. But there was only one chamber, and only one enormous bed that seemed to dominate the room and their thoughts.

It was one thing to share a bed on their travels; they'd both been exhausted each night and there had been that polite fiction of the next day's travels to excuse them from more than slumber. Now, either because their host had realized from his own experiences, as well as those of his friend Arden, to whom he'd lent this treaclemoon haven once before, that those in love found commuting between chambers a nightly bore, or because of his keen sense of humor, or even, Julian thought darkly, because of his penchant for meddling, they'd only the one room, only the one bed. If it was a comfort to have others about them to save them from themselves, it would be equally as much an embarrassment to have others know of their pristine wedded state. He couldn't request a separate room, and knew Eliza would not. And so it would do, if only because it would have to do.

"Delightful room," Julian said, with great enthusiasm. "See here, Eliza, it overlooks gardens."

"So it does," she said, stripping off her gloves.

After one anxious look toward the great feather bed, she shrank into a wing chair in such an uneasy fashion as to make Julian realize that he'd never known such chairs had corners before.

"I'll just wash up, then," he said, leaving her to whatever thoughts she wrestled with, wishing that he'd a valet to chat with, if not to help him dress, before he realized he was very glad he'd not brought the fellow along to see this charade of a wedding trip.

As water struck his face, he opened his eyes to look into his cupped hands and resolved then that he was done with charades, he would end this foolishness, for the splash of cool water had wakened him to reality. And the reality was that he was wed, and that was all there was to it, and, as Arden had once said about funerals: if it were done it would be best that it were entirely done—before he and his wife were unable to so much as comment on the weather, their favorite topic these last days, ever again. He dried his face and came out of the dressing room smiling, newly conversant, entirely glib, for now he'd a role he knew how to play.

"I've left you half a pitcher, now please bestir yourself, dormouse," he said merrily, "because I got a sniff of something with cinnamon when we got here, and I'm on fire to find out what it is."

She looked up at him at that, startled, for he sounded very like he'd done before all this coil they'd got themselves into. She rose quickly and agreed that it was cinnamon, and newly buoyed by newborn hope, as eagerly as a puppy called to heel after it has been left alone for hours, she laughed, professed her passion for ginger as well as cinnamon, and went to wash so she could return to him before his mood changed again.

She'd only the time to run her hands through her curls after she'd washed the dust from her face, but the glance she got of herself in the mirror satisfied her. The fleeting bits of sun that had got in under her bonnet had left her cheeks with soft tints of pink, and her hair, so carelessly fingered by the wind as well as herself, looked as though she'd passed hours to get it into such artful disarray. So she, too, was smiling when she came back into the room.

He walked down the stairs with her, and actually took her arm under his, and seated her at the table where their tea was laid out. Then he immediately exclaimed over the little cinnamon buns and spoke to her reminiscently about how the smell and taste of them reminded him of Christmas, and then of the islands, and then of how odd it had been to pass a Christmas in the tropics—now full of conversation as he had not been in all the past days.

She rejoiced, and laughed, and gobbled up the little cakes as though they were manna, though the sound of his voice was sweeter than any of them to her. Then he took her arm and led her on a stroll down winding garden paths, commenting on flowers with as much cleverness as he whispered to her about Arden's newly recruited gardeners, who were laboring over unfamiliar green things with as much seriousness as monks at matins, and never looking like the youngsters they were. He had her laughing so merrily she lost her bonnet, as he murmured the conversations he imagined the boys were having together as they worked—uprooting orchids as onions, and tenderly replanting thistles—inventing their imagined absurd horticultural comments in London slum accents with uncanny aptitude. Then she made him laugh, in turn, with her impressions of what the injured plants themselves might be thinking.

She was having such a great good time she wondered why she was still so uneasy. And it wasn't until they sat on a stone bench by a small ornamental fountain, alone except for some guardian statues, that she understood that her instincts were sharper than her ears. For as he entertained her, she sat and watched him, only now she could see that never once did he actually look at her. He was as bright as the sunlight that scattered a prism of colors from the dancing waters before them, but there was nothing but brightness behind his eyes, and nothing of the warmth of the sun or of love in his voice or his face.

The twilight came soon, but the evening lingered in the shadows at the edges of the lawns, for the days had uneven lengths now, with night as reluctant to come as the Viscount and Viscountess Hazelton were to see it. It was high summer, but even so the days were seldom so consistently fair and warm as this one had been. It might well have been that no one welcomed the ending of such a fine day, for all it was unlikely that many newly wedded young persons regretted the coming night as much as the handsome pair that sat in the gardens did.

No one would ever have guessed it.

For the gardeners, young and old, smiled at the sight of the pair of them, so handsome as they were, so well-matched as they appeared to be. Golden head and sunset one were close together, and their laughter tumbled and lilted like any late birdsong, as they moved at length, with grace and ease, back to the manor house down the narrow chalky garden lanes together.

But they spoke of things as inconsequential and light as birdsong, and they laughed for the sheer sound of it, both thinking they were convincing the other of the rightness of what both of them felt was so wrong.

She dressed for dinner in the idle hour alone that he subtly gave to her, on the excuse that he'd letters to write to be sure his own home was being set up for their arrival. She washed and redressed and stroked a comb through her silky curls, and then as she bent into knots trying to do up the back of her favorite gown, she thought that she'd always dreamed that her husband would do this for her on these, their first nights together. That it would be his long, capable hands on her buttons, doing them up regretfully, long after having seen and enjoyed what he was reluctantly enrobing again. And that imaginary husband had always been Julian. Her Julian. Not this slate-eyed, coldly handsome, affable gentleman that was so clearly making the best of a bad bargain. As she would too, she vowed, for it might be that something could come from all their efforts, if he cared enough to swallow his disappointment at what he'd been forced into and enacted the loving husband, she'd never stop him. But then, she thought, sighing, she could never stop him,

could she? Wasn't that how they'd gotten into this
situation?

Yet it might be, she thought as she rose from her
dressing table to go belowstairs so that he could come up
to their room on the excuse of having done with his
paperwork, it could be that his distance was no more
than a passing cloud, and that as the hours drew on, his
coldness would draw off and she would have, at last, the
only gentleman she ever loved, her Julian, with her again.
And if it were not to be so, then she decided it were
better that she pretend it was. She didn't believe that
would be difficult, if only he would look at her again.

He did, when they met in the small dining room for
dinner. And poured himself another glass of wine, and
saluted her, and thought, as he eyed her charming sprigged-
muslin frock, that he would have no difficulties this
night, no matter what the lowering mood he tried to
overcome. Because she was a delightful-looking little
creature, and if she were only as willing as she was
well-looking, he would be well-served. Harriet Wilson
herself was just such a tiny wench, he thought as he
recommended the roast beef and helped her to a slice;
that infamous courtesan had just such a tumble of auburn
curls and just such high full breasts. Although, he mused,
remembering, from what he'd seen from across many a
room—for he'd never cared to purchase what he could
receive as a gift, and even when offered just that, had
decided to take a road less traveled—his new wife had a
longer neck and a trimmer, more graceful figure, certainly a more lissome waist and neater derriere. And her
face, of course, her face was nothing to compare. Eliza
was a lovely sprite; Harriet had a reputation far more
exciting than her countenance—no, it was nonsense, there
was no comparison between those two faces, but then, he
was not in the mood for gazing at faces tonight. He'd a
certain task before him, after all.

After dinner they played at cards. She played the
spinet and he sang. They passed the hours laughing and
never listening to one another and he drank wine after,
as well as before and with, his dinner, but he'd a hard
head and felt nothing more than more eagerness for his

task for it, which was the reason he drank with such dedication. He made sure she had a sip or two too, and then they played at card tricks so as not to have to concentrate on numbers and suits. And after a time it was borne in on them that they neither of them could hold back time, and the night was full upon them when they realized that they must either sit up through the night or go to bed.

When they entered their room, he said nothing to her. There was nothing to say, after all, or at least nothing he could think to say that would speak louder than his embrace. He took her in his arms as soon as she turned round to see what he meant to do, and he kissed her with all the art and determination he possessed. And as he was a man of vast experience, she could think of nothing to say then either, but only lay back in his arms, looking at him, wondering how to go on now that he had begun.

She scarcely had time to worry, for if she did not, he knew very well what he'd set into motion. The moonlight was bright, and it made the room light as twilight, so he had no need of pausing to light candles, and he was grateful for it, since he knew that leaving her now would leave her time to wonder, and yet it was essential to him now that he see what he was about.

Each time a man made love, he thought, it was different, different as each woman he came to was, varied as each mood that set him to it was, because lust, he'd discovered, was no one simple thing. At least it was never so for him. This night he was compelled by reason as well as need, and so had to concentrate on what he did, and so the shape and look of what he touched was meaningful. For if he could not meet her eyes, and would not permit himself to think, then he had to see what it was that inspired him. But she had, he began to see, as lovely a body as he'd imagined, and he relaxed as he uncovered it, relieved, for the pink-and-white and budding amplitude he found would be inspiration enough for any man.

His kiss was warm and overwhelmingly sweet, his touch just as she remembered it to be, and as he lifted her to carry her to the high bed, Eliza felt gratitude and happi-

ness and a relief almost as overwhelming as the touch of
his lips, because he wanted her, because she pleased him.
They said nothing, but then, her emotions would not
permit it even if she could think of what to say, and she
only sighed as he eased her gown off, as those hands she
had wished for undid her buttons and encompassed her.
The feel of his hands and lips upon her breast was more
than she remembered, for it was entirely right now, it
was part of their union, and there was no reason for her
to do more than to rejoice and learn from him as she
gave herself to him. But she was, after all, for all her
love, an innocent, as unused to such desire as much as
she was to giving in to it. And there was, unfortunately,
a great deal of light in the room.

He had found her breasts to be as responsive as her
lips and had done with thinking. Her scent, her skin, her
generously curving figure had all carried him beyond the
need for anything but need, just as he'd hoped. In the
half-light, she opened her eyes on a gasp at a new touch
and saw his face as he bent to her, saw that there was
nothing there but concentration, nothing in those light
eyes but desire. For all that his touch was gentle and
sure, it was what she didn't see in his eyes that dismayed
her.

For it was as though she were baring her body to a
beautiful ardent stranger as his gaze and his hands roved
over her. And when he exposed her entirely, he stripped
away his cravat and shirt, all the while attending to her
with hands and mouth, as he started to undo his pantaloons and wriggle out of them. What she could see of his
body was strong and perfectly shaped; even unclothed,
he was not naked, any more than any statue in the
gardens had appeared to be, for he was clad in smooth
skin and splendid muscle. Yet unlike any statue, his
muscular form was lightly covered with a soft golden
down, and was warm—warm as the breath she felt at her
ribs, then her waist, and then for all her desire she was
suddenly timid with him, or whatever he'd become.

He was as intense as he was skilled, and spared her not
so much as a word as he proceeded, becoming suddenly
like some powerful machine set to its especial task, all

movement and momentum and deliberate action. She felt the ends of his soft overlong hair brush across her skin even as his mouth did, and looking down, saw his head, flaxen in the moonlight, and as he raised it, still saw nothing still but moonlight and determination shining in his half-closed eyes before he bent to her again.

It had all come about so rapidly, she wanted, needed, for all her matching desire, a word of love, a word of care. So she called his name to call him back to her, as though somehow, even inexperienced as she was, and close as he seemed to be, she knew he was too far gone from her now.

"Julian," she said.

"Yes, yes," he murmured, busy at her body, sure and deft and involved now, understanding she wanted something, unwilling to give more than he was, unable to look at her, "just stay still, love, do. This is very nice, isn't it?"

"Julian," she said then, half-knowing what she said, "look at me, please."

"Hush now," he muttered absently, but with an edge of anger to his tone, annoyed at the voice trying to distract him, though his hands remained gentle, as, fascinated, his gaze remained where his lips had closed over the puckering tip of a breast he'd breathed into life with his whisper.

"Julian," she pleaded, trying to get his attention to her face by her words, because all the passion she'd felt was being replaced with a new terror. There was nothing of love in this; this was getting beyond her. And yet she couldn't stop him—this was her husband; more than that, this was her Julian.

His hands had found a new delight, his lips a newer pleasure; this body he occupied himself with was sweetly scented and beyond lovely. He found his excitement growing even as slow caution fled, and if he hadn't felt the satin skin beneath him quiver with more than shock and less than ecstasy, and the pliant planes he was stroking becoming rigid as stone, he would certainly have continued, for he was very close to attaining what he'd sought, very near to ending what he'd begun.

But he was a man who valued females. He was a man who always required cooperation, even in his extremity. For all he'd been involved, he'd never been swept away. And so for all he'd deliberately deceived himself and locked out everything but his sense of touch and taste, he'd heard the panic in her voice, felt more than her shivers of fear. He knew, even as he rolled away from her to catch his breath and open his eyes to look at her at last, to his dismay, he knew exactly what he'd done, not done, and been about to do.

Odd, he thought as he reached for her again, this time to take her shaking body into his arms and hold her as chastely close as he would a child, his hands only upon her back, his lips only on her hair, odd how quickly the warmth of her body had faded, how his own heated desire had fled—her passion gone because she'd discovered what he'd been at, his because he'd allowed himself to see what it had done to her.

He'd tried to make love without love, and he'd fooled no one, least of all himself. He'd attempted Eliza as though she'd been a woman of pleasure, forgetting her innocence. And yet even that might have brought her pleasure, for he was adept, and never cruel. It was his denial of who she was that had frightened her, as much as it shamed him now. But now he accepted who she was. And so as he held her and murmured incoherent apologies to her, he began to feel his first true desire of the night, and it was so profound as to terrify him. Which was perhaps, he began to understand, why he'd deceived himself before.

"No, no," he said as she mumbled something about being sorry for being so foolish, as she begged him to continue and disregard her missishness, "let's forget that, you were right, Eliza, that was never a way to start out a life together, was it? It can be different, it ought to be different. I had too much wine, you were too lovely, what nonsense wedding nights are—and this is, in a way, our wedding night, you know."

"A fine wife I am," she cried, sitting up and putting her hands to her face, "forced upon you, and then cold as ice in your bed. Oh, Julian, I'm so sorry."

"A fine husband I am," he said, trying to take her back into his arms, "forgetting everything I know, everything you are, everything we are. This bedwork is very good stuff, Eliza, I know no better sport, actually. But it shouldn't be sport with us, should it? It should be part of our love."

She sat up very straight, and gazed at him, the events of the night, the worries of the last days, her disappointment in him and confusion with herself giving her courage to say what she'd meant to for weeks.

"But, Julian," she asked softly, deliberately, "is it love with us?"

There were a dozen easy conciliatory answers he could have given her; he was no fool, and it wasn't only his brilliant good looks which had lured women to his bed. But he'd done with giving her false coin and wanted this answer to be entirely true. He needed time to think of the perfect reply for her, as well as for himself. He dropped his arms, and sat back and sighed.

"A fine time," he said, "to ask that of a man, when he's sitting naked in bed beside you."

He laughed, to buy time, and because he thought, wryly, it was true.

She waited.

"We have a care for each other, Eliza," he said slowly. "I know no other woman I care for more," he continued, groping for truth. "No one, no power on earth would have made me wed you if I hadn't wanted to do so," he added, as though by heaping truth on truth he would arrive at some ultimate truth. "We can have more than we have now if we have time, and so I do believe," he said at last.

She understood.

"There *is* such a thing as divorce," she said softly.

"No," he said with finality, knowing, if she did not, society's penalty for that, and how it would mark her forever, loath to so much as discuss it, for reasons he'd not the time to think of now.

"But what if you find someone you love more?" she began.

"Or if you do?" he asked, and she fell silent, knowing

she never could, before he added, "I do not think it likely."

She was still very near to him, too near now to think of something right, or insightful, or at least clever, to say. And so she rose up, so perturbed that she forgot she was naked, and stepped down from the bed as he watched her warily. She walked to the window to look out into the darkness, and only realized her condition when a breeze from the half-open casement, a wisp of the soft warm summer-night air, caressed her skin as lightly as his breath had just so lately done. Then she dropped her hands to cover herself in classic confusion, and seeing from his growing smile how inadequate her hands were to the task, she, red-faced, wound a corner length of the billowing curtain around herself. And he laughed. And she did, and it might have been that she could have, indeed, had something healing to say, if she hadn't heard the sounds from beneath the window and looked out upon the unexpected, almost phantasmagorical arrival in the darkened drive below of a midnight coach and four.

"Visitors? Now?" she asked him, for he'd come bounding to the window at the sounds of a coach pulling up, the familiar sounds of hooves and wheels and jingling traces that he heard sometimes even in his dreams.

"It seems so," he answered, hastily pulling his clothing on again. "If it's not news of a tragedy that interrupts us tonight," he managed as he hopped on one foot, dragging a half-boot on, "the messenger will find it a tragedy, I promise you."

But at her worried look he stopped and cupped her chin in his hand and laughed lightly.

"Don't fret," he whispered. "Our friends have odd senses of humor, you know. And it isn't our house—who knows who regularly comes here in the night?" he said, although he knew no one with so vulgar a sense of humor, and no one with decency who'd visit anyone's home in the deep of night without good and urgent cause.

But her eyes searched his and her face had grown very white; he could see that it was blanched even in the moonlight. Although she had few people to love, all those she loved were far from her, and a midnight messenger rarely brought glad news.

He finished buttoning his shirt, and as he tucked it into the tops of his pantaloons, he thought of an excellent way to distract her.

"Eliza, love," he said sweetly as he combed his fingers through his hair, "I do like that drapery you've got on, very original indeed. But as you've dragged it across yourself to shield your lovely front from my lecherous gaze, and there's a grand full moon tonight, and your beautiful back is to the window, I imagine the coachman downstairs, lucky fellow, likes it even more than I do now."

And leaving her blushing instead of worrying as she scurried, bent double, away from the window, he chuckled and went from the room. But there was nothing but concern in his face as he took the stairs by twos and hurried through the darkened house to the grand front hall.

She stood in the hall, confronting the footmen and the butler, all in various stages of undress, all as confused and rumpled with hastily abandoned sleep as she was.

"Anthea?" he asked, disbelieving.

She looked at him with gladness, and then looked away with what seemed to be instant regret.

"My God," he said, coming toward her swiftly and taking her two cold gloved hands in his, "what's toward? What's amiss? Is it Francesca?" he asked with sudden dread, a dozen fragmentary thoughts of what could have befallen a lady who was with child occurring to him, and even more of what agonies his friend Arden would undergo if anything untoward ever happened to his dear Fancy.

"Oh, no . . . oh, no!" she said, gazing at him with equal horror as the force of his words took on meaning. "Or at least, no, nothing I've heard of. She was fine when I left her. But you see," she said, averting her eyes, which were, he noted, reddened with more than lost sleep, "I left her and the house the same day that you did. I went to the school, as I said I'd do, to collect up my things and wait for your summons, but . . ." She hesitated and then spoke her words in a rush. "The school was closed, all save for the caretakers, and I couldn't stay on, at least they weren't ready for me, and had no instructions to let me stay on, and I couldn't go back to the Lyonses, they don't know me, after all. After all, I am just a servant of a friend of a friend of theirs, really. And neither could I go to the duke for that reason, and he was likely already off to London for the coronation, and so I came to the only place I knew. To you," she finished in low tones, her voice breaking at the last.

His relief at hearing all his friends were well was so great that he stood silent for a moment. And if in the next, the gaps in her narrative occurred to him, for she was more than a friend to a friend, she had been bidden welcome at Arden's as well as Warwick's house, his vexation with finding her here on his doorstep this night overrode all else. For this night he'd planned to make Eliza his wife in truth, and had badly botched the matter with his untruths, and he'd planned to mend matters before the sun rose again. Anthea's unexpected visit overset that plan completely.

As a man who knew the ways of love as well as he loved them, he knew that the act he meant to begin tonight was only that—a beginning. The major and better part of it would have had to come in the next languorous mornings, and through soft whispers and touches and courtesies in the long afternoons and tender evenings to come, that would end in even more delicious following nights. It required time as well as privacy to make a well-brought-up young woman into a lover. Eliza would need all his attention, and only his attentions, until the thing made sense to her, until her senses could be filled with him and only him and the rightness of the new delights he meant to bring to her. There was no room for friends on a honeymoon.

But the fact was that Anthea was a friend, and if he understood in some fashion that she still hoped for more, he tried to forget that as well as his disappointment with her unannounced arrival. Because she was not only a friend, she was an unprotected female, entirely alone in the world. He was a gentleman first, and so a frustrated lover only second.

"Come, come in. You're welcome here, Anthea, I'll have a room made ready for you. Can we have a room made up for Miss Baker at once, dear Mrs. Wycombe?" he asked the housekeeper, who'd appeared, on a gleaming smile that made her wish to prepare a dozen rooms for him, at least twice.

After the dazzled housekeeper's immediate acquiescence, he turned to Anthea again.

"Have a bite to eat while you wait," he urged her, "and a sip of something to take the dampness from the night," he advised as he led her to a small salon that was hastily lit for them. But then, after he'd seated her, he left her in a different darkness, as he said, gently but decisively, "I'd join you, but Eliza waits for me. You do understand. But we'll both see you in the morning. Sleep well."

He wouldn't sleep well, he thought glumly as he went up the stairs to report to his wife. For he wouldn't begin something he couldn't finish correctly, and this matter between himself and Eliza was far too important to be done in harum-scarum fashion. He'd a great many fences to mend with his new wife. And if he could, and did, and then acted upon it as he wished, and as he'd need to do, he'd not have Eliza embarrassed in the morning, wondering if Anthea could see her new experience or emotions upon her face, as he'd heard new-made wives and newly unmade maids so often feared was the case. No, nor would be then subject her to the problem of making excuses for their times spent alone, or feeling as though she'd have to sneak away in order to make time to lie with him.

Still, he solaced himself by reasoning there'd be time enough in future, when they'd be alone together at his home, at last. When they'd found a place for Anthea, and a space for themselves. There'd be a lifetime. He didn't have to hurry things to their detriment.

But as he pushed open his door to see his new bride sitting up in his bed, apprehensive, he wished for a moment, before he explained matters to her, and then went to his solitary side of the bed to silently argue himself to sleep, that he'd had either less sensibility or more time before Anthea came.

As it turned out, he had time enough to ponder his decision regarding Eliza; he had, after all, an entire sleepless night. As she, of course, did too.

16

TRYING TO REMAIN inconspicuous while on someone else's honeymoon was very like trying not to be noticeable while lying in their bed—between them. Or so, Julian told Eliza that very next morning, he assumed it must be.

"Because," he said, lying on his stomach, propped up on his elbows, looking down into her face as he idly tugged at a small coppery ringlet that had fallen onto her forehead, just to watch it spring back again, "if we stay abed until late, Anthea will drift about the house by herself, trying to look as though she's got no idea at all of why we're late, and if we go down to an early breakfast, she'll gape at us and try to pretend she's not wondering why we're down so early. And tell me," he said, with his lips now following his fingers as they trailed along the perimeters of her wide-eyed face, "if I do now what I most devoutly wish to do, what you would do in an hour or two or three, meeting up with her at breakfast? Ignore me and make polite chat?" he asked, his soft voice mocking, driving the sense out of his words for her, for his touch always did that, and his entire body being so close to her in bed did that even more. "Ignore her? Send me meaningful looks of promise while chattering with her, or cut little glances at her while prosing on about something you think isn't too private with me? It's a devilish coil," he sighed, lying back on his own pillow with a groan, for he'd done little but think about Eliza since he'd come back to bed, and now her fresh little morning face was chasing all his decisions of the night from him. Then, too, there was something about the early morning and its usual effect upon healthy gentlemen that she obviously didn't understand at all, because now she sat up in bed enough for him to see that in the light of day her plain white nightdress was too thin to be pristine at all.

"Are you going to ask her to leave?" she asked, taking in a breath of alarm that made him look quickly to the ceiling.

"You haven't married a monster, Eliza," he reproved her. "No," he said, swinging his legs out of the bed and standing all in a motion as she hastily looked away and he realized he'd gone to bed in the dark, as he usually did, and she wasn't used to seeing gentlemen in their natural state. "No, I'm not so heartless," he continued, trying to be casual about the way he kept his back to her, stooped to pick up his shirt, and hastened to get into it, wishing for the penultimate time that they'd had time for intimacy, if only so that he could be more natural with her now, when he most needed to be.

"But neither can we continue, or begin, our married life together normally with her here with us. This is—was— supposed to be a private retreat for lovers. There's only just the two of us and her. Yet with all the rooms Warwick bragged about, there's not enough to give us privacy from one small lady guest, Eliza. Now, if we were in London, with a thousand people outside our window and a dozen more within the house, we'd have privacy enough for nightly orgies and daily revels, believe me. It's a paradox, but there it is. Think on it, will you? Until I come back. Because, lazy creature, you stayed in bed too late, and as I'm no gent, and used to being a selfish old bachelor besides, you shall just have to wait, and wait, and wait your turn . . ." he sang, his voice trailing off as he disappeared into the privy chamber.

But for all she might have liked to use the chamber for her own morning toilette, she was content to sit in bed, and wait, and think. Lord, she needed time to think, she moaned to herself, and she stretched out flat in bed and pulled the coverlets up over her face and wished she could leave them there forever.

Julian was being a complete gentleman, an entirely sensitive being, just what anyone would wish for in a husband. He hadn't finished making love to her because he realized he'd alarmed her. He hadn't asked Anthea to go away because he didn't wish to hurt her feelings. And now, he'd obviously no intention of further lovemaking, so as to spare Anthea's and her own feelings. Why was it, then, with him being so very sensitive and kind and noble, that she didn't believe any of it? Or if she believed his sincerity, didn't believe he was being entirely honest and sincere with himself?

He was being an entirely perfect husband, but a completely unsatisfactory groom. The dichotomy of this revelation left her feeling as flat as she was in actuality in bed. And so when Julian, done with his ablutions, and finding nothing in his bed but a vague shape beneath the coverlets, whipped them off, he saw her looking up at him, blinking at the sudden light like a small ruffled owlet. Then, for all he couldn't help but notice the exact shape of what he'd unearthed, she looked so much more enchanting than enticing that he was able to command her out of bed without too many more moments' hesitation. But he couldn't order her from his mind with such alacrity, and as he dressed he thought again of how young she'd looked, and how experienced he was, and what a devil of a mess he'd gotten himself into with just a kiss or two in the wrong place, and two or more on the wrong places.

They went down to breakfast together, arm in arm, chatting in murmurous voices, amiable as good friends on vacation, obviously in concert with one another, and so just as obviously, as least to their guest awaiting them at the table set for breakfast, not at all like lovers would be.

Anthea had not a great deal of experience with love or lovers, having spent her youth with undemonstrative parents and her young adulthood in girls' schools, but she knew Eliza, and she watched Julian's face as carefully as she might read a morning paper as they breakfasted together. There was nothing but poorly disguised worry in Eliza's eyes, and nothing but polite interest and a certain longing in Julian's whenever he looked to his wife. Anthea knew what the literal consummation of wedlock entailed. She understood the act well enough from her many long talks with occasional errant school-girls before they were dismissed from school for securing such knowledge so thoroughly. Although she was unsure of whatever else it might be for mature persons in love, she was convinced it hadn't been, in any fashion at all, for this newlywed couple. And despite all her best resolves, her spirits soared because of it.

Of course she could have gone to the duke's house in London, or better still, returned to the Lyonses' home in the Lake District. Both families had assured her of a welcome, and although she'd ample servants, Mrs. Lyons was incapacitated by early pregnancy and so would have been able to use an experienced schoolmistress's skills to the best purposes. All this Anthea knew. But to her own chagrin and confusion, she'd followed Eliza and Julian instead. She was no opportunist, she told herself, she wished Eliza no harm, she assured herself many times over on the long, lonely, doubt-ridden ride down to this honeymoon house.

If she'd seen any evidence that this was anything but a forced union on Julian's part, she'd have never come. Nor did she know herself what it was she sought or what she'd do if the unthinkable occurred in either way—if she sincerely believed she'd a chance for his heart if the marriage came apart, or if she'd take something outside of it if it didn't, and if it were offered to her. But then, she hadn't thought at all, she'd only traveled to Eliza's side in the same unthinking, driven way she'd have refused to put down an enthralling book before the last page had been read. And in much the same fashion, she decided now as she watched Eliza and Julian go about the business of breaking their fast in the most prosaic way, that as she was here now, so now here she'd stay. At least until she knew the way things were going.

"Shall we have a walk now?" Julian asked idly when he saw Eliza had done with her toast. "The weather's holding, it's a remarkably beautiful day, and Arden said he'd an orangery and a pond here, and knowing my man, I've wondered if he has the one in the other. No, not an orangery in a pond, that would be too much even for him . . . or so, at least, I think, so shall we see?" he said on a laugh as he rose and put his napkin down. But then he saw Eliza's look of consternation. And noting the direction of her gaze, he too saw the way Anthea flushed and put her head down, keeping her eyes on her empty plate, as though he'd said something smutty, as though he'd offended her. And of course, he thought with suppressed annoyance, he had.

For he'd made it an open invitation, hadn't he? But then, how could he not have? he wondered as he turned toward Anthea to ask her if she were coming. And when she looked up, guilt and worry and longing on her face, while a stammered weak refusal trembled on her lips, how could he then not offer her his other arm? He strolled out the door with his new wife and her old companion and friend, wondering, even as both his wife and her companion were, if it would have been better to have left the room with only his wife, even if then he would've had to look back to see her poor, neglected companion alone and ashamed, trying to look occupied in a house with no one else in it.

They ambled through the spacious grounds, commenting on the knot garden, admiring the rose garden, and remarking on how admirable the wildflower-filled meadows were. These sights inspired Julian to take up the reins and take the ladies in a curricle on a tour of the furthest reaches of the estate so that when they then went in to tea, they'd a great deal more to talk about than the marmalade and the lightness of the fruit scones.

After dinner, they discovered the further advantages of being a trio rather than a couple. They found they could sing three-part harmonies around the piano, play at whist instead of just patience, and Julian had two ladies instead of just one admiring one to guess at his charades. But after Anthea, with a great show of discretion, prettily begged weariness as early as ten in the night, though she was clearly even brighter-eyed than she'd been at ten in the morning, Eliza saw her husband's distraction and went off to their bedroom to await him there by eleven. Then Julian stayed by himself, standing at the mantel, staring into the dying fire until the new day had got itself well under way, by the clock on the mantel at least, for it was still dark as midnight outside.

"No," he said as he walked into his bedchamber, where his bride sat awake with a book that had been held open so long to one page that it had begun to gather dust there, "no, it will never do.

"Eliza," he said, sitting down on the edge of the bed and gently taking the book away from her and laying it down, but not so that he could then kiss her, as she'd dared to hope, for all she'd put on the prettiest night-dress she owned and had combed out her hair until it resembled a ruddy halo of soft curls, "Eliza," he said with a quirked and sad smile, "I'd have made a very poor sultan, I think. I'd have been so busily trying not to hurt any of my wives' feelings that I'd never have had time for doing any of the things I was supposed to do with them, the very things that make being forced to wear those puffy pantaloons and silly slippers with turned-up toes that come with the job worthwhile, I suppose. A great bloody eunuch is what I'd have been," he said roughly, before he sighed and stood and took a turn around the chamber as she watched him silently. "Excuse me, I've made a mull of it, and I'm not behaving very well about it either, am I?" he asked as he came to stand before her again.

"It's Anthea," she began to say before he cut her off by taking up her hands in his and shaking his head as he answered, "No, no, love, it's only partially Anthea, and partially it's you and I, you know. This wedding of ours was arranged with a lie—the fiction of our previous engagement; it's begun with a mistake—my abortive, badly botched seduction of my bride; and now it's been complicated with a mishap—Anthea's arrival. Three wrongs won't make a right. But I don't want to give it up. I want to begin it anew, with no lies or mistakes, because I think a marriage begun like that could survive any accident. Now, or at least as we are now, it's clear ours cannot. Let's start again, Eliza," he beseeched her, his eyes now dark as night mists, searching her face for reaction.

"Oh, yes!" she cried, staring up at him, for it was excatly what she'd been thinking. "Oh, yes, Julian, I agree, I think we must start over again."

"Good," he said with relief, nodding. "Then listen, because I've been thinking. No, don't worry, I've not been guzzling claret in the study to nerve myself to come up here and embarrass us both again. I'm sober and sure, so hear me out now. The first thing, I think, is for us to quit this place. It can serve us no purpose now, at least not the one it was designed for. As I said, I think London is the very place for us—we can get lost in a crowd there, and be alone together and be free there too, even if we're still forced to have company. But I think it best if you leave for there first, before I do. No, listen," he said, although she'd said nothing as she sat and stared at him, for this wasn't at all what she'd been imagining as a fresh start for them as she'd waited for him all these past hours,

"There'll be nothing but festival there now, summer or no, because of the coronation. I've been invited there and everywhere. 'Noblesse' is 'obleeged' to come, as Warwick says"—he grinned before he went on—"and I'm sure you'll want to commission a special gown or three thousand for the occasion, and you'll have to scurry to do that in time. Then too, once you're in London, you can see Anthea safely installed with Warwick or in any other household apart from ours. Or so I pray. And so," he said as he looked away over her shoulder, the first signs of vague unease upon him, "as I've some other business to attend to, I'll let you get there before me."

"I see," she said quietly, ducking her head to look down at her entwined fingers as they lay in her blanket-covered lap.

"Too well," he said softly, putting his hand beneath her chin to cause her to look up at him to see her hurt clear in her wide, misty amber eyes. "Ah, I'm a devilish poor liar, aren't I?" he asked as he ran a hand through his hair and admitted, "All right. I confess I'm just too uncomfortable sharing myself equitably with you two to keep doing so all the way back to London and in those first days there. And I'd have a devilish hard time seeing to Anthea's leaving us, without feeling like a brute for not insisting on giving her refuge whatever the inconvenience to me. You're her old friend, and a female, it's very different for you," he explained.

"And then, I do have something else that's important to see to," he said, looking at her again, his voice and his face full of earnest entreaty for understanding. "I want to devote myself to you entirely for a long, long while after we get to London, you see. But I've just discovered I'm close to where I need to be right now to finish up some troublesome business that I do have to attend to sooner or later. I think, given our unusual circumstances, it would be better to make it sooner than later, and so I thought to get it over with once and for all before I consign myself to eternal husbandry. No, that's animal-keeping, isn't it? Eternal wedded bliss, then," he said, trying to coax her to smile with him. "All right, little wife?"

Of course it was not. But she knew she'd no choice in the matter. She was no more really his wife than she wanted to agree to his bizarre proposal, but there was the necessity of pretending to both polite fictions in order to keep the most important one going. She knew no other thing to do but to seem to acquiesce.

"Certainly," she said softly, but then, because there were some things she couldn't pretend to, things that for her life she couldn't disguise, such as curiosity, and concern for him as well as his future with her, she asked quickly, before she lost the courage to, "Can you, will you . . . at least tell me what it is that you have to do first?"

"Ah, well," he said, relieved at her agreeableness, "it's a matter of business. We've a coaching line, Warwick, Arden, and I, as I'm sure you know, we've put you ladies to sleep with talk of it often enough. We've mines too, and foundries and sundries and ships and a dozen other enterprises," he said, becoming animated with his explanation, "but the coaching business is my especial care. And the point is, I do have a care for it now. There's something amiss with the tallies of monies going out and monies taken in. It looks fair enough on paper to those who don't know the business.

"But I'm a coaching man, lass," he said, his accents becoming hearty and common, "as well you know it, poor girl, and what I see on paper don't suit me, it don't strike me right at all. And as we own a line that plies the Brighton run, and there are three roads to Brighton, the most profitable of which is the one that runs through Cuckfield and Reigate, and we're not too far from the crossroads to it from where we are now, and everything's easier to do casually on the road than in London town, I've a notion to go and see what's happening. Not as the great Viscount Hazelton come snooping around to see how the books have been cooked, mind. But not in disguise, or much of one, either.

"Because I plan to look in," he said merrily, "in the guise of the coachie I once was. But this time not as a pauper-peer. This time I shall be a gent tired of the responsibility of his station. I'll go as a coaching-mad fellow out for a lark, out for a gambol atop one of my own coaches, madcap rogue that I am. There should be no difficulty persuading them that I only want to feel the reins in my hands again, for no other reason than folly, as a cut-up, a lark. Noblemen are notorious for their pranks. But then I can get a good look at the business too."

He fell silent, hearing his own words, realizing for perhaps the first time since he'd thought up the scheme that it was no lie. It was all a convenient escape and a retreat and he was no more than a foolish nobleman, after all. But though he suddenly understood, there was no way he could go back on the suggestion now, nor was there any way he wanted to do so. Because he did long for the freedom, and if not just a lark, he wanted, no, needed, a taste of the carelessness of the life he'd given up. Because his new life had suddenly become all too complicated and all too serious. He needed joy just as much as he needed time before he made an irrevocable commitment, or committed an irrevocable mistake.

"I see," she said softly, and she did. "Then by all means, yes," she said, smiling, proving one could smile when dying, "take care of business, Julian, and I'll be sure to settle things with Anthea. Is tomorrow too soon for me to go to London?" she asked.

"Is it?" he answered.

* * *

They passed the night together in one bed, but it was a dark night and a huge bed and so they could avoid each other. They dressed in the same room, but it had alcoves, after all, and so it wasn't until they sat at the breakfast table again that the newlyweds saw each other again, and what Julian saw he did not soon forget.

His new little viscountess was a splendid actress. Because she actually laughed, lighthearted as a girl planning a picnic, when she told Anthea of the fun that they were so soon to have in London. And then, clapping her hands together in glee, she announced that dear Julian was letting her go today! So as to be able to buy up all the ribbons and lace and silk and satin in London, she confided, so that she could be the star of the coronation—why, no one would have an eye out to see the King, they'd all stare at her so.

"And Julian will join us," she simpered, "as soon as may be, or at least as soon as he must, for he's fed to the teeth with my talk of feminine gewgaws and all my dress and other designs, and who shall blame him, poor fellow?" She giggled as she spoke airily of her plans with Anthea.

But her fine light brown eyes had nothing but reflected light in them, and she never once looked her husband's way all through the rest of that interminable summer breakfast. And immediately afterward, she set a maid to packing, and took herself away to supervise, or so she said, and so never saw him again until late in the afternoon, when he came to speak with her and she came to say good-bye to him and they met face-to-face in the hallway midway between their room and the study he'd paced since she'd left him.

They were as uneasy with each other as they were artificial. Because she smiled at once, and tilted her head to the side and told him that all was packed and stored and waiting in the coach and so she'd soon be off. And her only question was to ask how long he thought it might take for them to arrive in London. He didn't smile in return, but only took her hand, and then only assured her that it was less than an hour's ride, for otherwise he'd never have even thought to let her go on by herself. And when she still only looked up at him, he went on to reassure her of the things she didn't care about—telling her he'd arranged for two stout footmen to ride on the back of the coach to protect her, and another on the driver's seat fully armed, both with his instructions for the staff awaiting them at his town house, and with a brace of primed pistols.

There was nothing for her to worry about from thieves or from the unknown house awaiting her in London, but that never consoled her, because that hadn't been what she feared at all. But she had grown up a great deal in the past few days, and even more in the last nights, so she smiled and thanked him and wished him well, both then, and then later when he walked her out to the coach to see her off on her travels.

She never asked for any more specific time of his joining her than the "Soon" he promised her in a whisper as he kissed her cheek in farewell. And she waved as merrily as Anthea did as their coach pulled out from the long drive and they rode off, ending her brief, odd honeymoon and, she was convinced, her marriage as well.

For now she was entirely resolved. She'd never hold him to a bargain so obviously made in error or as a sacrifice. She still loved him too well for that. It was, after all, never his fault if he couldn't love her. She was unused to affection—too much all at once might have dismayed her as much as too little—but that he should so obviously only suffer her as wife was unbearable. She'd passed several sleepless nights since their vows had been made, and they, if nothing else, had convinced her that vows made in charity or as penance were never binding. There was such a thing as fair play. There might be pain later, but she was numb now, altogether decided on her course of action in future.

It might have been that there was another female waiting for him somewhere in the tropics, or America, that he'd his heart set on. He certainly would never have written to her about that. Or it could be that he had preferred Constance—as what man would not?—and he might have planned to follow her to town after he'd recovered from his illness, to try his luck with her. It might even be that he'd really wanted Anthea, and that was why she'd joined them and why he couldn't bring himself to rid them of her with even so much as a gentle word when she did. It might be that he merely didn't wish to wed yet. It hardly mattered. He clearly didn't want her.

She'd confer with a man-at-law when she got to London, and confide in no one else, for it was no one else's business, until the thing was settled. What was done so poorly must be undone. He was so beautiful that she knew no other thing that so delighted her eye, he was so clever that she could listen to him for hours, but he was a man, and a man should be free. There was no sense in keeping him, as one might keep some beautiful wild thing, caught and caged and always pacing, always dreaming to be free. Divorce was rare and as scandalous as it was infrequent, but it was possible. She'd see to it. That was her first order of business, for all she turned to prattle to Anthea about gowns and dressmakers as their carriage turned from the drive into the wide road to London, and she gave up her childhood as completely as she lost sight of the husband she'd never had and had just lost.

Julian stood in the drive and watched her go, and as he did, felt such relief as he'd not known for days. It was as if someone had rolled a stone off his heart. He could breathe again, he could think again, he could act without guilt and doubt. He was free.

Of course, he thought, it was only for a matter of days or weeks. He'd no intention of going back on his word before God or Eliza. But both seemed equally distant from him now, if also equal truths and wonders in his life. Eliza was beautiful, she was good and kind, and now she was his wife too. But now she was safe where she was going, and she would keep where she was going. And now he had what he hadn't before, not for once in all these harried days and weeks since he'd first packed and raced onward to return home again—he had time now. He'd make the best use of it that he could, in every way that he could.

With time to think, he could never act wrong. It seemed

he'd been on some weird precipitous slide since he'd set foot on his native land again. This taking care of business would be a good business for him. This last fling at a bachelor life would be an odd one too, for it would be celibate and spare, but he'd no more deceive his little Eliza than he would tolerate such treachery in himself. Too many females had wept in his arms over past misplaced trust, even as they betrayed another man. He'd heard too many men jest uneasily at their doubts about their wives even as they gave their wives more reason to doubt them. No matter why he'd undertaken this marriage, no matter how he'd imagined he might behave, marriage had always meant the end of other liaisons to him. Not only had he too often seen the terrible toll such foolishness took on man and wife, he'd seen the invisible toll it took on a man's soul, since the more a man cheated anyone he'd sworn to keep faith with, the less he knew truth himself when he saw it. No, such dishonesty was repugnant to him; a man was only as good as his word. For all he'd no real marriage, he'd not make it less so.

This respite was not for his body, but for his soul. He'd take the time to gather his thoughts and lay all his doubts to rest, or at least come to terms with them. When he came to Eliza again, he would come to her completely, both body and mind. She deserved that, and more, if he could possibly give it—at any rate, he would give no less. When the time came, he'd go to London and court her in style, and with as much honesty as he could. He'd all the time in the world now, for she was already his in name, and as he'd known since the day he'd met her, in her heart as well. But for now, at last, he was entirely free to think and to act by himself.

He strode back to the house to pack, because he intended to be quit of this honeymoon house before the sun set on it again.

17

THERE WAS NO PROBLEM. The coachman of the *Brighton Fancy* was only too pleased to take a paid vacation, courtesy of the handsome blond gentleman. He discovered, as a great many females before him had done, albeit in wildly different fashion, that it was always a pleasure to succumb to the Viscount Hazelton's blandishments.

"I'll keep me mouth shut too, but then, for that much extra coin, I'd keep me eyes shut walking a tightrope, sir," he assured his benefactor.

After all, it wasn't like taking coin from any of the rakish young gents that were always after him to so that they could get their hands on the reins, for that was even more profitable, but illegal. This gent he took the blunt from had been a coachie himself, was a notable whip, and if he were a madman too, he was coming down heavy for the privilege of driving himself to ruin. And besides, to quiet the last pangs of the coachman's conscience, for he was a good man, and a responsible one, he had no choice. The fellow he gave the reins over to owned the line.

There wasn't a whisper of misconduct surrounding the *Fancy,* but Julian was too wise to commandeer any of the coaches that had the most puzzling records. There were a few left that operated, at least on paper, just as they ought, at least on the Brighton line, for all of those on the Portsmouth and Southampton runs seemed compromised now. Any of these honest few, then, was the right one to take over and drive. He believed that he could hear and see more offhand from within the ranks of the innocent than from a week spent questioning the guilty.

The *Flash*, the *Charger*, and the *Colossus* were most to be avoided, as they had the most interesting bookkeeping, although in recent weeks the records of the previously blameless *Rover* and *Thunder* were becoming almost as odd. All of them went the same route as the *Fancy*, for that was the road of the Quality and those who wished to ride the same way, and so was the most popular, profitable run to Brighton. Wagons, farm carts, and slower vehicles used the two other roads, and a man could ride a coach on them and hear no more than rumors of the strange things happening on the stagecoach lines. Julian had come that way and had heard enough to know that he was doing the right thing. It seemed something was very wrong on his coaching line, if only because no man spoke freely of it. It was all "I hear tell," "It may be," or "Best not to know."

The books and the numbers in them spoke up loudly enough. It was a popular line and a frequented road, yet it showed little profit and more mileage, in terms of horseflesh used up, than it ought, unless there was something wrong with the road itself that caused cattle to age and weaken as they passed over it. Coaching horses were short-lived, hard-worked beasts; no one expected else. Owners supplied new horses as the old ones wore out, with seldom a question or a word of protest because of it. But this one owner was different because he'd worked as a coachman and had learned respect and compassion for the poor brutes that were the engines of the trade. He made special, unusual provision for the care and rest of the horses on his line.

Every owner expected a coachman to slide a little extra coin into his capacious pockets; that would never have troubled him. It was the unexpected number of replacement nags being used that had first alerted him to some irregularity. Only then had he checked the records more carefully, only then had he noticed that the line was growing less profitable, even as one of his competitors had gone out of business on the same route. Something was up, and Julian was pleased to be on the spot on the track of it instead of just pondering the matter from across an ocean or two.

He was even more pleased to be perched high on a stagecoach driver's seat again, despite the rain. It had been raining for five days now, ever since he'd taken over the *Fancy,* until he'd begun to wonder if the coach towed a small dark rain cloud along over it on a tether as it rolled along the road, like a child running with a kite. Yet it really made no matter; the joy of coaching, the delight of the road was evergreen with him, just like lovemaking was—it could be better, it had been worse, but it was never really bad, whatever the circumstances.

The motion, the speed, the rushing air in his face, rain-saturated or not, the feel of the power of the horses all held in one hand by separate tethers, but all working as one mighty engine carrying him ever onward, it was hypnotic and thrilling all at the same time. It was breath of life to him; he'd not felt so energetic for weeks. Then too, he'd a mystery to pursue as he drove. It was all just what he'd been searching for. Hard work for the body, a teaser for the mind, it kept him from thinking of anything else, it was a perfect diversion. Except when he realized it was, which was far more often than he'd have wished, because it was every time he wasn't concentrating on what he was doing. So he concentrated on the problem again, since his horses knew the road.

He'd made three runs so far, to and from Brighton, staying on at a small inn in Brighton one night, passing another at Reigate, avoiding another in London by handing the coach on to another driver at Reigate when he'd changed horses. The other coachman had been only too glad to do him the favor, and not knowing who he was, had generously shared the profits with him later, for the tips came in at the end of the run and the new passengers' bribes for small favors to be done en route were best at their departure on the return run from London the next day. But there was only time to be wasted for him in London, less chance of discovering something there, and more guilt for his proximity to all he'd escaped from there as well. And mostly, there was *something* at Reigate.

Whether it had been only in the innkeeper's eye, or in the atmosphere of the place, he could not yet tell, but it alerted him. Some of the drivers of the other coaches often stayed over there, and he'd got a good look at one of them, and even though the man worked for him, there was no way, shape, or fashion in which he'd have ever hired him on. He was nothing like any of the coachmen Julian had ever known on any continent. Small, cold, and sly he'd been, and every coachman Julian had ever met up with had been large of mind and body, as ever-ready with laughter as he was with a wench or a tipple. Even if they weren't, every coachman tried to appear so, for that was the standard and the ideal. He himself, Julian knew, was an uncommon sort of coachie; it had been remarked years ago, and would be again. That was why he had to make his discoveries quickly and move on before everyone on the line knew him for who he was. He didn't mind being considered a mad nobleman, but the game would be up when they all recognized him for one of the entrepreneurs of the Brighton line. He was singular, he knew it, and so knew he'd very little time.

It wasn't only his looks which marked him; he was congeniality itself on this errand, deliberately conspicuous. But how else could he speak with everyone? And so he'd never been more charming. Not only with his fellow coachmen and the guards, innkeepers and serving wenches and those whom he might be expected to pass his time with, but with the passengers, and every type of them, as well.

When his fares were forced to dismount at the foot of steep hills, at his practiced cry of: "Ladies and gents, please to step out with me so we can stroll along together for a spell. We must spare the horses, the hill is killing for them, you know," their groans soon turned to grins when they beheld their coachman, handsome as he could hold together, but not a bit of arrogance in him as he trudged up the hill with them, deep in conversation with the other passengers. That in itself wasn't so remarkable, but he didn't chat up only dashing young gents and would-be whips as so many of his kind did. No, just as often they'd see the slim, straight fellow in his long coat and low-brimmed hat with his head bent to one side, one hand on a near horse's flank as it toiled up the hill, and

the other hand securely under the arm of an old farmwife
—or it might be an ancient spinster or some other decent
unattractive female he listened to attentively as he assisted
her. That wouldn't go unremarked.

But every tongue bore a tale, and so just as often as he
had to listen to complaints about health, wealth, relatives, and bad weather, a well-placed question might net
him an unexpected answer from the oddest source.

It was a wizened baker's mother who told him the
rumor about how much rum—"Aye, good, aged and
black rum, and the best cognac too"—rode disguised
amidst the baggage on the Brighton Road these days.

A jovial merchant gave him a nudge in the ribs with an
elbow that took his breath away—as did his garbled tale
about the odd-looking gents who sometimes rode in the
coaches with glassy-eyed bits of muslin, females that
never had to get out and walk at the hills, because,
clearly, they couldn't.

And it was a peckish old lady who'd said, on a sniff,
that she wagered "some of the expensive fabrics, too
dear for the likes of me, that go from France direct to
London's fine ladies, never have dazzled the eyes of the
customs men, no, for all they're meant to snare those of
the gents of the *ton*"—or so she'd heard, and so she was
only too pleased to tattle.

At the start, he'd only the notion of finding the facts
and dismissing the miscreants who were putting their
hands in his pockets. But now, especially since some of
the wilder tales spoke of some of his coaches' cargoes
that didn't bear investigation by those with weak stom-
achs, he thought long and hard about laying information
with the Bow Street Runners. That was a step he'd never
take without consulting with his partners, especially since
his largest partner had the largest dislike of the law of
any man he'd ever met, only partially because he knew
better ways to dispense justice. And that was a step he
couldn't take without evidence.

So he drove his coach by day, and thought about his
other problems so much by night that now he was resolved to take on more day runs, and night ones on other
of his coaches too, in order to finish the business faster,

to be sure there was no room or time in his head for other thoughts until he was done with the business.

Julian pulled into the courtyard of the Belle and Bottle and drew his reins up. Tom Wait would take over from him now; the fellow was so eager for the job he came striding out of the Belle rubbing his gloved hands together.

"A cushy job, this," he chortled by way of greeting Julian, "hauling just the last leg of the journey, with a lovely night passed in London town, and then having only a morning's work so far back as Reigate again."

Jim worked the *Sporting Life* out of Brighton every third day for Chaplin, but was glad of the extra; he'd another baby coming, and an expensive girlfriend at the Crimson Cat further along down the road, too.

Julian grinned back at him and sprang down from his high seat as the teams were being unhitched. Some of the female passengers were disappointed at seeing their coachman being changed even as the horses were, but they'd the time to hurry out of the coach on the excuse of personally presenting him with a coin for his troubles before he left, and the pleasure of his weary smile and a bow for their trouble for it.

He swung off his Benjamin cape and hung it on a hook outside the taproom; it had been a long day and looked to be a long night coming. For he'd gotten a run from this inn to Brighton on a late-running coach, an old one he'd driven years ago, taking over from another coachman with a liking for liquor almost as keen as his love of money. No night runs were good, no sane coachman wanted them. On the best lines, it was a treacherous business on the dark roads. On the worst, it was a downright dangerous one.

Not only did the night roads hold dangers the day wouldn't hide, but the coaches were older, and the dark horses, unseen by the passengers and often not noted by the exhausted drivers, were likely to be mad, or blind, or half-dead brutes. And some of the passengers on those runs were often in similar case, for no one wanted to sit up all night when he could drive by day unless there was an urgent reason or he was too addled to care. Or he didn't wish to be seen. But his driver would spy him, and that was Julian's hope.

His other hope was that the concentration the job required would banish those other thoughts he refused to consider. The thoughts that were growing each night, disrupting his well-deserved sleep. Because so much as he adored coaching and his freedom and this mystery too, if truth be told, there was another truth he didn't want told. And that was that for all of its joys, this life lacked something now. Or he did. But something had changed, and drastically, for the pleasure was there, as always, but not as ever. Now it was something he had to keep remarking on to himself in order to enjoy to the fullest.

And, Julian thought darkly as he sat at a table and waited for the sensation of movement to stop and the floor to be still so he could decide what to eat for his dinner, once a man kept noting "What fun I'm having!" it was certain he wasn't anymore.

He flexed his shoulders to ease the pain there, and shifted on his hard wood chair to redistribute the weight there. He'd paid the toll for his relative inactivity days before, but sitting on a hard jouncing seat for long hours always made a man mind how he sat down after, and holding a fresh team on sharp turns in the rain made a man ache no matter how accustomed he was to using his muscles. There were other aches he could not ease, and he thought of them as he never meant to do until a low rough-edged voice asked, with enough innuendo to get a dead man's attention:

"And wot's it to be to take the chill from yer bones, luv?"

She was offering far more, from the tone of her voice and the tilt of her head and her smile. Dark-haired and dark-eyed and deep-bosomed, as her deep-cut dress made a point to show, earthy and interesting, but no beauty, this tavern wench, but such females seldom were. She was well-enough-looking, though. A man off the road took his pleasures where he could and seldom looked too hard at them, so it was rare to find a lass with more than the common run of looks waiting on tables, willing to sell or give more than food and drink to a fellow.

Dark-haired, dark-eyed . . . He gazed at her, remembering a wench in an inn not too dissimilar that he'd known so long ago.

"A hot Jamaican punch, Nan," he ordered absently.

"Wot?" she asked, her mouth dropping open. "A hot punch in July? Pull the other one, do. And I'm Mary, luv, Mary Ellen to you, if you like, and I might like, too, you never do know unless you ask, eh? So wot'll you have?"

Of course it was July, he remembered, it was only that he'd been far back in time and place to another place where it was winter, and a loving lass named Nan had served him everything he'd needed then. But she was gone now from the Silver Swan, an inn long down the road, raising a litter of Gypsy-dark sons for her new coachman husband, or so the innkeeper had said just the other day when he'd stopped, out of courtesy and curiosity, to see where he'd spent so much of his ill-spent youth.

"Oh, yes, July. Some rum punch then," he said softly, with none of the clever chatter he could summon so easily, and only the smallest smile he had, for he was weary and wanted no more than a drink from this wench today. Or any day, he supposed, lowering his head as though to tally his coins when she hesitated, caught by that simplest of smiles and lingering to see if more was forthcoming.

She was too dark, he thought as he noted the way her hips swung as she marched away to get his order, and too broad in every sense. But then, the curly-haired wench in Brighton had been too tall, and the freckled one in London too loud, while the fair-haired one in Hand Cross had been too soft-looking, reminding him of fresh dough, discouraging him despite how clean she looked, and the giggling one at the Compass in Crawley had been too hard-eyed for his tastes. And that was amazing, for he'd never looked so close to see so many defects in such females before—not even when he'd thought himself in love, so long ago. Because in that long ago he'd believed matters of the heart need not interfere with matters of the flesh. And they never had. But then, he decided, he'd not been married then, had he?

He sat up sharply despite his sore buttocks, and blinked. The thought of Eliza had crept up on him, assaulting him when he was least on guard. He'd been vigilant on the driver's box all these days, and just as determined to sleep on his pillow these past nights, but now, in the few moments he had for relaxation, it came to him, whole and unbidden again. It was true. None of it—not the pain or the pleasure—had the same meaning without Eliza sharing it. He missed the adorable little wretch abominably, he admitted.

Every new interesting thing that happened made him reach for a notebook to log it in so that he could write of it to Eliza, even though he didn't have to anymore, but he'd done it for five long years before he'd come home, and habit was hard to break. Everything he saw and heard, and everything he thought, he noticed now that he was noting in his head, storing it up for the day when he could bring it back to her in conversation. And that was never habit.

Because now he wanted more than her laughter and her delight with his cleverness. Now he wanted her in all the different ways he'd forced himself to ignore when he'd lain in bed, so near to her but far from her in his mind. Now, when it was too late, and growing later. Now that he was apart from her, he saw that he'd a lot to answer for, there was a great deal to make up to her, and a good bit more to permit himself. He could scarcely wait.

But he'd set himself a task, even if it was one he began to question his eagerness to begin, even as he began to doubt the very reasons why he'd insisted on undertaking it in the first place. That task had to be finished, or he'd feel an even worse fool than he was beginning to, if that were possible. But it wouldn't get done with doubt and regret. It was as well that he'd dared to take on one of his problematic coaches tonight, whatever the risk, having decided that the cover of night might help cover his aims, not knowing the decision had been made then because of the very eagerness to be done with the matter that he was feeling now.

But impatience bred mistakes, and overeagerness spawned mishap, so he refused to think of anything more now, and he was getting very good at putting things from his mind. Instead, he took down his drink when it came and ate all his dinner without tasting it, and then, as a damp twilight put out the light, he was glad to climb back on the coachman's seat when the *Thunder* arrived to take it the rest of the way on the night run back to Brighton.

The guard on the *Thunder* was closemouthed, and the inside passengers, two farmers and a peddler, too weary to speak. One of the outside riders was too terrified to talk, he only clutched onto his seat like grinning death, despite its being a relatively calm ride; another outside passenger spoke in such a thick dialect he might as well have been a Greek; and the third, a young rustic with a terrible complexion, never stopped asking questions about coaching long enough for the coachman to frame his own seemingly aimless queries about the reputation of the line. So if it weren't for the fact that the exertion chased all thought, unwelcome or not, from the coachman's mind when he finally reached his pillow, it would have been an entirely wasted night for him. But not so for the rustic youth and the terrified rider.

For their eyes had widened when he'd taken up the reins, and they'd exchanged glances when the coachman left his high seat, and as soon as he'd gone, they hastened to book fares back to London immediately, abandoning their original orders. Because now they'd something far more important to take back with them than the contraband cargo they'd come all the way down to the coast to secure. Now they'd this startling development they'd seen, so now they'd information, something their superior would doubtless want more.

The gentleman looked at her as though she carried some vile contagion. He actually tried to back away from her after she'd stated her business; she distinctly heard the bottom of his chair give a muffled scrape across the heavy carpeting. Before he could hide it and resume his neutral, pleasant expression, his round face gave a twitch of distaste and he looked like an infant with a colic.

"It can be done," he answered slowly. "It is possible. But it's also possible to poison wells—it is just that it is not frequently done, you understand. I think, perhaps," he said, smiling again, his professional tranquillity back in place, "You might think it over and return in a few weeks, a few months, perhaps."

But, unused as Eliza was to being looked at as though she were loathsome, for now that she was grown she was always being ogled, and in the past had only been ignored, she was well-used to being humored and patronized. She was a young female in a gentleman's world, after all. And so though the disapproval might have discouraged her into leaving quietly because she didn't know how to handle it, the lawyer's condescension only angered her. She did very well with anger.

"I am not contemplating poisoning any wells, sir, I am, however, quite seriously considering divorce. I take it you are unwilling to undertake the legal duties entailed?" she asked in her loftiest tones, raising her chin, peering at the gentleman as though he'd just done something unspeakably vulgar. She was copying every ancient hell-born termagant she'd ever seen dominating a social affair. And realized there might be a great deal of amusement to be gotten in growing old, after all, when she saw how hastily he pulled himself up and tried to placate her.

The lawyer was obviously remembering now that it was no less a nobleman than the Duke of Peterstow that had recommended her to him. He'd no wish to offend that gentleman, who while admittedly unusual, was as wealthy and influential as any in the kingdom. It was partially that which accounted for his sudden effort to charm her, and also that he was thinking that this beautifully dressed young woman could probably afford to be as eccentric as she pleased as well. But he had some scruples or he'd never have had the duke as even a sometime client, so he asked what he had to do before he allowed the conference to go any further.

"You understand, Viscountess, that there are only two means of securing a true divorce, or annulment. And as you say you don't wish to unduly embarrass your husband by declaring that he's insane or has misrepresented himself to you in some other wise, the final proof required for such an action must come from yourself?"

She leaned forward and sniffed. There wasn't a trace of spirits in the air, so it must be, she thought, that it was legal jargon and not inebriation speaking. She'd no idea of what he meant. He saw her frown of incomprehension and gazed at the ceiling. Delicacy, he told himself, was the key here, but for all he could dazzle with words, he wished she were a fishwife and not a nobleman's wife at the moment.

"Ah," he said, looking at the pen he'd picked up, "that is to say, there'd have to be a physician's examination and a sworn statement that you and the viscount had never been together as man and wife . . . in the biblical sense . . ."

As Eliza wondered how they'd ever get a physician to swear to something he'd never seen—for how was any doctor to know what she and Julian had got up to when they'd been alone?—the lawyer added, because he realized he had to, as he thought of a thousand curses for the education of well-brought-up females, "It's proof of your virginity that would be in question, my lady."

Well, she knew that, she thought crossly, before she remembered what exact sort of proof he was talking about, for she wasn't that ignorant, only that forgetful. Then, as she looked down to her toes and wondered if her face had really burst into flames or only felt that way, she summoned up all her courage and answered, strangling, "I understand. But it could be done, I assure you."

When she'd also assured him of a heavy retainer fee, he consented to begin to assemble documents. She was young and beautiful and her newlywed husband was out of town, the lawyer thought as he gave her his promises to begin work. The longer the matter was delayed, he thought, the likelier it would come to nothing, for if the young gentleman had eyes or senses, it would probably come to something sooner or later. And if it didn't, if the fellow couldn't change or wouldn't alter the situation—if he preferred other gentlemen or horses or mice, or whatever mad thing the decadent nobility was involved with these days—well, then, it would be for the best to file for this writ of divorce, for all it was as uncommon as it was a drastic measure to take.

Written proof, Eliza was relieved to hear, would not be necessary for some time yet. It only needed that she not live with her husband, and that she inform her husband of her plans. That, the lawyer insisted upon. And that, she thought, emerging from his offices with the sick feeling that she'd just done something unutterably obscene with him, instead of just hiring him on, was already being done. For Julian did not live with her, and likely never would again—at least, she'd see to that when they met again, when she told him her decision.

If she ever met with him again, she thought as she finally trailed back into Julian's London town house and dismissed the maid she'd had in tow.

"Eliza! Where have you been?" Anthea demanded, standing in the hallway, hands on her hips, looking very irritated.

"Lud, Anthea," Eliza answered gloomily, "you're not my mama, you know. And you're not my schoolmistress anymore either, and I'm not sneaking into my rooms from late-night foraging in the pantry with the other girls. Give over. I'd an errand to run," she said sulkily, removing her bonnet, "and only thought to let you sleep."

Anthea grew still. She and Eliza had become distanced, not by marriage, as she'd feared, but by this removal to London, which she had hopes for. It was better this way, she told herself, turning round, acting as though she'd been insulted by Eliza's harsh words. For when Julian returned, she wouldn't feel as if she were deceiving a friend when she saw him . . . but then she remembered: if the distance became too great, there'd be no "when," because she'd lose all the advantages along with the guise of friendship and would have to leave here.

"I only began to worry after you. I'm supposed to look after you," Anthea protested. "You might have told me where you had got to."

"It was a private matter, Anthea," Eliza said, stung by her onetime friend's tone of voice, "and as to that," she added, for she'd been brooding about this since she'd left Julian over a week past, "I remind you that you've been relieved of your duties, Anthea. I don't need you to look after me."

She was going to add, ". . . I don't need looking after so much as I need a friend now," for she did, but Anthea had not been acting very like that of late either, having been silent and almost secretive since she'd rejoined them. And worse, having been withdrawn since they'd left Julian. So Eliza only ended her complaint with reason, so it wouldn't look as though she were begging for friendship.

"I am, after all, a married woman now," she said.

But Anthea, anticipating another sort of answer entirely, and afraid of what it might be, equally as much as she guiltily feared she deserved whatever it might be, snapped:

"Are you, indeed, after all?"

"Am I what?" Eliza answered, grown very still.

When Anthea didn't reply, but only lowered her gaze and bit her lip, Eliza looked long and hard at her. Then she nodded, and raised her head even higher, for she'd just had practice in dignity at the lawyer's office, and if a difficult thing had to be said, it ought to be done with dignity. And this, she thought, the truth of it carrying her on, was a thing that ought to have been said before.

She might not have a marriage with Julian, but he'd been her friend for longer than Anthea had, and as he'd been her best friend, she'd still his best interests at heart. Why else would she be giving him up now? Aside from noble excuses, she admitted to herself, she was only human after all, and couldn't relish the thought of going ahead and blackening her name forever just so that Anthea could profit from her wretchedness. Some lady she'd never set eyes on, perhaps; she'd permit herself to think of his finding happiness with someone she'd never known. It might be mean-spirited of her, but she could at least bear that. But not Anthea, if she could help it—although, she decided, and that decision gave her imperious tone a slight quaver, likely she couldn't.

"I am a married woman now, Anthea," she said now, "as you should know—you were at my wedding. But for the life of me, I can't understand why you were at my honeymoon as well."

As Anthea gasped and began to pale, and before her compassion could outweigh her anger, Eliza unburdened herself of that which had nagged at her for days, and she added with little dignity but a great deal of sorrowing honesty:

"I think I'd rather sleep in a coach and live in a cellar than romp off on someone else's honeymoon with them, Anthea, I really think I would. It wasn't as if you'd nowhere else to go.

"My marriage is not perfect," she said, and paused for a brisk sniffle to forbid her own tears, "but it is legal enough, God knows. So whatever your reasons for following me, pray don't pretend you don't know if I'm married."

Anthea heard more than the words, and saw in her friend's face more than she'd wanted to see. For all of her nebulous hopes for Julian, she'd always believed herself to be more fair and honest with other females than most of her sex were. Because she'd understood the need for it in this unfair world, she'd seen the necessity for the kinship of all women. In Eliza's look of naked scorn she saw just what she'd done without any fantasy or rationalization to dress it up, and all because Eliza's sad and wondering words had given her no choice but to see it. And she was shamed.

Eliza got no answer, but then, she thought as her former teacher dropped her astonished gaze at last and fled the room, white-faced, there really wasn't any answer to be given aloud. It had all been there in Anthea's eyes, in her look of guilt and envy intermixed. It had all been there in her lack of an answer, actually, Eliza thought sadly.

The newly made viscountess ate her luncheon alone, and such was her state of mind that she didn't even send a footman to ask after her absent companion. If she'd lost Anthea, she thought, so be it. The only pain it caused her was a distant one, for all she'd loved her friend. Because she reasoned that if she herself had wanted another person's fiancé or husband, she'd have come out and said so instead of lurking or meddling with a person's honeymoon. The thing that bothered her the most was the thought that Julian might be angry with her for falling out with Anthea. No, she thought, curling up in a chair in the small salon, the thing that bothered her most was the thought that Julian might care about it at all.

She didn't go to her own rooms to select a gown for the coming night, because her spirits grew as dim as the late-afternoon light did, and she decided she didn't care to go out tonight after all. She'd been to teas and musicales and theaters in the past week. She'd dressed in satins and ruffles and the newest style of tightly fitted gowns for grand balls and the oldest styles of billowing ones for low masquerades. She'd held her head high and had been complimented loudly for her good looks as well as silently for her good *ton*, for putting a good face on what was obviously a bad marriage—for where, oh, where, was her wandering husband tonight, as the refrain always went when she turned her back. And now she'd had enough, quite enough, thank you, she thought, coiling deeper into the chair, so dispirited she wondered if the tears were worth the trouble of crying.

They weren't. She was dry-eyed and sitting in the semi-dark when the butler came to the door and peered into the gloom to tell her she had visitors.

"It is the Honorable Miss Merriman, my lady, and Mr. Be good," he said gently, for his new mistress was so small and valiant it fair made all the servants weep seeing how she tried to sail through London all on her own. The viscount ran the risk of being done in by his outraged staff when he returned—if he returned—the butler thought as he offered to light a fire, ignite the lamps, and bring any sort of brightness he could into the room for his brave little mistress.

"Oh, yes, thank you, and show them in, certainly," Eliza said. It was as unexpected as it was a delightful surprise, for Constance was very good to her these days, as was Ben-Be-Good, who was always with Constance. The two of them, as well as the Duke and Duchess of Peterstow, had insisted on accompanying her everywhere these past days, and it was to their eternal credit that they never made her feel extraneous, for all that she perceived both couples could do very well without her. Well, tonight they'd have to, she thought decisively, for she'd no intention of going anywhere, except eventually to bed.

But Constance didn't appear to be dressed for anything more than an afternoon call, and she clearly had no sort of entertainment on her mind. Ben had, as usual, nothing but Constance on his mind, and from his strained expression, he was just as troubled as she so obviously was.

"Eliza, where is Julian?" Constance said without preamble when the butler had left them alone.

"What is it?" Eliza asked at once, looking from one serious face to the other.

"Do you think you might tender me a reply and not another question?" Constance asked angrily, reminding Eliza where she'd got some of her impersonation of arrogance from.

"I think I ought to know what you're talking about," Eliza began, when Ben, on a sigh, deftly steering them both from the collision course they were on, said softly but quickly, "It's important that I get word to him. I've gotten some word myself that he might be in some danger."

Eliza's head shot up at that, and her nostrils flared.

"No, please, don't take alarm," he said smoothly, "for the danger can be avoided if he knows of it. It will all come to nothing if I can get word to him."

When she only looked at him pointedly, he went on reluctantly, "There are some villains who've been misusing his coach line to their own profit, that's all. He's gone in search of them, but I've just discovered, through various channels"—he paused, and thought wryly that neither of these two fair ladies knew how apt the word "channels" was in this case, for the sort of men who brought him such news ran in underground, underworld circles, low and secret, with their twitching snouts to the ground—"that unfortunately, they've discovered his presence first. If he knows this, he can avoid all difficulty. So I'd like to get word to him. Please."

"He stays at the Golden Fleece in Brighton some days, and the Owl and Garter in Reigate on others. He's written to me from both places," she explained proudly, for his letters were all that she had of him and she held them in high esteem. "What are you going to do now?" she asked.

"Get word to him, of course. Before anything happens, I'm sure," he lied smoothly. "I think I'll forgo Lady Henderson's water party tomorrow, if you'll excuse me, Constance. I think I'll take a ride down toward the sea instead. He travels fastest who travels fastest," he said on a grin, "and the best way to ensure a message being delivered right, as my friend Lion once said, is to do it the best way to deliver a kiss—yourself."

He'd laundered Lion's comparison, but the essence remained true and obviously Eliza agreed with him. For she seemed much struck and was still nodding in silent agreement when he begged to take leave of her to pack, and she recalled herself and bade both of her friends good night.

And then she packed.

After a long spell of rain, the afternoon cleared as it softened to twilight, and there was a clean road ahead, so for all that the long jaunt up from Brighton was no pleasure, at least the occupants of the *Bard* agreed, this trip had been no hardship. The coach was clean and relatively uncrowded, only three within and five without, and the horses they just put on at the change at St. John's Common seemed able to step nicely as well as together. The guard was sour-faced, but the coachman, although a dashing, uncommonly handsome fellow, seemed to actually know his trade.

And so there was a great deal of dismay when the coach rolled to a halt at the side of the road just after everyone had got nicely settled in again after their forced march up Reigate Hill, and they were ordered out—on the downturn! as the aggrieved passengers made haste to point out as they complained. But the blond coachman seemed not to hear their increasingly loud bellows about schedules and appointments and presumption and reporting him to the company if he didn't shake a leg, as he walked around the coach and inspected his horses and their harnesses, and finally got down on his hands and knees in the dust and ran his gloved hands over the wheels.

"A 'wobble' indeed!" one passenger protested when the guard tried to explain the coachman's odd actions after conferring with the mad fellow. "All coaches wobble!"

"Ah, but this wobble was different," the coachman said as he got up from his knees and came toward them with a bit of silver metal displayed on his palm.

"A coachman should know his coach as intimately as a lover knows his lady," he said thoughtfully, staring as hard at his hand as the puzzled passengers did as they crowded around him. "Pardon, ma'am," he said immediately, sweeping off his hat and bowing as he noticed his one woman passenger, a red-faced farmwife. "As a ladywife knows her garden, I should rather say."

"Aye," the woman said, laughing, "as good as she knows her own bunions, I ken," and they all laughed until he reported with some sadness:

"I knew that wobble wasn't in the road or the teams or the coach. It was in the wheel, and all due to this little bit of nothing, this axle bolt. See? Its threads are gone and in a mile or two, so should we be too, I think, all the way to hell and gone, my friends, likely on this downhill rush—off the road, and over the side, and into the river when the wheel spun off as we picked up speed. We'll walk, I'm afraid, until we can get another bolt this side of Reigate. But we're lucky."

There was little in his passengers' faces or commentary to signify their pleasure at their luck as they marched down the downslope of the hill. But the one woman among them patted the coachman's arm as he walked with her and kept her from making a misstep and rolling down like the wheel he'd just described.

"Never you mind," she told him. "We're lucky, there's truth. You know your business, lad. Or else you was born under a lucky star."

He shook his head, and though he didn't agree, he said

no more, for she was an elder and a female, and so people always said of him before they knew him better, after all.

But the two men behind the high hedges to the side of the road who sat on the horses that had followed the coach out from the inn at St. John's Common agreed with her. And so they turned their mounts on disappointed sighs and rode side by side back through the oncoming night, speaking in murmurous voices. For they knew it was always folly to leave anything to luck. Professionals never did, and they were proud to consider themselves that. And so next time, they agreed, they would not trust to it again, they'd have to recommend taking action.

18

"I'VE COME TO APOLOGIZE—but where are you going?"
Anthea asked, stopped in the doorway by the sight before her.

It was such an advanced hour of the night, she'd only dared scratch at the door because she'd seen a light shining from beneath it, and yet there Eliza stood, a disreputable-looking portmanteau dragged out and on her bed, and she was buttoning one of her old school cloaks about her neck. The drab high-collared garment hadn't seemed extraordinary in all the years that Eliza had worn it, but now it did, because it contrasted wildly with her fashionable coiffure, and looked as out of place as to be laughable against the backdrop of the elegant bedchamber.

"You needn't bother, I am the one who will be leaving shortly, you see," Anthea said when Eliza didn't answer, but only went on packing, flinging a pair of slippers into the old bag.

"Don't give yourself airs," Eliza said absently as she left the bed and went to search in a deep drawer for something. "You can stay on here until the cows come home. I've business elsewhere."

"I'm leaving and going back to school," Anthea replied in hollow tones, her voice somewhat thickened from weeping, but reassured by Eliza's air of briskness, she went on in a more forthright manner, "I'm not going to stay there forever, however. I see now that I am not made for such a life, I've obviously other ambitions. . . . I may well take on a position with the duke or even with the Lyonses in time. But, don't worry, I'm not at all interested in . . . deceiving myself about the viscount any longer."

That made Eliza pause. She glanced at Anthea, a questioning look upon her face. Then, as realization dawned, she laughed, looking in that moment as youthful and carefree and mischievous as she had when she'd worn that cloak for all those years before.

" 'The viscount'?" she mocked, laughing. "Oh, Lud, Anthea, what a time to come all over proper. You've been 'Julianing' him to death for weeks, and now that you've decided to be noble and give him up because you've remembered he's married to me, he's suddenly 'the viscount'? Well, don't bother," she said, her voice becoming distant as she turned her back suddenly in order to rummage for something deep in her wardrobe, "you'll have a fair shot at him any day now. I'm giving him a divorce. But," she said, emerging from the wardrobe with an old dressing gown in her hands, and ignoring Anthea's gasp, "I warn you, Anthea, he hasn't a care for you—not really. He only always wants what he can't have, I think. Doubtless he'll discover himself impassioned by me the moment he discovers I'm cutting him loose. Too bad, really," she said on a shrug, "for him, as well as for us. Yes," she said, looking at Anthea so coldly that the other woman took a breath in again, "*us*. Because, you see, I do remember how you used to go on about women uniting, helping each other against the cold, cruel man's world out there. And now that I'm actually 'there,' I can see you were right, even if you were wrong in how you tried to undermine me, you know. I can't blame you, though, for all I don't know if I'll ever forgive you.

"It's his looks, really, I think," she said in a musing tone, pausing to think. "For all he's clever and charming, it's definitely those looks of his. Would you have been so totally enthralled by him if he were a weedy little poetical type? Or a fattish fellow with thinning hair? I wonder . . . would I have been so instantly smitten myself? Would you even have cared to hear about him at all? Perhaps in time, when you got to know him—as I got to know him by his letters," she decided, folding her robe into ever smaller squares against her breast as she spoke, "but I really do think you'd have ignored him if you hadn't got a look at that locket I wore. I really do, Anthea, for all the girls had infatuations, you know, and you only shared in mine.

"Poor lad," she said suddenly, smiling gently at some errant thought as she stood and faced Anthea and yet seemed to be looking far away and beyond her. "How confused and distressed he must be when he discovers all his friends trying to become his lovers. Truly, it must be a problem. And it's really not his fault. He's very like Apollo in that, you know—or at least the Apollo you taught me about. Tooling about in his chariot all day, wanting no more than pleasure, dazzling goddesses and mortals and never caring about any of them for more than the brief shining hour he visits upon them. And I suppose never understanding how badly he hurts them, either. But for all that, there's not an ounce of cruelty in him, I think. Because I do think he suffers a little with each of them each time.

"I met him after the funeral of a lady who'd loved him, and he'd wept then, I think, as much for her as for pity that he hadn't loved her. Well, he won't have to weep for me," Eliza said determinedly, turning to vigorously stuff the robe into the portmanteau, "for I'm giving him his freedom, entirely. I don't fancy living on with him for the rest of my life, watching him feel guilty because he doesn't love me the way he thinks he ought. Divorce is a scandal— don't say it—I know it. But there are some gentlemen will want me even more for it, I think, don't you? There's nothing like wicked experience to catch some gentlemen's interest, or so I've noted, or else there wouldn't be so many popular females who are both homely and dull," she concluded, snapping the portmanteau shut.

"Eliza," Anthea said reprovingly, "this is never you speaking."

"Indeed it is—now," Eliza said, holding up her chin and tugging the heavy bag from the bed, looking like a runaway child, her former schoolmistress thought, and never like a viscountess, much less like the wise and embittered woman who'd just spoken.

"We all of us have changed, Anthea," Eliza continued. "We all of us have had to, I think. You never thought you'd let your passions rule your heart, much less your head, so that you betrayed not only yourself but also your best friend," and as Anthea dropped her gaze, Eliza added sorrowfully, "but you're not the only one. I never thought I'd so much growing up to do either."

"Well, then, Anthea," she said, hesitating, weighing the bag in her hand, seeming uneasy for the first time in their odd discussion, "I've a favor to ask of you. And I ask it for old times' sake, as well as for Julian's and mine. Please don't tell anyone, not Constance especially, nor Warwick or Susannah, where I've gone off to tonight. Say I've gone to Mama or one of my sisters, please, will you?"

"But where *are* you going?" Anthea asked.

"Your promise, please," Eliza said firmly.

"I cannot in all conscience give a promise I cannot see the consequences of," Anthea answered stiffly, on firm ground now, remembering the schoolmistress she was.

"Then say what you will, and good-bye," Eliza sighed, and began to walk past the other woman to the door of her bedchamber.

"Oh, very well," Anthea blurted, realizing she'd never be able to forcibly stop Eliza, as Eliza grinned, realizing that Anthea's curiosity must always outweigh her caution, or else she'd never have been able to be her friend for all those years.

"It's a promise," Anthea said resignedly when Eliza didn't answer. "Oh, very well, if you insist on being childish: I promise I won't tell anyone where you're going," she added when she continued to meet the smaller woman's silence and steady implacable stare. "But where are you off to?" she implored, hoping she might be able to dissuade her from leaving so that her rash promise would come to nothing.

"To Julian, he's in danger," Eliza said simply, and as Anthea gaped, she continued, with some worry coloring her voice, "Ben-Be-Good said he's tracking some villains but that they'd got wind of it and so he's to be warned. I think I ought to do that. And as I know where he'll be tomorrow evening, and as I can catch the daybreak coach to Brighton if I leave now, I'll go at once."

"But isn't that dangerous?" Anthea protested. "Why not let Ben-Be-Good do it?"

"He says he will. But he said something else that made me realize I won't be sure of it unless I do it myself. And I must be sure, because then I doubt I'll see him again for a very long while. Because then I'm off for home. Alone, quite alone, my parents won't be there, but they're never there anyway. They hate the solitude of the place. But I don't. I need it now. I'm not even taking a footman or a maid, because I wish to cut myself off from this life entirely for a spell. Entirely," she repeated with some emphasis, before Anthea could volunteer her services as companion again.

"And I don't want anyone to know, because I don't wish to be stopped. It's as simple as that," Eliza said as she hoisted the bag again.

"But it's dangerous—traveling alone in any case—and with villains afoot especially," Anthea stammered.

"I won't be molested in a public stagecoach—not the way I intend to look, I assure you," she said, making Anthea doubt her even as she tossed her head and set her myriad auburn curls to dancing. "And Julian's not likely to do that either, no matter how I look," she said with bitter mockery. "And then I'm off to the safest place on earth. I'm not altogether helpless either. Julian had a wonderful assortment of pistols in his study downstairs, you know. And Hugh taught me how to use one a hundred years ago. See?" she said proudly, dragging a small silver pocket pistol from a deep pocket and admiring it before she slipped it back in again.

"But then it might be dangerous, after all," Anthea cried.

"I suppose it might," Eliza said a bit recklessly, looking more the schoolgirl every moment.

"But then why are you doing it?" Anthea asked, distraught. "Purely for mischief? But you're too old for that now, Eliza."

"Indeed, I am," Eliza answered sadly, all her brashness gone, but then, just before she left the room, she added, with a shrug and on a little laugh, "But I'm doing it just because I'm too old for childish pursuits, don't you see? I'm doing it because I love him, Anthea, and there's an end to it," she said gruffly. And then she left.

But she hurried down the stair and hastened to have a sleepy footman summon a carriage to take her to the coaching terminal at the Bull and Mouth, for the sun would be rising soon and there were miles to travel, and she'd learned that she couldn't altogether trust Anthea, promises or not. Indeed, she'd learned by bitter experience of late that she could trust no one but herself. And obviously, not even herself, she thought nervously as she clambered into the carriage, for now that she was alone and on her way, she was as alarmed by her decision to leave as Anthea had been, and a great deal more frightened besides.

"The girl can't move a finger, 'n that's the honest truth," the palsied little old man whispered, " 'n when she were awake, 'n tried to steady herself, 'n concentrated hard on holding her glass, her eyes crossed, one almost kissing the other, I swear it, 'n then she giggled when the water spilled down her chin, there's a scandal for you."

"Jug-bitten?" the blond coachman asked idly, turning his own glass of rum round in circles as he bent over the table talking to the garrulous old fellow as the *Rover*'s teams were being changed. Julian didn't have to take the reins of the *Thunder* for several hours yet, but the ancient fellow had been one of his most talkative fares on the trip out from Brighton the other day, and now, having discovered the attentive coachman taking his ease in the common taproom, the old man was regaling him with what he'd noted going on during his trip back again. A retired peddler who passed his time plaguing his remaining children with his incessant visits, it was rare for the quavering old man to find someone who'd listen to him, and he was as excited as he was grateful for Julian's interest. But not as grateful as Julian was as he listened with as much attention as secret delight. This was exactly the sort of firsthand news he'd wanted to hear so that he could see what was going forth on his coaching line for himself at last.

For he'd heard quite enough by now. No one minded a little moonraking: some few items got at the dark of the moon, brought along untaxed, amongst documented cargo on the line. And no sane owner expected a coachman or guard not to do the odd favor for a friend, or to make the extra penny where he could. But when such doings became so common it was becoming clear that passengers and legal freight were intrusions on the general run of business, it became a bad business, however lucrative it was. Or so at least it was to decent men. And so it was to Julian.

Then, too, he'd heard tell of the use of his coaches for not only the common run of illegal goods—liquors and silks and art objects—but also lively and ugly trade in those things even the moon didn't care to illuminate, passing from London to the coast and back again. These were objects of frailer constitution—for there were dark tales of the frequent transport of forbidden flesh: live for foreign delectation, newly dead for the domestic use of certain doctors. White slavery and body-snatching, whores from London to the sea, cadavers from the docks to the medical schools, the quick and the dead for fast profit—it was a bad business and getting worse. He'd heard enough to act; he wanted to see for himself, so he listened closely. But as he had to be sure, he refused to act hastily.

"I've seen females, aye, even dashing-looking young ones, drink themselves so blind they couldn't hold their next glass," he said now, as calmly and consideringly as if they were discussing the price of rum and not a young woman who lay, even as they spoke, in the back of the *Rover*, drugged to her eyes—if the old man could be believed.

"Ho!" the old man said wisely, putting one shaking, knobby-knuckled finger aside his nose. "As if I couldn't smell it a yard away, lad, 'n me putting away a bottle or two together in my life before the quacks forbade it. No, Lord love you, lad, I may not be a learned man, but I was a peddler in my day 'n I got around. For all the other nodcocks in the coach look away 'n carry on like they was disgusted, with all their lifted eyebrows 'n noses, that female didn't have a drop, I'd swear to it. A bonny little thing too, not in the common way, 'n not the sort to go larking off with those two rapscallions that's got her in tow, neither. Now, they're London-bred maggots, those two—they'd make a soul cross the street on a dark night in the pouring rain, I can tell you. Hearken, lad—it's just as they have it in the melodramas, 'n I never thought to clap my eyes on such goings-on. Got her drugged 'n getting her to the docks," he whispered even lower, " 'n they'll be at selling her off to Gawd knows where—wherever they got use for a pretty piece who can't get home no more, I expect."

"Let's see, then," Julian said, rising.

"Ah, you have a look, lad," the old man said in a hasty mumble. "I'd only get in the way," he explained, looking about the taproom anxiously, proving how he'd gotten to his great age intact.

The *Rover* was almost ready to roll again. Two fresh teams had been hitched to her traces, and the coachman, a burly red-faced giant, was drinking down the last of the tankard that the innkeeper had brought to him. The guard, obviously bent on entering the inn to order all the strays back into the coach so that they could be on their way again, marched right past Julian as he paused on the doorstep looking out to the stagecoach. As the coach had arrived, Julian had absently noted that its guard couldn't play a true note on his tin. At the time, he'd thought it might have been that the poor fellow suffered from a head cold or too much liquor, since no guard in his health or right mind could resist a tuneful entry to an innyard. Now, as the cold-eyed fellow shouldered past him, he saw that it might only have been lack of ability that had silenced the horn.

Because he'd never met any stagecoach guard before that would ignore a coachman, on the job or not, on the road. Theirs was a convivial profession, and that was one of its unalterable truths. And for all he'd left off his driving cape, Julian's other clothing—from the tie of his neckcloth to the shape of his half-boots and the cut of his loud waistcoat—spoke of his position as well as a waybill might have done, to those who could listen, and he pondered this for a second after the fellow had gone into the inn without a nod to him.

Then he walked to the coach, keeping its body between him and the guzzling coachman, seemingly idly inspecting the rig, until he came to the door. Then he looked in, and then he pulled the door open and stared in.

One of the men, a grizzled fellow with dirty linen, looked up and out and then away again. The other, bulkier and younger, sat back, staring into space—perhaps, Julian thought, he'd had a bit of what the girl that sat between them so obviously had gotten quite a bit of. For the old man had been right. No spirits Julian knew could transport the girl to wherever she'd gone in her mind right now. Had she been sleeping, however exhausted, she'd have stirred, or opened an eye as the door flew open. Had she been drunk, she might have groaned or even murmured. In either case, she wouldn't have lain there, propped up in her seat, head lolling to the side, eyes rolled up and mouth hung open, snoring like a dying old man.

She was dressed cheaply but serviceably, her ample body decently covered in plain muslin, and she'd a quantity of fair hair, a turned-up nose, and a round freckled face that could have been comely if it weren't so unnaturally ashen. She might well have been pretty in a buxom, wholesome sort of way when she was in her senses. But she was not, and not by a long chalk. Her companions, however, soon demonstrated that they were.

" 'Ere! You comin' in or just lettin' the flies in?" one of the roughly dressed men demanded, as the other squinted into the light Julian stood silhouetted against.

"I thought," Julian said softly, "that the lady might like to come out and stretch her legs."

"Lady? Oh, 'er. Nah, lazy slut. Sooner stretch 'er neck, my lass," the older man replied, putting his arm round the girl. "Thankee just the same. Now, close the door, like a good fellow, eh?"

"No," Julian said calmly, "because I do wonder just whose lass she is, actually."

"She's my wife, 'n 'is sister," the man said at once, " 'n wot's it to you?"

"Few men drug their wives to the eyes in order to sell them at the docks for use in foreign bazaars, and fewer brothers help them to do it. And," Julian said pleasantly, making a gesture with the pocket pistol that appeared in his hand that caused both men to sit up straight, "far fewer coachmen allow them to do it, I think."

"Now, now, what's toward?" a heavy voice said at Julian's ear, and from the way both men relaxed, Julian stiffened.

"Madman here thinks I've dossed my Jennie, 'e does. Fancy that." The grizzled fellow laughed, looking pointedly at the huge coachman who'd come to stand at Julian's side. "She 'as a dram or two an' Robin'ood 'ere comes to the rescue. She'll 'ave a laugh at that when she sobers up, she will."

"He says we're going to sell her at the docks," the heavier man reported slowly and carefully, whether because he was incapacitated by drugs or nature, Julian couldn't tell, but he frowned as he went on explaining, "He says as to how she's going to be sold in foreign bazaars. Nobody told me foreign—" he went on sullenly, before his companion slewed his head around, and glaring at him, silenced his complaints, for it seemed some rudimentary sense of patriotism had been offended as his moral code had not been.

"That's a laugh," the coachman said in hearty accents. "Ain't it, Bob?"

Both men looked dumbly about the coach to see whom the coachman had addressed, until he added, with some impatience, and more emphasis, "To think that you'd have to give your lass anything to get her like that, eh, *Bob*?" As realization that he was supposed to be "Bob" dawned on the older man and he began to smile and nod, the coachman added, "Now, put that pretty pistol away, lad, for I've my guard with a carbine at your back. That's better," he said, smiling merrily as Julian's hand went down. "I don't know what line you pull for, friend," he said then, shaking his head sorrowfully, "but I can tell you I don't let any funny business onto this one. Now, let my passengers be, eh? Bob and Jennie here ride with me often, and I've never seen her sober yet."

"Nor me!" the older man declared, getting into the spirit of the game, although his heavier companion frowned and looked suspiciously about himself, obviously still confused as to who this mysterious "Bob" could be.

With his words, the older man gave the comotose girl a quick hug about the shoulders, which caused her head to drop down abruptly, lolling as though it hung from a broken neck, and there was a moment's silence until he said brightly, "Ah, she'll be better in the morning, mate, not to worry."

He planned to end this business soon enough, Julian thought, but he didn't know if it would be soon enough to help this poor creature in the coach, for she was already well on her way to her doom. Though she wasn't dressed as a trollop or a girl in the trade, it was unlikely that she was entirely innocent. Although it was possible, innocents were rarely kidnapped and snatched from the streets, even in London's worst districts, unless they were far lovelier than this one, unless there was some other score to settle. More probably she'd been lured, or lied to; most usually these poor young chits were seduced and abandoned to their fate. This one could have been promised anything from a better position to a good marriage before she'd had the celebratory drink that leveled her. But whatever the bait had been, she'd never expect to wake to a life of eternal servitude, degradation, and early death. And so, however soon he knew he'd be able to close this dirty business down, it was hard for Julian to leave now, knowing he was abandoning even one last lost girl to such a life.

But how could he call the coachman a liar, when there was a carbine pointed at his back?

"I say," a deep plummy voice interceded. "Coachman! I echo this gentleman's doubts. For all the unfortunate person in the coach may well have often imbibed in the past, I take leave to tell you, sir, that I doubt it is alcohol which so affects her now. No," the loud voice went on, causing both the coachman and Julian to swing around to see where it issued from. "And my dear father, now deceased, was himself a physician of some note. Never have I observed such stupor from mere alcohol. Observe her eyes, note her pallor, mark how she breathes! I was meaning to bring it to your attention, sir, on the ride down, but awaited her recovery. Now I must agree with the young man, and take leave to insist the girl be examined by a physician, and at once."

It was a huge old man who addressed them. A giant of an old gentleman, wearing outmoded clothes and an antique of a moth-eaten box wig. But he had a fine gold watch fob and an air of command, as well as a loud and carrying voice, and he seemed very much outraged. The *Rover*'s coachman narrowed his eyes. Julian widened his.

"And who might you be?" the coachman demanded.

"I am Sir Toby Fenton," the gentleman declared with as much pleasure and pride as he might have said, "I am the King of England," and then he paused, as though awaiting their fear and trembling, or amazement, or any other sort of outsize acknowledgment of this name. When none came, he went on, undismayed, "And as magistrate of my district, which you are shortly to drive through," he added, with a nod to the coachman and a hard look to the two men in the shadowed interior of the coach, where they sat like unspeaking stones now, "I am afraid I must insist on your cooperation.

"Take the girl out, please," he said with nothing like a request in his voice, "and place her within the inn while a physician is summoned. Or I shall have to summon the sheriff or the militia to the purpose."

There was only a second's hesitation. And then the coachman's face split into a wide grin and he waved his guard forward, crying loudly, "Come along, Sam. Help me with the 'lady,' just as his honor says."

When a stifled cry from within the coach, high-pitched enough to have been the girl's, if she'd been lively enough to have uttered anything but breaths, was heard, the coachman went on, loudly enough to have been heard in the next district, although he supposedly spoke only to his guard, "C'mon, hop it. I've a schedule to meet. We'll leave the lady here, and have the sawbones see her. You'll never mind that, will you, Bob?" he asked, poking his head into the coach, his broad shoulders and big back blocking all that then transpired within.

"Here she is," he said a moment later, emerging from the coach with the girl hanging from his arms like a rag doll. "She don't weigh more than a mite, so never you mind, Sam, I'll tote her in myself, just you load the passengers up now."

As he walked with the girl, and the formidable Sir Toby Fenton raised a quizzing glass to get a better look at his burden, who appeared even sicklier in the full sunlight, he said over his shoulder, "Bob and her brother have business in Brighton, so they'll be going on with me. He'll pick her up tonight, he says, when she's sober."

"Very well," Sir Toby said, following in his footsteps, "but I shall stay on until the doctor arrives. I conceive it to be my duty."

When the coach was refilled and the guard up on back again, the coachman, having deposited the girl in a bedchamber of the inn, took a step up on the wheel to get to his seat. Sir Toby placed a huge hand on his arm, staying him. The coachman spun round, a look so desperate and cornered on his face that Julian, standing in the courtyard, tensed his muscles and reached for his pistol.

"A moment," Sir Toby said imperiously.

In that moment the silence was so intense that the sound of one of the horses exhaling was loud as rolling thunder.

"I paid full fare, coachman," Sir Toby said. "I should like either a refund of my monies, or a written transfer, if you please, fellow."

The coachman began breathing again, reached his hand into his pocket, and without setting an eye on the coins he held there, dropped a number of them into the waiting outstretched hand of the haughty old gent.

"And good day to you, sir," he mumbled, along with some other things fortunately unheard, as he clambered up to his seat. He raised his whip and snapped it with unnecessary vigor, causing the horses to startle and the coach to start forward with a jolt, before it rumbled away at top speed, its remaining passengers volubly complaining.

Sir Toby and Julian stood silent, watching it leave, until it was gone from sight entirely except for the settling road dust it left behind it. Then Julian turned to the old gentleman with a frown.

"Sir Toby," he said, "would have rather been burnt at the stake than appear in public in such antiquated rig. As I recall, he was too much a tulip of the *ton* to have done more than sneer at that waistcoat, for example."

"True," Arden said, looking down at the sadly shiny black waistcoat he wore, "but as it's been five long years since he walked this green earth, his clothes were all out of style anyway, by now. They were at the bottom of the trunk too—and covered with camphor. If anyone had to smell of those crystals, it should be the officious old gent, don't you think? And 'Uncle Charlie' wouldn't have sounded half so weighty as 'Sir Toby' did, would it?"

"Excuses, excuses, Lion, my pet," Julian said, shaking his head in sorrow. "It's just that you never liked playing at being that fop, did you? You always preferred portraying the toplofty old gentleman, especially when you had to make an impression. Oh, Lord, Arden," he said then, with a wan smile, looking very young again, "you came in a good time. I was in a corner. You've appeared before me in many costumes, in many countries, in many guises in our days traveling the world together, but never, I think, so advantageously as now."

"Oh?" Arden answered as they strolled back to the inn and he swept his high wig off and scratched at his crop of tawny hair. "And what about that time in Cádiz? When the general arrived home and the lieutenant came to tell him of his new orders just before he was about to open his wife's bedroom door? Or the time in Rouen, when the wine merchant found Sir Toby himself about to buy a massive amount of wine, for export, of course, just as he was going to open his daughter's bedroom door? Or that time in The Hague—"

"Shall we say," Julian interrupted, "the most advantageous time outside of a bedroom and leave it at that, my friend?"

"Very well," Arden agreed, shrugging out of his worn jacket and seating himself, in his shirtsleeves, in the now almost deserted taproom, "I can think of better ways to pass the night, anyhow. Here's one—look, the nice coachie gave me three times my fare for getting off here. I'll buy us a few rounds of ale—rescuing damsels is thirsty work. I don't think she'll come round until morning, myself. Looks like opium to me. Best leave her with some banknotes and a written one as well, and a word in the landlord's ear for when she rises, in case she can't read. He looks honest enough, for all he receives gallowsbirds as coachmen if the money is right, but I think I can frighten him more than the other fellow does, so it will even out. I'll see she's sent home unharmed when she wakes. I don't think her 'husband' or 'brother' will return," he mused, "but much as it pains me, we might as well tell the local law about it too, for safety's sake. Now, what else do you want done, my boy? Mind, I won't do floors or windows, my lumbago won't allow it," he cautioned as he took out a handkerchief, dipped it into a glass of water he'd obtained, and began to remove the gray, pasty powder from his face.

"Arden," Julian said, unsmiling, "how did you get here? And don't answer, 'by coach,' because now that I'm over being relieved, I'm worried. How many others know my whereabouts, and the reasons for them?"

"I know most things, not all," Arden replied lightly, but then, seeing how grave his friend's face was, he sighed and spoke without a trace of humor. "Ben got word to me that you were on the trail of trouble but that it had tumbled to you first. I had to come down, fast as I could, and traveled by stagecoach, in disguise, rather than in my own coach and skin, so as to keep an ear to the ground and an eye on things, undiscovered, as I did. Ah, well, don't look so honored and moved, it's not all for friendship's sake, I'm a partner in this mess, am I not?"

"And always the sort to worry about funds, is that

what you're saying? Never mind," Julian said on a radiant smile, "I'll spare you the hugs and kisses then, but not the thanks. Because I am grateful to you, my friend. You saved me from making a foolishly premature ending to my adventures just now when I decided to play an impromptu Galahad. But although I'm glad you didn't, you might have saved yourself a trip if you only wished to warn me. Because I've a notion of some trouble coming. After all, when you ask a great many questions of a great many people, you're bound to eventually get some hard answers. As it happens, tonight's my last run to Brighton—and only because I'm promised to it."

His face became set and his voice grim as he went on, "It's more than moonraking and trade in stupefied wenches, Arden. It's contraband of every sort—and every filthy sort of business villains can traffic in. But now that you're here, shall we shut them down?"

"Of course," Arden said. "It only needs that I know the name of the head, for in such things strangling the body don't kill the beast. I want to break its neck. We'll see how best to do it after I meet up with Ben. Where is he, by the by?"

"I've no idea," Julian answered in surprise. "I haven't seen him since we both were guests at your house. Was he supposed to be here?"

"Oh, aye," Arden said softly, so softly that Julian grew still again. "By now, certainly. I was the one who was going to surprise him. I think, my friend," he said, "that I'll ride along with you tonight, because it may be that for all it's a fair night, there's trouble on the road ahead."

"Be easy," Julian said on a smile he never felt. "There are two more coaches due in here for a change of horses before I'm to take over my old coach, the *Thunder*, to Brighton tonight. Who knows who will arrive before then?" he asked as he signaled to the serving wench.

The *Tempest*, out of London, out of horsepower and with a coachman out of patience with a quartet of drunken young rakes on his rooftop, stopped over at the inn for a change of horses. It disgorged a farmer and a farrier and a small boy who was tearfully reunited with his grandfather. A cursory check showed it retained only a merchant, his wife, their daughter, and the drunken rooftop quartet. And after it took on a clerk and a poor young tradesman, it lurched off into the gathering twilight, the outside revelers' discordant singing wafting back to Julian and Arden, who watched it go.

Soon after, the *Royal George* rattled up and let out a grumbling rotund husband and wife to stay on at the inn until morning, when the wife declared she might tolerate a coach ride again, as well as a pair of elderly sisters who comforted a roadsick old widow as best they could before they took off for their own homes. It still held three sailors and a pair of schoolboys and their uncle outside, and none within now, nor did it take up any new passengers, since night was coming on. The widow had a ticket all the way to Brighton, but such was her distress that the coachman was only too glad to give her money back so that she could travel on with the *Thunder* if she recovered by the time it left, or with the devil—the coachman's disgusted face clearly showed as he left her threatening to faint if she didn't get every ha'penny back from him—if she didn't.

But Ben was nowhere to be seen, nor had either coachman spotted him anywhere down the line from London.

"It's not full dark by a long way, the *Thunder* leaves on the first star," Julian reminded an uncharacteristically subdued Arden. "There are always private coaches, you know."

The first faint glimmer of a star near to the melon slice of a bone-bright moon was struggling through the late purple dusk when Julian climbed up on the *Thunder*'s high seat. The *Thunder* carried only packages and boxes, a jug-eared farmboy and a sleepy intinerant worker on top; the widow, recovered enough to toddle into the coach, had enough room to herself to be roadsick or heartsick to her heart's content, for she rode by herself within. Arden paused, one foot on the wheel, as though by so waiting he might catch sight of the lost Ben. And miraculously, even as he heaved a great sigh and began to swing himself up, the faint clatter and rattle and stammer of stones thrown from onrushing coach wheels came clear to their ears in the hush of the deepening night.

An elegant chariot and four came racing into the courtyard soon after, its blooded steeds' heads high and eyes rolling from their hard ride. Julian and Arden waited until it rolled to a stop, Arden already rehearsing sarcastic rejoinders for his youthful friend Ben for managing to commandeer such a turn-out, and Julian lost in admiration of the horseflesh that pulled it.

Arden, relieved enough to be angry with Ben's tardiness, drew in a breath to blast him for coming so late, and then lost it on a silent exhalation as the door swung open and a lean figure leapt out onto the cobblestones and strode to the side of their coach.

"I can't let you alone for an hour without you fall into some hopeless morass. What am I to do with you?" the tall, slender gentleman scolded as he stood, his hands on his lean hips, booted feet apart, managing, by some incredible means, to look down his long nose at Julian and Arden as he stared up to where they sat perched on the driver's seat above him.

"Warwick!" Julian shouted, beginning to laugh, until he remembered all the circumstances of this odd meeting, and then he held his tongue and his breath as Arden quickly asked, "Have you seen Ben, Warwick?"

"Of course," the duke answered with some irritation. "Why do you think I had myself driven like a leaf before the wind to get here? The lad's dead to the world in a ramshackle inn near to St. John's Common, but not permanently so, thank heaven. He's got a bump on his head, and he'll wake to a bad taste in his mouth—but not for the rest of the night. Because unless I miss my guess, he's had a drink of something more than what the villains poured all over his clothes to deceive passersby as to his condition. But at least he'd the sense to send word of where he was bound before he met with his misadventure, and so I knew just where to travel to prevent more mischief."

"Thank you for your concern, Warwick," Julian said,

smiling, "but didn't you think Arden would be enough of a bodyguard for me?"

Even in the growing haze of twilight, Warwick's expression was clear to read. His next words came softer than the look that grew in his eyes.

"Oh, yes," he said, "doubtless our good Lion could protect you from Ali Baba and all his forty thieves, Julian. As doubtless you could preserve him in turn. But it was never either of you that I worried about. You see, it's Eliza that's gone missing, and from what I was told, I supposed I'd find her here with you. Never say she's not here?"

But their sudden dumbfounded silence was answer enough for him.

19

THE TWO OUTSIDE passengers in their high seats hesitated before speaking. The *Thunder* was supposed to leave at first dark so as to arrive in Brighton with the new day, but here they sat, already late, and their coachman seemed unwilling to begin the journey.

Only three things stayed their protests, for they'd paid good coin, even if it was only half-fare, for the privilege of riding on the stagecoach. One was the fact that the coachman seemed more a gentleman than a coachman and certainly more of one than either of them was. The second was that he was conferring with a gent that seemed to be more of a gentleman than the king himself. And the third was that the third gentleman they saw before them was roughly the size of a small mountain and looked none too amiable at the moment. As the darkness deepened, the two passengers exchanged little side glances with each other and then found their boots overwhelmingly interesting even as they lost their tongues.

"Is there any reason to suspect Eliza's come to see me?" Julian asked Warwick, his hand knotted tight over his whip. "She might have gone anywhere, mightn't she have?"

"Oh, she might have, but she didn't. Or so Anthea Baker said. She'd been sworn to silence, but I found a cogent argument and she's a remarkably reasonable female," the duke answered.

"You have a wealth of cogency," Arden commented, as Julian fell silent. "I hope the poor lass's arm don't ache too much."

"Barbarian," the duke commented amiably enough, although he kept a concerned eye on Julian. "I never had to resort to so much as the threat of force. She felt guilty enough for her part, and I had real concern for Eliza on mine. We've been through the nonsense of the folly of keeping one's word when danger threatened a young lady once before, and so I told her, and so you should remember, Arden—for it was your own intrepid Francesca who once mistakenly tried to keep her machinations a secret. We intervened then, as we shall now."

"But if Eliza were coming here, she would be here by now," Julian said softly.

"So she would," Warwick agreed. "So, then, I imagine she went to Brighton to await you there. For I'd no word of her or anyone that looked like her stopping off on the road so far today, and I'd many mentions of poor Ben to put me on his trail. Come," he said, "my neck's getting stiff looking up at you two oafs, and the night's getting on. I'll leave my carriage here and ride on with you. As Arden's taking up my part of the seat as well as his own, I'll ride in the coach, thank you. Put me on the waybill, please, Julian, and be quick about it . . . unless you mean to shoulder me and swallow the profits for yourself."

"No!" Julian said suddenly as the elegant duke turned to enter the coach, stopping him in his tracks. "No, I think not, now. I think," he said slowly and thoughtfully as he leaned low to speak for Warwick's and Arden's ears only, "that you ought to wait here for Eliza, Warwick, in case she eventually does come along. If she's at Brighton, I'll find her; if not, you can tell her to wait for me here. And you, Arden, would be better to keep our duke company, and then too, that way"—he seemed to think quickly as he went on—"you'll be able to see Ben early in the morning if you stay on here tonight. Yes. I think that's the better way. Because I've got to leave now, these two poor souls on the top are yearning to go but afraid to open their mouths, and they've the right of it, because we're behind schedule. But I can be there and back quickly enough, and there's never a need for either of you to come along with me. Best remain."

"Best get up a great deal earlier in the morning than me, Julian—and I woke at dawn," Warwick retorted, "if you want to do better than that."

"I thought I taught you better," Arden mourned, looking at Julian and shaking his head.

"You find a flaw in my reasoning?" Julian asked angrily.

"I find it perfect," Arden said, "so perfectly obstructive, in fact, that all your wild horses couldn't drag me from this seat now that you so clearly don't want me to come with you."

"Imperfect," Warwick disagreed. "For one, Eliza's obviously not arriving here tonight anymore, and a note would suffice for the possibility of her coming in the morning. For two, I do not need, and have never needed, company while sleeping—or at least not such as Arden's—and once and for all, Julian, since you are being so almighty noble, it's obvious you expect difficulty, and no power on earth will dissuade me from being part of it."

"But you're both married men and have children now," Julian said in a harsh whisper, "and shouldn't be taking any sort of foolish risks."

Warwick stood very still and exchanged a look with Arden. Then he drew himself up.

"A mans' having children is supposed to prove quite the reverse of what you so obviously think of our manhood, Julian. You really ought to have that talk with him, Arden. I think if you leave off the birds and lighten up on the bees, and concentrate more on the mechanics of the thing, he'll finally get the idea. No, Julian, my pretty," he said more seriously, "I'm coming along with you, and would if I'd fathered a dozen children, for I wouldn't be much of a father to them if I ran from a friend's danger, would I? For it's the fathering of them that counts, you know," he said on his sad, sweet smile, "not the begetting of them, really."

"Well-said, Duke," Arden rumbled approvingly, as the two topside passengers, hearing the title used, sat up straighter and were thankful that they hadn't kicked up a fuss after all, and then slumped, resigning themselves to sitting up half the night on top of the coach while the coachman parlayed, for nobility took odd fancies and it was just their luck, after all.

But it wasn't long until the coachman began turning his horses, and the guard, numbed with boredom, or more likely with drink, as was usually the case with him, remembered to pick up his tin and blow a few notes for the form of it.

"Are there any inside passengers?" Warwick asked before he entered the stagecoach after giving his own coachman directions.

"Only one. And she's no trouble. Only a widow. A heavily veiled and grieving widow. I wish you joy of her, for she snivels and speaks in whispers when she's not swooning," Arden said.

But then, even as Julian raised the whip, Arden grew silent, thinking on what he'd just said. And after the whip came down in a light kiss on the wheelers' shoulders, Julian turned to stare at him with disbelief and a wild surmise clear to see on his face in the glow of the carriage lamp.

"Madam," Warwick said as he opened the coach door, "your pardon, but I believe we share this coach now."

A sniffle and a muted sob greeted him from the interior of the coach, where the black-draped little woman sat, and taking that for leave to enter, Warwick climbed in, seated himself opposite the grieving widow, and crossing his legs, leaned back.

"Never fear, dear lady, I shan't impose on your privacy, but as we are to share this long journey to Brighton, I thought it might make you more comfortable if I made myself known to you," he said easily, once the coach began moving. "Allow me to introduce myself. I am Peterstow, Warwick Jones, Duke of Peterstow. And you?" he prompted.

A muffled "Mrs. Rampf" or "Dampf" or "Humph" was heard, and he nodded pleasantly, and asked, despite his recent disclaimer of offering conversation, "Have you been bereaved very long, my dear? Or is it only recently that you lost Mr. ah . . . Ramph?"

A broken sob and another sniffle and a handkerchief, which, being white and being raised by a dark glove to a veiled face, seemed to fly up by itself in the darkness, were his only answer. A few moments of utter silence followed before he spoke again.

"Come, you can do better," he said sweetly. "Give us a tale of woe. Was it bubonic or the hangman that deprived the world of dear Mr. Humph, Eliza?"

"But I didn't say anything! How did you know?" a shocked little voice cried after a moment's pause.

"Just because of that. It was solely because of your uncommon discretion," Warwick said with amusement, "for widows, my dear, are only too eager to tell how they got that way. It's like asking someone who's been bedridden for a month what his sickness is like—or asking a middle-aged female how it was having babies. It's simply an irresistible subject to them, you see—they find speaking of it endlessly fascinating. No one else does, of course, and so a real widow would have been treating me to deathbed scenes and the exact nature of the unfortunate fellow's final crisis before I got a second older. Julian will likely make himself a widower when he discovers you here, you know," he added just as pleasantly.

"I had to come," she said with some passion, her words causing her veil to puff out. "He was in danger."

"*Is* likely in danger," Warwick corrected her. "So then why didn't you discover yourself to him and tell him about it?"

"When I got off the coach, I saw Arden with him," she said miserably, her voice coming from the depths of her deep coal-scuttle-shaped bonnet, "and so I knew he already knew what Ben had said, and I knew he'd be warned, as well as aided. So I decided to go on as I'd come, in secret, and go on to Brighton, and then go home from there. My home," she said with some emphasis, "for we, Julian and I, have no home together, you see. No, and no future either," she added on what was a real sniffle and muted sob this time.

He stood in a half-crouch, and despite the swaying coach, swung easily into the seat beside her, and without interrupting his easy movement, took her immediately into his arms, where she immediately wept, as he'd expected, against his shoulder. But then, after her sobbing stopped and her bonnet was thoroughly crushed, there was a silence, and then a little flurry as her head shot up.

"Please don't tell him," she said suddenly, trying to sit

up straight. "I can't make you promise, and won't try," she said unhappily, "for I see that those I know are loose with their promises when they think a person's best interest are involved. But please—"

"I won't tell him," Warwick said into her ear as he patted her back. "Lie back and rest now," he said. While he thought: I doubt I'll have to tell him if I know my man. And then thought: And rest, for, alas, if I do know my man, I'm afraid you'll need it for what lies ahead.

They drove on in silence. Until Julian turned his attention from the darkened road to swear under his breath, but not at the horses.

"A whispering, heavily veiled widow," he said flatly, "and we were so busy looking for Ben before that we never thought to investigate . . . How like the little madcap, though . . . Good God! I hope not."

"If wishes were horses, beggars would ride," Arden said sadly. "There's nothing to be done about it now, so since we're not beggars, lad, look to your horses."

And because he'd no wish to look anywhere else, Julian did, and they drove on through the long summer night.

The teams hadn't been driven hard, but still the change had to be made at St. John's Common. And after he'd visited the taproom and the privy, Julian had the rehorsing of the coach to see to to keep him occupied. He determined not to look within his coach or mention the matter again until he arrived safely in Brighton, and then, he thought darkly, ordering a horse back into the stable because of the limp he detected even in the dark, then he'd certainly kill her for her deception, if not for the way it was fretting him to death.

He had no doubt now. The widow was the right size and, beneath her voluminous cloak, likely the right shape. Moreover, she avoided him like the plague, drifting around corners when he turned his head, stepping quickly out of his line of sight if she happened to catch herself crossing it. Then, too, he'd watched Warwick, out of the corner of one eye, and then the other, as he'd escorted the petite widow to the inn for a rest and a bite to eat and a glass of something revivifying, and watched him wait for her after her use of the privy house out in the back of the night-black yard. Then he'd seen him usher the lady back into the coach. And for all his politeness, Warwick was not in the habit of playing nurse to strange females, single, married, or widowed, young, old, or incapable—at least not since he'd wed.

But they'd come most of the way, they were only a few hours from Brighton, he'd not let himself think of anything but the road now, Julian vowed to himself as he saw Arden stop for a word with Warwick and one to the widow, and then thought that he might just kill his two friends as well, when this interminable night was done.

But the longest night finally resolves to day if one manages to live through it, and the darkness began to lift even as Julian's spirits began to rise. For he'd been so bent on his thoughts, Arden so silent beside him, and the topside passengers so quiet as they tried to stay awake so they wouldn't drop off literally, by drowsing, losing their grip, and flying off the roof, that he hadn't noted the inky blackness receding until he became aware of new light.

Now he could make out the shadows of trees beside the road. Dawn was coming. Gray mists were rising like dead souls on Judgment Day from the road surface all around them. Clayton Hill lay directly ahead. The passengers would get out and walk up the hill and greet the rising day at the top of it, and try to look from there clear to the sea and the end of the danger of this worrisome adventure. The thought of the sun always lifted his heart. He smiled—until he looked down to the road again.

A great tree lay across it.

But he knew, as he pulled up on the reins in his left hand and his right hand slipped into his pocket, that far more lay ahead.

"Not wise, sirs. Hands out in front, please! Oh, not cleverly done at all," a voice cried from out of the mist, freezing Julian's heart as well as his hand, as Arden, too, stopped mid-motion as he reached into his jacket.

"Hands out! I've got too many friends with me, all

looking down their rifles' stocks at you. Come, come, out and down in front of you, gentlemen, so that we can talk. Ah, better," the man said as the blindingly gray mists parted for him to be seen walking, gun in hand, from the side of the road to the side of the coach, his armed accomplices following.

He was a heavyset, florid fellow, well-dressed and neatly barbered, not quite a fop, nor in the Corinthian style, but rather looking like a prosperous businessman, although his neckcloth was in too high a style of fashion for staid commerce, and his gold fobs too many and heavy for true elegance. He was grinning hugely as he looked up at them.

"What a haul," he said appreciatively. "Not only the viscount but, by God, the reports was right! Lion 'isself! Himself," the man corrected himself, frowning before he grinned again, as though he regretted his brief lapse of accent so obviously brought about by his enthusiasm and delight.

"Welcome, Sir Lion," he said. "I've heard of you, and seen you, of course, but never hoped to meet you—like this. My name's William Peep, 'Will Peep' to my mates, and if you haven't heard of me, I'd be surprised. Because I did for Sam Towers, and you knew him, and I persuaded old Fishhouse Evans, he who ran most of Shoreditch and took the odd corner of Billingsgate, to emigrate—all the way to Australia—in chains." He chuckled. "I've took over most of Portwine John's ken, most peaceably, since he'd a notion to get on with life. Oh, I done away with a lot of bad fellows, and I'll have it all soon, since Ben-Be-Good's turning gent . . . and since now, of course . . ." He stopped abruptly and shook his head as though amazed at himself for letting his attention wander from the business at hand.

"And now, of course," he said, grinning, "please to get down, gentlemen. I can tell you the rest eye to eye. You can hand the reins to my man here, Viscount. Come, come," he said impatiently, "you're neither of you fools. I've six good men with me, and two more at the side of the road, all armed. Your guard's mine too, you know, and too drunk to mind if he wasn't. Bravado will do nothing but end it quick-like . . . quicker." He scowled, for his vocabulary was slipping even as his patience was, and it was difficult to see whether it was that loss of his hard-won polish or Arden and Julian's hesitancy that vexed him more now. For both men stayed still on the high driver's seat, obviously weighing their options.

"The fellow in the coach is being took out, and the lady too—here, you two fools on top," he shouted to the petrified topside passengers, who sat breathless, as though hoping they'd been forgotten, "if you haven't wet your pantaloons yet, and even if you have, follow the coach-man and the big man down after they hop it. Come on, time's wasting," he said, gesturing with his gun, all pre-tense of humor gone now. "Your one choice is to walk up the hill yourself, or be driven up. And it's a ride you'll never know you've took if you don't move it now!"

Julian leapt down lightly, and landed near to Will Peep. Arden followed soon after, and then they stood in silence, noting Warwick being prodded round by another man with a gun until he stood beside them, his arm round the window, now silent as the grave herself. The two topside passengers came soon after, and then the six of them stood, ringed round by an equal number of their captors in the bleak gray of rising dawn, midst pointed rifles and the swirling, shifting morning mists.

"The thing is all timing," Will Peep said in straightfor-ward fashion. "You came home at the wrong time, Vis-count. I'm not interested in coaching in the common way of things, I got into it by accident, and stayed in by design. And my design was to move on and buy my own line, in time. But you came back and started going over the books too close. Pity, really. If you wasn't a coaching man yourself, you'd have never twigged to it, I promise you, for I was that careful. Whatever," he said on a shrug, "you did, and made matters worse by coming to have a look before I could move on, and so I'm sorry, my lord, but you're in the way now. Nothing personal. It's business, you see. Lion here'll tell you that."

"I do see," Julian said calmly, "and understand. But certainly these others"—he gestured, and stopped when he heard indrawn breaths and saw how many weapons

that one sweep of his arm caused to be leveled on him—
"are ignorant as they're blameless. No need to keep
them, I'd think, bad business to, actually, I'd imagine."

"Then you'd be wrong," Will Peep said curtly, "for
they're in it now, ain't they? Too late, too bad. And
doing Lion here would do my reputation a mort of good,
it would."

"The Runners would find it shined up your reputation
even more," Arden commented dryly, his deep voice a
sudden shock to the surrounding men, for it seemed the
mere sound of it caused them to redirect their weapons
to him.

"You know better than that," Will Peep said with a
trace of annoyance. "Bow Street will hear just the same
as everyone else, but they can't act on what they hear,
only what they can prove. And proof of all sorts will be
left with Ben-Be-Good, or at least left in his room, for
them to find when he finally wakes up. I've left another
fellow with him, to be sure he don't wake for a week.
Your man's been sent back to London, Duke," he added,
looking beyond Julian and Arden. "Don't think I forgot
you, your grace—I didn't get where I am by forgetting
nothing," he said, his pride allowing him to forget his
elocution lessons without distress for once.

"I think you've forgot that 'doing' a duke of the realm
might bring you more renown than you'd care to have,"
Julian mused, sounding entirely calm, although from where
Eliza stood beside him she could see his hands knotted
into fists at his sides.

"But it's Ben's the rogue, remember, and if not him,
for I'm letting him live only to see him squirm, why,
then, it'll be the good Lord gets the blame, as usual.
Here, you're a coachman," Will Peep said merrily. "When
the nags bolt and a coach goes out of control, and is
thrown off a hill, and everyone gets their necks and
worse broke, who's to hang for it? God 'isself? Ain't a
noose big enough, is there?" He chuckled.

"Now, come along," he said, sobering. "We waited
long enough for you, as it is. Soon day coaches will be
passing, but by then, all they'll do is stare at the terrible
accident they'll see. We're going up the hill together, and

it's a good long ways. 'Please to get out—the hill is killing for the horses,' " he cried in glad mockery of the eternal coachman's command, before he said in uglier tones, "And for the passengers. It's too heavy a load for the horses, mate, you're right. So we'll walk to the top together, before you get in again and we say good-bye. Ah, where's my head? First, put out your fives. We'll tie them up neat, to be sure. Don't worry," he said as his men stepped forward with lengths of rope, "we'll untie them after, when you won't need them no more on this earth. And don't fool yourself none, Lion," he warned, looking up at the big man, "them that survives the tumble won't escape Matt Fist, aye, the ugly one behind you—he snaps necks like kindling for sport, so best pray you're gone by the time he checks the wreckage for business.

"Come along, now," he ordered impatiently as his men began to tie the passengers' wrists, "day's coming, I've a long ride ahead if I want to be in London by night."

"There's no need to take the lady along with us on our wild ride, now, is there, gentlemen?" Warwick said in mild accents, with only the slightest emphasis on the "gentlemen" as he held out two long wrists for the wrapping.

Julian tensed as Will Peep walked around to the widow, who stood, head down, face obscured entirely by her trappings of deep mourning. Will reached out and snatched her deep hooded bonnet off, releasing a welter of sunset-colored curls and causing the men all about them to catch their breath when she raised her white face to them, her large, angry eyes glowing like topazes in the rising gray light.

"S'truth she's a stunner!" Will Peep said with chagrin, tilting her chin up in his hand. "Wish I'd of known it afore this. But makes no matter," he said sadly, dropping his hand, and recovering himself. "She'd fetch me a fortune here and more abroad, but she'd be a deal less fetching without a tongue, and that's the only way I could let her go. A waste," he said longingly, still looking at her, "but I don't dare risk keeping her even a night. She's likely an educated female, and even the stupidest sluts has their ways of making trouble."

Will Peep sighed. And then caught his breath, for a small silver pistol had appeared in the lady's hand as if by magic, and she held it against his waistcoat, prodding his heart.

Then in a moment it was gone, swallowed up in Julian's own hand, which had snaked out from the side to capture it. And then in a twinkling it was turned round, handle out, and offered to Will Peep. And as Eliza stared, astonished and confused, at Julian, he said, on the saddest smile she'd ever seen him wear:

"A half-hour can be a long time when it's the last one you have, Eliza. I couldn't let you lose even that. There were two carbines aimed at your back, and another at your head, you see. You'd never have got to pull the trigger."

The jug-eared farmboy began weeping softly as his hands were bound, and Julian tried to put out a hand to comfort him, only desisting when he realized how tightly his own were now tied. But he stood so close to Eliza she could feel his body touching hers, until Will Peep pushed him forward, for he obviously meant for Julian to lead their final parade. Arden and Warwick were entirely still, belatedly relieved of their concealed pistols now, as Julian was, and probably, Eliza thought, thinking as feverishly as she was.

For she couldn't believe this would be the end of it. It was too cruel to think that the milestone she stood near that read "London forty-four miles" might be her tombstone. It was hard to believe the duke's wit and influence couldn't save them, nor Arden's slyness and experience, nor even Julian's courage and spirit. Or that none of this would avail them any better than her own abortive effort with the pistol, prayers, and tears. She'd always believed that the wicked could never prosper, aside from the fact that being young and accustomed to tomorrow, she'd never really believed in endings at all.

Julian stood tall and straight, and seemed curiously undisturbed, for though he was pale, his head was held high and his face was composed, his light eyes unshadowed by terror. But he never looked back to her as he began walking, and that hurt her almost as much as the fact that they'd begun moving up the hill, their coach following slowly, as the tree that blocked the road was dragged away. He'd taken off his many-caped driving cloak because of the warmth of the morning, and it lay upon the driver's seat. With his hands bound behind him, he strode on, his back straight, shoulders back. But a feather, some foolish tiny white feather from a pillow or a quilt, was caught on his tightly fitted jacket, and it clung to the blue superfine surface on the back of his shoulder, and that was what Eliza fixed her eyes on. For that one bit of lint on his finery made him so human and vulnerable that at last she felt the tears come. At that, Warwick's shoulder on one side and Arden's on the other upheld her, so that she could continue to walk.

And then Will Peep put up a hand and signaled to his minions, and two of them darted into the mists at the side of the road as the others stood stock-still and made their prisoners pause. For there was a new rolling, rattling sound, a sound of hooves and a clatter of springs growing louder, and Will said in a hushed command, "A word, and whoever they are, they go with you—but sooner!"

The rising light showed a team of handsome grays, dappled and smoky as the swirling mists that they emerged from, pulling a dashing high curricle. Two sporting young gentlemen sat on the driving seat, and two more sat behind, and when they sighted the stagecoach and its party ascending, they pulled up and hailed them with shouts of delight.

"Oh, good show!" cried the driver. "What luck!" he caroled. "Well-met! Lost and at sea in these demned mists of morning, and now here's a jolly coachman before us! Good sir, do you know the way to the Baron Hood's manor in Wivelsfield? We've been up and down and round about, bashing along all night, looking for the place. Here," he called, reaching into his many-caped driving coat and taking out a map; he shook it, and being backed with buckram, it then unfolded almost to the ground before him. "We've been through Clayton and

Ditchling and Streat, and Hell itself, I think—oh, pardon, Miss—but could you give me a hint, sir?"

"Be pleased to," Julian said, when Will Peep nudged him deep in the ribs, "if I could but have a look at the map."

The young man leapt down, and as his friends looked curiously at the dispirited group before them, he conferred with the golden-haired coachman. If he thought it odd that the fellow kept his hands behind him all the while, and only motioned to the right road with his head, he said nothing, but only folded up his map smartly when Julian had done, and thanked him profusely before hopping back up on his seat.

Eliza almost wept anew to see him raise his whip, as she heard no word coming from the three gentlemen she trusted. But she realized they were right. It would be cruel to involve the carefree young men, for all it would pain her to see them go free when she herself was bound here, to stay here, perhaps for eternity.

But her tears were stayed. Because only seconds later, another rattling, spinning sound was heard and the growing light revealed another sporting carriage rolling up beside the first one, this one also filled with a jolly quartet of dashing young gentlemen.

"Oh, here, Jeremy! We're found!" the first young gentleman cried, putting aside his whip. "And right on time, all right! This obliging coachman's put us right. Come look, we've been going in circles!" and leaping down again, he strode to the second curricle to consult with its driver.

As the *Thunder*, its driver and passengers, and their captors hesitated on the slope of the hill watching the young gentlemen conferring in front of them, the early-morning quiet was broken by the sound of more oncoming horses and wheels, and then a tuneful yard of tin. The rapidly evaporating night mists soon thinned to show the bulk and shape of another stagecoach looming up behind them. Will Peep frowned, his rapid thinking clearly showing on his face, as the *Defiance* out of London, its name writ large on it, pulled up behind them, even as its coachie shouted heartily, "Ho! *Thunder*, make way! Get an early start, and see what happens? Traffic tie-ups on the road."

And as Will Peep grew a furtive wide-eyed look, and Arden and Warwick exchanged glances, Julian began at last to let his smile begin to quiver at the side of his lips—as the sound of another coach clattering down the fog-shrouded hill was heard. Then the *Spitfire*, from Brighton, pulled by heaving horses, burst from the filmy mists to let the first rays of the morning sun shine on its fittings—even as the coachman from the arriving *Royal George* shouted for them to make room, and a spanking new calêche stuffed with grinning young gentlemen drove up beside it, while the guard on the rapidly arriving stagecoach *Perseverance* gave out a "Halloo" to clear a path—which almost drowned out the whoop that the burly driver of the *Dreadnought* gave as he reined up directly after the sparkling new *Vixen*, whose teams were dancing to a lathered halt, just after the *Tempest* pulled up short.

Out of the night and into the morning swept a cavalcade of stagecoaches, all filled with beefy, wide-shouldered guards and drivers, hanging out the windows, clinging to the tops, not a paying passenger among them; while such an assortment of private coaches, gigs and tilburys, drags, landaus, and britchkas kept appearing, manned by elegant London gentlemen, that the air was filled with the confusion and sounds of horses, carriages, laughter, and horns.

But then one voice cut through the air and silenced all the noise.

"Now, step back, you blackguards," the coachman on the *Defiance*, closest to the *Thunder*, shouted, "and drop your weapons if you want to live to hear the end of my sentence. Aye, you—Will Peep, you dog! For we've more guns than Wellington's finest amongst us, and more bare hands than that, and would just as soon tear you apart as waste bullets, so drop them now, you dogs!"

As Will Peep's men stared at their leader and saw him hesitate, the coachman from the *Defiance* continued, "And have no hope for the curs you left at the side of the road, just now or before, for we've seen to the first hours past, and have the others in hand right now."

Will Peep didn't drop his weapon. He threw it down.

Then the coachmen came boiling out of the stagecoaches and picked up the weapons that were falling almost as fast as Eliza's tears were, and came up to Julian and his fellow captives, and with much tut-tutting and a great deal of sympathy, untied them, even as their fellows were tying up Will Peep's men with little sympathy and more dispatch.

Julian rubbed at his wrists and took one step to Eliza, and without saying a word, simply enfolded her with his left arm and held her tightly, while he put out his right hand for the nearest coachman to shake.

"You knew?" Arden asked, as he saw Julian's broad grin.

"You didn't need us?" Warwick asked in thoughtful wonder.

"I always need you, my friends," Julian replied, "and I didn't know. I hoped. I knew there'd be trouble on the road, and so I passed the word. But I didn't dare say if I only hoped, and I never expected such a turnout!"

"A word passed to coaching men is heard," the *Defiance*'s driver interrupted to say. "We're a tight-knit fraternity, sir, never doubt it. There aren't many of us, some few thousand only, against the hard world, so we hold together. We look after our own."

"I'd begun to wonder," Julian said. "I was late, and wondered if I had been forgotten when I saw I'd the road to myself."

"Better that way by a mile," the coachman from the *Spitfire* put in. "That way we got them all together."

"But I can tell you, brother," the *Dreadnought*'s driver said, "you were never alone. We kept watch all the way. We was getting bored with the waiting and watching, aye, these London gents were hot to have at it, it was only our wisdom held them back."

"Aye," laughed a slender fellow in a spanking driver's coat with buttons as big as sheep's eyes, "your wisdom and your forearms. Lord, you coachies have a muscle or two!"

"The Four-in-Hand Club out in full regalia," Warwick said on a sigh. "Obviously, the villains never had a chance."

"Mock if you will, your grace," said a carefully coiffed gentleman who recognized the duke, "but we'd not have missed being in on it for the world. There ain't half enough good amateur whips in this world, either, you know, and the viscount's something of a legend to us, being part of both worlds."

"Time enough for a chat-up later, lads," a gruff coachman said briskly. "We've work to do. You London fellows lead the way, if you please, sirs, back to Preston and The Seven Sisters. We'll meet you there by and by, and have a drink to celebrate. In fact, I believe we'll make a day of it, I just believe we will."

"Capital idea," seconded another from far back in the crowd, as Julian's eyes widened and he said, "My God! The *Highlander* off the Great North Road! Why, the coaching world's here! The transport of all England will be held up for a day!"

"Aye, maybe," a dour coachman agreed, "but after a few angry letters to the *Times*, in time it'll be forgot, this day all stagecoaching stopped—the day of the coachies' convention. But not by us. It's time," he cried out, as the other coachmen began to cheer, "for the fraternity to have a holiday."

"But as to Will Peep and his men . . ." Julian said as the coachmen began to urge him and his passengers into their carriages, each arguing the merits of his particular rig.

"As to that," the driver of the *Defiance* said, for he seemed to have become their spokesman, "some of us will stay on for a while to see to them. He'd planned for you all to go over the hill, and indeed, looks to me like the *Thunder* is none too sturdy a coach. You've insurance on it, I hope, my lord?" he asked Julian politely.

Eliza gasped. All this time she'd been so glad that her heart had been filled to bursting, but now dread clutched at her again as reality intruded. "But that's murder!" she said before she could stop herself, and Julian looked down at her, frowning with concern.

The *Defiance*'s coachman looked somber, his heavy brows knitting over his dark, thoughtful eyes.

"Those men are a bad lot, missy," he said heavily,

"and what they was up to was no good for no one, especially not for coaching. A man—and a woman too, missy—has got to feel safe in a stagecoach, has got to be safe in one too. We can't have kidnappings and killings and suchlike on our roads, and we mean to take care of it in our own way."

"But the Bow Street Runners . . ." Eliza said, as Arden frowned as well, remembering something he'd heard, until the coachman continued, "We took care of the fellow they set to your friend, Mr. Be-Good, and the Runners will not be the wiser. And if they twig to something, why then I expect they'll be only too glad to let it pass. The fellows need killing, and unless I miss my guess, none know it better than the Runners."

"Oh, aye," Arden agreed feelingly.

"And if they get onto something . . ." the *Defiance*'s coachman said, smiling slightly, "why, I doubt they'll ever find a tree that big—no, not half so big as to hang half the coachmen in the kingdom from."

"But . . . they . . . the coach . . ." whispered Eliza, looking to the *Thunder*, where Will Peep and his men were being herded, afraid to ask what she felt she must know.

". . . will have its scheduled accident. But never fear, little lady," another coachman said consolingly, "this time the horses will go free of it before it tumbles. We're not murderers, you know . . . only executioners," he added softly as she was led away by Julian.

"A toast!" some of the gentlemen from the Four-in-Hand Club shouted after Julian, Eliza, Arden, and Warwick arrived at the inn where all the coachmen were scheduled to meet. Warwick and Arden came with the *Vixen*, Julian and Eliza with a private chariot, while the other two passengers from the *Thunder*, glad of their skins and not wanting to know more of what clearly shouldn't concern them, had been only too pleased to take to their heels and be gone, by foot, to their destinations.

But the four other survivors had been brought to the inn in triumph. The gentlemen chatted and shook hands all around with several dozen well-wishers; Eliza stood wide-eyed. And now that all the other coachmen had returned silently from whatever it was that had happened at the crest of the hill they'd all originally met at, the landlord was rushing about with libations. For now the convention of coachmen was begun in earnest.

Eliza had not once spoken to Julian since her discovery, nor he to her—there simply hadn't been privacy or time for it. Now she'd reason, even as she stood within the shelter of his arm, which he'd never withdrawn, to be glad of it. For now he raised his glass, but he only said:

"A toast then: Thank you, my friends, from my heart, for saving my life—and my heart," and then at last, at that, he looked down to her, and held his glass up to her, as the coachmen all flourished their glasses and cheered.

"Oh, poor stuff, Julian, you're better to look at than hear. Let our poet speak for all of us. Arden, please," Warwick commanded, and an appreciative silence fell as the big man was given a hand to stand up on a table to address the multitude of them.

"To the coachmen of Britain," Arden declared, lifting his glass high, "who excel at 'Phaeton's own task.' 'He drives with Phoebus' self, the chariots of the sun,' " he deftly quoted, before he thundered, "And so may he do until the sun itself goes out!"

A great cheer went up, and glass clinked with glass as the assembly became a great party, with laughter rising with the glasses as the day came up to full light.

After a while, on a little shy smile, Eliza slipped out from under Julian's arm to seek, she whispered softly, a ladies' convenience. He nodded, and watched her leave with a long and measured look. And then he bent to whisper a word into the ear of a nearby coachman, who nodded, and rose at once, to circulate among the other men at the inn.

Julian and Arden and Warwick, united in friendship and pleasure as they'd feared they might be in death only hours before, laughed and drank and grew grave only when a newly arrived traveler from a regularly scheduled coach burst into the inn to tell breathlessly of the terrible accident that morning at Clayton Hill—that had ended with the *Thunder*, out of London, staved in, and all aboard her perished.

But by then it was almost noon, and by then some of the merrymakers were already wandering off and out into the broad sunshine to inspect and compare coaches and rigs and to acknowledge the real day. It was then, as the crowd in the taproom thinned, that Arden noted something he feared his friend Julian had not. A look to Warwick showed he'd noted the same thing. And then, after Arden had a turn in the sun in the front yard, and Warwick in the back, they met again in the common room. It was the duke who finally interrupted Julian as he listened to a coachman reminiscing about the old days on the high road, and begged a moment of his time to take him aside.

"Julian, do you know where Eliza is?" he asked quietly. "I thought to find her in this crowd, but she's nowhere to be seen."

"Oh, she is somewhere to be seen," Julian said, closing his eyes as he downed his ale. "On the high road to the coast, I expect," he said after he'd done.

"Oh, so you've sent her on," Warwick said with relief and a bright, satisfied nod to Arden.

"No," Julian said. "She stole away, just as you thought. But she's bound for her home on the Isle of Wight."

"Alone, again?" Arden roared.

"Again." Julian winced. "But safe enough, as my ears aren't. Good God, Arden, deafness will run in your family if you're not careful. Relax, gentlemen, I know where she is, and whom she's with, as well as where she's bound this time. This is my world, after all, remember?"

"Aye," Arden said more quietly, "but I'd have thought you'd go after her."

"I shall," Julian said, putting down his glass and signaling for another, "but I've time and to spare, my friends. She'll need the time too, I expect, to get where she's going. Well," he said, his gray eyes alight with laughter, "she left on the only conveyance that would accept her, I made sure of that. No coachie will take her up—on my orders. And I know where she's bound by her queries. No, she left on the one stage I put in her way and left at her disposal, that was going her way. She'll make good time and will be watched after, until she's let down in a field, with another friend of mine—never fear—unbeknown to her, near to her destination. But not too near," he said dreamily, his eyes half-closed in pleasant thoughts.

"Then," he continued, "her only connection will be my friend Gypsy Frank's wagon that I sent word for him to reroute this morning. It's never too hard to reach him if you know his route, you see. Yes, a lovely conveyance—pulled by eight horses and moving so slowly with its load, like all wagons, that Gypsy Frank has to walk beside his draft horses all the way. But it's better for her than walking—on the downhill, at least. Oh, I've seen to it that I've a great deal of time in which to catch up, but I don't choose to until she gets to her childhood home again. And then I think I'll let her have some time alone."

As his friends grew still, shocked at his heartless tone, he grinned like a youth and added, "Time for a bath, at least. For Gypsy Frank's hauling swine to market this trip. But she can always sit outside, if it don't rain. That might teach her to think carefully before she acts again."

"Good Lord, Julian," Warwick sighed, shaking his head, "will she ever forgive you?"

"Ah," Julian said, suddenly gravely serious, all the light in his face and eyes gone out, "but that's the least she has to forgive me for—the very least since we began this wonderful marriage of ours. I only wish it were all so simple to mend as that. And I only pray," he said fervently, "that it's only twice as hard. And believe me, I shall pray," he added, unnecessarily, from the stricken look that crossed his face, "since I find I've never wanted anything more in the whole of my foolish life."

20

HERE, WHERE IT ALL BEGAN, she thought, was rightfully where it all must end. It was here, and on just such a day, a clear mild summer's day, that he had first enchanted her. And it had been some sort of bewitchery, Eliza decided, for all on that summer's morning, with the breath of the meadowsweet perfuming the air, and the slight salt tang of the nearby sea and her own tears in the air to temper the sweetness, she had breathed in his presence and had never been free of him since. It was time, she decided.

So she rose from the grass and walked to the top of the rise and stared down at the blue-and-bottle-green-patchwork sea, and pulled the pendant from off her neck. She paused only to look just once more at that incredibly perfect painted face upon it, and then she raised her arm high.

"No," he said, and she spun round to see him come slowly up the rise behind her, as she'd somehow known he would, this strange dreamlike morning.

"No," Julian said. "Let me do it, please."

He took the pendant from her now-nerveless hand as she lowered it to her side.

"Yes," he said, and only that, as he looked at it. She hadn't seen him since the day she'd run away from him at the inn near to Brighton, and yet they neither of them spoke a word as he took her hand in his. Then he took her with him, tugging her along as he slid down the side of the sandy rise, skidding and slipping, the sand giving way beneath his feet as he created a staircase of shifting steps for her to follow in, until they came down, at last, to the level of the strand, and the murmuring sea.

He drew her all the way to the water's edge, and then he took the pendant and flung it far, even as she gasped and regretted it, as she watched it rise and glint and fall, at last, far out, to sink, on a splash, into the sea.

"There now," he said, looking after it. "I should have done that years ago. Let some men of science unearth it when the earth is old and the seas have dried up. And let them wonder how the world could have gone on with such perfect-looking, impossibly lifeless men upon it. It was never me. My folly lay in the fact that I was once flattered, even as I was amused by it. *One* of my follies," he said, still staring out to where it had fallen.

"But she . . . she loved it, and you," Eliza said, despite herself. For now that the pendant he'd given her when they'd met all those years before was gone, she dared speak of the woman who originally had it created, the woman who had wanted to wear it until he'd rejected her love, and who then had renounced him, and in fleeing him had gone to her death in the sea. Or so the other townsfolk had whispered at the funeral, for he'd never written or spoken to her about it. He'd only consoled her that same day of his lady's funeral for her own loss—of her dog, her best childhood friend, as well as for the oncoming loss of her childhood itself, for she was about to be sent away from it to grow to be a lady, if she could, and a woman, nonetheless.

"She was my mistress," Julian said now, "and I never loved her. I never had a mistress before, or after, because if her love left me with anything other than regret, it was the realization that love can't be bought, not even the semblance of it. After that, I contented myself with only buying flesh, or negotiating for it. I'm sorry," he said, looking down at her with a strange smile, "but you'd never believe I lived celibate ever after, and I certainly didn't. And I won't try to gammon you. But I did live loveless ever after, or at least, illusionless after that. Until, of course, I met you," he said.

But now she'd gotten over the shock of seeing him, and now the mystical mood was gone, along with the pendant . . . it must really have been enchanted then!

she thought, before she dismissed the fancy altogether to deal with her reality, and raised her chin.

"Give over, Julian," she said quite calmly. "I've left you and I mean to go on leaving you to your life, and to get on with mine."

"But they are the same," he said, still holding her hand tightly as he turned his head to look down at her.

"Oh, no," she said, shaking her hand free, though there was a minute when she feared she'd have to fight him for possession of it, until they looked like two children squabbling by the sea. And perhaps it would have been better if they had, she thought, for his face was bereft of laughter now, still and solemn, his gray eyes as light as the clouds in the summer sky, much bleaker than the sun-drenched waters.

"No, no, Julian," she said, looking down as she started to walk along the margins of the water where the sand was smooth and hard-packed, easier on her slippers because she did not sink with each step, but harder because she could feel the dampness and the shape of each sharp pebble beneath her thin soles. But that was all to the good too, for the discomfort kept her mind from the sting of her words.

"Marrying me," she went on as he waded along beside her, because he walked nearer to the water, as though he wished to keep her from the dangers of the open sea, "was a kind and considerate, gentlemanly act. It was entirely the correct thing to do—but not the right thing at all. I understand that society doesn't care about the rightness of a thing so long as it is correct, but I do."

She found the courage to face him and stopped in her tracks.

"You don't love me, Julian. And I won't hold you to vows made in courtesy. . . . But your boots! They're being destroyed! If you don't move out of the water, you'll have winkles growing on them instead of gold tassels!" she cried, relieved that the hardest thing had been said, glad now of the excuse to change the subject as she did her position, as she danced back up the beach again.

She'd worn no bonnet and her hair glinted like some wild-berry wine in the sun, her face was alight with laughter, her white dress was whipped round her slender form by the sea winds, and he was glad of an excuse to run after her and catch her up and hold her in his arms. Then he strode up the beach with her as she protested, and then clambered up the breach he'd made in the earth coming down. And he might never have released her when he got up to the top of the rise again if she hadn't struggled to be free of him.

Too close, she thought, turning around to compose herself, remembering the hard strong arms she'd escaped, the scent and feel of him causing her to actually shake before she took control again. If the thing had to be ended right, she must not get so close, she reminded herself, as he said, as he stood still and watched her:

"It's always my boots you worry about when we meet, it seems, as I recall. Now, and on your first wedding day. I'm touched that you care about my clothes, but I'd prefer it if you worried about my heart instead."

Ah, but you haven't really got one, she thought, but only said, because she never wanted to hurt him, only let him know she did indeed care, "Julian. Don't gammon me. I know you very well. Five years of long-pages'-worth well. Your heart, my friend, is whole and sound."

"Still vexed about the swine, eh?" he asked, grinning.

If they'd been on better terms, if they hadn't been married, she thought, she'd have clouted him for that. As it was, she glowered at him, and merely said as airily as she could:

" 'Swine' is giving them airs. Which they had. They were pigs, and nothing else. But Gypsy Frank was a merry fellow, and believe it or not, I enjoyed being with the other passengers on the wagon, milkmaids and fishwives being a pleasant respite from society ladies and gentlemen. There was a great deal of hay to sit in, and the day was clear. And breezy," she emphasized as he chuckled, "but no, I don't bear grudges . . . especially about something so important as this," she added as the smile slipped from his face.

"It will never do," she sighed, looking down at her slippers and out to a tree, and anywhere but at him as she spoke. "This 'marriage' of ours won't do. And I think you know it, but custom and loyalty and masculine nonsense don't let you say it. If you're worried about my 'disgrace,' which I think you really are, rather than that 'heart' you go on about; if you're afraid of my being a wicked divorced woman with noplace in the world to go and no one to go to—why, don't. I've had a word or two with Hugh. Yes, he's here . . . well, he lives here," she said crossly as he stared at her, slow anger replacing his sadness.

She sat down abruptly, sinking to the grass in a flounce of her skirts, needing a distraction and a reason to occupy herself. As she settled herself, she let her fingers search absently in the young grass. When she found a small daisy, she decapitated it and pulled at its tiny white petals as she continued to speak.

"Hugh wondered why I'd returned alone. I've been here two days, you see, and I've known him forever too, and while I didn't say anything specific, he guessed a great deal. *He* wouldn't ostracize me, Julian. In fact, I do believe he'd marry me again. That is, again-really, even if his parents had the pip. Which they would," she said in softer tones, remembering the looks of suspicion and outright disfavor she'd been treated to by her rejected onetime suitor's kin.

"Do you want to marry him?" he asked, his voice far away, and when she dared to look, she saw only his boots, braced far apart, for he stood above her, and she couldn't look higher. She pretended the sun behind him hurt her eyes, and glanced away, shading them with her hands.

"No, no," she said crossly, "but the point is that I could if I wished, so you needn't fear I'll end on the shelf if I don't want to. And I'm sure there are others like Hugh, and perhaps in time . . . But I don't wish to marry anyone just now, which is as well, for it takes forever to get a divorce, you know. Well, and if you don't, I do, because I went to see Warwick's man-at-law in London.

And there's never a need to say a bad word about you, not really, I have only to prove that we haven't . . . that I'm not . . . that I'm still a maid," she said finally, with determination. "It needs only that you agree, and we can set the thing in motion.

"I don't," he said.

He sank to one knee directly in front of her, and now he could see that she could not meet his eyes, so he bent to her as she turned her head.

"Eliza," he said, "we are man and wife. I want us to remain so. I didn't 'have' to marry you. I could have gone back to Jamaica, or abroad. Or I might have waited for things to pass, or made up some circuitous story. I've known many young ladies, and though I'll never regale you with the tales, trust me that I've eeled my way out of matrimony before. I didn't struggle in the net, I was well-pleased to wed you. I wish to remain so. I love you."

All this while, she'd listened with her head averted, a look of pained discomfort clear upon her features. But at the last, she snapped her head about and stared directly into his eyes. Her own were blazing with anger.

"*That*, you do not!" she cried. "You like me very well, Julian, and I know it, and never doubted it. But you do not love me."

"Lord! What do you want, heart's blood?" he asked, running his hand through his hair in exasperation. "I tell you I do. I think of you all the time, wretch. On the stagecoach, I had but to see an odd-colored bird and thought to tell you of it. I heard a foolish bit of prattle from a passenger and thought: Ah, I must tell Eliza this, she'll adore it! Anything new that happens, I store up, and our old discussions and arguments always drift into my mind to renew when we meet again. You're my heart's friend, and more, its companion, since things take on more meaning when I share them with you, and seem to have little purpose if I can't."

He was so close, his words so warm, but she knew what he hadn't said, even if he didn't, so she only smiled sadly and tilted her head to the side, looking so charming it was all he could do not to reach out for her, but he knew she must have her say.

"Oh, we're friends," she agreed, "and have been, I think, since the day we met. You know," she said sadly, musingly, "this island is supposedly as haunted as the mainland is. But we're so little, we must have smaller ghosts. There's a house just down the road where they say there's a little blue girl who walks through the night through eternity, grieving for her dog. In truth, there is, or so they say," she said, looking to him earnestly. "I've never seen her, but I saw the shadow of another child here this morning, a plump little redheaded girl, just as dead and gone, and grieving just as much, but I saw her in the sunlight—just there—because she was me. She's gone now, entirely. She was your friend, but I've taken her place, and I'm your friend too . . . and, Julian, I've grown up enough to know not to impose upon friendship."

She smiled sadly and patted his hand as it braced him, knuckled to the grass. Then he surprised her. He got down to both knees, and she would have cried out to warn him of the damage the grass would do to the knees of his fine light charcoal-colored pantaloons, and only stopped when she remembered his complaint about her consideration for his clothing. But he looked so fine in his white shirt, blue jacket, and intricately tied cravat, perfect going-away clothes, she thought, that she disliked seeing them spoiled. Then he took up both her hands in his as he knelt before her.

"You accept the linkage of our minds, but I tell you, Eliza, that I yearn for that of our bodies too. Oh, blush, yes—do. But for yourself, depraved creature, not just me, because I know that's been in your mind too. I haven't taken you as my wife completely, but that doesn't mean that I haven't wanted to. Or that I couldn't for any reason except for my own fear, whatever excuses I made. And what amazingly paltry ones they were, even if I tried to believe them: you were too young, I was too old, you were too flighty, we were too tired—but it all was that I was too craven, Eliza. Because it was fear. Even when I had you in my arms, I see now that I tried to make love to you with my eyes open and my heart closed—lest I lose it entirely. I think that's it," he said consideringly, as though he hadn't thought of all this on the long journey to her, hadn't gotten it all straight in his mind before he dared see her again.

"I waited for love so long, you see," he said, "and all along never knew what a coward I was, because I was afraid that by losing my heart I'd lose my head and my will as well. It doesn't matter now. It's too late. It happened when I wasn't looking. I simply can't live without you.

"And, oh," he said, growing grave again, looking deep into her wide and astonished eyes, "if you're worried about my living—my continuing to live, that is—if that's it . . . I assure you, the doctors say I'm likely not going to get the fever again, and if I do, it will be less severe, and lessen each subsequent time. I'll hire on a valet to help me through it if it comes again—it needn't worry you," he tried to assure her, misreading her jolt of surprise. "I'm not a sickly man, Eliza. I promise you I wouldn't insist on tying you to an invalid. Believe me. I may be older than you by a good bit, but I'm healthy, and wealthy, if not particularly wise. Two virtues out of three are the best I can do, I'm afraid," he said on a wistful smile.

How beautiful he was, she thought as he sat back on his knees and waited for her answer. She would always remember him so, as he looked before her in the sunlight now. She noted again, with wonder, his handsome clothes, the well-proportioned frame they covered, the sensitive hands and wide shoulders. The sun set his hair to a shining crown above that still and watchful, entirely—yes, the only appropriate word, she thought—beautiful face of his. And so when she spoke, it was at first of that, his beauty.

"Do you know," she said softly, her own brown eyes filled with truth, "that when I told that tale that day of the judgment of Paris to the children, I thought of you? I thought then that Anthea and I and Constance were like the three goddesses, only we were just three foolish women awaiting your decision as to which of us you preferred—until they asked me if Paris looked like you, and I remembered that mortal men seldom do. Apollo, more likely. But how hard it must be to become a good man with such a face before the world. And how easily you must find love, always.

"But it's not just your face, Julian, for I believe that a face only mirrors what's within, and that if you were put into a monster's skin, within a week it would be a lovely monster indeed. Why, so it always was in school—the prettiest girls on first sight often became much less so when I came to know them, while the plainest grew beautiful to me, if they'd beautiful souls. So it's never only your face, Julian. You're a remarkable man. And deserve a remarkable wife. One you love."

"I am unremarkable," he said, shaking his head in a slow negative, as he'd begun to do as she spoke. "My friend Warwick has more wit, Arden more bravery. I am fortunate in my friends, and, I think, unlucky in my appearance if it makes you doubt me. I'm no immortal hero, not in the least godlike," he said with anger, as though this was a thing that had plagued him once too often. "Shall I cut off my nose to spite this deceptive face? Or is it that you fear I'll continue to take up the invitations it has always got me? Then don't waste as much as a moment wondering about that. Even if I didn't disdain infidelity as unworthy of a decent man, you, Eliza, have unmanned me entirely, at least when it comes to other females. I don't want them, any of them, since I found you. It's that simple. But I want you. You are the three goddesses in one: beauty, wisdom, and strength of character, all neatly wrapped in one little person. No contest, no judgment is necessary.

"Once I only wanted to wed in order to have children of my body. My God," he said wonderingly, "was it only that short while ago? Was it so long ago then? How you've turned me round—I can't even tell the time anymore. But now I know, since Miss Mary and Arden have taught me so well, that it's not necessary—I can get any number of children of my heart. Except that I haven't my heart anymore. You've got the whole of it.

"Can't you see?" he asked, touching her cheek gently. "Love, like death, I suppose," he said, smiling faintly, "takes men unawares, in different ways, at different times, so some of us don't know what fate's dealt us until the final stroke. I've been hard hit," he explained, speaking the absolute truth that he'd learned when it had fallen on him like a thunderclap to deafen him to all else these last days since she'd left him—when he'd discovered she'd taken everything he'd ever wanted in life with her.

"I want you, Eliza," he repeated.

"To show me what 'fun' lovemaking can be?" she asked in a strange voice, and when he frowned, she reminded him, "As you once told me it was."

"Oh, it will be more than that," he promised her. "I was halfhearted last time, impeded by my own confusion. This time nothing hinders me. I intend to show you more than 'fun.' "

And then, because he felt he could never say all that he meant, he leaned forward, took her into his arms, and kissed her. She didn't resist him as her words had made him fear she would. In fact, he kissed her for a very long while, because her lips were soft and sweet and more than yielding, and it seemed to him she sighed against his mouth in surrender of more than her lips. So when he let her go, he wore a look of triumph, and his heart felt full to bursting, as for once the demands of his clamoring body were as nothing to the joy that sprang up in his heart.

And then she spoke. His kiss had set her senses reeling, and she'd let them dance, because she'd known that when they were done, more than the kiss would be over.

"Thank you, Julian," she said, rising to her knees and then to her feet as he looked up to her in confusion. "You are a good and gallant man. Clever as your friend Warwick, and brave as Arden, but better than both, I think, because you are like them as well as being yourself, all three together too—bright, brave, and good. At least so it seems to me. You'll always be my friend. And I do love and appreciate you. Too much to remain wed to you. You must find love, and I think you will one day.

Never throw away that chance on me because of friendship, because of 'honor.' Because we females have a sense of honor too, and mine demands that I set you free.

"Good-bye Julian," she said, and, smiling, turned from him, and, smiling, because for all it hurt her, she knew it was for the best, she left him there, behind her, and walked away.

And then she heard him call.

"Eliza," he shouted. "No. Don't go. Don't leave me."

But she didn't stop until she heard his next strangled cry, for then he said, muffled, broken, half-heard, but clear enough to her:

"Eliza. Help me."

When she turned back, afraid for his life, for there'd been such agony in his voice, she saw him, still kneeling there, his face as white as death, his eyes gray as oncoming night, as he stumbled up to one knee.

"Help me," he pleaded, astounded by his own pain, for he was lost. "I don't know what else to say, God help me, Eliza, what would you have me say?" he asked, lifting his haunted face to her. "How can I show you my heart short of cutting it out and opening it up? I love, for the first time in my life, I ache with love, and yet I've never had to court a lady so, much less the woman I love. So how do I do it? What would you have me do? Tell me, and I shall. But don't leave me, my God, don't leave me. I could not bear it."

There was that in his face that she had never seen, not even when he lay racked with fever. There was that in his eyes which she'd never wanted to see, and because she felt he'd never want her to either, she ran to him and fell to her knees and held him so that the tears would fall where they would never be seen. She held him close, his cheek to hers, one hand on his wide shoulder, the other to the back of his head, as if for all his size he was her child, this man she'd have given her life for, even if it required she cut him out of her life with all the pain she'd feel if she cut out a part of her own flesh.

"Eliza," he said, his lips in her hair, his arms coming

tight around her, "don't leave me. My God, I need you, I love you so."

And that was all, really, she thought, that he had to say.

But he went on: "You don't have to love me as I love you—indeed, I don't know if you can," he said on a shaky laugh. "My little friend, my heart. But I'm never such a fool as to marry where there's no chance of mutuality. I love you too much to insist you stay on where you can never love. I do know you, and I believe you already love me in many ways. I'll earn the rest. Hush, listen, I'll be good to you, so kind, so devoted you'll have to hire on outlaws to get me away. I want to live with you and laugh with you, and teach you the kinds of love I already know—those of the flesh, which can be a joy, I promise—while all the time you'll continue teaching me those of the spirit, that I never knew until I admitted you into my heart."

He was still then, and neither of them spoke, as, knee to knee on the grass, they clung together. And then she felt a sigh like a shudder rack him, and he said at last, in a wondering voice, as he drew back to look at her again, "We met right here those years ago, and never left each other, not really, you know. I never loved another after, and I believe it was because I'd already found you, whether I knew it or not. Stay with me, Eliza. Please."

"I never left you, Julian," she said simply. "Didn't you know? And even if I had gone, I would never have left you. Now, I never will. Poor boy," she said on a little laugh, for she was that sure of him, at last, and the joy of it was just occurring to her.

The color was returning to his face, and if his cheeks were damp, it was as well, for her own eyes filled now, but with the sudden delight of knowing he was truly hers. He kissed her then, at first lightly, and then his arms came around her again, only to leave as his hands began to hold her in ways that had nothing to do with the sort of comfort they had offered each other only moments before. There, in the sunlight, his lips were on her mouth, her cheek, her neck, while his hands touched her breasts and waist and hips, until he moved his lips away from her and gazed down at her as she lay half on his lap, half upon the grass.

"I'm not a god, or some sylvan deity either, you know," he said, half-laughing, looking to her tumbled hair and skirts, glad that she lay across his lap so that the broad light didn't show the whole extent of his enthusiasm to her, since she was yet, as he remembered all too well, a maid, "and so I can't be entirely comfortable like this, love. But this is your island," he added when she didn't answer, but only gazed up at him dreamily, "so we'll stay if you think no one will come along."

"Because," he said, bending to her again, "I really think it's time, my love, to end this troublesome matter of your maidenhood, and begin our married life. And it's nothing to do with legal matters," he added as he brushed his lips across the smooth skin covering her collarbone, "or perhaps it is, because if I can't have you soon, I think I'll run mad and you'll have to have me clapped up in Bedlam. I once foretold you'd have to divorce a fellow to show you were in love with him—but I'd really prefer you do something else. Something simpler, and much more enjoyable. So, if you agree, and you're sure no one's coming . . ." he said, slowly pulling the top of her gown down and admiring what he uncovered.

Until the import of his words overcame the incoming message to her senses and she sat up with a squeak.

"We can't . . . out here!" she whispered frantically, pulling up her dress, looking about as if she expected to see an army of voyeurs leering at her.

He grinned like a boy. "Then . . . where?" he asked.

How quickly, she marveled, he'd changed from despair to desire. But then, so she'd done too. It was like snatching at life after an encounter with death. It robbed her of her shyness too, this sudden lust for life and love with Julian.

"My house is nearby," she said. "Will you come home with me?"

They ran, hand in hand, past the graveyard near to where they'd met, passing the ghosts of old and lost loves as they quickened their footsteps. And when they came down the long winding path to her childhood home, she paused for only a second to draw in her breath, and then took him by the hand, in through the front door.

They paused for a moment in the hallway, and she introduced him to the old butler and the cook and the man-of-all-work and the few servants who'd been left on to attend to the house since the master and mistress were never there, all of whom had come to see if their young visiting mistress was in need. She was, but not of them, and when they'd left, grinning, assured of their little lady's safety and reassured as to her happiness, she turned to her husband again.

She was going to ask him if he wanted tea, or port, or something stronger, or a few sandwiches or perhaps something more, suddenly shy with him again, and afraid to ask for what she wanted, for she'd neither the words or the experience for that. But he, her dear friend Julian, knew her better than that, and helped her, as he always had. He only held her hand and asked:

"Where is our room, Eliza?"

Oh, doubtless he knew her, she thought, after they'd got to her room, for he knew enough to draw the shades against the blatant day before he took her in his arms. And then in the shaded room, he knew how to make her yearn to be free of her concealing clothes, and then again, in the shadowed bed, knew how to remove his own so as not to alarm her, not to interrupt the slow, smooth flow of what he was helping her to build with him.

This time he did not separate his body from his mind, this time he gave up his vigilant watch over his secret, inner self. And while he dared not forget his expertise, he discovered for the first time what it was like to make love to a woman, as well as her body. The joy of knowing that this lovely little well-shaped body was Eliza's, this breast he touched was hers, and that gasp of pleasure he gave her was her speaking to him in words beyond words, brought him almost beyond pleasure before he'd gone half so far as he'd gone in the common way, with all the nameless women he'd thought he made love to before. For this, he discovered, lingering with her in his pleasure, slowly uncovering to her, her own, was making love—the rest had all been some sort of pleasant exercise, no more. This was more than he'd ever known, for all that he'd known so much.

As it was all of it new to Eliza, so then it was, too, to Julian. The one was being taught the infinite possibilities of the body even as the other was learning the limitless pleasure of the mind. Yet as Eliza reveled in all the new sensations, she couldn't forget that this was her Julian with her, his golden head upon her breast, his hands where she'd been taught even her own must not go, his long strong body upon hers. However different it all was, as his body was, as hers became in his hands, none of it was frightening or wrong, because this was Julian, her dearest, oldest friend. This time it was no icy-eyed stranger, soundlessly and impersonally at work upon her body. No, this time he never stinted with his words or smiles. Nor did he ever call her his easy, impersonal "love," but always and only his "Eliza," as though he never wished to forget that, not even for a second.

And for all he knew her body better than she did, from practice with so many others, he wouldn't profane their love by remembering now, even if he could remember them now if he tried; he found his greatest joy in knowing that this was his Eliza moving with him, welcoming him, allowing him the greatest intimacy she'd ever known, just as it was rapidly becoming the greatest he'd ever experienced.

His body was as beautiful as she remembered it to be, and she only wished she pleased him half so well with how she looked and tried to learn to behave. She told him this, bit by bit, when she could, as best she could.

"Oh, Eliza,"—he smiled against her heart—"you could not be lovelier and need not do more for me than to love me."

She told him she did, but scarcely needed to—he'd understood entirely the unspoken language she'd been speaking all along, all unaware.

When he knew he could no longer wait, when she lay beneath him, troubled because for all the pleasure, there was still something she knew remained, although she could not quite envision it, only then he moved her to ready her. Then he bent to her and whispered more than half-words of instruction, or words of praise and love:

"I'm sorry, Eliza," he breathed. "This last must be, in order for this to be complete. But it's hard, even for me, to know that although this will give me my greatest pleasure, it may give you discomfort, at least this once. Bear with me, love," he whispered, sighing, shivering with the anticipation of delight as well as distress, confused at that paradox, before he thought of no more than relief.

Because then he moved to her and entered her, and forgot everything but that this was his Eliza. For she wrapped her limbs around him and hugged him closer after one small tensed spasm of denial, telling him he was welcome even as she then gave him complete welcome.

But at first it did anger her, as it surprised her, this burning pain where there should have been sheer joy. Then she was glad of it, because it was necessary. It emphasized the way her Julian, her real and golden, warm and breathing lover, was burning his way into her heart and body, branding her forever. With wonderful perversity, it became a pleasure to add to all the other pleasures that he gave her. So, too, when she felt his ultimate rapture, and saw his head thrown back, his face transfixed by joy, and then heard her own name tumble from his lips even as his body gave up its last shudder, driven like a stabbing flame within her, she also knew her greatest content.

How perverse this physical love was, she mused after, as he held her closely. How magnificent this bonding, she thought, as he kept her close, and told her of his love, and promised her much more than bonding next time.

Then he gave her far more. He propped himself on his elbows and looked down to her face and smoothed back her tumbled hair.

"Eliza," he said, "all the pain and doubt and confusion

are vanished. All the wandering too. Do you know, had you never been born, I would never have known peace. If I know nothing else, I know that."

Then they said nothing more, but held each other close, like children in the night, and comforted each other in many ways, for the rest of the day and then all through the night.

21

"It seems to me," the very young gentleman said in such a reasonable tone that anyone who did not know him would not have known he was arguing, "that children are the ones who ought to be allowed to stay up to see the new years in, because they have the most in common with them."

"Yes, both being ignorant, fresh, and infantile, I do see your point, you unlicked cub," the young gentleman's father, who did know him very well, agreed. "You will now go to bed, and I assure you you'll find that your elders have not savaged the new year or frightened it away—1822 will have twelve daylit months remaining for you to commiserate with it in."

"Really, Randolph," Francesca said on a sigh, eyeing her elder son with the same affection she'd given to her newborn one when she'd seen him off to bed hours before, "you've gotten your extra hour, pray do not push for more. And with such an argument!"

"I had none better," the boy admitted ruefully.

"Clearly, it's not a career in politics for the boy," Warwick commented, "too much guile for the church, too much sense for the army, and too much honesty for law. What will you do with the lad, Arden?"

"I'll grow to be just like my father," Randolph declared, which caused Arden to cry, "Heaven forbid!" as the company whooped with laughter.

But it didn't take much to make them laugh tonight, although for all they'd bottles of champagne out on the sideboard, they'd not taken very much wine yet. It was the festivities themselves, it was the company they were in, it was their lives themselves which made them giddy with happiness tonight.

They'd all stayed on for the fortnight of Christmas with Arden and Francesca, since the lady couldn't travel with ease, having so lately delivered herself of another son, although she'd done it with great ease. But the house in the Lake District was roomy. Unlike London, where the snow fell solely to impede traffic, here it fell expressly to look lovely on the topiary, as well as to give the many assorted children living and visiting there a world to sculpture and slide and skate upon. And it gave their elders an excuse to enjoy luxuriating indoors after they'd been out.

Now dinner was done. The fires crackled in the several hearths throughout the huge house, the children were all of them abed (except for those clever enough to stay awake in stifled merriment, in secret celebration in the nursery together), and the adults sat in the grand salon and waited for the new year to arrive.

A newly svelte Francesca sat within the circle of her husband's arm, the Duke and Duchess of Peterstow were near to them on a wide settle, and the Viscount Hazelton and his viscountess stood on opposite sides of the fire, arguing over whether the chestnuts were done yet.

"By all means," Eliza said, "if you like them raw, snatch them out. I'll leave mine in a few moments longer so that they don't sprout after I eat them, thank you."

"Certainly," her husband agreed, "charcoal is good for the digestion, I hear."

"Children," Warwick said idly, "do you think we might have a few seconds off from warfare in which to greet the new year?"

Julian consulted his watch. "Time enough to roast Eliza a little more, I think. The new year's not due in for several moments more."

"I'd rather hear your resolutions, before it's too late to revise them when you find you can't keep them. Susannah?" the elegant duke asked his lady wife.

"I resolve not to get angry at you until I know for a certainty whether you're teasing or not," she said, biting her lip to keep from laughing as her husband's lean face grew ruddier than the firelight accounted for, as he remembered an extremely personal jest they'd shared in their bed in the night.

"Vixen," he said appreciatively, "nicely turned. And I resolve not to tease so much—not quite so much, that is. And you, Arden?" he asked ignoring his wicked duchess's whisper of, "Oh, surely not."

"None necessary," the large man replied on a contented sigh. "I cannot see any room for improvement."

"You might try for one that has to do with stopping lumbering friends with infants—we've got so many we'll have to build another house just for them, or we'll have no room for our own," Julian complained.

"Oh? Sits the wind in that quarter?" Arden asked with great interest, as Eliza and Julian exchanged bright glances. But Julian was saved the effort of making a blistering retort when Warwick added musingly:

"And certainly, my dear host, there'd be a small space for a resolution concerning boring on about roots and composts and drainage systems to old friends when all they do is admire your roses."

After which Francesca put in something to do with one's husband perhaps resolving to restrain himself from midnight forays on the kitchens which set all the servants to accusing each other of pilferage the next day, and resolved herself not to slay him for it. And Susannah murmured a word about one's host might resolve not to encourage children to question everything under the sun—as Arden did a fine impersonation of virtue outraged.

"Eliza, my one true friend," he began as she turned around and gave him a measuring look.

"And one to do with matchmaking," she said pointedly, and he fell silent.

"Oh, yes . . ." "Quite so," the muttering began, until Arden said, with what well may have been honest contrition, "No need to resolve that, I've already done. Ben told me to mind my own business in straightforward fashion, and Constance ignored me altogether, as a lady should. They may keep company without resolving matters between them until the new century rolls around, for all I care now. I certainly won't meddle further."

There were various hoots of derision, silenced by Arden's quickly asking, "And your resolution, Julian?"

"I resolve," he said, taking up a peeled chestnut his

wife offered him and chewing it without a murmur, even as he feared his teeth would break on it, "to do what Eliza asks."

"And that is?" Arden prompted.

"To be himself," she answered honestly, before she tasted one of his uncooked chestnuts herself and began giggling.

"Ah, no more, I can't bear it," Warwick pleaded. "One of my firmest resolves was to avoid sticky sweets. Please let the newlyweds alone."

"At any rate, the clock is moving onward," Arden said. "We'll take your resolve to do anything Julian asks, as read, Eliza, and raise a glass to it, and the new year. Another year into the decade gets well underway in a few minutes, you know, we're fairly galloping into the thick of the century. Let's have a toast, please, Duke," he said as the butler moved an assortment of grinning underage footmen in with trays of champagne glasses.

They all stood.

"Ah, yes," Warwick Jones, Duke of Peterstow, said, taking up a glass and thinking as he held it. Then:

"To the past! That which brought us here together," he offered, remembering all his doubts and loneliness, even as he smiled tenderly at his duchess, who'd put an end to it.

"Yes. And to the present too, that which we share," Arden cried, hugging his lady close, to let her know he'd never known such content.

"To the future! And what it will bring us," was the toast Julian gave them as his gaze caressed his bride and their smiles promised all that was to come.

"Hear, hear," they cried, before Eliza raised her glass to salute them.

"To love!" she said.

And they all drank to that.

A new realm of romance and passion—
in Signet's Super Regency novels . . .

The GAME of LOVE
EDITH LAYTON

author of the award-winning *Love in Disguise*
*A fiery beauty dares to yield to her passion for a
handsome stranger with a shadowy past . . .*

Beautiful Francesca Wyndham was taking a
gamble when she fell in love with Arden Lyons,
a gentleman who was clearly anything but a
gentleman when it came to winning what he
wanted: a hand of cards, a test of strength, or a
lady's favors. Though Francesca knew nothing
about this man . . . though his past was a dark
mystery . . . she dared to pit her innocence
against his expertise. It was definitely a game
where passion took all. . . .
